WEEPERS

(A NOVEL)

Forthcoming novels by Nick Chiarkas:

Nunzio's Way

Black Tiger Tea

Blue Bounty

WEEPERS

(A NOVEL)

NICK CHIARKAS

Three Towers Press
MILWAUKEE, WISCONSIN

Published by
Three Towers Press
An imprint of HenschelHAUS Publishing, Inc.
www.henschelHAUSbooks.com

Hardcover ISBN: 978159598-389-3
Paperback ISBN: 978159595-390-9
Audio book ISBN: 978159598-391-6
E-Book ISBN: 978159598-392-3

Publisher's Cataloging-In-Publication Data
(Prepared by The Donohue Group, Inc.)

Chiarkas, Nicholas L.
Weepers : (a novel) / Nick Chiarkas.

pages ; cm

Issued also as an ebook and an audiobook.
ISBN: 978-1-59598-389-3 (hardcover)
ISBN: 978-1-59595-390-9 (paperback)

1. Child witnesses--New York (State)--New York--Fiction. 2. Police murders--New York (State)--New York--Fiction. 3. Missing persons--New York (State)--New York--Fiction. 4. Courage--Fiction. I. Title.

PS3603.H537 W44 2015
813/.6   2015933657

Author photos: Amy Jester Photography

Cover design by Dan Fleming

Printed in the United States of America.

Dedicated to
Judith E. Olingy
My wife and IR

In memory of
Harry E. Oxford, Jr.
(October 27, 1944 – August 14, 1966)

And a big thank you to the rest of the gang—
Angelo, Anthony, Barbara, Billy, Bobby, Bruce, Carl,
Carol, Cathy, Chico, Denise, Dennis, Diane, Eddie,
Georgia, Harriet, Harry, Howie, Jimmy, Joey, John,
Johnny, Lydia, Marie, Mary, Mike, Natalie, Rennie,
Richie, Robert, Ron, and Tommy
—for always being there with me,
on those streets, so long ago.

And all the children are insane.
— The Doors, *The End*

There can be no courage unless you are scared.
— Eddie Rickenbacker

AUTHOR'S NOTE

The Two Bridges neighborhood of Manhattan's Lower East Side is the setting for Weepers. In the 1950s, "Two Bridges" defined the slums moldering between the Manhattan Bridge to the north and the Brooklyn Bridge to the south. The collection of narrow streets and trash-lined alleys slithered through the decaying brownstone tenements with common toilets—one per floor—and was among the most notorious neighborhoods in the city.

Perched on the midnight-edge of the Two Bridges neighborhood were the Alfred E. Smith Housing Projects. The Projects were a no-man's land: no history, no common bond, and no rules. Bordered by the South Street docks, Catherine Street, Madison Street, and St. James Place, it was the most dangerous part of an already dangerous neighborhood. I grew up in those projects.

Weepers is a work of fiction. Names, characters, places, and incidents are the product of the author's imagination or are used fictitiously. Any resemblance to actual events, locales, or persons, living or dead, is coincidental.

1951

CHAPTER ONE

"If it moves toward you, you're food."

"Angelo, don't get too far ahead."

"I won't, Papa."

Angelo had never been happier. It was the night before Christmas, he was with his father, and it was snowing. Not a chilling, icy snow, but a powder of flakes—perfect forms floating to the streets of New York.

The few maple and ash trees that stood watch along the cement playground on Cherry Street were dressed in white, with crystal-gloved fingers reaching down to the silent sidewalk. Those brittle bushes that had managed to survive another summer pouncing of playful children now nestled comfortably under a downy white cover.

Angelo heeded his father's warning and shortened the distance between them. Even at seven years old, he knew these streets were unsafe. This was, after all, the Two Bridges section of Manhattan's Lower East Side.

"Doesn't it look just like that glass ball that snows when you shake it on Nonna's table?"

"Yeah, but a little colder." His father followed behind at a steady pace, pulling a two-wheeled metal shopping cart filled with brightly wrapped Christmas gifts.

"Yeah, it sure does, but a little colder." Angelo giggled and turned to grab for a particularly large flake that see-sawed down like a feather from a pillow fight. The ash on his father's cigarette brightened momentarily.

Like a dragon, his father streamed smoke from his nostrils and the corner of his mouth. Mixed with the vapor from his breath, it left a brief trail before disappearing behind him.

"Wouldn't it be funny if Nonna looked at her snow globe and saw us walking?" Angelo asked in an effort to continue the connection with his father. "What would she say?"

"Jesus, kid, I don't know." Angelo's father took a quick drag on his cigarette and flicked it into the snow. "Try to catch a snowflake on your tongue."

"Okay." Angelo danced in circles with his opened mouth to the sky.

"Don't cross Catherine Street without me."

"Okay, Papa."

"How's that eye doing?"

Angelo instinctively touched the left side of his face with a wet mitten. "It's okay. It don't hardly hurt no more."

"Good." His father's voice was suddenly stern. "But, like I said, it was your own fault."

Angelo didn't respond. He was absorbed by the memory of sterile pads on his eyes, the aroma of tomato soup and alcohol in the hospital, and his mother's weeping.

"Hey, you hear me?"

"Yes, Papa." Angelo again felt the snowflakes on his up-turned face. "My fault. I know, Papa. My fault."

"You better believe it's your fault."

Angelo's father was not a big man. Mostly he seemed calm, though Angelo had witnessed just how rapidly things could change with little provocation. He'd learned to read the cues quickly and respond accordingly. He was pretty sure he didn't need to respond at that moment, but threw back another "I know, I'm sorry, Papa," just in case.

Angelo walked alongside the burgundy brick walls of Knickerbocker Village. Beyond the narrow park to his left that separated Cherry and Water Streets, he could see the Journal-American newspaper building. The Journal's loading platform on Water Street, usually lively with shouting men and the comings and goings of trucks, was quiet. Instead, three Christmas trees stood on the platform, each beautifully decorated with colored lights and an illuminated gold star on top. "How come nobody stole the trees, Papa?"

"They belong to Uncle Nunzio."

Angelo nodded.

After a slight pause, his father spoke. "Angelo."

"Yeah?"

"That stuff I said...it wasn't your fault, kid. None of it was your fault. You're a good kid, Angelo. Beats me...it just beats me." His father shook his head in private puzzlement.

Angelo stopped walking and turned around.

His father winked. Angelo smiled and resumed his dance in the snow. Beyond a veil of falling snow, Angelo could see black-jacketed, shadowy figures moving within the projects. Two standing there. Four more moving together, a white mist kicked up at their feet.

"Papa, see those guys?"

"Don't worry about it. They're just punks."

"I wish I was a lion. Pompa said they're the king of the jungle."

"He would know."

Angelo's attention alternated from the black-jacket shadow-punks to the Christmas lights dancing in the projects' windows. "Will Uncle Johnny be home before the new baby comes?"

"Probably."

"I bet he ain't scared of the projects. I bet he ain't scared of nothin'...just like you, Papa. Just like a lion."

At the corner of Cherry and Catherine, Angelo stopped, waiting for his father to catch up. He looked back up Cherry Street and was stunned. Less than twenty feet away, the cart stood alone in the snow. Angelo stared in disbelief. He ran to the spot where his father should have been. He grabbed the handle of the cart, looking down at the abandoned presents.

He knew his father had been right there pulling the cart. He squeezed his eyes shut tight, opened them, and still his father would not appear. He turned in circles, scanning the quiet street for some sign of where his father had gone. His foot slipped. He fell. He got up. Nothing. No one. Not a sound.

"Papa," he shouted into the silent night. "Papa!"

No response. Not even an echo. The solid brick walls of Knickerbocker offered no clues. No cars moved and no footsteps could be heard. Nothing. Just the cart standing there filled with Christmas. He was alone.

"Papa, please!"

Angelo fell to his knees in the snow and cried into already soggy mittens. In a breath between sobs, he heard something. The hairs stood up on the back of his neck and goose bumps flooded his small body.

"*Aspetta, aspetta,*" someone whispered. Just that. Hushed, deep, and nothing more.

Startled, Angelo jumped to his feet. Eyes wide, his head whipped around. There was no one. Terror tightened its grip as he looked across the street at the projects. Like hyenas spotting a lost lion cub, the black-jacketed punks were moving cautiously toward Catherine Street. Toward him.

Angelo looked at his own building, 20 Catherine Slip, on the edge of the projects, about a block away. He locked his grip on the shopping cart in a failed attempt to pull the cart with him. It was too heavy and the punks were coming.

The boy already knew the first rule of the jungle: *If it moves away from you, it's food; if it moves toward you, you're food.* He took a deep breath and released the handle. The cart toppled onto its side as he ran as fast as he could toward home.

Angelo cut diagonally across the snow-covered street without looking toward the black-jacketed punks, for fear it would slow him down just enough for them to get him. He kept focused on his building. The cold air and snow were clouding his eyes and burning his lungs, but 20 Catherine Slip was getting closer. He tripped on the edge of the sidewalk in front of his building and fell face down, sliding in the snow. Even while skidding, he was getting up, finding his footing and running. The entrance was now in front of him and he flew through the door and into the lobby.

Slipping in a puddle of melted snow, Angelo slammed into the wall of mailboxes to the left of the door. Amidst the muted cacophony of Christmas music from several first-floor apartments and the scent of pine and pie, he noticed for the first time the sound of his own crying. Fearing that his sobs might attract predators, he tried to control himself, planning the safest route to his fifth-floor apartment.

Not the elevators. They were unreliable and he could be trapped. He cautiously entered the stairwell. Grabbing the banister, he dashed up the first flight of stairs. A sharp pain from the cold air burned through his lungs and heart. *Only to the fifth floor*, he thought. His ankles felt like weights as he continued up, pulling himself along with the banister as fast as he could.

His breathing was shrill and strained rounding the third floor landing. The acrid smell of urine replaced the stale stairway air as he stopped abruptly at the fourth-floor landing. He didn't recognize the man who lay on the floor with his head and shoulder propped against the wall. Any other time, Angelo would have run down a floor to the elevator or back stairway. But tonight he had no time for detours and he was running out of steam. He had to keep going.

Angelo moved cautiously, stepping over the thin, extended arm. The young man did not move. White crusts covered the stranger's lips below unblinking eyes. Angelo's eyes remained locked on the ghostly figure as he turned toward the next flight of stairs.

Angelo grabbed the banister and snapped his head toward the fifth-floor landing and safety. Once there, he slammed open the firewall door and shot down the hallway to his apartment. He threw himself against the locked door and pounded.

"Mama, Mama, hurry, Mama!"

After a moment that felt like a lifetime, his mother opened the door and reached down to him. Angelo collapsed into the harbor of her arms.

"Angelo, my baby, what is it?" She kneeled and embraced him in the doorway. She looked at her son, and then past him. "Where's your father?"

Angelo, unable to speak, cried and gasped for air. His mother lifted him over the threshold and inside the warm apartment as he tried to control his sobbing.

"Frank!" she shouted, but her brother was already behind her.

"What's goin' on?" Uncle Frank asked.

"Calm down, my baby, tell us what happened." Her tone comforted Angelo. For the first time since he'd turned to look back up Cherry Street, Angelo felt safe. The warmth and smells of home rolled over his body like a tonic.

Anna Pastamadeo's black hair accented her warm and worried gray eyes.

"Mama, we have to find Papa."

"What do you mean 'find Papa'?"

"He disappeared on Cherry Street. Just gone. We have to go find him."

Uncle Frank grabbed his leather jacket off the closet doorknob. "Cherry Street...you see anybody, anything I need to know?"

"A voice...I don't know." Angelo choked down a lump of fear. "P-Please find my—"

"Anna, lock the door and call Pop. I'll be right back."

Angelo heard the stairwell door open and close as his uncle went into the night.

His mother locked their apartment door. "Okay, Angelo, okay." With some effort, she lifted him up, wet clothes and all, and carried him to the living-room couch. The room was lit only by the Christmas tree in the corner near the window. She held Angelo in her lap, swallowing him in the sanctuary of her embrace.

There, in between sobs and shivers, he told her what had happened. Angelo knew she had to swallow hard and hold on. He knew she remained calm for him.

He told his mother all of it—the Christmas trees at the *Journal-American*, catching snowflakes on his tongue, his father saying he was a good kid, hearing someone say *aspetta*, the gifts tumbling into the snow—all of it.

"Your father said you were a good kid? He said that?"

"He really said that...to me."

"Huh... and after he was gone you heard *aspetta?*"

"Yeah. The cart fell over. I couldn't pull it. And then I ran home. I just left."

"Don't worry about it, Sweetheart. I'm glad you left it there and came right home."

"No. Mama, I left Papa. I should've looked for him. I got scared and left him."

"You did right, Angelo."

"I got scared of the punks with the black jackets and I ran."

"Punks with black jackets? Knights." His mother nodded. "Did they hurt your papa?"

"No. They were in the projects. I just got scared of them and all. And I ran home instead of looking for Papa. I should've been with him. Walking with him."

"Angelo, you did just what you were supposed to do. Uncle Frank will find out what happened." She gently unfolded Angelo from her lap. "Come to the kitchen. I'll call Pompa."

Angelo nodded. Pompa, his grandfather, would make things right.

* * *

Angelo took a hot bath, put on his pajamas, and was halfway through a slice of bread when Uncle Frank returned with the shopping cart and damp presents.

"Did you find Papa?" Angelo choked back despair.

"Not yet, kid. Angelo, I found these cookies in a napkin on the presents."

"They're from Mrs. Monahan."

"Angelo." Uncle Frank kneeled on one knee. "Tell me exactly where your father was the last time you saw him."

"Right where the cart was."

"Did you notice any cars coming down the street?"

"No."

"Don't answer so fast, Angelo. Close your eyes. Try to picture it, kid."

Angelo closed his eyes. "No, no cars. No people. Nothing." He opened his eyes.

"Okay, when you turned around and Mac—when your father was gone, do you remember any empty parking spots?"

Angelo closed his eyes tighter this time and pictured the cart standing there on its own. He remembered looking around for his father, but nothing about the cars parked along the street, except they looked like rolling, snow-covered hills.

"I don't remember any empty spots. I'm sorry."

"Don't be sorry, that helps. Do you remember anything else that seemed different when you turned around and your father was gone?"

"No, I was scared, kinda still am a little."

"Ah, hey, kiddo. Don't you worry about nothing. Your Uncle Frank's here and I ain't quitting 'til I find him. And, Angelo, I'm not going to let anything hurt you."

"Angelo," his mother said softly, "it's time for bed now."

"But, I wanna help find Papa," he protested as he turned from his uncle to his mother.

His mother's and uncle's eyes met for a moment.

"If you wanna help get a good night's sleep. Tomorrow, think about what you saw. You know, with your eyes shut, and trying to picture what you might have seen."

"Okay, Uncle Frank."

"Now I need to talk to your mother. You go to bed, and don't worry about nothing."

Uncle Frank's stubble was scratchy and he smelled like cigarettes and Old Spice. But his hug made Angelo feel safe again.

Instead of turning into his bedroom down the hall, his mother led Angelo to her bedroom.

"You sleep in here with me tonight, Angel."

"Okay, Mama." Angelo climbed into the large bed and under the thick comforter, a hand-me-down wedding present from his mother's parents. He rolled over onto his back as his mother brought the cover up to his chin.

"Angelo, are you sure you heard someone say *asperra*?"

"I think so, Mama."

"You know it's Italian. It means—"

"Wait."

"That's right, Sweetheart. It means wait. And that's what you heard?"

"That's what it sounded like."

"Okay, Angel. No more tonight."

"Mama," Angelo said as his mother turned out the light, "I'm sorry."

She stopped short in the doorway. Backlit by the hall light, Angelo could see her frown. "Angelo." She walked back to the bed. "You have nothing to be sorry for. Nothing."

Bending over him in the dark, she placed a hand on either side of his face—carefully avoiding the fading bruise near his left eye—and kissed him on his head. A stray tear moistened his forehead.

"Wait here." She needlessly adjusted his cover. "I'll get something for you to drink."

"What?"

"Something Pompa used to make for Uncle Frank and me when we couldn't sleep."

"And for Uncle Danny, too?"

"Danny, too." She smiled. "You say your prayers and I'll be right back."

"Okay."

In minutes, his mother returned. She placed a glass on the nightstand and then helped Angelo sit up. Holding the glass to his mouth, she said, "Here, drink this."

"What is it?"

"Warm milk, some honey, and a touch of brandy. It will help you sleep, Sweetheart; now drink it down."

Angelo took a sip and made a face. His mother held it back up to his lips until he was finished, then placed the empty glass back on the nightstand as he nestled in beneath the covers. Gathering her skirt in front, she lay down next to him and began to hum a familiar tune while gently stroking his head.

He stirred when he felt her get up. She touched her lips to both his eyelids and his forehead. "God grant you peaceful dreams, my baby."

After she left, Angelo listened to the muffled voices through the closed door. When Pompa arrived, he heard his mother's voice augmented by her fear.

He could hear enough to know she was telling Pompa the story he had told her. He heard her say, "*Aspetta, aspetta!* Angelo heard it."

"Shhh, Anna. You'll wake the boy," Pompa said. "Frankie, what do you make of the gifts still being there?"

He heard Uncle Frank say, "That bothers me, too, especially since Angelo said some Knights saw him." Uncle Frank continued in little more than a whisper. "I figure the Knights saw something that scared them enough to keep them away."

Angelo tried to stay awake, but exhaustion and the brandy took hold of him and, through silent sobs and clinging fears, guided him into dreamless sleep on that chilly Christmas Eve.

1957

CHAPTER TWO

"And then there's the edge thing."

"Tea, Annabella?" asked the priest as he entered his spartan office at Saint Joachim's Catholic Church. He was holding a heavy silver tray in both hands. On the tray were two cups, a pot of strong black tea, and a beautiful buttermilk porcelain plate crowned with silver-dollar-sized shortbread cookies.

Father Joseph Bonifacio was fifty-two years old, five-foot-eight, and built like a fire hydrant. The small scar that split his left eyebrow publicized his Golden Glove youth. He had a gentle smile and while his brown eyes invited trust, it was his matter-of-fact edge that served him best on these wicked streets. He wore a black, short-sleeved shirt with an embroidered cross on the pocket. The top button of the placket was open and the white pontiff's tab askew.

Father Joe, as he liked to be called, deftly kicked his office door shut with the heel of his right foot and moved to the large, well-worn wooden chair behind his desk.

"Annabella," Anna repeated. "You're the only one who still calls me that, Father Joe."

"Hard to believe, you're still the most beautiful flower in this neighborhood."

This was exactly what Anna wanted. She'd made the appointment to talk about Angelo, but she also needed to be reassured.

Rosemarie Moran, her best friend and neighbor, had been worried about Anna's lingering melancholy and convinced her to see Father Joe. Anna agonized but made the appointment.

"Well, thank you. But frankly, it's hard to trust the judgment of someone drinking hot tea on a day like this," she said. "It must be eighty degrees out there."

"Eighty-two. I have always admired the way hot tea can, at the same time, comfort you and stimulate conversation." Father Joe placed the tray on his oversized, uncluttered wooden desk. Without looking up, he poured tea into the two cups and passed one across his desk to Anna, who was seated in a smaller wooden chair in front of the desk.

The aroma of black tea mixed favorably with the lingering scent of cigarette smoke and incense. Until Father Joe closed his door, she was listening to the radio playing in the outer office. Now she could faintly hear Elvis Presley singing "Loving You." Elvis made her feel good. Sinatra made her feel lonely. But it was Johnnie Ray who pierced through years of restrained sadness and stirred her soul.

"Thank you for the tea."

"How's your mother, Anna?"

"She's fine. So's my father," she added a little too quickly. Fearing that she sounded like she wanted to dispense with small talk and get on with why she was there—which indeed was the case—she added, "I'm taking Angelo and Adam there for dinner tonight."

"Your parents are good people."

"I know."

"And Mac's brother, Johnny, how is he?"

"Johnny's okay. He's still afraid to leave the apartment. He spends his time cleaning that rifle he brought home from the war, exercising, reading, and looking out the window. I know the people in the neighborhood call him 'the ghost.' He's very pale, but healthy and strong—and he adores Angelo."

"You know I could still have him stay with me."

"We've been through that...and anyway, he helps me as much as I help him. He's good company."

"Okay, so Anna, dear," he said, with an understanding smile, and taking a cautious sip of tea, "talk to me."

Anna sighed. "Father Joe, you've known Angelo since he was born—"

"Ha! I've known you since you were born." He picked up an open pack of Camels that had been resting against an empty ashtray on his desk and offered a cigarette to Anna.

"Thanks, but I'm quitting." She watched Father Joe light his cigarette. "Angelo is wonderful. I know, every mother feels that way about her child, but Angelo had this light behind his eyes."

"Had?"

"He's changing. Becoming more like...like where we live...the projects. He'll be thirteen in two days, and I know a lot of this could just be growing up, but I'm worried."

"It's only natural that Angelo is changing. Remember when he'd first learned to walk? He would take a few steps and then look back."

"Yeah, but now when he looks back, he's looking for his friends, and believe me, his friends are not the best influence on him."

"No, Anna, he's looking back to make sure you are still there," Father Joe said in a comforting voice. But then he added, "Are you?"

* * *

Angelo, usually alert to danger, especially after delivering groceries, mumbled to the sidewalk as he sauntered against the summer heat back to Bookman's delicatessen, failing to notice the five teens closing in on him as he walked along Monroe Street. This was not the first time a kid returning from a delivery with money in his pocket was targeted. But he was quicker to recognize danger, and to dodge it. But not this time.

He finally spotted them out of the corner of his eye as he started to cross the wide, trash-laden thoroughfare running adjacent to the Manhattan Bridge—Pike Street. The teens walking along Pike toward Monroe Street were wearing sky-blue shirts with a small image of Popeye on the left front pocket.

These were South Street Boys—Popeyes. All of Angelo's senses kicked in as two of the South Street Boys broke off to circle behind him.

Angelo figured that by the time he got across Pike, the other three would be less than six feet to his right and moving quickly toward him. If he ran now, so would they, and it would be too close to call. Plus, even though the two behind him were pretty far back, he would have to run to his left, toward South Street, where there would surely be more South Street Boys. No, he needed to get back to Bookman's, and that was straight ahead.

He would not look directly at them; the only thing he had going was that they didn't know that he knew. He needed something. Some advantage. But no matter what, this was going to be a hard run. Angelo knew he was quick; he just needed an edge. They moved toward him. And then it came to him.

Angelo turned toward the three South Street Boys on his right and, looking past them, waved and shouted, "Uncle Danny, wait up." It worked. The three boys stopped and turned toward no one, but in that moment they lost their momentum, and Angelo was flying down Monroe Street.

"Get him!" one of the South Street Boys shouted, and the teens were in angry pursuit.

Angelo dashed down Monroe toward Market Street with three of his pursuers thirty feet behind him. The two who had circled to his rear earlier gave up and slowed to a fast walk. The slap, slap, slap of Angelo's sneakers echoed as he ran under the Manhattan Bridge. The bridge's dark refuge was home to several bums crouched in black alcoves, rats digging through trash, and a decomposing cat under a blanket of humming and crawling insects. Here, the soggy summer scent surrendered to a wall of urine, excrement, and decay. He tried to hold his breath, but his breathing was already strained.

"I gotcha, ya little shit," cackled one of the alcove residents, reaching out toward Angelo. A startled Angelo spun out of the way but in doing so lost his advantage, and the three South Street Boys were now gaining on him.

He recovered his bearings and bolted on course and out from under the bridge. Taking a deep gulp of air, he hit Market Street at an angle, just in case a car was coming. It was clear. He crossed Market with his pursuers now trailing by less than twenty feet.

The boy ran up the stoop of the first tenement on Market and Monroe. The entrance door to the tenement was held open by a trash can. Two older women sitting on the stoop moved to the side as Angelo shot past them. Hand-over-hand on the banister, he pulled himself up the steps two at a time, the South Street Boys one flight below and gaining.

Angelo slammed open the metal door to the roof with a bang! sending an explosion of pigeons scattering into the overcast sky. He bolted onto the roof and ran toward Catherine Street.

Angelo knew the roofs the way a smitten sea captain knew the ocean. He ran from roof to roof, some lower than others. He leaped alleyways and airshafts. And he did it without slowing down a bit.

On one of the roofs, six teenagers on blankets were packing up from a day at "tar beach." Their radio was still on and Angelo could hear the Del Vikings singing "Come Go with Me" as he increased speed. He was now at full gallop; he was clicking, and he felt like he could fly.

His pursuers, not as certain of the terrain and uneasy on these open, fenceless roofs, slowed down.

"The kid's a roof rat," one of the Popeyes said. "We'll never catch him up here."

By the time Angelo reached the roof next to St. Joseph's, on the corner of Monroe and Catherine Streets, his pursuers had given up the chase.

Angelo panted, drenched with sweat as he walked over to the edge of the roof facing Monroe Street. He took little steps until his toes were perfectly even with the rim of the roof. Chin on chest, he looked straight down and imagined falling. Window by window, floor by floor...falling. Vertigo tugged at his belt.

Angelo lifted his chin and looked straight ahead at the building across the street. A woman in a window watched him with more curiosity than concern. She sat in a chair pushed against her open window. Her elbows rested on a pillow placed on the windowsill.

Turning his attention back to the street, Angelo asked himself, "May I take another baby step?" "Yes, you may," he answered and edged out over the roof about an inch. His stomach churned. His arms were limp at his sides. Angelo smelled a storm coming. His tongue tasted like turpentine. He could see people sitting on stoops and walking along Monroe Street. A young priest across the street stopped walking and looked up at him.

Angelo looked straight up at the sky—gray sea foam rolled over the tenements toward him. He felt even more lightheaded. He recalled his father saying, "Angelo, don't get too far ahead." Papa. He took a deep breath, backed away from the roof's brim, and jogged over to the roof on Catherine Street next to Book-man's. He ran down the four flights and through the front door of the tenement. And there, at the top of the stoop, Angelo became immobile at the sight of Liz Brennan.

Liz and two of her girlfriends were standing on the sidewalk in front of the stoop. Liz lived in this building. She was fifteen, wearing tight jeans with folded-up cuffs and a pale-blue short-sleeve shirt. He heard her say hello to the priest he'd seen from the roof. Angelo loved her voice.

He was frozen there on top of her stoop when she turned toward him. Surprised to see him coming out of her building, she smiled. Angelo swallowed hard. He smiled timidly and walked down the steps of the stoop, more nervous than at any point during his recent race from harm. But he would not run now—not even if a Buick were going to fall on him.

"Hi, Angelo," Liz said as he walked toward them.

"Hi," Angelo said, still a bit breathless.

"He's cute," one of the other girls said, ruffling Angelo's hair. "Wish he were older."

"Bye, Angelo," sang the third girl.

"He's sweet," Liz said to her friends.

Angelo waved without turning around as he walked away from them and into Bookman's.

* * *

Anna was stunned by Father Joe's question and stared at him for an uncomfortable minute, shaking her head. She finally said, "Am I there?"

"I'm asking if you—"

"Me? Am I there?" Anna leaned forward. Her hands gripped the arms of the wooden chair. "How dare you imply that I'm not there for my boys. You have no—"

"How dare I? We have always been like family. I was there when you were born. You are like my own daughter. How dare I if I were not willing to talk to you about this."

"I don't want to talk about me. I came here to talk about Angelo." Anna started to get up. This was not going the way Anna had imagined it would.

"We are talking about Angelo, Anna. Sit down!"

"I don't want to talk about me," she said, trying to redirect the discussion while sitting back in her chair. It was too late to leave.

"We have to. It's in Angelo's best interest." He took a long drag off his cigarette and blew the smoke into the air away from Anna. "Are you there?"

Anna eyes filled with tears. It seemed like an eternity before she replied, "I don't know."

Anna didn't remember Father Joe putting his cigarette out and leaving his chair behind his large desk. She did not remember him walking around to where she was sitting, or her chair being moved. But suddenly her chair was turned away from the desk and he was kneeling on the floor in front of her, his strong arms wrapped around her shoulders and neck. She was leaning forward with her face buried under his chin and she was softly crying. He held her as she cried.

Anna hated crying in front of anyone. She was raised with brothers and could hold her own. She hated being thought of as weak. Pitied. Patted like a child. She pulled herself together.

Regaining control over her dragons, she forced them back down into the shadowy prison of her stomach. "I'm sorry—"

Father Joe took a bright white handkerchief out of his pocket and patted her eyes. He kissed her forehead and handed her the handkerchief. He lifted himself up and into the empty wooden chair next to her.

"I'm just a little emotional right now—"

"Anna, I don't want you ever to say, 'I should have been there for Angelo.'" He looked directly into her dissolving, pepper-gray eyes. "It's not too late for you and Angelo. I just want you to tell me how you really feel."

"I'm unraveling."

"Let's see, you're a thirty-one-year-old woman without a husband, working a full-time job at the *Journal-American* while raising two sons and taking care of your brother-in-law for the last six years. And you're doing all this day after day while living in the projects. Frankly, Anna, I couldn't do it. I would have unraveled a long time ago."

"Sooo?"

"So, let's talk honestly about you and Angelo and Adam."

"Primarily Angelo."

"Okay, Angelo. But Adam will learn from Angelo. And from you." Father Joe watched as Anna's gaze found the floor. "What am I missing, Anna?"

* * *

Father Robert Casimiro headed down Madison Street toward Roosevelt Street and St. Joachim's. His head turned from side to side, taking in the swirl of movement. The smells of sausage, onions, and peppers grilling at the corner stand. The sound of children laughing and daring each other to jump from the swings they were pumping in the concrete playground attached to Public School Number One. He stopped for a moment to watch a group of boys playing punchball on the same playground. He'd been in New York for less than twenty-four hours and already loved the city.

Father Casimiro was twenty-eight, almost six feet tall, and fit. His coffee-brown hair, which he groomed by wetting it and shaking his head dry like a dog, laid in any direction it wished. Ever since Father Joseph Bonifacio's keynote address at Saint Lawrence, Father Casimiro wanted to work with this inspiring and dedicated priest. And long before that, he'd wanted to work in the slums of New York's Lower East Side. Both dreams came true.

He continued to stroll along Madison Street. Two men sat in lawn chairs in front of a funeral home. He smiled at them and nodded.

"Hello, Father," said the larger man, removing a cigar from his mouth and returning the priest's nod.

"Good afternoon, gentlemen," Father Casimiro said, looking back and smiling as he inadvertently walked into a boy. The boy, who looked like he was in his mid-teens, was carrying a white paper cup filled with lemon ice.

"Hey, watch where you're goin', pal," the boy said as he stopped and looked at the priest. The boy was wearing dark pants and a black T-shirt with two narrow red stripes going around the collar and the edge of the short sleeves. On the front left side was a small crest with the boy's name, Jimmy, in red script below it. Two other boys wearing black T-shirts came out of a grocery store carrying lemon ice and stopped behind Jimmy.

"Here, hold this," said Jimmy, handing his lemon ice to Andy.

"Hey, Jimmy, he's a priest." One of the boys took the lemon ice and looked at the other.

"So what?" Jimmy said. "He still should apologize. Ain't that right, priest?"

"You bet," said Father Casimiro. "I was looking around; I apologize. Are you hurt?"

"Am I hurt? You believe this guy?" Jimmy said to his two friends, who immediately started laughing. "Hey, Father Clumsy, if I was hurt, you'd be on the ground, priest or no priest."

"Well, I'm glad you're not hurt, so…" Father Casimiro said, hoping to end this encounter and get on with his walk.

"So? You new here, Father Clumsy?" Jimmy asked.

"Yes. I'll be working with Father Bonifacio. Maybe you know him?"

"Yeah, we know Father Joe."

"Well, good. I'll be at the Cherry Street Settlement, and I hope to see you boys there."

"Oh, so now you're a wise guy, huh, Father Clumsy?"

"Casimiro," the young priest said with a bit more firmness.

"What?"

"Casimiro. My name is Father Casimiro, Jimmy." Father Casimiro's initial shock by the hostile audacity of this young man melded into impatience at Jimmy's rudeness.

"I don't give a rat—"

Jimmy stopped talking and looked over Father Casimiro's shoulder.

"You all right, Father?" came a voice from behind the priest. Father Casimiro was surprised to see the large man with the cigar now standing next to him.

"Oh, yes, thank you."

The three boys walked away and toward the projects. Jimmy's arms were raised in mock surrender. On the back of the boys' T-shirts was a coat of arms crossed by a sword and a pitchfork. Written above the coat of arms, in red letters with a white outline, was SATAN'S KNIGHTS. The three boys reached the projects side of the street and were immediately surrounded by a dozen Knights. Andy returned Jimmy's lemon ice as Jimmy gazed back at the priest. After a moment, Jimmy turned back to the group and together they all entered the interior of the projects and vanished.

The large man said, "So, Father, I heard you're new here. Listen—"

"Milwaukee," he said, shifting his attention from the projects to the man talking to him.

"Milwaukee. Listen, you said you're gonna be workin' with Father Joe, right? You stick close to him. Oh, and Father? Not for nothin', but watch out for those guys."

"Satan's Knights?" Father Casimiro pointed a thumb across the street. "They may need my help."

"I'll tell ya what they need, but then you might not let me in church no more." The man laughed, patted Father Casimiro on the shoulder, and walked back to his friend and lawn chair.

By the time Father Casimiro reached Roosevelt Street, he had regained his composure. A pounding stream of water spewed from a fire hydrant across the street. Several kids played in the water while two others were using a garbage can cover to direct the arc of the discharge.

"Hey, Billy, hold it up," one of the kids shouted as Father Casimiro approached.

"Gotcha." Billy directed the stream downward. "G'head, Father. We won't getcha wet."

"Thank you." Father Casimiro waved his appreciation to the boys across the street and felt only a welcomed mist carried on a breeze as he walked by. He loved the sociability of the brown-stone tenements tied together with clotheslines spanning alleyways. He took in the entire symphony of the neighborhood— the shouts, the laughter, the hum and echo of the melody—as he continued walking.

When he reached 22-32 Roosevelt Street, Father Casimiro stood for a moment in front of the Romanesque architecture, looking up at the four large stained-glass windows of St. Joachim's Church. He smiled like a mischievous child and entered the building.

Father Casimiro walked up one flight of stairs, then along a mutely lit hall and into Father Joe's outer office. A pleasant-looking middle-aged woman with a Lucille Ball hairstyle and a blue floral swing dress was watering a tall bamboo plant in the far corner of the room.

"Are you Sally?" Father Casimiro asked.

"Huh? Oh, my, yes, I'm Sally." Sally placed her cigarette on the rim of a large, crowded clay ashtray on her desk and walked toward Father Casimiro. She nervously switched the watering can to her left hand and extended her right. "I didn't hear you come in. You must be Father Casimiro," she said, shaking the young priest's hand. The ceiling fan overhead pushed the stale summer air through a mixture of perfume and cigarette smoke.

"I'm a little early—"

"Early, late, doesn't much matter around here. Father Joe is with a parishioner." Sally nodded toward the closed door with a wooden crucifix above it as she walked back and put the watering can on the floor next to the bamboo plant. "Want me to tell him you're here?"

Father Casimiro could hear muffled conversation coming from behind the closed door to Father Joe's office. The radio on Sally's desk played *A Thousand Miles Away*, and for the first time, he felt a little homesick. "I'll just wait."

"Glad you're here, Father." Sally crushed her lipstick-kissed cigarette in the ashtray, making certain it was out. "I'll see you in the morning."

"Saturday?"

"I'm here most every day. Please close the window when you two leave; it's supposed to rain tonight." Sally seemed to slow down as she lifted a framed photo of a young soldier, kissed it gently, caringly placed it back on her desk, and just as caringly draped an onyx rosary over it. Then, as if startled back to the moment, she quickly emptied the ashtray into the trashcan, turned off the radio, slung an iris-embroidered blue and white handbag over her shoulder, said, "Goodnight," and walked out.

"Goodnight," Father Casimiro said to Sally's back.

* * *

Inside Father Joe's office, Anna had composed herself. "I won't talk about it. Not now."

"Anna, I can assure you, in thirty years as a priest, I've heard it all."

"But not about me. Just help me stop the unraveling. Tell me how I can fix it all."

Father Joe nodded. "When we were kids, me and your father, he taught me how to play pool. He was terrific. I was just okay. One night, we were in this little pool room on Canal Street and I said, 'Pomp, give me some pointers?' He watched me make some shots and then he said, 'Joey, pool is all about the distance from the cue tip to the cue ball, which should never be more than two inches. And those two inches are all you can control.'"

"So what're my two inches?"

"Let's find out. But let's take our first steps on ground where you feel safe. Tell me only what you want to tell me. We'll talk again and again. Okay?"

"Okay." Anna was suddenly aware the radio had been turned off in the outer office.

"Unraveling," Father Joe repeated. "But not unraveled. So, how about you and me and God put our heads together and stop this unraveling. What does it feel like?"

"I feel like I'm off course, abandoned...vacant... my best years are gone and now I'm just falling apart. All of my emotions are right here in my throat." Anna placed both hands on the front of her neck. "The slightest thing, a song, will start me crying. It's getting more difficult to hold it. It's hard to explain."

"You're doing fine. Go on."

"I have so little patience with my sons. I let the boys get away with stuff because I just don't want to deal with it. Then I get angry with myself for letting them do whatever it was, and I yell, 'Don't do this; don't do that, just sit quietly.' Later, I feel bad about being too tough, and so it goes." Anna blotted tears with Father Joe's handkerchief.

"You haven't been to church since Mac disappeared."

"Just about." Anna gave her eyes one more swab. "But right now I'm more concerned about Angelo."

"Anna, unless someone else is going to raise Angelo, you have to pull yourself together."

"I'll do anything for my boys."

"Good. Start by coming to church again."

"I'm not so sure God will take me back."

"He already has, Annabella. We should meet every week... more if you want to."

"I think...that would be good," she said slowly, thoughtfully nodding.

"Let Sally know what works best for you. I will arrange my time to your convenience, and if you can't come here, I will come to you. Okay?"

"Thank you."

"No problem. Now, talk to me about Angelo," he said, lighting another cigarette.

"I need to understand what's going on with him."

"Okay," Father Joe said. "I'll tell you something about the boys around here. When I was growing up in this neighborhood, I had four friends. Your father, Nunzio Sabino, George Keller, and Nick Gostopolas. Nick's daughter is a friend of yours, right?"

"Yeah, Rosemarie's my best friend. She lives in my building. Her son Spiro and Angelo were in the same class in PS-1, and now they're both going to PS-65. They start the seventh grade a week from Tuesday. So what about you, and my father, and...?"

"The five of us were inseparable. All for one and one for all. Even today, we all keep in touch. We play cards on the third Tuesday of every month."

"Ever since I can remember, my father has told me stories about you and him and Uncle Nunzio. And you know I love Uncle Nunzio—he's my godfather. But he is who he is...the Boss, and you're a priest."

"Yeah and Nick was a cop. But Anna, I'm not talking about what path you have chosen. I'm talking about what you are. And we are friends. No matter what. Period." Father Joe walked over to the browning black-and-white picture hanging on the wall of five barely teenage boys with their arms around each other and smiling. He took it off the wall and walked back to Anna. "By the time this picture was taken, we knew who we were."

"But, so young?"

"In this neighborhood, we grow up quickly. But in the projects...no comparison."

"What do you mean?" Anna asked.

"There is a kind of social order in this neighborhood and it's worse in the projects," Father Joe said. "By the time a boy hits his teens, he's either prey, predator, or he has mastered his environment."

"Mastered his environment?"

"Yes; he is respected by the weak and the predators. This is a very difficult line to walk for anyone. Your father, Nunzio, Nick, George, and I made it, primarily because we had each other. We had our friendship."

"Father Joe, you became a priest, my father works at the meat market—"

"I know what you're going to say. But, like I said, it's not about what you do; it's about what you are. Nunzio Sabino and your father are stand-up guys. And so am I."

"But Uncle Nunzio's no priest."

"No, he's not. But I'll tell you something, many of the priests and almost all of the politicians I know I wouldn't trust with a nickel, but I'd trust Nunzio with my life."

"But, my Angelo is just a child."

"Uptown, yes. In this neighborhood, maybe, maybe not. But in the projects, no. If Angelo fits in perfectly uptown, he will draw needless and dangerous attention to himself in the projects, where he has to exist every day. I hear the fourteen- and fifteen-year-old kids from the projects talking about who's better than whom. But they don't use school grades, sports, or merit badges to distinguish themselves. They use a 'who can beat up who' rating system.

"That's the system that Angelo is stuck with right now. He must learn to navigate through that system without becoming a victim of it. He must appear tough but not act tough. He must have a sense of himself but not be too self-conscious. He must have a sense of humor that doesn't offend or make him seem silly. He must understand the first secret of courage, which is to appear unafraid, even when you're scared to death. He doesn't live uptown. Anna, listen to what I'm telling you and rely on the fact that Angelo is a good kid, and you have given him judgment and strength. He comes from good people."

Anna nodded.

"Okay, let's take one thing at a time. Tell me what he's doing that concerns you most."

"What concerns me most...," Anna repeated almost to herself. "It's hard to pinpoint. For the first couple of years after Mac disappeared, Angelo had terrible nightmares. I would hear him cry out at night and I'd go comfort him. Sometimes I would find him looking out of his window at Cherry Street and crying. Then one night, about two years ago, I had put the boys to bed and felt certain they were asleep. I poured myself a glass of wine and sat on the floor in my living room listening to music and feeling very alone...and, I guess, sorry for myself.

She continued. "Anyway, there I was sniveling. I don't know how long he had been standing there, but when I looked up, Angelo was standing next to me. He started to cry and I held him. He told me he was sorry for screwing everything up. He said he was going to be brave and not be a screw-up anymore."

"A screw-up?" Father Joe shrugged his shoulders.

"He told me that's what Mac used to call him. A screw-up." Anna shook her head. "Mac told him that he screwed up our whole life and that he would always be a screw-up."

"Anna, you never told—"

"I never knew." Anna covered her mouth with her fingers.

"Why would Mac say something like that to Angelo?"

"Father Joe, you are one of the few people who knew how Mac felt about Angelo."

"But, I always thought with time—"

"With time? Oh, Father Joe, Mac never accepted Angelo. He never hugged him. Never kissed him. I can't remember Mac ever saying a kind word to Angelo. Except...the night he disappeared, Angelo told me that Mac said he was a good kid. You can't imagine how much that means to Angelo. He holds on to that."

"What does Angelo think happened on the night his father disappeared, Anna?"

"That somehow he was supposed to take better care of his father that night." Anna sighed in frustrated disbelief.

"He was only seven. Why in the world—?"

"I know, I know, but it's part of what Angelo feels and what makes him, well, him. And then, sometimes he thinks Mac left because of him."

"Because of him?"

"Yeah, that must be the 'screw-up' thing, I don't know. Anyway, that's probably why he holds on so tightly to his father saying he was a good kid."

"Anna, does Angelo know about the Zara brothers?"

"No." Anna's gray eyes turned black and her jaw clenched. "No. Nothing about that."

"He must be told. We need to talk about telling him...but not right now."

"I know." Anna averted her eyes, momentarily lost. "Anyway, after the night Angelo saw me crying, no matter how much I tried to convince him that he wasn't a screw-up, that my crying had nothing to do with him, that it was okay to cry—he just became more distant. No—not distant, exactly—more like he's trying to be strong for me. He's taking on the responsibility of protecting me. He keeps his fears locked up, you know? And he doesn't cry anymore. I know he's troubled, but he won't talk to me about it. I say, 'Angelo, you're still a kid; it's my job to take care of you.' And then, there's the edge thing."

"Edge thing?"

"One day, I'm taking the subway with Angelo and Adam. As the train came into the station, most people backed away from the edge of the platform. Not my Angelo; he walked to the edge. I mean right to the edge. He stood there as the train roared in a couple of inches in front of him. I said, 'Angelo, what's the matter with you? Back up.' Then the other day I looked out the window and saw him crossing the street. A car was coming. It looked like he was going to walk right into the car. It just missed him. Like a bullfighter. And he just kept walking."

"Did you ask him about this?"

"He said he likes getting close to the edge. But sometimes I think he might—"

"I wouldn't worry too much about that, Anna."

"Don't tell me not to worry. Tell me it's normal, he'll outgrow it. All boys do that stuff, but don't tell me not to worry. Please."

"You're right. Let's start by putting it in the context of his other behavior."

"Other behavior...sometimes he goes to that spot on Cherry Street, where he last saw Mac, and just stands there looking around and talking to...no one...himself. My mother saw him a couple of days ago walking in circles around that spot and talking to the sidewalk."

"How often does he do this?"

"Couple of times a week. It's like he gets something in his head and he has to go back there and look around."

"Have you asked him about this?"

"No. I don't want him to think... It's hard for me to reach him sometimes. I'm afraid of losing him, I mean, losing him further inside himself."

"Where does he usually hang out?" asked Father Joe.

"When he's not working, mostly he hangs out with his friends at the Cherry Street playground, or the penny arcade on Mott Street, or at Mo-Mo's."

"Anna, you have to risk talking to Angelo about your concerns, for his sake. And please encourage Angelo to hang out at the Cherry Street Settlement."

"I'll try."

"Actually, a new priest is coming to run the Settlement."

"Oh, no, are you leaving?"

"No, no...Father Casimiro will be working with me. He's young, bright, and will be a great mentor for the kids."

"Father Casimiro," Anna confirmed.

"He arrives today. With your permission, I'll give him some background and tell him to expect a visit from Angelo tomorrow. I'll talk to Angelo Sunday after Mass. You'll be there?"

Anna nodded. "Please tell the new priest whatever you want."

Father Joe put out his cigarette and they both stood up. "So, Sunday is Angelo's birthday."

"Yes, thirteen." Anna kissed Father Joe on his cheek and squeezed his arm. "Thank you."

"God bless you, Anna." Father Joe opened his office door and saw Father Casimiro in the reception area. "Oh, Robert, I'm glad you're here. I was just mentioning you to my dear friend. Robert, this is Mrs. Pastamadeo. Anna, this is Father Casimiro."

"So good to meet you Mrs. Pasta-ma-deo."

"Anna," she said, extending her hand to the young priest.

"I look forward to seeing you again, Anna," he said shaking her hand.

"Me, too. Well, I must run. Thank you, Father Joe."

"Thanks for coming in. My love to your family."

Anna walked out of Saint Joachim's and into the late afternoon veiled sun. The smell of incense and candle wax was quickly replaced by the humid scent of sewer and summer flowers. Walking along Roosevelt Street, she clenched her fists tightly at her sides, clinging to a sliver of renewed hope. The hint of a cautious smile shaped her mouth as she bit down on her lower lip.

CHAPTER THREE

"Now I gotta do it tonight."

Bookman's Grocery Store on Catherine Street had a long, L-shaped, five-foot-high counter that ran from the left of the entrance door to the very back of the store, where it turned right. It was there, at the short end of the "L," where the counter was three feet high, that Mr. Bookman waited on customers. The long part of the "L" enclosed capicola, prosciutto, ham, olive loaf, pancetta, salami, roast pork, a platter of hot dogs and Italian sausages, and other meats, including pickled pig's feet. There were also provolone, Swiss, and American cheeses, as well as mozzarella balls floating in a bowl of milk. These and other fresh goods were visible through a glass front.

Along all the walls were twelve-foot shelves stacked with groceries. The large, heavy cans of tomatoes, five-pound bags of sugar, and large boxes of Oxydol, Cheer, and other detergents shared the bottom shelves with cases and boxes of products to replace items as they were sold. Cases of Ballantine, Pabst, and Budweiser beers and soda that were not in the walk-in cooler were kept in the cellar. The higher shelves contained such items as Campbell soups, Quaker Oats, and smaller cans of Crisco. These were accessed by a long wooden pole with a metal claw at the top.

When Angelo returned from his delivery, Mr. Bookman was at the far end of the counter talking to a customer. Angelo walked down the narrow path between the counter and the shelves. He stopped at the freestanding five-foot-high magazine rack that was halfway down the aisle.

Angelo liked getting a first look at the new comics, especially *Gunsmoke* with Kid Colt, *War* with Sgt. Sawyer, and *Battle Front*, which this month featured "Colonel Chang's Last Chance!" But it was the cover of *Mystic* that caught his attention with a pair of eyes floating in midair and staring into an elevator that stopped on "The Thirteenth Floor." He would, on occasion, swipe a comic. But he would buy—because it was too big to steal—a week-old copy of Life for Uncle Johnny. Bookman charged him ten cents for the outdated magazine, which went for twenty cents new. The new Life was in so he could buy the August 12th issue with May Britt sticking out her tongue on the cover.

"Angelo! I'm not paying you to read. Did Mrs. Parks give you the five dollars for the groceries?" Mr. Bookman shouted.

"Yes, sir." Angelo heard a glass jar break.

"Now look what you made me do. Good grief, boy. Come around behind the counter and clean this up. And don't you forget to give me that five dollars."

Angelo walked around the counter. He had hated the job from his first day. But working at Bookman's was part of his plan.

Bookman's normal musty smell, subdued by fresh bread, suddenly included the scent of olive juice. Angelo picked up a cleaning rag and a small trash can and was walking the length of the counter toward Mr. Bookman.

"Come, boy, hurry up. And bring me a small jar of green olives. Right behind you."

"Got 'em." Before Angelo got to the turn in the counter, he saw a dollar bill lying on the floor. Angelo picked up the dollar and turned the corner. Mr. Bookman was standing just slightly in front of a small puddle of olive juice, olives, and broken glass.

"Give me the olives and the money and clean that mess."

"Here ya go, Mr. Bookman. And I found this dollar on the floor over there." Angelo handed the olives and the six dollars to Mr. Bookman and dropped to his knees to clean the mess. "Mr. Bookman, did the Pillsbury guy get here yet?"

"No he has not, and you can't leave until he makes his delivery." Mr. Bookman was shaking his head and shrugging his shoulders. "Is there anything else, Mrs. Fleming?" Not taking time to open the cash drawer that was built into the counter, Mr. Bookman stuffed the bills in his right front pants pocket and wiped the dust off the jar of olives with his white apron.

"What a nice, honest boy you have there, Mr. Bookman."

"Thank you, Mrs. Fleming, Angelo is an honest lad. But a little dim."

Angelo looked up and saw the tip of the dollar bill sticking out of Mr. Bookman's pocket. Angelo continued making cleaning noises with his left hand, as he reached slowly with his right toward the tip of the dollar.

"You should reward his honesty," said Mrs. Fleming.

Angelo's hand was closer. He knew that if Mr. Bookman looked down now he was finished. He kept moving toward the dollar.

"I always do," Mr. Bookman lied.

Angelo was close to the dollar when his hand started to shake. He pulled his hand back, took a long, deep breath, and squeezed his hand shut. Opened it. It stopped shaking. He took another deep breath and let it out slowly, as he again reached for the tip of the dollar.

"Well, you're a good man, Mr. Bookman."

Angelo was holding the tip of the dollar between his thumb and index finger and began to slowly pull the dollar out. Mr. Bookman was shifting his weight from side to side, a habit developed over years of standing for hours exchanging chatter.

"Thank you, Mrs. Fleming."

Angelo knew that Mr. Bookman was going to open the cash drawer any second, and he would probably put the pocket money in the drawer. He moved more quickly.

"That will be seven dollars and fourteen cents, Mrs. Fleming."

The dollar bill was free and in Angelo's hand, but the five-dollar bill, two more singles, and a quarter followed it out of Mr. Bookman's pocket. The quarter plunged for the floor. Faster than Mr. Bookman's addition, Angelo caught the quarter with the rag in his left hand, while the bills see-sawed down to the olive juice.

"Here you are." Mrs. Fleming closed her handbag. "The exact amount."

Mr. Bookman took the keys attached to his belt. He found the one for the cash drawer and started to look down.

Angelo was about to throw the rag on top of the puddle, when a shout from the front of the store caught Mr. Bookman's attention.

"Pillsbury. Delivery!"

Angelo hurriedly stuffed the damp eight dollars and twenty-five cents in his pocket and finished cleaning the spill. A distracted Mr. Bookman opened the cash drawer, deposited the seven dollars and fourteen cents, and closed and locked it again, without checking his pocket.

"Thanks for coming in, Mrs. Fleming, and have a nice evening."

"You, too, Mr. Bookman."

Angelo's heart was slowing down again. He swallowed hard.

"I'm coming, Mike," Mr. Bookman called back as Mrs. Fleming left the store. "C'mon, Angelo. You need to lift the doors." Angelo shoved the trash can to the side and followed Mr. Bookman out of the store.

"What do you have for me, Mike?" Mr. Bookman asked, as he again looked through his keys. The cellar doors lay flat together and locked on the sidewalk to the left of his entrance. There was only one key for that lock and Mr. Bookman kept it on his key chain. He kneeled, removed the lock, and stood up.

"Seven boxes," Mike said. "Where do you want them?"

Angelo lifted both heavy steel cellar doors and laid them flat open. Mr. Bookman and Mike headed down the steep steps and Angelo followed. Mr. Bookman put the open lock on top of a large box marked Ronson Corporation at the foot of the steps.

"Here, put one of them near the stairs to the back room. Angelo needs to unpack it for the shelves. You can stack the rest over there." Mr. Bookman counted the boxes as they came down.

Angelo casually and circuitously made his way back to the Ronson box. There he removed an open lock from his pocket. It was identical to Mr. Bookman's lock. As Mike carried down the last box, and was between Angelo and Mr. Bookman, Angelo quickly switched locks. He put Mr. Bookman's lock in his pocket, being careful not to close it.

"That's it," Mike said. "I need you to sign the paperwork, and I could use a cold beer."

Angelo went up first. At the top of the stairs, he saw a cop looking at Mike's truck.

"This guy making a delivery here, kid?" the cop asked.

"Yes, sir," Angelo said. "Mr. Bookman, there's a cop up here looking for Mike." Angelo hoped that hearing this, Mr. Bookman would grab the open lock without giving it much notice.

"Good evening, officer, you're new on this beat aren't you? I'm Mr. Bookman; this is my store. Is everything okay?"

"You have a hydrant right here," the cop said.

"That's my truck, officer; I'm leaving as soon as I get the paperwork," Mike said.

"The doors are closed, Mr. Bookman," Angelo said.

"Angelo, fine. Fine. Now, go down the cellar through the store and unpack that box. I swear this kid's an idiot." Mr. Bookman was shaking his head. "Officer, why don't you stop in, let me make you a sandwich or something?" Mr. Bookman said, as he walked over to the cellar doors and locked them with Angelo's lock.

"Now I gotta do it tonight," Angelo whispered to himself.

CHAPTER FOUR

"Just below the boiling point."

At 5:30 p.m., Father Joe showed Father Casimiro to one of the wooden booths at Mo-Mo's Pizzeria on Madison Street. Seven wooden booths lined the right wall. On the left wall were three small tables for two, a jukebox, which was playing The Jesters's *So Strange*, and two more small tables. At the end of the path between the booths and tables was a four-foot-long counter. A teenage boy and girl were the only other customers and sat in the middle booth.

"How's this?" Father Joe pointed to the booth closest to the counter.

"Good," Father Casimiro said.

A voice from behind the counter shouted, "Be right with ya."

"No rush." Father Joe took out his pack of Camels and extended them to Father Casimiro.

"No, thanks, I'm quitting."

Father Joe lit a cigarette and pulled the ashtray closer. "I know I said we'd be going to my favorite spot in Chinatown, but I decided on Mo-Mo's instead for two reasons. First, a boy I will talk to you about likes this place."

"And second?"

"This boy's mother—who has not had an easy life—is concerned about him."

"And this boy's mother would be your dear friend, Mrs. Pastamadeo?"

"Very good, Robert."

"When you say Mrs. Pastamadeo—Anna—has not had an easy life..."

"Six years ago her husband, Mac, disappeared. At the time, Angelo was seven and Anna was pregnant with Adam. Anna had promised Mac that his brother Johnny could live with them for as long as he needed. Johnny was a Korean War hero who had no physical injuries but suffered from combat stress. We all offered to take him in—me, her parents—but Anna promised Mac and that was that."

"Is Johnny dangerous?"

"No. Johnny has a form of agoraphobia—he's afraid to leave the apartment. He hasn't stepped outside since he arrived there in March of '52."

"So her difficulties began six years ago?"

"Anna's difficulties began about fourteen years ago, on Thanksgiving." Father Joe was facing the takeout counter, and saw Morgan Mosby approaching the table. "We'll finish later."

Morgan was twenty-nine years old. His skin was a rich, deep chocolate and his eyes were polished indigo marbles—more stone than soft, more mirror than window. His upper body was well defined and all muscle. But Morgan's legs, from well above his knees, were gone. He perched on a flat piece of hard wood with a black leather cover.

Four swivel wheels allowed Morgan mobility. In each hand, he carried a wood and leather block. He used these blocks to push himself along. On each side of his wooden board, which he dubbed "Morgan's scooter," was a hook upon which to hang his push-blocks. And in the front of his scooter was a basket to carry whatever he might wish to bring along.

In the kitchen were a ramp and rail that brought Morgan waist-high at the takeout counter. An Army .45 automatic hung on a hook below the counter. There were also several strategically placed mirrors, a switch that locked the front door, and a custom-ized dumbwaiter that provided transportation between his upstairs apartment and the pizzeria kitchen.

"Good to see you, Father Joe."

"Morgan, this is Father Casimiro. He'll be working with me, and I wanted to introduce him to the best pizza place right off the bat."

"Good to meet you, Father Crazy-mirro." Morgan held out his large hand.

"Good to meet you, Morgan," Father Casimiro said, shaking his hand.

"So, how do you like my joint?"

"What is it that makes this place better than the pizzerias on, say, Mulberry Street?" Father Casimiro immediately felt comfortable with Morgan.

"Good for you, Father Direct," Morgan said, as *Little Darlin'* came on the jukebox. "Answer me this, what's that song you hear playing?"

"That's easy, it's *Little Darlin.'*"

"By?"

"By the Diamonds," said Father Casimiro.

"Ha! The Diamonds are just a white cover group. What you're hearing is *Little Darlin'* by the Gladiolas. They wrote it and sing the soul into it. But the only place you can hear it, and any other real music south of Harlem, is right here at Mo-Mo's Pizzeria. And our pizza is as good as our music."

"The Gladiolas?" repeated Father Casimiro. "Are you sure?"

"Am I sure? Order a pizza, check out my jukebox, and if I'm wrong, the pizza's on the house," Morgan said with a big, warm smile.

"Speaking of pizza, we'll have a small pie and two egg creams," said Father Joe.

"You got *Church Bells May Ring*? asked Father Casimiro. He liked the game.

"By?" asked Morgan.

"The Willows, of course."

"The Willows? Well, listen to him. You damn sorry right I got the Willows on my box. Where you from, Father Direct?"

"Milwaukee."

"Milwaukee?"

"Wisconsin—"

"I know where Milwaukee is. I just didn't think you had any colored folk out there, 'cept Hank Aaron."

"You bet we do, and both of them like the Willows better than the Diamonds."

"Ha! That's good! This man's all right, Father Joe. Both like the Willows," chuckled Morgan as he made his way back to the pizza ovens.

"Good for you, Robert." Father Joe smiled. "Or do you prefer Father Direct?"

"I prefer Father Direct over Father Clumsy."

"Father Clumsy? Who called you that?"

Father Casimiro wanted to tell Father Joe everything that happened today. But he knew that everything he marveled at was just part of the background to someone like Father Joe, who grew up here. So in an attempt at a detached tone, he told Father Joe about his encounter with the large man and the three young Knights. "They were only fifteen or sixteen and yet they, especially the one named Jimmy, had all the poise of a stage actor. They were impressive—in a bad way—but impressive."

"That would be Jimmy Bowman. He's fifteen. You have to be fourteen to be a Knight."

"They have rules?"

"Indeed they do."

"I remember reading about a crippled kid getting killed."

"A terrible thing—Michael Farmer, fifteen years old and crippled by polio, murdered up on the West Side by the Egyptian Kings." Father Joe sighed. "This summer, kids have been killed all over the city. But down here on the Lower East Side, the birthplace of street gangs, things have been kept...'under control' might be too strong...how about, 'just below the boiling point'? Father Kim Myers, the vicar over at Trinity Episcopal, managed to get a peace commitment from the Dragons, the Sportsmen, the Enchanters, and the Chino Squad. Kim has convinced all four gangs to attend the Trinity Mission. I've convinced the Cobras, the South Street Boys, and the Yellow Jackets to attend the Cherry Street Settlement. You'll be working with them and a lot of other kids from the neighborhood."

"Joe, thank you for the opportunity to work with you."

"That's very nice of you, Robert, but the truth is, I need you here. We are needed here...there's much to do. This has been a particularly difficult summer."

"You didn't mention Satan's Knights."

"The only gang I've not been able to bring over is the Knights. And, frankly, I don't hold out much hope, but I'm not ready to give up just yet." Father Joe shook his head.

"Good. I read in today's *New York Times* that the police commissioner disagreed with the mayor over what to do about juvenile gangs and delinquency."

"It's city politics and a lot of bravado."

"But the kids. It's so sad."

"Today's *Times* also reported that this is the thirteenth consecutive day without a single polio case in the entire city. There's good news for kids, too. Having you here is also good news for them. So forget about the mayor and police commissioner. You and I are going to create more good news for these kids. Okay?"

"You bet."

"Have you been over to the Settlement house?"

"I stopped by briefly. Any final word from the city about St. Joachim."

"I'm afraid so—the city's going to close St. Joachim."

"Close, for sure? I know you were concerned about that during my interview, but I never thought they'd close it."

"It's certain, Robert. But it doesn't necessarily mean they're going to close the Settlement, and whatever happens, I promise you'll land on your feet."

"That's not my concern." Father Casimiro blushed. "Why close it? When?"

"Well, the plan is to close it next month. But I'm hoping a friend of mine might buy us a little more time. We'll talk with him on Sunday. The why is that the city plans to renovate the area around the Brooklyn Bridge. In addition to new approaches to the bridge, there are plans for a twenty-one-story co-op and a new police headquarters. Anyway, it means that all the buildings in the way, which includes St. Joachim's, will be torn down."

"What about you? I came here to work with you."

"I'll be around."

CHAPTER FIVE
"Sometimes people just disappear."

Anna was still encouraged by her talk with Father Joe earlier in the day as she fixed dinner for her brother-in-law, Johnny, and his two Korean War buddies. Ben and Henry brought Johnny to Anna's apartment in March of 1952. They told her they would send money each month to help care for him. Anna protested, but they insisted. Ben, the older of the two, told her that they owed their lives to Johnny, and that this was something they needed to do. Money had come every month since that first visit. And she had to admit—but only to herself—that it helped.

Anna invited them to visit—so in addition to a surprise visit here and there, on the last Friday of every month, Anna insisted on fixing dinner for Johnny, Ben, and Henry. She would then take Angelo and Adam to her parents, giving the three war buddies room to remember and forget.

After preparing dinner, she took Angelo and Adam to her parents' place to have dinner with them and her two brothers. Frank, her older brother, was thirty-three years old and owned the Lilly's Spirits liquor store on Catherine Street. Her younger brother Danny was nineteen and worked for Frank.

Pompa sat in his big chair, smoked his pipe, and told the boys what it had been like in Africa when he was in the Army. Anna liked the sweet cherry smell of her father's tobacco. Last year, Pompa had brought home a Motorola TV, and tonight Gene Autry was on at six o'clock. They all looked forward to these Friday-night dinners.

In Nonna's small kitchen, Anna and her mother performed a well-practiced and perfectly choreographed ballet with seafood, fusilli, spices, and pots, each complementing the other's rhythm. Over and under and around, creating sizzles and smells that made everyone's mouth water. It was delicious magic.

"Mama," Anna said as she grated Romano and Parmesan cheese. "I met the new priest at Saint Joachim's today."

"Father Casimiro," Nonna said.

"Yes. He seems so young."

"He's twenty-eight."

"He seems much younger."

"A woman your age shouldn't say that out loud."

"Thirty-one isn't ancient."

"I didn't say it was." Pointing to the large pot on the stove, Nonna said, "See if the macaroni is done."

"It's perfect." Anna moved the pot to the sink and grabbed a colander.

"So you went to Saint Joachim's today?"

"Yeah...to talk to Father Joe."

"Oh, yeah? About what?"

"Just stuff."

"You can talk to Father Joe, but not to your mother, about this stuff?"

"Ma, it was like I went to confession."

"In confession with Father Joe you met the new priest?"

"Ma, please. As I was leaving, Father Joe introduced me. It was no big deal."

"No big deal? You haven't been to church in what, six years, and now suddenly you go to church to talk about God knows what, but you can't talk to your own mother? And this is no big deal? Here, taste, what does it need?" Nonna held a wooden spoon with tomato gravy and a shrimp on it to Anna's mouth.

"Ooh, hot...ahh," Anna said, sipping the gravy and eating the shrimp. "A little more black pepper and some white wine, maybe half a cup."

"I got red in there. Now white?"

"Yeah, half a cup."

"So you're going back to church with us?" Nonna added white wine directly from the bottle.

"Nonna," Adam shouted from the living room. "Pompa said we can't watch *Rin Tin Tin* tonight. He said we gotta watch *Beat the Clock* instead."

"Pompeo, don't be a scutch. They can watch the tin-dog show," Nonna called back. A crash of laughter came from the living room. "What I say?"

"*Rin Tin Tin*, Ma. And yes, we're going to church."

"Wonderful. Wait 'til your father hears; he's gonna be so happy. Did you tell the boys?"

"I told them on the way over."

"Good. You come over on Sunday after church, and we'll fix bracciole and a nice cake for Angelo's birthday. And we can talk."

"Mama, please. I don't need this right now."

"Need what? Bracciole, cake, and talk. What's to need?"

"I'll come over on Sunday and we'll see what we will see." Anna sighed.

"Good. We'll talk then."

Anna looked up past the ceiling to God and shrugged.

"Come, boys," Nonna said as she poured a mixture of cream soda and red wine into two glasses for Angelo and Adam. "*Mangiare.*"

* * *

"Gentlemen, how's that pizza?" Morgan called from behind the takeout counter.

"Best pizza I've ever had," said Father Casimiro.

"As compared to what—Milwaukee? You tell me that again after you tried some places on, what's that you said before? Oh, yeah—Mulberry Street."

"I will, Morgan, but this was still the best pizza I've ever had."

"You have good instincts, Robert; you're going to make a difference."

"Again, I am very fortunate to be here."

"There is much to do here, Robert. Too much for even two priests, I'm afraid."

"But you've been handling St. Joachim and the Cherry Street Settlement by yourself?"

"Not always. A few years back, I was working with a more senior priest, Father Culley, who watched over St. Joachim while I devoted myself to the Settlement."

"Where is he now?"

"I haven't kept up with him. Last I heard, he made Monsignor and was ministering to a desk—a fitting flock for Culley—uptown."

"Well, you're not alone anymore and I'm anxious to jump in. But I got us off track. You wanted to talk about Mrs. Pastamadeo and her son?"

"If you're finished eating, I suggest we talk as we walk around the neighborhood." Father Joe, with a Camel dangling from his lips, carried the pizza platter with one slice to the counter and paid for the meal. The Diablos were singing "The Wind" as Father Casimiro followed with the dishes and the glasses.

"It's always a pleasure, Father Joe, and it was nice meeting you, Father Casimiro."

"Take care, Morgan." Father Joe opened the door.

The summer night heat, damp smells, and colliding voices filled the air and swirled around Father Casimiro's head like a carnival. "Which way should we go?"

"Let's go left, Robert. This is Madison Street; we're walking toward Catherine Street. On the right, over there, is PS-1; straight ahead and to the left are the Al Smith projects."

"I walked this way when I bumped into the Knights."

"Let's see who else we bump into. We'll make a left and walk down Catherine to Cherry Street." Father Joe lit another Camel as they turned the corner.

"How old is Angelo?"

"He'll be thirteen on Sunday." Father Joe blew smoke toward the darkening sky.

"Thirteen. I saw a kid today. Now, I know that Angelo is probably a common name in this neighborhood, I mean—"

"Not that common. Tell me what you saw."

"As I walked down Monroe Street I looked up at a roof near St. Joseph and saw this kid standing on the edge. It looked like he was thinking about jumping. Some guy said to me, 'Don't worry, that's Angelo. He's a roof rat.'"

"That was our Angelo," Father Joe muttered. "The edge."

"The edge?"

"Something his mother said to me earlier today."

"So tell me about Angelo," Father Casimiro said, as a red and black 1955 Pontiac with its top down screamed past them.

"Yo, Father Joe," the young driver yelled, waving. One of the three girls in the backseat turned and whistled flirtatiously.

"I'm certain that was for you, Robert." Father Joe smiled and waved back.

The boy in the front passenger seat was lost in *Rock Around the Clock* blasting from the radio. The car stopped abruptly and backed into a parking spot near St. Joseph's church.

"Not Knights, I'm guessing."

"Yellow Jackets. Those are Knights." Father Joe pointed across the street to a dozen teens all wearing black T-shirts, walking together in the projects. "So, about Angelo...where to start?"

"His mother is not just another parishioner to you."

"Good place to start. Anna's father, Pompeo, and I grew up together, like brothers. So, Anna is like my own daughter."

"What happened fourteen years ago? You started to tell me in Mo-Mo's.

"Well, let's back up a couple of months. Fourteen years ago— almost to the day—I married Anna and Mac. They were so young, so in love."

"Mac?"

"Michele Pastamadeo."

"So Mac is short for Michele?"

"He picked up the nickname Macaroni as a kid because of his last name, Pasta-madeo. He never minded; it was all in fun. It seems like everyone has a nickname in this neighborhood."

"Oh, so Mac is short for Macaroni."

"Yeah, but not that easy." Father Joe slowly shook his head and looked down. He took a last drag off his Camel, dropped it, stepped on it, and twisted his foot from side to side, crushing it into the pavement. "What I'm going to tell you now must stay between us; it must have the sanctity of a confession."

"Of course, please."

"Three months after Anna and Mac were married, Anna was helping out at the Settlement house serving Thanksgiving dinner. We were finishing up; it was late. I left to deliver a dozen meals to neighborhood shut-ins. She stayed to clean up."

Father Joe removed another a cigarette from the pack, tapped it gently on his left thumbnail, and placed it in his mouth. "I left."

He shook his head and then lit the cigarette. He took a long, composing drag as they walked. "About an hour or so later, I finished my deliveries and headed back. When I got there, I reached out to open the front door, when Remo and Ignazio Zara shoved the door open and ran right into me on their way out. I grabbed onto Iggy, the older one, and I said, 'What are you guys doing here?' Iggy said, 'Nothing, Father, just eating macaroni.' Then he pulled away and they took off laughing. I walked in, Anna was on the floor, curled up and bleeding. They had raped and beaten her."

"Dear God." Father Casimiro squeezed his friend's forearm. "So you recognized them?"

"Yes. The Zara brothers were from Oliver Street. They, Stan Primo, the Tonello brothers, and the Cruz brothers started Satan's Knights back in '42." Anyway, I got Anna to Beekman hospital. I stayed there all night with Mac, Mac's brother Johnny, who was about fourteen, Anna's parents, and her brother Danny, who was only five at the time. Her older brother Frank was overseas, in the army. I told them everything—the Zara brothers running out of the Settlement house and what Iggy said. Robert, it was one of the toughest nights of my life."

Another deep drag on his cigarette. "Anna lost a lot of blood but obviously pulled through and named the Zara brothers as the attackers. She gave the police a formal statement on that Sunday morning. I didn't hear from the cops until Sunday afternoon, when I got a call asking me to come down Monday morning to talk to the detective on the case. I did that and confirmed that I saw the Zara brothers running out of the Settlement."

Lightning illuminated the ships docked along the South Street piers straight ahead of them, followed by a loud crack of thunder. Several people sitting on benches along Catherine Street got up and headed for shelter.

"Hey, Fadda, hi'ya doin'?" a bum in a light blue and yellow checkered, short-sleeved shirt shouted from the projects side of Catherine Street. He was standing facing them and urinating between two parked cars.

"Doing good, Sammy." Father Joe waved. And to Father Casimiro he said, "That's South Street Sammy, one of the original 'South Street Boys.'"

"Did you tell them what Iggy said?"

"No." Father Joe took a long drag and flicked the cigarette into the street. "That Monday morning—before I talked to the cops—Jason Carter, the Settlement caretaker, as usual went over to open the Settlement at five a.m. It was still dark so Mr. Carter didn't notice the Zara brothers until he was right there in front of the Settlement-house stoop."

"The Zara brothers were there?"

"They were facing each other, kneeling with their backs against the large posts on opposite sides of the stoop. Two gargoyles kneeling, eyes wide open, mouths smiling, tightly closed, just staring at each other. Mr. Carter started to say something to Iggy before he saw the blood...so much blood. Then he noticed that Iggy's hands were tied behind his back. Both boys were tied to the posts in this...this kneeling position. They were cold ghost dead."

"But, you said their heads were up, smiling at each other?"

"Their heads were tied to the posts in an upright position, exposing the deep purple gashes on each of their throats. Rags were tied around their mouths—actually, they were so tight that they were in and around the mouth, pulling the cheeks back in what appeared to be a bizarre smile. Over the rags, their lips were fastened shut by large safety pins. These pins went through the top lip and out through the bottom lip and then closed."

Father Casimiro stepped back and leaned against a Hudson parked in front of Lilly's Spirits. He felt lightheaded. Another crack of thunder. He welcomed the first few drops of rain.

"You okay?"

"I think I need a cigarette."

Father Joe took out two Camels, lit them, and gave one to his new colleague.

Father Casimiro inhaled a long drag, held it, and then sighed the smoke at the sidewalk.

"Come with me." Father Joe took the young priest by the arm and walked him into Lilly's. Squeals and laughter came from the Pontiac down the street as the convertible top ascended against the rain.

The man behind the cash register in Lilly's said, "Hey—I got it—two priests walk into a liquor store and—"

"Funny," said Father Joe. "Where are Frank and Danny, Jokes?"

"Over at their mom's for dinner. I'm covering for them."

"That's right. Anna mentioned that this afternoon."

"Okay, how 'bout this one—a forgetful priest walks into a liquor—"

"Jokes, you're a funny guy, but all I want is a shot of whatever is open back there."

"No problem. How 'bout a couple of Imperials?"

"Great. This is Father Casimiro; he's my new partner."

Jokes poured Imperial whiskey into two small glasses and slid them across the counter. "Here ya go, Fathers."

"Thanks." Father Joe handed a glass to Father Casimiro.

"I'm really okay, Joe. Really."

"Yeah? Good, but I haven't formally welcomed you to New York yet."

"Hey, wait for me." Jokes poured himself a couple of fingers.

"Welcome to New York, Robert." Father Joe held his glass up.

The two priests and Jokes clicked and emptied their glasses.

Father Casimiro smiled an unassuming "Thank you." He walked over to the glass door and looked out at the street. The sudden heavy downpour had changed to a light rain. "Can we keep walking, Joe?"

"It's rainin'," Jokes said.

"It's an easy rain."

The two priests thanked Jokes, cupped their cigarettes, and stepped out into the night rain. They walked to the corner of Catherine and turned left on Cherry Street in silence.

Father Casimiro took a drag on his cigarette and broke the silence. "Pins?"

"Safety pins. As you could imagine, poor Mr. Carter was rattled. He called me from the Settlement house. I told him to call the police and wait inside. I would be right there."

The two priests walked with their heads down against the rain.

"You saw all this?"

"Yes, I got there just before the cops. When the safety pins were finally removed, they found uncooked rigatoni—macaroni, in each man's mouth."

"Macaroni? It might take me a little time to get used to the way things are here."

"This is not the way things are. It's shocking. You're not supposed to get used to it."

Father Casimiro felt relieved, not just because his reaction wasn't viewed as naïve, but because the world still made sense. When awful things happened, it was even awful here. "Was he—I mean someone—arrested? Was there a trial? What happened after that?"

"What happened after that was no one called Mac 'Macaroni' ever again." Father Joe took one more drag off his cigarette and tossed it into the gutter. The cigarette bobbed and rolled in a narrow stream along the curb, splashing up and around the tires of parked cars.

"So you didn't tell the police what Iggy said because he was dead?"

"That and it was over. I didn't want to bring more heartache to that family, to Anna."

"But the police must've suspected it was Mac."

"Mac came up with a good alibi."

"Joe, you covered up a murder."

"Right and wrong are blurred here, Robert."

"Not in God's eyes."

"You're right. You'll be a needed gauge for me, Robert."

"What about the press? Friends?"

"With the exception of the other Knights, the Zara brothers had few friends, and most people thought they got what they deserved. Everyone else lost interest."

"Their family?"

"Well, that was very sad. Their father kept trying to convince the police to go after Mac. He died of a broken heart—actually, a heart attack on August 25, 1947."

"You remember the date?" said Father Casimiro. The two priests crossed Market Street.

"It was Angelo's third birthday."

"And the rest of the family?" The two priests continued up Cherry Street and under the Manhattan Bridge. Several bums were curled for the night in their black alcoves. Father Casimiro looked around as he heard the scurrying of small creatures.

"Well, that left just their mother Fabia and sister Angie, who by then was twelve years old. Right after her husband's funeral, Fabia took Angie and moved to her family's home in Italy. They never came back."

"What about the gang, the Knights?"

"A good friend, whom we will have coffee with on Sunday, convinced Hector and Danilo Cruz, the new leaders of the Knights, that it was not in their interest to go after Mac, Anna, or Anna's family. Danilo, the most reasonable of the Cruz brothers, was killed in Korea in 1950."

"Coffee Sunday. Swell."

As they reached the Cherry Street Settlement, the rain was little more than a mist. Father Casimiro stared at the large posts on either side of the stoop, imagining what the Zara brothers looked like, facing each other, strapped to those posts. The Settlement had two tenement buildings on its left toward Pike Street and three empty lots on its right. A sign on the front door read CSS welcomes all on Saturday, August 24. Please stop by and meet Father Casimiro.

"Wait a minute; Angelo was born on August 25, 1944?"

"That's right."

"And, the attack on Anna was in November of '43," Father Casimiro continued slowly.

"Angelo was born nine months after the rape."

"You mean that—"

"Anna's certain that Angelo's Mac's son. But no one was ever able to convince Mac of that. Anna—all of us—tried talking to him."

"And Angelo knows all of this?"

"No, he knows none of it. He just knows his father was never warm toward him."

"He must be told. Sooner or later, he's going to hear something."

"I'm talking to Anna about how to best do that. Do you want to head back—maybe through the projects?"

"The projects, sure," Father Casimiro said. Even though the idea made him uneasy, he was with a priest who had grown up here.

"C'mon," Father Joe said as the priests retraced their steps.

"So it's not bad enough Angelo is growing up in those projects, but bang, right from day one, he's got this stigma that even his own father embraces instead of him," Father Casimiro said, raising his voice.

"My, my, you've been unleashed." Father Joe talked about the night Mac disappeared and Anna taking in and caring for Mac's brother, and her drifting away from the Church.

"Well, clearly it was retaliation by the Knights," Father Casimiro said.

"Our friend is convinced it wasn't the Knights."

"Can you tell me our friend's name?"

"Sure, I'm sorry. Nunzio Sabino. We have been friends since we were kids."

"Why is he so certain it wasn't the Knights?"

"Several former Knights work for Nunzio, and one of his top guys, Gene Viola, oversees them and they keep the Knights in line. They looked into it and said, 'No chance.'"

"What about the authorities?"

"They say this happens. Sometimes people just disappear. Husbands run off, sometimes with a mistress—which Mac had—

and sometimes alone." They crossed Catherine Street. South Street Sammy was curled up, under damp newspaper, on a bench in the small playground. "That's where Anna lives, fifth floor." Father Joe tilted his head toward 20 Catherine Slip as they walked between the building and the playground and into the darkening ghostly core of the projects. "C'mon, we'll weave our way through them."

"So did his mistress know anything or was she gone, too?"

"She was Frank's first stop, but she didn't have a clue." Light from too few lampposts along their footpath flickered and hummed with insects and electrical problems.

"Joe, do you believe that Mac would just leave a pregnant wife and a seven-year-old son on Christmas Eve?" Father Casimiro was very aware of the movement of black shirts in and out of the shadows around them.

"After Angelo was born, Mac began to drink too much. He became abusive and took a mistress. But no, I do not believe he just left."

"So what happened to Mac on Christmas Eve six years ago?"

"That is still a mystery," Father Joe said. "I told you that Angelo said he dropped the cart with the presents in the snow and ran home? He also told Frank, Anna's older brother, that there were no empty parking spaces on Cherry Street that night."

"So?"

"When Frank found the cart, it was standing upright and all the presents were piled in it," Father Joe said, lighting a cigarette and offering one to Father Casimiro, who turned it down.

"So, Angelo didn't drop the cart?"

"Oh, he dropped it. The presents were damp and the snow around the cart still showed an imprint of where it fell. Also, a parking space near the cart was empty except for some vomit in the snow. Not a surprise—someone overindulged on Christmas Eve, threw up, and drove off. Or threw up and walked away before or after the car left. Who knows? It wasn't Mac, at least not while Angelo was still there. And it would take more than a drunk to overpower Mac. There were several different footprints around the empty spot. And tire tracks from the spot headed down Catherine toward South Street. Frank asked folks in the bar on the corner but nobody remembered anything."

"So that's it?"

"Well, Frank thinks he might have a lead."

"Did he tell the police?"

"The police told him." Father Joe blew white smoke into the dark night. "Frank joined the cops in '46, one year after his army discharge. He was going to get married, so he rented a three-room apartment at 10 Monroe Street in Knickerbocker. But his wife-to-be ran off with someone else. I don't think Frank ever got over it. He was a cop on his way up, lots of commendations. Then, in 1950, he quit. But he still has friends there, and they keep in touch."

The priests were interrupted by a shout from one of the windows in the projects: "Harry, you son of a bitch, you get back here. Harry! You hear me? Harry?"

"Ah, the music of the city," said Father Joe. "Anyway, last week, Frank gets a call from his former partner, who says he has a snitch doing time upstate who, in trying to cut a deal, said he was in prison with a guy who bragged about a hit he did on Christmas Eve 1951, on Cherry Street. Frank's former partner is getting the snitch out of prison next week and will arrange a time for Frank to talk to him."

"Sounds promising."

"There have been so many dead ends that it's hard to be hopeful."

"So Frank went from being a cop to buying a liquor store?"

"Originally it was Catherine Street Liquor, owned by two childhood friends of Frank—Gus and Lilly. In '48, Lilly was shot and killed during a holdup. Gus changed the name to Lilly's Spirits. When Frank left the cops, Gus gave him a job at the store. Then in '54, Spiro killed himself. He never recovered from the loss of Lilly and ended up leaving the liquor store to Frank."

Chapter Six

"The ghost is in the window."

Friday night dinner at Nonna's was more than a delicious meal—Angelo and Adam got to watch some of their favorite TV programs: *Rin Tin Tin* at seven-thirty, followed by *The Adventures of Jim Bowie*. At eight-thirty, Pompa switched to channel five. As *Racket Squad* began, Angelo, his mother, and Adam hugged and kissed everyone goodbye and headed for home. Nonna and Pompa lived close to St. Joachim's on Madison Street. It would be a shorter walk to cut through center of the projects, but it was safer to walk around them.

The rain had slowed to a few intermittent drops. The air was balmy, and the sky was a banded blend of black, plum, and ash-blue. Angelo took in a deep, soothing breath as he walked with his mother and brother along Madison Street.

As they turned right onto Catherine Street, his mother said, "Angelo, I want you to stop by the Cherry Street Settlement tomorrow."

"Ma, tomorrow's Saturday, I have to work at Bookman's." Angelo looked across the street at his lock on Bookman's cellar doors. A blue 1950 Nash Airflyte came from behind, flew past them down Catherine Street, and stopped next to a group of teens.

"After work, Angelo. The new priest, Father Casimiro, wants to talk to you."

"What about?"

Across the street, near St. Joseph's, a group of teenage boys and girls were standing around a Pontiac convertible as the driver lowered the top. They were listening to music, laughing, and goofing around. The blue Nash had pulled up behind a Dodge Coronet to welcoming cheers and shouts. Both cars were filled with teenagers and were double-parked alongside the

Pontiac. Hanging below the rear license plate of each car was a black plate that read Yellow Jackets in yellow letters.

"About you attending the Settlement."

"Oh, man, none of my friends go there."

"Just talk to him, Angelo. Please?"

"What's his name again?" Angelo heard the shattering of glass as a beer bottle smashed against the street behind them. The laughter and chatter became muted as Angelo and his family continued to walk home.

"Father Casimiro. And he seems very nice."

"But you're not saying I have to start going there no matter what, right?"

"Angelo, just talk to him."

"But you're not saying—"

Seven teenage boys, all wearing the black shirts of the Knights, were walking toward Angelo and his mother and brother.

"I am just asking you to talk to him."

"Can Tate come with me?"

Tate Kramer had been seven years old when he and his mother moved to the projects. The Kramers lived two floors below Angelo. In the first grade, Tate—a year older, taller, and more awkward than his classmates—quickly became a target of cruel comments and pranks. So Angelo went out of his way to befriend Tate. Mostly the teasing stopped and Angelo and Tate became best friends. Over the next few years, Tate grew less awkward and more athletic. He looked up to Angelo, admired his courage, quick mind, and wit, and was unwaveringly loyal to him. They both cherished their friendship.

"Thank you. And, yes, it would be fine if Tate went with you."

The Knights stopped, blocking the sidewalk in front of Angelo and his mother and brother. The Knight in the middle walked up to Angelo's mother. Fear and rage began to build in Angelo. His stomach ached.

"You live in these projects?" the Knight asked.

"You know we do, Ernesto," Angelo's mother said in a firm voice. "Get out of our way.

"Oh, now I recognize you, *querido*." Ernesto looked her up and down, to the giggles of his fellow Knights. Then he said to Adam, "What're you lookin' at?"

Adam pointed to the gold half-dollar-sized medallion hanging from a gold chain around Ernesto's neck.

"You like that?" Ernesto held his medallion toward Adam. "Tell ya what, I'll let you hold it if you let me hold your mama. She likes Knights holding her."

"Leave my brother alone." Heat rushed to Angelo's face; he stiffened and moved forward. His mother grabbed his wrist and Adam's hand.

Ernesto took a step toward Angelo. "What the fuck did you say?"

"Leave my brother alone. I ain't scared of you."

"You better be, shithead, or you might disappear like your old man."

Angelo's mother said. "Are you going to move or do I push through you, Ernesto?"

"Not just her, Ernesto." Rosemarie walked out of the building and toward them. "Now you and your brave Knights have to fight two girls. Right here in front of our building."

"I told you guys, don't mess with project chicks. They will sound on you and fuck you up." Ernesto laughed.

"Take your brother upstairs," Angelo's mother said to Angelo.

"No, Mom, I want—"

"Ernesto," a Knight interrupted. "The ghost is in the window."

Angelo, along with the Knights, looked up at the fifth-floor window. Uncle Johnny was watching them. *He does look like a ghost from down here*, Angelo thought.

"You should tell your shithead kid that your husband was the one that killed his father. Next time, *querido*, I'll let you hold my medallion, too." Ernesto turned left and headed deeper into the projects, with the other Knights following. Angelo watched them disappear into the night. He was embarrassed, frightened, and angry.

As they entered their building, Adam asked, "Mama, that man called you *queri—*"

"That man's a punk," she said. "Just forget it. You want to stop in, Ro?"

"Sure, just for a minute," Rosemarie said.

After a few moments lost in dark thoughts, Angelo's mother said, "Thanks for coming down, Ro." She unlocked their apartment door. "Boys, it's almost nine o'clock. So, go wash up and get ready for bed."

"Mom, what did he mean about your husband killed my father?"

"There's something wrong with him, Angelo—he's stupid crazy. We'll talk about it tomorrow. It's late and I'm tired. Okay?"

"Okay. Can I talk to Uncle Johnny before bed?"

"Of course." She could hear the creaking of Johnny's rocker as she locked out the world from her modest apartment. "But not too long."

"Okay, Mom." Angelo and Adam ran toward their room.

The dishes were washed, the trash was gone, and the kitchen was clean. On the table was a thank-you note written on a white envelope containing the monthly cash from Ben and Henry. She picked up the envelope, shook her head, and smiled. Anna poured two glasses of red wine and sat at the table with Rosemarie.

Angelo knocked and walked into his uncle's room. Uncle Johnny rocked in his chair and looked out of the window. A pack of Lucky Strikes and an ashtray sat on the window sill. When Johnny had first arrived, doctors said he was suffering from shell shock. He would spend almost all of his time in his room.

Although Johnny still wouldn't leave the apartment, it was Angelo who brought him out of his room more often and, in many ways, out of himself. Johnny's favorite times were cleaning his old army rifle, looking out of the window, reading, doing his exercise routine, and the half hour he and Angelo talked before Angelo went to bed.

"Thanks for the *Life*," Uncle Johnny greeted Angelo with a smile.

"No problem."

Angelo lay askew on Uncle Johnny's bed with his feet up on the wall. Uncle Johnny was an average-looking man, but paper pale—a stark contrast to his dark hair and eyes. And he was steel-cable thin. His consistent workout routine had created a man who seemed to be made more of iron rods than skin and bone.

"Them Knights hassle you guys?"

"Nah, they were just making sure we lived in the projects."

"You really believe that?"

Angelo just shrugged, knowing Uncle Johnny would not pressure him for a truthful response. He made Angelo feel interesting. "A few South Street Boys chased me today, but I outran them on the roofs."

"I'm surprised they even tried to catch you up there. What did Ernesto say to you?"

"He said he could make me disappear like my father. Do you think he killed my dad?"

"No. Ernesto was only twelve or thirteen back in '51. But tell your Uncle Frank what he said anyway."

"He said Mom's husband killed my father. Mom said Ernesto is stupid and we can talk about it tomorrow."

"Yeah, he's just bustin' your chops. What, Angelo?"

"I just stood there when they blocked us. You would've done something, huh?"

"I would've done what you did—got them home safely."

"Uncle Johnny, could you teach me to fight? I mean, I can fight pretty good. But all I do is throw punches, or swing my belt around, or wrestle around on the street. I don't really know what I'm doing. I'm going to be thirteen on Sunday. I need to know some stuff."

"I can teach you some stuff—but not to fight. Someone very special taught me how to end a fight, but not how to fight. If you want to learn to fight, talk to Father Joe. He was Golden Gloves. Angelo, boxing, wrestling...there are rules in fighting; it's a contest, a sport. *Capisce?*"

"I think so. But I don't care about the rules; I just want to learn how to fi—how to handle myself if someone picks a fight with me on the street. You know?"

"Yeah, okay. When someone picks a fight with you, what are you thinking about? What's going through your head? 'Cause that's where most of the fight is."

"Well, I'm nervous. Especially if people are watching. I don't want to cry or look dumb."

"So how's a fight start?"

"I wait for the other guy to start. Then if he pushes me, I push back, and it's a fight."

"What if those South Street Boys had caught you today? Would you've been nervous if people were standing around?"

"Not as much, 'cause they outnumbered me. So if I lose, you know—"

"Okay. First lesson—you're thinking too much about you. You're too worried about what other people are thinking." Uncle Johnny tossed his pack of cigarettes to Angelo.

Angelo caught the pack of Luckys. "What the—?"

"What were you thinkin' about?"

"Nothing. Just listening to you."

"Nothing and yet you caught the Luckys. How'd ya look when you caught them?"

"I don't know, I didn't think—"

"Same in a fight, stop thinking so much about how you look. Concentrate on targets—eyes, nose, neck, lungs, groin, and knees. We'll work on this. Got it?"

Angelo nodded and tossed back the pack of cigarettes.

"Second lesson. If he puts his hands on you—or if he's about to—you end the fight. You don't push back or push first; you end it. That means you usually get in very close—like you're going to kiss him—and you're gonna use your elbows, hands, fingers, feet, knees, whatever you got. This is not a sport, contest, or a game. *Capisce*?"

"Yeah, I think so. Can we start Monday?"

"We already started." Uncle Johnny studied Angelo for a moment.

"What?"

"You wanna talk to me about what else is bothering you?"

"No, not yet." Angelo was always surprised by his uncle's ability to tell when something was troubling him. "I better get to bed." Angelo hugged his uncle's neck and kissed his cheek. "G'night, Uncle Johnny."

"Goodnight, kid."

Angelo looked back as he left the room and saw Uncle Johnny take a Lucky out, tap it lightly on the pack, and stick a splinter of toothpick deep into the tip.

Angelo recalled Uncle Johnny telling him that when he had been a prisoner of war he was only allowed to smoke one cigarette a day. He used to stick a splinter into the tobacco—careful not to pierce the paper—to slow down the burn. Uncle Johnny's experience as a POW, he once explained to Angelo, was also why he seldom smoked while talking with Angelo. "Time went so slowly and there were few pleasures in the camp, so we learned not to combine them," he explained. "I don't want anything to interfere with my enjoyment of talking with you."

Angelo heard the sound of rocking and knew that his uncle was now enjoying his Lucky.

Chapter Seven

"You are like us—a predator."

Angelo lingered on his back, squeezing the sleep out of his eyes as they adapted to the darkness. The reflection of his window stretched and darted across his ceiling as a car passed on the street five floors below. He checked the clock on the nightstand between his bed and Adam's. It was two in the morning.

"You think you got everybody fooled, don't you?" he recalled his father saying. "Well, not me. I know you. You're a screw-up, and sooner or later, everybody will know it."

Even in the dim light, Angelo could see his five-year-old brother curled on his left side, sound asleep. The room, like the night, was stale and muggy. Angelo's T-shirt was damp and clung to him unevenly. He reached up and tapped the cowboy-and-Indian-print curtain, pretending a breeze came through the open window above the nightstand.

A cold tremor rolled over his body as he sat up. His stomach tightened. Matching cowboy hats were hanging from horseshoes, one over the head of Adam's bed and the other over Angelo's. He kneeled on his bed and pulled the curtain to the side. Angelo looked out at Catherine Street. He shivered.

"Damn punk coward," he whispered to himself. The street below still glistened from the previous night's rain. The reflected headlights of a passing car bounced like basketballs against his window. A couple of people walked toward Knickerbocker. Muffled voices. The bar on the corner was closed. People throughout the projects were asleep. Peaceful. He sat on the edge of his bed and pulled his socks on with trembling hands.

Angelo climbed off his bed and walked to the other window in his room. "Oh, God, please stop this shaking." His brother turned in his bed but remained asleep.

Across South Street, a ship sat still in the East River. He loved the saltwater-and-fish smell of the river and the sounds of foghorns and bells. He thought about the times his father had to work all night on the ships. Sometimes, after his mother fell asleep, Angelo would get out of bed and stand at this window trying to see him. He wondered if his father was working on a ship someplace right now. Maybe right there.

Distant shouts drew his attention toward the Journal-American building across the street. He saw men working around the three red trucks parked under the lights of the loading platform. His breathing moaned and heaved. He took several deep breaths.

He grabbed his jeans off his chair. A quarter and a lock fell out of the pocket, clanging and tinkling on the hard linoleum floor.

"Huh, what?" Adam was now awake. "What time is it?"

"Two." Angelo pointed at the clock on the nightstand between their beds. "Go back to sleep, Adam boy." He took off the white T-shirt he was wearing and slipped his dark blue T-shirt over his head. He put his jeans on, tucking in his T-shirt and adjusting his garrison belt so that the buckle was off-center to the left.

"What're you doing?"

"I have to go do something." Angelo was now sitting on his bed facing Adam and lacing up his black high-top PF sneakers. I'll be back before you know it. Look, I stuffed some junk under my cover so if Mom comes in, she'll think—"

"What's that lock for?" Adam sat up and folded his legs in front of him.

"It's part of my plan." Angelo moved to his brother's bed and put his arms around Adam. With a little pressure, he pushed Adam back down and covered him with the thin, faded blue sheet. "This is a secret just between us brothers."

"I won't tell."

"Good boy."

"Promise you'll come back."

"I'll be back real quick."

Angelo's throat felt thick. He lifted Adam back into a sitting position on the bed and hugged him. "I'll never leave you, Adam. Never."

"Swear to God?"

"I swear to God. Now go to sleep, and I'll wake you up when I get back."

Angelo again laid Adam down and covered him with the sheet. He put the quarter back in his pocket with the eight dollars. He also put the lock, the key, his apartment key, and his blue bandana handkerchief in his pockets.

Angelo stuffed his handball gloves in his back pocket and walked out of his room. The door to his mother's room was halfway closed. He turned left and started down the long hallway past Uncle Johnny's room, the bathroom, kitchen, and living room, until finally he was facing the apartment door. He quietly unlocked and opened it, checked again to make sure he had his key, and closed the door behind him. He was out. Alone.

After his father disappeared, Angelo's fear of being thought of as a coward exceeded his fear of the projects. Now, he actually took pride in living—surviving—in what most people thought was the worst place to live in New York City. These were his projects, and Angelo moved through them with a cautious comfort. But this was his first voyage alone into the shadowy soul of the projects at night.

He took a deep breath, walked to the stairwell, and pushed open the heavy door. He turned his back to the stairs and, gripping the banister with both hands, leaped and ran down the five flights backwards faster than most kids could make it forwards. When he was alone, he always went down these stairs fast—they were scary. This time, he was lucky—no bodies, no people, no rats, nothing.

He went down the couple of extra steps to the left and out the back door. As he hit the muggy early morning air, he began to shake again. He held on to the side of the building and took a deep breath through his nose and slowly let it out of his mouth. He did this three times, like Uncle Johnny showed him. He let go of the building and looked at his hands. They were steady.

Angelo started along the meandering three-block-long footpath. As he pursued the interior route through the projects, he stayed along the edge of the shadows. He knew there could be swabbies or junkies hiding deeper within the shadows, just waiting for him to get close. He sensed they could see him. They were watching. Waiting. He tried to pierce the darkness while also following Catherine Street in the distance to his right. He could smell urine. He felt a bony hand touch his left leg.

"Here, sweetie, here," hacked a voice in the shadow.

He pulled away. Angelo sniffed the air and listened to the night. His eyes moved like beacons over the landscape, marking means of escape—fences he could climb, intersecting footpaths, more shadows. He continued cautiously, tasting and sniffing the salt of the night.

Angelo thought about being kidnapped by swabbies. Being forced to work the ships in another country. Being killed before his thirteenth birthday on Sunday. Never seeing his mom or Adam again. He undid the heavy Indian-head buckle of his black garrison belt and wiggled the studded and hand-woven belt out of the loops on his jeans.

He stared at his belt. It was beautiful. It had taken him three days to create, burning holes with a hot nail along the edge and down the center. He had woven plastic ribbon around the edge of the belt and secured alternating large and small silver conchos and studs along the center length of the belt to where the buckle holes started. A short loop of rawhide, for Angelo's wrist, hung from the tip of the belt. And then there was the heavy Indian-head buckle that had a hook on the back to fasten closed.

Angelo had patiently honed each of the corners of the brass buckle stiletto-sharp. When he slipped the rawhide loop over his wrist and then wrapped the belt around his hand—once, sometimes twice—with the brass buckle hanging, it became his Excalibur.

He wrapped it around his pants, but on top of the loops, keeping the heavy brass buckle off-center to his left. He would now be able to access it more quickly. He put on his gloves to protect his hands and improve his grip in case he had to climb or fight. He pushed on with purpose.

As Angelo passed the small cement playground on his right, the glow of a solitary lamppost smoked down through a mist of mosquitoes and washed over the shoulders of a young man in a stained blue-and-yellow-checkered shirt. He sat forward on the bench with his face in his hands. Two guys wearing Knight T-shirts were standing in front of him.

One of the Knights was talking and slapping the seated man on the head almost playfully. But Angelo knew they were not playing. He saw the flash of silver from the straight razor the other Knight was holding. As he got closer, he saw a reflected glint of gold from the amulet worn by the Knight doing the slapping. Ernesto, he remembered. As he passed within twenty feet, separated only by a four-foot-high chain-link fence and a double row of waist-high bushes, the two Knights stopped and looked at him. Angelo looked back.

The savannah belongs to the lion. Two adult male lions scratched at their captured prey as an adolescent male cheetah crept past. Cautiously, the cheetah watched the lions as he continued to glide through the shadows. And then their eyes met. The lions stared and tracked the young cheetah. "Does he recognize our superiority in the savannah?" The young cheetah's eyes locked onto the lions. "Look away too soon and they will see I am frightened. Hold my eye contact too long and they may think I am challenging them. I know I can outrun them. Stay alert." One of the lions raised its eyebrows, sending the message, "What are you going to do, Cheetah?"

The cheetah shrugged faintly and almost indecipherably shook its head just once while maintaining eye contact. Sending the message, "I am just passing. I offer no challenge. But I am not afraid, Lion."

The lion returned a faint nod. "Pass, then. You are like us—a predator."

In that moment, Angelo understood something about himself within the social order of the projects. And the heat of it coursed through his blood like an elixir.

As Angelo continued past them, the man in the stained shirt looked up at him through defeated eyes, his face covered with blood and dirt. Angelo's stomach stiffened as cool sweat slithered under his gloves and along his spine.

The four-foot-high pine hedge bushes near the buildings were taller and fuller than those outlining the playgrounds. These bushes, trees, and buildings cast the deepest shadows. Along this syrupy, dark periphery, Angelo continued his pursuit. He sniffed the sticky air and continued to stalk the edge of darkness. The Knights went back to slapping and taunting. He moved beyond their concern. He scanned for creeps prowling the projects after dark. And for cops. At night, the cops patrolled the outside perimeter of the projects, but they would come in if necessary.

Across Catherine Street he could see Knickerbocker Village. Lilly's was closed. The red and black Pontiac convertible was parked and quiet and the Nash and Dodge were gone. He wished he were in his bed asleep, like so many others at this hour. Like Adam. Safe.

Two men emerged from around a bend in the footpath. They walked toward him. Their white T-shirts glowed in the dark. Swabbies.

Angelo's eyes shot toward the tall bushes. It was too late to hide. The swabbies separated. With the footpath between them, they flanked Angelo. He swallowed hard.

They continued to close on him. Angelo slowed down as his options narrowed. His heart throbbed in his temples. Closing. He unhooked his buckle and gripped the end of his belt as it fell away from his waist. The rawhide ribbon dropped around his wrist. His stomach clenched. He swung the belt once around his right hand and gripped it tightly. The heavy buckle narrowly oscillated below his right knee.

The swabbie closing on his left reached into his pocket and removed a knife. Angelo took a very deep breath. The swabbie on his right was now moving in toward him.

Angelo shortened his steps and, with the unsettled agility of a cautious cat, he readied Excalibur for the fight.

Uncle Johnny always said, "Every soldier has a plan 'til he gets shot." Angelo's plan was to use his belt buckle on the swabbie with the knife first, keep the buckle going fast and clip the second swabbie while moving forward, and then bullet between them deeper into the projects. Angelo's mouth tasted like copper. He swung his belt like a propeller, building momentum. They were close. Closer. His belt made a deep wooooo sound as it circled faster and faster.

The swabbies slowed their advance. Their eyes looked ... frightened.

Wooooo.

Both swabbies suddenly turned and ran.

Angelo was stunned and about to congratulate himself when just as suddenly six Knights came from behind him and chased the swabbies.

A Knight snarled and shoved Angelo against the tall bushes. "Those are the two guys."

The swabbies and pursuing Knights disappeared into the darkness. Their shouts became more muffled. Angelo cautiously returned to the footpath. He bent over and took several deep breaths and then continued along the edge of his fear.

* * *

Housing more than four thousand people, the twelve buildings that made up the Al Smith projects towered ominously, like immense mountain trolls guarding their acres of brick and cement. One of these buildings, 54 Catherine Street, loomed above the tenements and stores that lined the somber sidewalks and alleys of Catherine and Madison Streets.

Harold and Emma Vorgage occupied a front apartment on the eleventh floor of 54 Catherine Street. Emma was lying in bed awake. Yesterday was their fortieth wedding anniversary and it slipped by without notice, except by Emma. She couldn't sleep. Instead, she thought about being courted by young men who no longer remembered her name. Turning heads that no longer turned. She was now simply one of life's asides. All her princess dreams lost.

Emma's quiet tears, arthritis, Harold's snoring, and the summer heat conspired to keep her awake. Finally surrendering to it all, Emma left their bed and walked to the bathroom, where she washed her face. Then, staring into the mirror a little too long, exposing her vital lies, she quietly wept.

Emma wiped her eyes dry, took three aspirins, and went into her kitchen. She poured red table wine into a water glass. She lit a cigarette, grabbed an ashtray, walked to the small window, and sat on an old stepstool against the wall. She gulped her wine and inhaled long, slow breaths of smoke. Ignoring the ashtray she placed on the windowsill, Emma flicked her ashes out of the open window. She gazed despairingly at the steamy, summer night streets still wet from last night's rain.

She examined the two rows of cars parked along Catherine Street and drifted back to a time when there were more horse-drawn carts than cars in this neighborhood. She smiled as she thought about the ragman who still came around on a horse-drawn cart. The sound of the clump, clump, clump of the horse followed by the squeaky wheels of the cart transported her back to a time of love and enthusiasm. The iceman still came around but he just got himself a truck. Too bad, she thought. Too many cars. Too many people.

Emma's reminiscence was broken by the sound of laughter coming from a man and a woman as they walked past Doc's Drugstore, Bookman's Grocery, and Linda's Luncheonette. His arm draped around her shoulder and her arm around his waist. "Tramp," Emma said to no one. "Look at them flaunting their appetite. Trash, both of them." The couple entered a tenement next to St. Joseph's church and their giggles echoed momentarily along Catherine Street.

Emma saw the headlights of a blue Plymouth on Madison Street turning left onto Catherine and heading for a parking spot on her side of the street across from Linda's Luncheonette. She could hear the voices of boys and girls coming from the car's open windows. "I know that car. That's that Bobby Rizzo down on nine. Teenagers. Hoodlum trash. This whole country is going to hell." Emma gulped her wine and took a long drag on her cigarette as she watched the car park and listened to the chatter.

* * *

Angelo was now passing the tenements and shops between St. Joseph's church and Bookman's grocery across Catherine. The earlier teenage gatherings left their signature of debris on the now-silent sidewalks. It was time to start across the street. He froze as a large, white dog—it actually looked pale blue in the shadows—led two other strays past him. They could be dangerous, but tonight, like the Knights, they passed with a purpose that did not include him.

Once the dogs were gone, Angelo darted for the tall hedge bushes and shadows on the side of 54 Catherine. He kneeled there for several moments and listened, watched, and sniffed the air, but didn't move. Angelo thought he heard voices coming from the blue Plymouth parked on Catherine Street. He shook it off. It was time. He pushed through the bushes and ran across the street bent over at the waist. When he got to the front of Bookman's, he hunched down on his knees in the shadows against the storefront.

Angelo removed his right glove, reached into his pocket, and took out the key to his lock on Bookman's cellar doors. He opened it, removed the lock, and put it in his left front pocket. Bookman's real lock was unlocked in his front right pocket.

Angelo put his glove back on and lifted one of the doors. Holding the heavy steel door up with one hand, he entered Bookman's basement, quietly closing the door above him.

* * *

Emma was pasted to her window. She thought about waking Harold but he would ruin the whole thing. Probably call the cops. "Who is that boy?"

* * *

Angelo lifted the cellar door just a crack at first, and then as quickly as he went in, he sprang up and out of the cellar. A puff of charcoal-gray smoke followed him out. He closed the door hurriedly and locked the cellar door with Bookman's lock. He checked up and down the street, and then, bending over at the waist with a nervous smile on his face, he started to dart back across Catherine Street toward the projects.

Angelo was halfway across Catherine when he suddenly felt as though he were underwater and the pressure was building unbearably on both sides of his head. Angelo's entire body was numb. And then he noticed that his feet were straight out in front of him.

Angelo was actually flying in a sitting position across Catherine Street. No sound. Numb. His arms flailed helplessly in circles. And then the silence was shattered by roaring explosions—loud and soft, loud and soft—as if someone were turning the volume up and down repeatedly. Painful echoes of thunder rolled in Angelo's ears as he hit the pavement, bounced up and forward, and into a car parked at the curb on the projects side of Catherine Street.

He slid down into a sitting position with his back against the front wheel. His vision was blurred, but Angelo saw the heavy steel cellar doors, still locked, skittering across the street and right at him. He somehow managed to scoot to the side as the heavy doors skidded and screeched inches to his left and slammed into the parked car.

Angelo tried to stand up and in that instant, the numbness was replaced by pounding spasms of pain and nausea that knocked him to his hands and knees. He thought he saw the blue Plymouth backing up toward him; he heard someone far off in a tunnel call his name.

Angelo was so overwhelmed by the fear of being caught that, in spite of the pain, he again attempted to find his feet and flee. His right foot gave out under him and he cried out as he fell on his right knee. Like a wounded animal, he got up, hopped, ran, stumbled, fell, got up, stumbled, and somehow made it back to the projects. He staggered and plunged into the hedge in the shadow of 54 Catherine Street. There he would hide, assess his injuries, and die quietly out of sight, if he must.

* * *

The explosion sent Emma screaming to the bedroom to wake an already startled Harold. "Harold, Harold, the street is on fire! We're being bombed! Harold!" When she looked out of the window again, she saw the blue Plymouth back up, stop, and then bullet down Catherine Street and turn left on Water Street. She poured more wine in her glass, lit another cigarette, and waited for the fire trucks.

CHAPTER EIGHT

"Stay in the shadows."

"**A**ngelo, Angelo can you hear me?" an angel whispered. No, not an angel. A girl. Close. She smelled of lilacs and baby powder.

He tried to open his eyes.

"Angelo," whispered the voice. "Angelo, can you hear me?"

Angelo opened his mouth to speak.

"Good, but now you don't have to talk, shhhhh."

He felt something soothingly damp on his face. Cool water on his lips. He moved.

"Shhhhh. Be still, Angelo."

Darkness...Angelo was suddenly aware of voices and movement around him. The smell of grass, pine, soil, and smoke. With some effort, he opened his left eye. He saw a blurry haze of green and black. A great weight prevented him from opening his right eye. He reached up and removed a damp, stained kerchief. Beyond the blood and dampness, the kerchief smelled like lilacs and baby powder.

He wiped both his eyes. It was coming back to him. As his vision cleared, he looked around. No angel. No girl. He was lying curled up in the shadow behind a clump of dark bushes. He heard the scream of sirens. The air smelled like smoke.

He lifted his head and peered through the branches of the pine. A crowd stood with their backs to him looking across Catherine Street. He lifted his head higher and saw that Bookman's, the drug store next to it, and a couple of parked cars were billowing black smoke and remnant flames as fire trucks flooded them with water.

Two police officers talked to people in the crowd. More neighborhood onlookers—men wearing T-shirts and pajama pants, women with trench coats over nightgowns, slippers, and kerchief-covered heads full of curlers—continued to gather between him and the firefighting performance. Among them, several Knights stood with their backs to him and the tall hedge bushes. The fire mesmerized them all. The shimmering crowd unknowingly concealed him. The dense interior of the projects behind him was secluded and offered additional cover.

Angelo crawled behind the line of bushes along the building toward the interior of the projects. The clamor and shouts and the smell of smoke behind him were becoming more distant. At the far end of the hedge, he stood up. His right ankle shrieked in pain and he fell back. Sitting, he undid his sneaker, tied his bandana tightly around his swollen ankle, and retied his sneaker. He stood, wobbled a bit, and put most of his weight on his left leg. Still, the pain from his ankle brought tears to his eyes. His back was scraped raw. His face was a collection of paper cuts, and his head was a deep-drumming haze.

He limped along the concrete footpaths woven through the complex of brick buildings, cement playgrounds, and fenced-in skeletal shrubs and trees, carefully staying in the shadows. As he hobbled, he took inventory of his injuries. Although he had many cuts, bruises, and bumps, nothing seemed to be broken except maybe his ankle.

Angelo heard what sounded like whimpering. It was close. He quickly ducked behind a hedge to investigate just as a group of Knights walked passed him toward the fire. He found the source of the whimpering—the pale-blue dog he had seen earlier. The dog seemed to be hiding from the chaos. Angelo crawled to the prone dog and stroked the side of its face and neck.

After a moment or two, Angelo made his way back to the footpath and continued to shuffle through the jungle, trying to ignore his pain. Knowing his defenses were now limited, Angelo removed his garrison belt and wrapped it around his gloved right hand with the heavy buckle hanging ready. Several people so intent on getting to the fire before it was completely out passed within a few feet of Angelo without noticing him.

Angelo was now alongside 10 Catherine Slip. As he walked past the small playground where he earlier encountered the two Knights with their prey, he half expected to see some remains. Nothing. A couple of bums slept on the benches, but no one else. Three Knights, wearing their black T-shirts, came out of 10 Catherine Slip and were headed right toward him. Angelo stopped walking, tightened his fist around his belt, and started to back up. Suddenly, a hand on his shoulder pulled him deeper into the shadows.

"Shhh," came a voice from behind him.

Angelo didn't move as the three Knights walked past him. When they were out of sight, he turned to see who grabbed him. He expected a swabbie, but instead he was looking at the black T-shirt of a Knight. Below the crest was the name Marty in red script. When he looked up, Angelo was both relieved and shocked to see South Street Sammy.

"Sammy, where'd you get that shirt? They'll kill you."

"That Ernesto and them took my shirt and put it on this guy." Sammy pointed to the name on the Knight shirt. "Then they beat him bad."

"Why, if he was a Knight?"

"Ernesto asked him about Hector and Willie. They called him a fink."

"Who's Willie?"

"Dunno. But Hector is the—"

"Yeah, I know who Hector is. Hey, thanks for saving me just now, Sammy." Angelo reached in his pocket and pulled out a dollar. "Here ya go, take this."

"No, no, you always good to Sammy, no problem."

"I wanna. Please, take it."

"Okay. But Sammy trade you." He gave Angelo a dirty gold coin.

"Thanks, Sammy." Angelo put the gold coin in his pocket. "I have to go. And you better get rid of that shirt." Angelo continued along the path toward 20 Catherine Slip.

"Stay in the shadows, Angelo," Sammy rasped.

Angelo, surprised and pleased that Sammy knew his name, turned and smiled. But Sammy had already disappeared into his own shadow.

Angelo was now approaching 20 Catherine Slip, his building. He traced his steps along the footpath to the back door. It was open. He went in and through the second door and then it was a quick right and up the steps, using both hands to hold the banister like a crutch. His belt buckle, still hanging from his right hand, tapped against the wall.

By the time he reached the fourth floor, he thought he was going to be sick. He held on and finally made it to the fifth floor. He stopped in front of his apartment, wrapped and buckled his belt around his waist, put his gloves in his back pocket, and removed his apartment key from the front pocket of his jeans.

Holding his breath, Angelo unlocked his apartment door, entered, and closed and locked it behind him. The apartment smelled safe. He removed his sneakers, but left the bandana wrapped around his ankle. Carrying his sneakers, he limped to the bathroom, where he locked himself in and turned on the light. He started to breathe again and then looked in the mirror.

His right eye was a half-closed, violet golf ball. Two Band-Aids covered the cut above his right eye. There was also a cut on his swollen lip. His nose and right ear had been cleaned. His right ear still felt as though it was filled with water. He touched it— ringing and tenderness. After washing his face, hands, and arms, he took off his stained jeans that now had tears in both knees. The gold coin dropped out of his pocket and onto one of his sneakers. He picked up the half-dollar-sized coin. There was a gold link attached to its edge. Two child-saints were on the face of the coin, and on the back was engraved Ernesto 1938.

Angelo looked at the medallion and smiled. He slid it back into his jeans. He removed the bandana; his ankle looked like a plum. As the blood rushed back to his foot, Angelo nearly cried out. He finished undressing down to his underpants. He noticed a little blood on his sneakers and shirt that also had a faint smoky smell. He rolled his clothes into a single large ball and carried them to his room.

When Angelo limped into his room, Adam was sleeping. He put the ball of clothing under his bed. Then he leaned over Adam and kissed him on the forehead. Adam opened his eyes, smiled, and rolled over, drifting back to sleep. After clearing the stuffing he used as a body-double from his bed, he put on the T-shirt and crawled under his light-blue sheet cover. He would make himself wake up at five o'clock and get out of the apartment before his mother woke up and saw him. He was supposed to be at Book-man's by seven thirty on Saturdays, and he needed to show up like he didn't know anything happened.

He lay on his back and stared at the ceiling. He pulled the blue sheet up to his chin and made a soft about-to-cry sound but was able to swallow it. Angelo rolled over onto his left side, facing the wall, with his back to Adam. He brought his knees up to his chest and covered his mouth with his hands and sheet. His eyes welled up, but he managed to choke down another cry-lump.

CHAPTER NINE

"Don't you move."

T he sound of the shower woke Angelo. He pulled the sheet off his face and turned toward his brother's bed. Adam was still asleep. The clock on the nightstand showed six-thirty. He had overslept. If Uncle Johnny was in the shower, the sound was going to wake up his mother. Not good. Angelo climbed out of bed and tiptoed with a painful limp to the door of his room.

He leaned into the hall. Through the open door, he saw her bed was empty. He needed to get out of the apartment before she could get out of the shower. He hobbled back into his room, reached under his bed, and pulled out the ball of blood- and dirt-stained clothing. He held his breath and pain as he hurriedly put on his torn jeans and buckled his belt. He sat on the floor to put on his socks and sneakers when he heard the familiar squeak-thump signaling the end of the shower.

Angelo sprang to his feet, pain subdued by adrenalin. He grabbed his socks, sneakers, and shirt and limped out of his room and down the hall. His ankle screamed in protest but he kept going. As he passed the bathroom, he heard his mother humming a song. He heard the bathroom door open just as he reached the apartment door. He hopped more quickly. He hit the apartment door a little too hard. Pain filled his eyes.

As Angelo closed the door, he heard his mother call his name. He knew she knew he heard her, and he felt bad about not responding. But it would be much worse if he had to explain why he was half-dressed in bloody, ripped clothes. He used the back stairway just in case she came out of the apartment. He made it down to the third floor landing before he stopped to finish dressing.

The lobby was empty except for Tate, who was sitting on the floor with his back against the mailboxes reading a *Grim Reaper* comic book. When Tate saw Angelo, he stood up, folded the comic lengthwise, and stuffed it into the back pocket of his jeans.

"Whoa! What happened to you?" Tate looked Angelo up and down.

"I told you, I was "

"Yeah, yeah, I know you were gonna torch Bookman's. But, what happened to you?"

"It blew."

"It blew?

"There was a fire engine and some cops last night."

"There was a fire engine? Hey, I think I heard the sirens. That was you?"

"Yeah."

"Yeah?"

"Tate, you really gotta stop repeating me. What are you doing here?"

"What am I doing here? I wanted to see that you were okay. You look terrible."

"I'll live." Angelo was touched by his friend's concern. He had only told one person about what he was going to do, and that was Tate. Tate had wanted to go with Angelo. To help him. To watch out for him. But this was something he had to do alone. "I have to come up with something to explain why I look like this. Anyway, I'm glad you're here, Tate."

"No problem. So what should we do?"

"I'm gonna get hit by a car."

"You're gonna get hit by a car?"

"Tate."

"You're telling me you're gonna get hit by a car—oh, side slap down?"

"Right."

"You want me to do the headlight?"

"Yeah, and then you have to go to Bookman's, act surprised about the fire, and tell whoever is hanging out there that I got hit by a car. I'll go upstairs and tell my mom. Okay?"

"Got it. So when we go out of the building keep your head down, in case somebody is lookin' out the window. You don't want anyone to see you like this before the car hits you."

"Good thinking, Tate. Put your arm around me like we're whispering. You know, cover me as much as possible. You ready?"

"Yeah but if those two Band-Aids above your eye ain't from before last night, you better ditch 'em." Tate, with a good-thinking smile, tapped at his own right eyebrow.

"Oh, man. Yeah, thanks." Angelo pulled off the Band-Aids. "I'll toss these outside. I might need to lean on you to walk. You ready?"

"Yeah, let's go before someone comes down." Tate nodded toward the elevators.

They walked out of the building with Tate covering Angelo.

"Tate, don't look up even if my mom calls us from the window." Angelo took a deep breath mostly to try to relax, but also because he loved the smell of morning. It was the start of another warm day but a slight breeze promised it would not be as hot as yesterday. The boys moved directly toward the street.

Across the street, several people stood around the news-stand. A few people walked up Catherine Street. An elderly man came out of 20 Catherine Slip behind them but more slowly.

Angelo spotted a black Packard coming toward them. "Okay, this is the car."

"Right." Tate ducked between two parked cars.

"Grab that." Angelo pointed at half of a brick resting against the curb.

"Here it comes, ready?"

"We'll hit it at the same time." Angelo limped crouched to the back of the parked car while Tate moved to the front. "Now."

Angelo slapped the back side panel of the Packard with both hands, bounced back against the parked car, and rolled over its rear fender as the Packard screeched to a stop. At the same time, Tate slammed the brick into the front right headlight, shattering the glass, and saw that the driver was alone in the car. He then ducked around another parked car, stood up, and ran to Angelo, shouting, "That car just hit my friend!"

Tate got to Angelo first. "You okay?" Tate bent down and handed Angelo shattered headlight glass.

"Yeah." Angelo rubbed the glass on his left arm.

Tate put glass in Angelo's hair as Angelo wiped street gravel on his face, and then started to get up. By then the driver was out of his Packard and rushed to Angelo.

"My God, are you all right?" the middle-aged man shrieked. "I was a little lost. I was looking around. Where did you come from? I didn't even see you. Are you okay? Let me take you to a hospital."

Tate held Angelo up as a small group of neighbors gathered around them.

"Angelo, you want me to get your mother?" someone called out.

"No, no, I'm okay," Angelo called back while starting to brush himself off. Several cars stopped behind the Packard to see what happened.

"Kid, please, let me help," the driver pleaded. "I didn't even see you."

"Forget about it," Angelo said. "It was my own fault."

"Angelo, you should have a doctor look at you. You don't look so good," cautioned Mrs. Perez, a neighbor.

"You sure you're all right?" the driver asked again. "I would be happy to take—"

"No, nothin'—I'm sure. Go ahead, don't worry about it," Angelo said as Tate started to help him back to his building.

"Wait, please," the driver said, stepping in front of the two boys. "Please at least let me give you something." The driver put two ten-dollar bills in Angelo's hand.

"Thanks, mister, but you really don't—"

"Please take it. It'll make me feel better."

"Okay. Thanks. Hey, Tate, do me a favor go tell Bookman I'm not sure if I'll be at work today," Angelo said in a voice loud enough for others to hear.

"Sure, no problem. Can you get upstairs okay?"

"No, no, no," Mrs. Perez interrupted. "You help Angelo home. I'll go tell Mr. Bookman what happened and that Angelo will not be at work today."

"Thank you very much, Mrs. Perez," Angelo said and then looked at Tate.

"Angelo," Mrs. Perez said. "Tell your mother—"

"You!" Angelo's mother charged out of the building, pointing at the driver, but then she looked at Angelo and screamed, "Angelo! Oh, my God, look at you!"

"Ma, I'm fine. Just some—"

"You," Angelo's mother growled at the driver. "Don't you move."

"It was my own fault, Ma," Angelo said, as his Uncle Frank sprinted up to them.

"Frankie, look at what that son-of-a-bitch did to my Angelo."

Frank's dark eyes locked onto the driver like a panther moving in for the kill. "Stay," he said to the driver, who grew pale and began shrinking right there in front of Angelo.

"Ma, Uncle Frank, I said it was my own fault."

Rosemarie walked out of the building and up to Angelo. "What happened?"

"That dead man hit him with his car." Angelo's mother pointed at the pale driver.

Uncle Frank kneeled to examine Angelo's swollen ankle. "Probably not broken, some torn ligaments, though." Uncle Frank touched the bloodstains on Angelo's pants and then looked up at Angelo. Angelo averted his eyes.

"Okay, get out of here," Uncle Frank said to the driver.

"What are you doing, Frankie?" Angelo's mother asked.

"Like Angelo said, it wasn't the guy's fault."

"You know that from looking at Angelo's ankle? You must've been some cop," she said, a little too flip.

"I was." Uncle Frank stood up and looked at Angelo's puffy eye. "Any problem with your vision—dots, lines, blurry, anything?"

"No."

"You lose consciousness even for a couple of seconds?"

"Um, no." Angelo saw the Packard speed away as the crowd began to disperse.

"This hurt?" Uncle Frank rubbed his thumb across the cut above Angelo's right eye."

"A little."

"Anna, I'll take him over to Beekman," Uncle Frank said.

"Why? What's wrong? I'm coming."

"I don't think anything's wrong. I just want to be on the safe side. But I only want Raffino to look at him. So please go upstairs, stay with Adam, and call Dr. Raffino. Tell him to meet us at Beekman. Then call Danny at the store and tell him where I went. I'll call you as soon as Raffino's finished."

"What if it's more serious than you think?"

"I'll call you and I'll tell Danny to drive you down to Beekman."

Mrs. Perez said, "Angelo, I'll tell Mr. Bookman. Anna, I'll stop by later."

"Thank you, Rita," Angelo's mother said. "Frankie, you call me no matter what."

"You got it. Come on, Angelo. Lean on me. I'm parked right over there."

"I'll wait with you, Anna," Rosemarie said.

"Thanks, Ro. Let's go upstairs. I'll make us some tea."

"Hey, Angelo, I'll come see you when you get back," Tate said.

"Uncle Frank, can Tate—"

"No. I think it's better if it's just us, Angelo."

"Later, Tate," Angelo shouted back to his friend.

CHAPTER TEN
"Be cool, hermano."

I n 1943, when Ignazio and Remo were killed in front of the Cherry Street Settlement, Satan's Knights had only twelve members. By 1950, the year Danilo Cruz was killed during the Inchon battle in Korea, Satan's Knights numbered close to fifty kids. And by 1957, Satan's Knights had a membership of more than a hundred. Hector Cruz was the gang's leader.

Because of Hector's influence, Satan's Knights rented a two-bedroom apartment on the ground floor of 10 Catherine Slip. While all members were welcome, only senior Knights—those nineteen or older—were given keys. Hector and his wife lived on the tenth floor of the same building in a three-bedroom apartment. His two younger brothers, Rico and Ernesto, lived with their mother in a three-bedroom apartment two floors below Hector. Hector was making enough money to buy a house anyplace he wished. But this was his empire and he was smart enough, and paranoid enough, to watch it very closely.

Early Saturday morning, Hector told the eight members who made up the Knights' council, including his two brothers, to meet at 8:30 a.m. Rico and Ernesto were to meet him at 7:00 a.m. in front of their building so he could talk to them first.

"What time you got?" Hector walked in small circles, examining his reflection in his deep-brown wingtip shoes. His light-tan shirt was pressed and, as usual, buttoned to the top and neatly tucked into his dark-brown creased and spotless pants.

"Hector, let me run upstairs and get him." Rico squinted up at the building. He loved his brothers and was determined to use his education to guide them out of the projects and into a life of leisure and luxury.

"Am I talkin' to myself or what? What time is it?"

"Seven-oh-five. But he'll be here—"

"*Me importa un comino*. Walk me to Linda's; I want some coffee." Hector started walking toward Catherine Street. "Gotta smoke?"

"Sure." Rico took a couple of quick steps to catch up to Hector. He removed a pack of Cavaliers from the pocket of his white short-sleeved shirt. Rico's shoes were highly polished and his black pants were pressed. But unlike his older brother, Rico wore his shirt unbuttoned and outside his pants, with a clean, white, sleeveless T-shirt underneath. Rico and Hector smoked and walked toward Catherine Street, the silver taps on their shoes clicking in accord.

"Ernesto pisses me off—I said 7:00 a.m., am I right?"

"What's goin' on over there?" Rico pointed to the small gathering in front of 20 Catherine Slip.

"How should I know?"

"Hey, what happened?" Rico asked Mrs. Perez as she walked past them.

"A boy got hit by a car," Mrs. Perez said.

"He okay?"

"He looks pretty bad, but I think so." She continued to walk up Catherine.

"Hector, what's up?"

"I got a call from Sabino's guys about the fire at Bookman's last night. I told him, 'No Knight did that.' Now I'm hoping that we had nothin' to do with it. But I gotta ask, am I right?"

"The fact that you have to ask is itself a problem."

"See, you're the only one that gets that. We got over a hundred guys. When I say do somethin', they do it. When I say don't do somethin', they don't do it. Otherwise we got just another gang, instead of Knights. Am I right?"

"That's right." Thunder rolled in the distance. "We might be in for another shower."

"Good—it'll wash away all this crap. *Cerdos.*" Hector pointed at the broken beer bottles and trash in the street near the red and black Pontiac. "You showed me that we can get rich with this gang, but only if we act smart. Am I right or am I right?"

"Look, we'll grab some coffee and figure this out."

As they got closer to Linda's, the smell of smoke, still lingering in the warm morning air, became more acute. Rico saw a cop talking to a young priest and some neighborhood people a few doorways past Linda's, in front of Bookman's. He was pointing to the open cellar roped off with police DO NOT CROSS signs.

"Let's take a quick look." Rico walked past Linda's and offered another cigarette to Hector. Hector and Rico lit their Cavaliers and walked up to the group. The small gathering parted as Hector and Rico approached.

"So what's the story?" Rico asked the cop.

"Fire in Bookman's cellar last night," the cop responded flatly. "You guys know anything about it?"

"Somebody get killed?" Rico asked, nodding his head toward the priest.

"No, no, nobody got hurt—very lucky," said Pete, an elderly man in the gathering. "The explosion woke up Mr. Bookman, it did. He lives above the store. He got everybody out."

"You know who did this?" Hector asked the cop.

"That's his job." The cop pointed at the man in the wrinkled tan suit across the street.

"Who's the old dame the dick is talking to?" Hector asked Pete.

"Emma. That's Emma Vorgage from 54. Yeah, Emma," said Pete.

"She see what happened, Pete?" Hector asked.

"She knows everything that goes on, Emma does. She's a busybody, Emma Vorgage. Your mother's known her for years. How is your mother? Good? Your mother's good? She's good people, your mother."

"Yeah, she's fine," Hector said.

"Good. Tell her ol' Pete sends his best. Good people, your mother."

"So what's a priest doing here?" Rico asked the young priest.

"I'm Father Casimiro. I work with Father Joe, over at Saint ..."

"I know Father Joe," Rico said. "But, you're not from around here."

"No, I'm new here. And you are?" Father Casimiro held out his right hand.

Rico took the priest's hand. "I'm Rico. This is my brother Hector."

"Charmed," Hector said sarcastically.

"That's an interesting medallion you're wearing." Father Casimiro pointed to the gold half-dollar-sized coin on a thin gold chain around Rico's neck.

"This? It's from my mother...for luck." Rico said, taking off the medallion and chain and handing them to Father Casimiro. "I think those kids on the front are saints."

"It's beautiful," Father Casimiro said. "Yes, Saint Justus and Saint Pastor. And on the back is Rico 1934. I assume that is your birth year?"

"Yeah, my mother had one made for each of us, her sons. Show him yours, Hector."

"I don't know him well enough to show him mine. Maybe after a couple of dates," Hector said impatiently, still watching the detective and Emma. "Can we go now?"

"You know anything about those saints?" Rico asked Father Casimiro.

"They were brothers from Spain. They refused to deny their Christianity—even after being tortured—so the Governor of Spain had them beheaded. Saint Justus was nine, and his brother Saint Pastor was thirteen. After he was beheaded, St. Justus stood up with his head in his hands." Father Casimiro handed the medallion back to Rico.

"Whoa! You hear that, Hector?" Rico replaced the medallion around his neck.

"Yeah. Casimiro—that's not Italian," Hector stated as if he were responding to a question.

"Spanish," said Father Casimiro.

"Yeah? So are we. Cruz," Hector said. "Now if you're finished, Rico . . ."

"Linda's okay?" Rico asked the cop.

"Fine. I had coffee there earlier. You guys hear anything, give us a call."

"Are you kiddin' or what?" Hector said as he followed Rico to Linda's.

Rico opened the smoke-stained glass door to Linda's Luncheonette, they stepped inside and turned to go to the counter on their right. The aroma of charred air from outside now mixed with cigarette smoke, toast, and coffee. Several customers sat on round, rotating stools along the long counter. The chatter quieted down momentarily.

"I'll be right with you guys," a waitress called to them from halfway down the counter.

"Make it snappy, Sweetheart. I want two containers of coffee, black and a regular, to go," Hector called back to the waitress, who was pouring coffee into Bobby Rizzo's cup. Bobby looked briefly at Hector, then returned to his toast and conversation with Will Garrard.

"What are you looking at?" Hector shouted at Rizzo. "Yeah, you. You got a problem?"

"No, no problem, Hector," Rizzo said.

"Okay, Sweetheart, so drop what you're doing and get my coffee now. Nobody's going to mind," Hector said to the waitress, who immediately prepared two cups of coffee to go.

"Here's your coffee, one black and one regular." She placed the coffee on the counter in front of Hector and Rico.

Rico wanted to apologize to the waitress, but instead, he gave her a whaddaya-gonna-do-he's-my-brother smile, and simply said, "Thanks."

"Yeah, thanks. And Sweetheart, my friend Rizzo there will pay for them. Ain't that right, shithead?" Hector said in a loud voice, as Rico picked up the coffee.

"Happy to, Hector," Bobby Rizzo said evenly.

"Let's walk over to the handball court," Hector said as they left. "It stinks over here."

Rico kept the black coffee and handed the regular to Hector. As they crossed the street toward the projects, the detective and Emma walked toward them.

Rico was spinning the plates that guided the Knights toward success. He took care to catch the wobble and add a gentle graze—a rotation. Plate by plate, day after day, required his constant attention or the plates would fall. Which he knew was inevitable—in the end, gravity would win, the plates would tumble, and the Knights would become just another street gang.

He had to hold it together until he could get out. He wanted to marry his girlfriend and move upstate. Brewster would be nice. But here he was, still in the jungle. Still looking over his shoulder for a cop or a bullet. Still spinning the plates. He told himself that he stayed because of his mother and brothers. He needed to ease them out of this neighborhood. But it was also the potential of big money that kept him around. Kept him waiting. Risking everything.

Rico wondered what this detective wanted and how Hector would react. Everything could change quickly. His tongue tasted like sand.

Through pasty lips, Rico whispered to Hector, "Be cool, *hermano.*"

Rico slowed down as the detective and Emma closed the distance between them. He almost stopped, but the detective's eyes told him he was not the target. Rico turned in step with the grace of an ice skater as the detective and Emma walked past him. He watched them stop in front of Linda's Luncheonette. The detective and Emma peered into the window but stayed out front talking.

"You gotta relax, *hermano.*" Hector chuckled.

"Yo, Hector...Rico." Ernesto walked toward them. "Wait up."

"Yeah, right," Hector said to Rico as they walked into the projects.

"He was a popular governor," Rico said, looking up at the statue of Al Smith, as he and Hector walked into the playground. "He fought for decent housing for poor people."

Rico liked to remind Hector that he, Rico, was the smart brother. That Hector should rely on him for guidance.

"What? Who?" said Hector.

"Al Smith."

"Well, the joke's on him, 'cause the projects ain't decent housing."

"Hey, Hector." Ernesto caught up to his brothers. He was wearing his black Knights T-shirt, gray slacks, and black shoes with a high shine.

"You know the Bowery used to run alongside the projects, but they changed the name of it to Saint James Place because Al Smith was a parishioner at St. James Church." Rico continued to annoy his brother. "So the Bowery is still the Bowery except for the couple of blocks that run alongside the projects—"

"What are you, the morning fuckin' news?" Hector snapped.

Rico smiled.

"Who goes to St. James?" Ernesto asked.

"What time did I say to be downstairs?" Hector asked Ernesto.

"I don't know, about seven. How come you guys never wear Knights shirts anymore?"

The three brothers turned left into the handball courts. The handball court area was a freestanding multiple-court concrete wall enclosed by a twelve-foot-high chain-link fence. The only opening faced the statue of Al Smith.

The courts were empty except for two boys who Rico figured were about ten years old. They played stickball against the far court. One boy held a section of broom handle like a bat in front of a two-foot-square, chalk-drawn strike zone on the wall. The other boy, the pitcher, threw a pink Spalding high-bounce ball at the square, and the batter swung away.

"About seven?" Hector repeated as they stopped walking. "About seven? Don't bust my balls, Ernesto—I ain't in the mood. When I tell you seven, you be there no later than seven."

"I was there. What, I can't be a couple of minutes late?"

Hector put his coffee on the ground and shoved Ernesto against the wall. "You was there? When I talk, do you just hear palabra? No, you can't be a minute late. Got it?"

"Yeah, I can't be late." Ernesto stepped away from the wall, took a comb out of his back pocket, and combed his straight black hair back. "Got it."

Rico noticed that the two kids at the far end of the courts had stopped playing stickball and were watching Hector.

"Hey, come 'ere," Hector shouted at the kids as he walked toward them.

"Leave them alone, Hector." Rico knew the detective was still across the street.

The kids looked at each other and then at the fence. The kid with the ball squeezed it into the front pocket of his jeans. The other kid tried to throw the stick over the fence. It hit the top of the fence and bounced back into the court area.

"Don't run. I know who you are. Come 'ere," Hector said.

But it was too late. The kids cleared the twelve-foot fence and were a block away by the time Hector got to the abandoned stick lying on the ground. He picked it up, laughing.

"You see those kids climb that fence?" he called back to his brothers. "I swear they could fly." Hector held the taped end of the stick and swung. Woooshhhh, woooshhhh. "Nice stick."

"Let me see it," Ernesto said.

Hector tossed the stick to Ernesto and picked up his coffee.

"So what's the meeting about?" Ernesto asked, swinging the stick. Woooshhhh.

"The fire at Bookman's," Rico said as he looked across the street. The detective looked briefly at the handball courts. To Rico's relief, he seemed more interested in talking with Emma.

Ernesto shook his head. "Why? Do they think we did it?"

"The meeting is to find out if any of our guys know anything about it," Hector said, taking a final drink of coffee and retrieving the stick from Ernesto. "Pay attention, okay?"

"Yeah, but I don't think any of our guys did that."

"Good. That's what I want to hear," Hector said, tossing the empty coffee container into the air and hitting it with the stickball bat. *Woooshhhh, whack.*

"Ernesto, why ain't you wearing your medallion?" Rico asked.

"What?" Ernesto looked down and touched his chest with his right hand.

"Don't worry about it. Your brother's just writing a book about Spanish saints," Hector said. "You probably left it home."

"There were Spanish saints?" Ernesto said, searching his pockets for the medallion.

"Rico, what about Marty? You talk to him yet or what?" Hector asked. "Did he say anything about me and Willie?"

"Hector, I still don't know why you would tell anybody about Christmas Eve."

"I told you, I was drunk and shooting off my mouth...I trusted Marty. I fucked up, okay? Is he a problem or what?"

"Jack, my cop friend, is going to find out who his contact is and what the cops want, stuff like that. Meanwhile, Jake and Dave talked to Marty last night. I'll catch up to them after the meeting. The plan is to give Marty bullshit to pass along to the cops. We have an opportunity here. *Entiende, mi hermano*?" Rico said as he finished his coffee. He looked at the sky as rolling thunder delivered its threat a bit closer.

Hector nodded. "*Entiendo.*"

Rico crumpled up his empty coffee container and pitched it toward Hector, who prepared to hit it with the stick.

"I might know somethin' about Marty," Ernesto said.

Hector let the container drop near his foot without taking a swing.

Rico looked at Hector.

Hector shrugged.

"What would you know about Marty?" Rico asked Ernesto.

"I told Dave you changed your mind," a now-nervous Ernesto said to Rico. "And, that you wanted me to meet with Marty instead of him and Jake."

Rico's eyes met Hector's.

"Rico, let's all try to be cool here, okay?" Hector said.

Rico nodded and looked at Ernesto. "Did Dave tell you what he knew about Marty?"

"No, what for? This guy Dave, he got no respect for us Cruz brothers," Ernesto said. "He said to me, 'Hey, let me tell you what I know, kid.' He's talkin' to me like I'm a dumb kid. So, I said, 'Let me tell you what I know. You're a shithead,' I said. 'Now take a walk,' I told him. I can find out what I need to know for myself."

Rico was livid. Ernesto was out of control and Rico could no longer keep him in check. He needed to think. Rico walked over to the handball-court wall, put his back against it, and slid down. He rested his arms on his knees, put his head back against the wall, closed his eyes, and said nothing. The morning smelled like rain and the coffee aftertaste was bitter. Brewster was fading. It was all starting to come apart.

"I told you I wanted Rico to handle this," Hector said to Ernesto. "Am I right?"

"Okay, yeah, but you wanna know what we found out or what?"

"We?" Hector said.

"Me and Ronnie showed up in the small park instead of Dave and Jake. We talked to Marty until two, two-thirty in the morning. But it paid off, 'cause we found out that—"

"That he didn't tell the cops anything but some crap, trying to cut a deal for his brother in prison upstate," Rico interrupted in a detached tone while still sitting with his head against the wall and his eyes closed.

"Yeah! Right."

"He had to do this. Not just for his brother, but also for his mother; it was breaking her heart to have his brother in prison," Rico continued unemotionally.

"Whoa! That's it," Ernesto said looking around.

Rico continued, "The nosebleed wasn't a Knight long enough to really know you or Ronnie the Razor." Rico looked at Ernesto. "He thought if he told you what he told Dave, you'd understand and wouldn't beat him so bad. And if you guys were anybody else, Marty would've been right...hold it, did you and Ronnie beat the shit out of him or, or—"

Rico stood up and walked over to Ernesto. He held Ernesto's shoulders and stared into his face. Ernesto's eyes darted for sanctuary. "You crazy fucks killed him. Didn't you?"

Rico shoved Ernesto away. All his work. The careful balance. The need to have absolute control over this gang. He couldn't even control his little brother. Rico walked back to the wall nodding as all his instincts foreshadowed the twilight of Satan's Knights. He had to stay calm...sort this out. His thoughts were interrupted by *woooshhhh,* crack, and a painful wail.

Rico turned and saw Ernesto holding his right elbow...and then the blur of the stickball bat in Hector's hands.

Woooshhhh—crack! Rico heard Ernesto's shins shriek.

Ernesto dropped hard onto his knees, tears streaming from his eyes.

Rico looked across the street. A double-parked truck shielded them from the detective.

"Am I the Boss of this gang or what?" Hector shouted. "You fuck—when I say meet me at seven, you fuckin' be there before seven. Am I right or what?"

Woooshhhh—crack! The stick caught Ernesto across the small of his back. Vomit splashed out of his nose and mouth. He screeched as his right shoulder hit the pavement.

Rico dashed between his brothers. "Okay, okay...Hector, enough."

Ernesto tried to crawl away.

"Where you goin'?" Hector pushed past Rico.

Woooshhhh—crack! The stick caught Ernesto on his back. He belly-flopped flat down on the cement. His face scraped against the ground and blood oozed from his nose.

Rico grabbed for Hector.

Hector dodged him and raised the stick again.

"Enough!" Rico threw his arms around Hector and pulled him away. "Enough."

Hector gained control over his temper and backed away from Ernesto. "Okay, okay."

"Gimme the stick." Rico took the stick and threw it toward the far fence. He walked over to Ernesto, who sobbed into a sitting position. "Ernesto, can you hear me?"

"Yeah. What the fuck? My arm, it's all numb."

"C'mon, I'll help you up." Rico took hold of Ernesto. "Let's go over to the water fountain." Rico was anxious about the small cluster of spectators gathered outside the fence. "Hector, a hand here, huh?"

Hector and Rico got Ernesto to the drinking fountain. Rico took out a handkerchief, wet it, and wiped most of the blood off his brother's face. The side of his face was swollen and cut. His ear and lip were puffed and his right arm was badly bruised.

"He'll live," Hector said. "We'll clean him up better at the club."

Rico, eager to leave the onlookers, nodded. "I'll get Doc Fritz to come take a look."

Thunder cracked. Rico welcomed the merciful sheets of rain that followed and washed the blood from Ernesto's face and dispersed the small cluster of spectators.

"This is what you call staying cool?" Rico said to Hector as the three of them walked hunched over against the rain toward 10 Catherine Slip.

"He just pissed me off. It's his attitude, like you always say. So finish the story, Ernesto. Is Rico right? Did you guys kill Marty?"

Ernesto squinted toward Rico, Hector, and back to Rico as they walked through the interior of the projects toward 10 Catherine Slip.

"I ain't gonna do nothin'," Hector said. "We just gotta know what happened. Here, Rico, you walk between us. Okay? Is Rico right?"

"He died. We didn't mean to kill him. We just got a little carried away. But it's cool."

"It's cool?" Hector mocked.

"Yeah, we found out what we needed to know first. Like Rico said. Right, Rico?"

"No, you didn't find out what we needed to know. I just told you what I figured Marty told you."

"What difference? It's the same thing, right?" Ernesto looked at Rico for confirmation.

"Ernesto," Rico said in a stern, instructive voice. "If you let Dave tell you what he found out about Marty, he'd have told you that Marty doesn't have a brother."

"You shittin' me?" Ernesto stopped walking. "So, what's his story, then?"

"He's killing me," Rico said to Hector.

"I know...me, too."

"What? What?" Ernesto slipped on some slick pavement but was held up by Rico.

"That's why Rico was gonna turn Marty," Hector said. "To use him to feed the cops bullshit information about the Knights. And to find out what he already told the cops. That's why Jake and Dave were gonna meet with Marty last night. Is any of this making sense to you yet?" Without waiting for an answer, he asked, "Where'd all this happen?"

"In the little park, over there, near 20. Like I said, we were there for a couple of hours." Ernesto repeatedly squeezed his eyes closed and licked his lips. "Me and Ronnie got there first. And—okay, this part's funny, okay—Ronnie took this ratty, puke-stained, blue and yellow checkered shirt off a bum—South Street Sammy, you know him. He was lying on the bench. So when Marty comes in, Ronnie makes him take off his Knight shirt and put on Sammy's shirt. Funny as shit. Anyway, Jimmy Bowman and Ray Cotton helped us dump the body. Don't worry, they're good Knights—they ain't gonna fink us out."

"Four of you, now." Rico shook his head. "Where's Marty's Knight shirt?"

"I don't know. I think we just threw it in the bushes or somethin'. Who cares?"

"It has Marty's name on it, right?" Rico said.

"Yeah, but nobody saw anything."

"Ernesto, look around you. You see all those windows? You never know who saw what. What's certain is that somebody saw something and will tell somebody else. I just don't want them to know Marty was there, and then he left without his shirt," Rico said.

Ernesto nodded. "I'll find the shirt."

"Were you wearing your medallion last night?"

"Yeah, sure ... oh, shit."

CHAPTER ELEVEN

"Wash away the night."

The ride to Beekman Street Hospital went better than Angelo feared. To hide his anxiety, he fawned over his uncle's new car and made small talk.

Uncle Frank backed into a parking spot, turned off the car, and faced Angelo. "You had a Band-Aid on the cut above your eye, the blood on your clothes is dry, and your shirt smells like smoke. You want to tell me what happened or you don't, that's up to you. Right now, all I care about is how you're doing. So you must level with Dr. Raffino. He is an old family friend and a damn good doctor. You paying attention, Angelo?"

"Yeah. I'll do whatever you say."

"Good. You hesitated when I asked you back there if you passed out. Whenever, whatever happened—did you pass out?"

"Not right away. But, I guess so. Just for a couple of minutes."

"Okay, tell Doctor Raffino exactly what hurts where and how much. I'll tell him you lost consciousness for a couple of minutes."

"What if he wants to know what happened?"

"He will. I'll be with you. You just tell him what hurts where. Got it?"

"Yeah."

"Come on, I'll help you inside." Uncle Frank opened the car door for Angelo. "Lean on me, kid." Uncle Frank held Angelo as they walked into the hospital.

* * *

Angelo sat forward on the examining table in a small room, wearing only his underpants. Dr. Raffino cleaned Angelo's cuts and scrapes. He leaned over and smelled the back of Angelo's head. Angelo held his breath.

"Today's paper said a doctor was elected President of Haiti," Frank said to Dr. Raffino. "I keep saying you could be the next mayor of this city."

"Duvalier. But the election was rigged, which is the only way I'd win an election. Lean forward, Angelo. Frankie, I heard Bookman's burned down last night."

"No kidding," Frank said evenly.

Angelo remained stone silent.

"Come here, Frankie. See these bruises? Now look at the back of his neck. These are burns. See the hair down here near his neck. Smell it," Dr. Raffino said.

"How's he doing Doc?"

"Lucky, I think. Angelo, put on one of those robes over there. You can leave your clothes; you'll be coming back. Frankie, take Angelo downstairs. I want some pictures of his ankle, leg, and hip. I'll call down. You know where to go?"

Angelo climbed off the table. He put the robe on without making eye contact with either his uncle or the doctor.

"Yeah," Frank said. "I've been there once or twice."

"When he's done, come back up here."

"C'mon, Angelo. Sit in the wheelchair. I'll give you a ride," Uncle Frank said.

Angelo sweated in anguish. He wanted to shout out the truth and get it over with. But he just sat in the wheelchair, looked at his feet, and remained silent. Suddenly, it hit him. At first he was fearful that Uncle Frank would grill him. But riding down in the elevator in floor-staring silence really unnerved him. He knew his uncle was putting it all together.

"Uncle Frank—"

"Not here. Later...in the car."

I'm gonna have a heart attack before I get outta here.

* * *

"Well, Angelo," Dr. Raffino said, reviewing the X-ray. "In addition to several bruises and burns, you've torn a ligament in your ankle. There may be a hairline fracture as well, but that will mend itself. I'll wrap that ankle and get you a crutch...one should do."

"I have to use a crutch? I'm starting junior high and the other kids—"

"I understand. I'll get you a cane, but you must use it."

"I will, thanks."

Dr. Raffino looked into Angelo's eyes, which made Angelo gasp in anticipation. "I'm not going to stitch the cut above your eye...it seems to be healing fine. I'll just dress and cover it. All in all, you're a pretty lucky kid. So don't look so worried."

* * *

Hector, Rico, and Ernesto walked into the club-apartment at 8:20 a.m. The other six members of the senior council were seated around the table.

"Look at that, Ernesto—they're already here for our 8:30 meeting," Hector said as the three brothers, soaked from the rain, dripped past the table toward the bathroom.

"What the hell happened?" said someone as they walked by.

Hector said, "Mike, go get Doc Fritz over here—"

"Hold up, Mike," Rico said. "Hector, I'm going to clean him up and take him to the hospital. You don't need us for the meeting, right?"

"G'head."

"Hector, Doc Fritz is a good idea if you can have him meet us at Beekman so he takes care of Ernesto with no questions," Rico said.

"I'll see to it. And I'll fill you in when you get back."

Rico took less than five minutes to clean up Ernesto. "Come on, Ernesto."

"As I was sayin', anybody know who hit Bookman's?" Hector asked the table.

Rico stopped in the doorway to listen.

"No. But no chance it was a Knight," somebody said.

Rico closed the door behind him.

* * *

Ernesto perched sideways in the front seat of Rico's car. His back was toward the door, hunched forward, right arm limp in his lap and his left arm around his waist. And he rocked. Despite everything, Rico loved Ernesto. He remembered how scared Ernesto was of the projects when he was a little boy. How when he was frightened, he rocked. He assured his little brother that he would always take care of him.

Now he wondered when it was exactly that Ernesto lost his way. "I should've done something sooner, Ernesto." Rico took two Cavaliers out of his pack, lit both, and gave one to Ernesto.

"Thanks. What he gotta beat me like that for?"

The windshield wipers slapped back and forth as Rico drove toward Beekman Street. "'Cause he's nuts. You know that."

"Rico, you think I'm in trouble here? You think the cops are gonna find out anything?"

"I don't know. But I think it's a mistake to underestimate cops."

Ernesto blew a long stream of white smoke toward his feet. "I'm sorry for what I did."

"I know. Was anyone else around when you and Ronnie were...talking to Marty?"

"No, just Sammy and maybe one other bum. But, this kid—you know him, Angelo Macaroni—walked by at about two."

"Alone?"

"Yeah, alone."

"Was he going home?"

"No, he was walking away from 20."

"Did he see you?"

"Yeah. He saw us real good."

"Did you see him come back?"

"No, we left."

"Ernesto, when we get back, you get your guys out there and find that shirt."

"Right, Marty's shirt."

"And find your medallion. Your name's on it...and maybe Marty's blood."

It was still raining when Rico pulled up in front of Beekman Street Hospital. He helped Ernesto out of the car.

"I'll take you inside, then I'll go park. Come on."

* * *

Angelo's right ankle was wrapped, a bandage covered the cut above his eye, and he used the cane as he walked through the lobby of the hospital with his uncle. Just before they reached the exit, Ernesto and Rico walked through the door. The four stopped face to face in the lobby.

For a moment, Angelo wondered if the guy in the checkered shirt had beaten up Ernesto. Ernesto whispered something to Rico and nodded toward Angelo.

"How you doin', Frank?" Rico said.

"Rico." Uncle Frank always sounded like he was in charge of everybody.

"You the kid that got hit by a car in front of 20?" Rico asked Angelo.

"Yeah."

"Angelo, right?" Ernesto asked.

"Yeah."

"C'mon, Angelo, your mother's waiting for us," Uncle Frank said.

"I'll see you around, Angelo." Ernesto coughed.

Angelo nodded as he left Beekman Street Hospital with his uncle.

* * *

On the drive back, Uncle Frank stopped at a Delancey Street clothing store. Angelo sat in the car while Uncle Frank ran into the store. Angelo watched as the rain stopped and the wipers squeaked against the dry windshield.

He opened his window. The air smelled like Jones Beach. He closed his eyes and could almost hear the sound of seagulls and surf. He remembered how the hot sand burned his feet as he carried hot dogs and sodas with Uncle Danny and Uncle Frank. He recalled how they searched for their blanket among the thousands. And his mother, standing like a lighthouse, waving them safely toward their small portion of beach. Laughing—

Uncle Frank returned with a shopping bag.

"They didn't have a dark-blue T-shirt. This was the best I could do." Uncle Frank turned off the windshield wipers and handed the shopping bag to Angelo. "I'll dump your clothes for you when we get home. I don't want anybody lookin' at them too closely."

"Thanks, Uncle Frank." Angelo looked at the new jeans, light -blue T-shirt, black high-top PF sneakers, underpants, and socks. "You knew all my sizes."

"Of course, kid—you're my nephew. I love you."

* * *

"Tell me straight out. You were too vague on the phone—what did the doctor say?" Angelo's mother said as soon as Angelo and his uncle walked into the apartment.

The fear in her eyes brought shame to Angelo's heart as his mother embraced him. "It's okay, Mom. Right, Uncle Frank?"

"No big deal," Uncle Frank said. "Like I said on the phone, some torn ligaments in the ankle, bruises, might have a hairline fracture—"

"Fracture? You never said a fracture. Where?"

"His right ankle, hairline. Maybe."

"What are they going to do?"

"Nothin' to do. Everything'll heal fine. He just needs to take it easy for a few days."

Angelo hated seeing his mother this worried. "Uncle Frank, can I take this off now?" Angelo started to remove the Band-Aid from above his eye.

"Yeah."

"I'll do that, Angelo." His mother held his face in her left hand and gently removed the covering. She kissed the injury. Angelo didn't look at his uncle.

"And he should unwrap his ankle when he takes a bath, goes to bed, anytime he's not walkin' on it," Uncle Frank said. "He should also use the cane for a few days."

"Mom, is it okay if I take a bath?" Angelo wanted to get away. To be alone. To wash away his guilt and to think.

"Sure, Sweetheart, just soak for a while."

"Thanks again for the clothes and everything, Uncle Frank." Using the cane, Angelo started toward the bathroom with the shopping bag of clothes.

"No problem, pal."

"Clothes?" his mother asked.

"Yeah, I got him a couple of things."

"Oh, Angelo...Mrs. Perez stopped by and said there was a fire at Bookman's last night and it's closed. Maybe out of business."

"Yeah, we heard," Uncle Frank said. "What time was the fire?"

"About two-thirty, three o'clock this morning," his mother said.

Angelo did not respond but continued toward the bathroom. He needed to be alone.

"Angelo," Uncle Frank called.

Angelo swallowed hard. "Yeah?"

"Put everything you have on in the shopping bag and leave it outside the bathroom."

"Okay, Uncle Frank." Angelo did not turn around. "Thanks."

Before going into the bathroom, Angelo limped into his room and hid the kerchief that smelled like an angel and Ernesto's gold medallion between his desk and the wall. He emptied his pockets and put his money and comb in the desk. He still had his lock. He put the lock in the desk under some comic books.

Angelo put his soiled clothes in the shopping bag and left the bag outside the bathroom. The hot water was wonderful. The smell of soap and steam filled his head. He actually felt the pain leaving each of his bruises as the soothing bath and silence coddled him.

Angelo soaked while Uncle Frank left with the shopping bag of soiled clothing. He wanted to spend the rest of the day in the bath so he would not have to tell any more lies or act surprised about what he knew only too well. He lay quietly in the tub and let the warm water wash over him. Wash away the night.

He drifted into daydream. He was a wounded marine lying on a faraway beach after saving hundreds of lives. He was a hero. People in the projects would tell their kids breathtaking stories about Angelo for years to come. His adventure was interrupted by a knock on the door.

"Angelo, can I come in?" asked Uncle Johnny.

"Sure," Angelo called back.

Uncle Johnny entered, closed the door, lowered the lid of the toilet bowl, and sat on it sideways with his back against the wall, facing Angelo. "You okay?"

"Yeah, that car just kinda skinned—"

"I don't mean about the car. Me and you, we don't need birdseed. I was looking out the window. I saw how you...got hit by the car. And you weren't all bruised up when you went to bed last night. But this morning, you're a mess. And now I hear that Bookman's burned down during the night. How bad are you hurt?"

"Mostly just a little." Angelo hoped that this would be enough. He was tired of making up lies. He was tired of being afraid. And he could never fool Uncle Johnny.

"Good. This is what was bothering you last night? You wanna talk about it?"

The way Uncle Johnny asked told Angelo that he wasn't being pressured. "Maybe later about...what I did...but not now. If that's okay?"

"No problem. Whenever you want."

"Thanks. It was dumb...what I did, I mean."

"If it's what I think, it was a real pit stop in stupid town. And...we were very lucky."

"You mean I was lucky."

"We were lucky. There are a lot of good people who love you, Angelo. They would die for you. What do you think would happen to them if something happened to you? You risked all our lives. All our happiness. We were lucky. Understand?"

"Yeah." Angelo frightened so many people. People were finding out about him. His father was right.

"Don't drown." Uncle Johnny left the bathroom.

Angelo covered his mouth with a warm, wet facecloth and cried.

Chapter Twelve

"No one walks to a fire slowly."

Bobby Rizzo and Will Garrard walked out of Linda's Luncheonette and into the rain.

"Let's grab the girls and head over to Palisades," Bobby said to Will. "We can hide out in the Showboat until the rain stops—it ain't gonna last long."

"Hey, Rizzo," a man's voice came from behind them.

Bobby's heart stopped. He whirled around, certain he would be face to face with Hector Cruz, but instead saw a middle-aged man in a bad suit walking toward him.

"Jeez, who did you expect?" the man asked. "You and Will got a minute?"

"If I say no, will you go away, Officer?" Bobby said, feeling relieved and anxious to redeem himself in front of Will.

Bobby, Will, and the detective ducked into a doorway, out of the rain.

"It's that obvious? I mean, my being a cop?" the detective asked.

"Oh, yeah. How do you know our names?" Bobby felt in control, strong.

"That's what you pay me for. I'm Detective Hartz. I understand you saw what happened here last night." Hartz took out a small pad and a pen.

"What happened?" Bobby said.

"Someone set fire to Bookman's while you were sitting in your car right over there." Detective Hartz pointed to the car now parked in the space Bobby's blue Plymouth occupied for a short time last night.

"That's not my car. I have a Plymouth. It's parked over on Market."

"Yeah, I know, a blue one...parked right there last night," Detective Hartz insisted.

"Hey, if it was parked there, it would still be there. That spot's good all weekend; why would I move my car to Market Street if I already had that spot?"

"You didn't want to be caught in the area."

"I got nothing to hide. I saw a little of the fire. But that's it."

"Tell me what you saw."

"Me and my buddy here were out pretty late. We were driving down Market Street looking for a parking spot when we heard an explosion. So I parked my car and we walked over to where the explosion came from and joined the crowd watching the show."

"The show?"

"Yeah...the fire, the firemen, you know. We watched for a couple of minutes and then went home. That's it. Right, Will?"

"Yeah, right," Will confirmed.

Detective Hartz put his arm around Will's shoulder like he was his best friend and mentor. "I'm going to teach you a couple of detective tricks today, Will."

Bobby and Will exchanged glances.

"Now watch Bobby's face," Hartz said to Will. And then to Bobby, he said, "That's it?"

"Yeah, that's it," Bobby said. "What?"

"See the way he shook his head from side to side like he was saying 'no'?" Detective Hartz said, in a pleasant, instructive tone. "And how he blinked a couple of times and avoided my eyes? He's even turning a little red. You see, Will?"

"I don't know...kinda."

"What?" Bobby said.

"What time was it when you heard the explosion?"

"About two-thirty, two-forty, something like that," Bobby said, looking at Will.

"Yeah, about two-thirty," Will confirmed.

"What were you two doing out so late?" Detective Hartz took his arm off Will and started scratching in his pocket-size pad.

"Tryin' to pick up dolls. That's not against the law, is it?" Bobby asked.

"Did you get lucky?"

"Hey, that's a little personal." Bobby chuckled, trying to change the mood.

"There were girls in the car when you parked it over there. Where'd you meet them?"

"No. We didn't get lucky and, no, there were no girls in the car, and we didn't park it over there." Bobby flushed. His mouth felt dry and sticky.

"That's right—you heard the explosion one block away on Market Street while you were parking the car," said Detective Hartz.

"Yeah. It was loud." Bobby leaned out of the doorway and opened his mouth to the rain.

"Then you walked over and joined the crowd watching the firemen?"

"Right." Bobby was still nervous, but he thought this conversation was wrapping up.

"Let's see if I got this," Detective Hartz said. "Pay attention, Will—this is the good part."

Bobby's stomach tightened. He tasted glue when he swallowed.

"First there's an explosion. And then in less time than it took you to walk one block, there was a crowd and firemen?"

"We were talkin', probably walkin' slow, you know?" Bobby said too quickly.

"No one walks to a fire slowly," Detective Hartz said with a pleasant smile.

"Look, I can't explain it—"

"I can," Detective Hartz said. "First, you told me that you heard the explosion while you were looking for a parking spot. But then you agreed with me when I said you heard the explosion while you were parking the car."

"I just got confused. It's like I—"

"Save it. Pretty good, huh, Will?" Detective Hartz winked and smiled.

Will nodded.

"You know how I know you're good kids? You don't know how to lie to a cop yet. What I know for sure now is that you know something about this fire and that, for whatever reason, you don't want to tell me about it. Let's see some identification, boys."

"Identification?" Bobby knew he was nailed. But he wasn't going to rat out Angelo; Danny Terenzio was his friend and Angelo's uncle. Bobby could tell Will was chewing the inside of his lower lip.

"Yeah, like a driver's license, maybe the registration for the pretty blue Plymouth. You know, the one with smoke dust on the back window. Over on Market."

Bobby wanted another chance. He knew he could sell this without giving up Angelo. The detective seemed nice enough. Through sticky lips, Bobby said, "What do we need to—?"

"I'm afraid there'll be no grabbing the girls at Palisades for you boys today. You're going to be busy at the station house. Cough up that ID and let's take a ride. My car's over there."

"Ah, come on, Detective Hartz," Bobby pleaded as he, Will, and Hartz huddled in the doorway next to Linda's Luncheonette. Bobby desperately wanted to keep the conversation here instead of going to the police station. "Have a heart, Hartz."

"Cute. Okay, like I said, I can tell you're good kids. You got one more shot."

"Okay, okay." Bobby knew this had to sound good without giving up Angelo. Angelo's Uncle Danny was not just Bobby's friend, but one of the toughest guys in the neighborhood. Even the Knights didn't mess with Danny or his brother Frank. "About two-thirty, we were parked right over there like you said."

"We?"

"Me, Will, and our girlfriends." Bobby felt Will staring at him. "So we're sitting there talking, and I see this guy come out from alongside 54 bent over at the waist but moving fast across Catherine."

"Could you make out anything—age, clothing, anything?"

"It was dark, I'm pretty sure it was a guy, but the way he was bent over, I couldn't see anything. So I said, 'Will, did you see that?' and Will looks out the window and says something like, 'What's he doing?'"

"Go on."

"Okay. This guy gets to Bookman's and he unlocks the cellar—"

"Bookman said he has the only key," puzzled the detective out loud.

"Well, he must've been a professional." Bobby strained to send a mental message to Will, to keep it close to the truth and back him up. "Because he opened the lock in no time."

Detective Hartz took a quick look at Will. "How's he doing?"

"Good."

"Go on." Detective Hartz returned to his notes.

"He went down the cellar and closed the doors above him. Then in a couple of minutes, he was up and out. He locked the cellar doors and bolted across Catherine toward 54."

"And then?"

"And then, boom! Shit flying everywhere. I say, 'Let's get out of here.'"

"Why?" Detective Hartz looked dead into Bobby's eyes.

"It scared me. And we're out a little too late for the girls' parents—"

"Too late for all our parents," Will added.

"Yeah, right, plus I was worried about my car with all the crap flying around. Anyway, I'm not sure of all the reasons, but we...I got out of there."

Will added, "We asked the girls if they wanted to see the fire...they wanted to go home."

"Yeah, they're scared that with the explosion and all, their folks would be awake. So me and Will, we walked them home and then went to see the fire. We watched the firemen for a while and then went home. That's it. Really, I swear that's it."

Detective Hartz said, "You think he's telling the truth this time, Will?"

"It is the truth; I was there."

"So who do you guys think did it?"

"Look, we don't want trouble. We told you what we know for sure," Bobby pleaded.

"No trouble. Take a guess."

"The only guys who would have the balls to do something like that would be...Knights," Bobby said, eager to strike a blow at Hector.

"Satan's Knights?" Detective Hartz clarified.

"Yeah. But like I said, we ain't sure. And we don't want no trouble with the Knights. I mean, we ain't sure who it—"

"If I asked the girls you were with what happened last night, what would they say?"

"They'd say they never want to see either of us again. But everything else would be the same," Bobby said. "It's the flat truth, detective."

"Much better, Bobby. Huh, Will?"

"It's the truth." Will nodded.

"You gonna let us go to Palisades?" Bobby asked.

"Yeah, I just need the girls' names and numbers."

"Ah, please don't call them. Can we just tell them to meet you someplace? Please, we leveled with you. C'mon...." Bobby implored.

"Tell you what. Go get the girls. I'll be in Linda's having coffee. Don't make me wait too long, and you'll still have time for the Tunnel of Love. Okay?"

"Great. Thanks, Detective Hartz. We'll be right back."

Chapter Thirteen

"No matter what, I'll always be on your side."

A t 5:30 p.m. Angelo's mother, Uncle Johnny, Adam, and Angelo sat at the kitchen table and enjoyed a slumgullion stew and crusty Italian bread.

"Father Casimiro called when you were taking a bath to see how you were doing," Angelo's mother said. "He knows you can't go to the Settlement tonight but I told him you would be there for the dance next Friday."

"The dance?"

"Yes, and please encourage your friends to go. I volunteered to help. Adam, you can come, too."

"Um, can I just stay home with Uncle Johnny?" Adam asked.

Their conversation was interrupted by a knock at the door. Angelo's mother got up and went to the door. She returned with Uncle Danny. "Look who stopped by to see you, Angelo."

"Uncle Danny!" Angelo and Adam shouted with elation.

"Angelo, Danny wants to talk to you alone," Anna said.

"When?" asked Angelo.

"Right now, Champ," Uncle Danny said.

"What's this about?" Angelo's mother asked.

"I'll tell you all about it later, but first, Angelo."

"Let's go." Angelo grabbed his cane and limped over to Uncle Danny.

"Danny, he needs to be careful with his foot—"

"He'll be fine, Sis. He's with me. We'll be right back."

* * *

Angelo climbed into the front seat of Uncle Danny's 1953 Pontiac. "Where we goin'?"

"Just down to the pier. We can keep the windows open, catch a breeze, and talk. Okay?"

"Sure. What about?"

"When we get there."

Uncle Danny's car crossed South Street and stopped at the entrance to a pier blocked by a heavy chain with a DO NOT ENTER sign on it. Uncle Danny was about to get out to drop the chain when a dozen South Street Boys surrounded the car.

"Well, who do we got here?" a South Street Boy said as he sauntered up to Uncle Danny's window. "Danny T. How ya doin'?"

Uncle Danny nodded and pointed his chin at the chain.

"Hey, Angelo, good run yesterday up on the roof—what happened to you?" another South Street Boy said as he leaned in Angelo's window.

Angelo recognized him as one of the three South Street Boys who chased him yesterday. "I got hit by a car this morning."

"Hey, Paul, lower the chain. I'll leave a couple of Popeyes here to make sure nobody surprises you."

"Thanks."

Uncle Danny's car plunk-a-da-plunked over the heavy, flat timbers to the secluded end of the pier. He turned off the car.

Angelo could hear the East River splashing against the moaning wooden stanchions below. He inhaled a sea breeze and could taste the salt. *I wonder what my dad is doing right now. If he's alive, I bet he's smelling the same sea air.*

"No matter what, I'll always be on your side." Uncle Danny turned in his seat to face Angelo. "I figured I knew you pretty good, but I'm missing something."

"What? What's wrong?"

"Last night, you blew up Bookman's Grocery Store."

"Uncle Danny—"

"Shhh....I don't want to catch you in a lie, so let me tell you what I know. You did this at two-fuckin'-thirty in the morning. That you were out alone, in the projects, at two-thirty is scary enough, but you go and blow up a store and almost yourself. And I figure you got hit by the car this morning 'cause you needed a cover story for all your bings and bangs. How am I doing so far?"

"I..." Angelo stared out at the river.

"Yeah, so I need to ask you some questions. Look at me." Uncle Danny gently turned Angelo toward him. "I want to help you, so I have to know. Did someone make you do it?"

"No."

"Have you done this before? Set fires, blow stuff up, anything like that?"

"No."

"Good, good. Okay, so then was it like something inside was making you do it? A voice inside your brain, or something?"

"Nooo. You think...I'm nuts?"

"What am I supposed to think? You been working for Bookman how long—two years?"

"Almost two years. But look—"

"Did he hit you, or touch you...If he put a hand on you, I'll kill him."

"No, he never touched me. He told Mrs. Monahan—you know, from Knickerbocker—that my mom was trash."

"Bookman told Mrs. Monahan that my sister was trash?"

"Mrs. Monahan stuck up for Mom; she said that wasn't true. Then he said he knew stuff about Mom and the Knights." Tears welled up in Angelo's eyes. "So Mrs. Monahan said she didn't care what Mr. Bookman knew. She said she didn't like that kind of talk and didn't want to hear another word. Then I ran out of the store."

"You were there? That sonofabitch said that in front of you?"

"I was there, but he didn't see me."

"When did this happen?"

"On my ninth birthday."

"Four years ago? So what happened four years ago, Champ?"

"Mr. Bookman let Mom have groceries when she didn't have any money and then she would pay him later, you know?"

"Yeah, and he would add on twenty percent. Go on."

"So we were in there to pick up a couple of things. Mom was holding Adam and waiting in line, and I was reading comics over on the side."

"That's why he didn't see you."

"Right. Anyway, it was Mom's turn, and Mrs. Monahan was behind Mom, but Mr. Bookman said, 'What would you like, Mrs. Monahan?' So Mrs. Monahan said, 'Anna is next,' and Mr. Bookman said, 'She won't care,' and Mrs. Monahan said that *she* cared."

"Good for her."

"So after Mr. Bookman gives Mom her groceries—I guess she thought I was waitin' outside 'cause she walked past me—I heard Mr. Bookman say, 'You don't have to do that, Mrs. Monahan—the trash belongs in the back.' That's when Mrs. Monahan said she didn't like that, and you know." Angelo wiped his face on the front of his shirt.

"Did you ever tell your mom?"

"No way—it would just make her feel bad."

"Okay, so what does that have to do with what you did last night?"

"Four years ago, I...I punked out. I didn't do nothing." A rush of saliva filled Angelo's mouth and gurgled his words. "So I waited, and then about two years ago I asked Mr. Bookman if I could work for him. I didn't care how little he paid me or what I had to do. I wanted to figure out how to get even with him for calling my mom trash."

"Why this?"

"Last week, the inspector came by. Mr. Bookman always makes me hide when they come 'cause I'm too young to be working. Anyway, while I was hiding, I heard the inspector say, 'You better get some fire insurance because if this place goes up, you'll lose everything.' Mr. Bookman said he'd get some next month. And, so that was it. A fire, before next month."

"How'd you get in? Not a chance Bookman would give you a key."

"I bought the same kind of lock and—"

"And Bookman locked up with the duplicate that you had a key for, and you had his real lock to put on the cellar doors when you were done."

"Right. But I never meant to blow the place up; I just wanted to burn it down."

"What did you use to set the fire?"

"Matches, old rags, and two milk bottles filled with gasoline I siphoned from a car. I hid the stuff in Bookman's cellar."

"Gasoline?—with all the crap Bookman keeps down there—Oh, that would explain the boom that knocked you on your ass." Uncle Danny put both of his hands on his head. "Do you know how lucky you are that you weren't killed?"

"Yeah. I know it was stupid."

"Stupid? Angelo, you could have killed the people living in the apartments above the store, even if it was only a fire. Why didn't you talk to me about it?"

"I was there when he called my mom trash and I didn't say nothing' to him—I didn't do nothing 'cept run out and cry in bed that night like a baby."

"You were only nine years old."

"I was all Mom had that day, in that store, and I ran. Like when my dad disappeared. I ran. I had to do it. Just for me to know I did something."

"You never said anything? You just waited four years to get even, and then you did what you did last night. That's all of it?"

"That's all of it. I swear to God."

"Okay." Uncle Danny grabbed Angelo by his shoulders, pulled him close, and gave him one of his famous bear hugs. "Damn it to shit, Angelo, you never stop surprising me. I'm scared for you. You should've told me ahead of time—you almost got yourself killed—*pazzo.*"

"Nobody got hurt, did they? I mean in the fire last night. I didn't even—"

"Nobody got hurt."

"How'd you know? Did Uncle Frank tell you?"

"I know four people who saw you do it. One of them told me."

Angelo thought he was being so careful. "Were they in a blue car?"

Uncle Danny nodded. "Plus a couple of people are pissed about it."

"Who's mad?" Angelo was squeezing his cane.

Uncle Danny stared at Angelo. "Most importantly, Uncle Nunzio is pissed. This is his neighborhood. But he doesn't know it was you, so now he thinks maybe some other guys are trying to move in on him. You understand?"

"I guess so." Angelo felt dizzy. Nobody ever wanted Uncle Nunzio pissed at them.

"Plus, he's supposed to make sure nothing like this happens. He's the insurance. His guys are all over the place trying to find out who blew Bookman's."

"I'll tell him it was me." Angelo couldn't breathe. "Is he gonna kill me?"

"Nobody's doing nothing 'til I talk to Frankie and Pompa about this. And, no—Uncle Nunzio ain't gonna kill you."

"Do you have to tell Mom? I don't want her to know what Bookman said."

"Kid, my sister's smarter than all of us put together. You really think she don't know?"

"Mom knows?"

"I'm sure she'll figure it out. You should tell her first."

Angelo's stomach dropped. "Oh, man. But not tonight."

"Let's get home." Uncle Danny started his car and backed off the pier.

"What should I tell Mom? She's going to want to know what we talked about."

"Oh, yeah, listen. I joined the Army. I wanted you to be the first to know."

"That's what I'm supposed to tell Mom?"

"It's true. I really did join the Army. You're the first to know; I'm going to tell Pompa and Nonna tonight when I get home."

"You really did?"

"Yup, first Fort Dix in Jersey. Then I go learn how to jump out of a plane."

"Like Uncle Frank and Uncle Johnny."

"Yeah, that's right. Well, here you go, Champ." Uncle Danny parked in front of 20 Catherine Slip. "I'll walk you up."

"You don't have to."

"I know, tough guy. But I want to."

"Are you going to tell Mom about the Army?"

"Nope. I want you to do that. I'll just make sure you get in, and then I'll blow."

"I'll miss you, Uncle Danny. I mean, when you're in the Army." Angelo and his uncle walked into 20 Catherine Slip.

"I'll tell Frankie to bring you along when he visits me at Dix."

"Will you send me a patch or something?"

"Bet on it. Patches and other stuff." Uncle Danny put his arm around Angelo's neck. "Hey, there's your elevator. Let's run for it."

"I can't, my ankle—and I gotta use this cane."

"Okay, let's hop for it."

Uncle Danny and Angelo hopped for the odd-floor elevator. Uncle Danny kept blocking Angelo to prevent him from winning the impromptu race. Angelo could only giggle in protest.

* * *

Angelo and Adam climbed into their beds at nine o'clock. Anna sat on the edge of Adam's bed. She knew that even while Angelo was reaching for the future with one hand, he was holding on to his childhood with the other. She sang an Italian lullaby to her sons.

Anna kissed her boys, washed up, poured herself another glass of Chianti, said goodnight to Johnny, and went to her bedroom. This was her time. Her time to dream, to travel to different places and different times. Before the rape...before the beatings. When she thought Mac was her prince. When the gentle magic of love ached and calmed. When she was beautiful in his eyes. Before. She promised herself no one would ever strike her or her boys again. No one. But now it was time for flight of imagination. Lost in a book or just thoughts of past delights—real or imagined—or a future enchantment. This was her time—just for her.

CHAPTER FOURTEEN

"When they look at me, they see an army."

Sunday, August 25, was Angelo's thirteenth birthday. As Anna had promised Father Joe, she took Angelo and Adam to the nine o'clock Mass at St. Joachim. They met Pompa, Nonna, Frank, and Danny in front of the church and walked in together. A sense of security, belonging, embraced Anna. It was a routine she knew and could float through. And it gave her time to reflect.

Anna thought about the last couple of days—her talk with Father Joe on Friday, Angelo getting hit by that car yesterday. She was troubled. She told herself she was just worried about Angelo. But something wasn't right. She could taste it.

She thought her brother Frankie would have ripped off the driver's arms, but instead he just let him go. And then Frankie buys Angelo all new clothes. Nice, but...why? she wondered. And since when do we throw away dirty clothes, even ripped? Something was just not right. Danny dragged Angelo out of the house last night, during dinner, just to tell him he joined the Army? Anna promised herself that she would let Angelo enjoy his thirteenth birthday. She would try to bite her tongue until tomorrow.

After the service, Father Joe met them at the door. He introduced Anna's parents to Father Casimiro. They talked between waves of "good mornings" to other parishioners.

"Angelo, can I talk to you for a moment?" Father Joe asked.

Anna watched as Angelo followed Father Joe to a quiet section of sidewalk. They talked for less than five minutes before they made their way back to her and her family. After wishing Angelo a happy birthday, the two priests moved on as Father Joe continued the introduction of Father Casimiro to the others gathered around.

Pompa and Frankie led the way home deep in conversation. Behind them, Danny walked with the two boys. Adam danced in playful circles, tagging Angelo and Danny while Angelo tried to hit him with his cane. Anna and her mother walked behind Danny. They were all heading to Nonna's for good food and gifts. Angelo's birthday celebration.

"Papa seems troubled; is he okay?" Anna asked her mother.

"His nose was out of joint all night. I think it's this Army business. Did you hear your brother joined the Army?"

"Yeah."

"He gives me such *agita*. What, it's so bad here he's got to join the Army?"

"I don't know, Ma. I haven't talked to him about it. What did he tell you?"

"What did he tell me? Goodbye. That's what he told me."

"Really, Ma, what did he say? Angelo, be careful of your ankle, use the cane. Danny!"

"Okay," Danny shouted back as he reduced his playfulness with Angelo and Adam.

"He said he felt pulled. All that *Terry and the Pirates* stuff he reads."

"*Terry and the Pirates*?" Anna watched her father and Frank. She tried to hear what they were saying. But they were too far ahead as they turned right on Madison Street.

"The comic. You know, Terry and—"

"Yeah, I know, but what's that have to do with joining the Army?"

"Oh, so when did he ever explain anything to me? When did any of you ever explain anything to me? I'm still waiting to find out what Father Joe said that got you back to church."

"Ma."

"All I know is what I told you," Nonna said, showing her palms to Anna. "Your brother is such a *jadrool!* You think he would talk to Frankie first. No, not him. He sees a poster, badaboom, he's in the Army. So, this is what I know. Nothing."

"Was it one of those Uncle Sam Wants You posters?"

Nonna stopped walking. "Danny."

"Yeah, Ma, what?" Danny asked breathlessly, the two boys pulling on his arms.

"Wait, boys, please," Nonna said to Angelo and Adam. "Danny, tell your sister what poster pulled you into the Army."

"It didn't pull me into the Army, Ma. I said I just felt a pull inside, you know? But it was a very cool poster."

"Ahh, now with the cool again," Nonna said to the sky.

"Ma, please," Anna said as they all started walking again. "Danny—"

"It's at night, and there's a paratrooper all alone, floating down, probably into enemy territory, with all this stuff hanging on him," Danny said. "He looked in control. Like he could do anything, just him, all alone. I wanna feel like that guy. You know, Sis?"

"Yes, I know. Wow, my little brother, a soldier."

"Thanks, Anna." Danny picked up Adam and ran with Angelo hopping in pursuit.

"Angelo, be careful—your ankle," Anna shouted after them.

"Anna, he doesn't need encouragement. Look at him, he's still more boy than man." Nonna shook her head as she followed her husband and Frankie into their apartment.

The smell of slow-simmering sauce lured everyone into the kitchen. Pompa put three tablespoons of the gravy in a small soup dish, broke off a piece of bread, and made his way into the living room. Frankie and Danny followed suit and Anna fixed two dishes for Angelo and Adam.

"Peanuts?" Anna said, pointing to the bag on the counter in the kitchen.

"The boys are goin' to feed the pigeons," Nonna said, shrugging her shoulders and tilting her head in a *who knows?* manner. "They're gonna meet your godfather in City Hall Park."

"Uncle Nunzio? Why doesn't he just come over?" Now Anna was really concerned.

"Why? Why anything? So they will all sit on wooden benches and talk and feed the pigeons," Nonna said, stirring the gravy and then lifting the wooden spoon to Anna's mouth. "Anyway, it'll give us a chance to talk."

"Wonderful, Ma." Anna sighed, sipping the gravy off the spoon. "Tell me what's going on. I want to know why Frankie bought new clothes for Angelo. Danny coming over—"

"Shhhh. I'll tell you when they go. Don't ruin Angelo's birthday."

"Ma."

"When they go."

* * *

Angelo and Adam loved City Hall Park. It was eleven o'clock and shadows crisscrossed the maple-lined footpaths. People smiled as they walked by and pigeons skipped and danced to an inner song. It all seemed so far away and yet it was only a twenty-minute walk from the projects.

Angelo and Adam sat on either side of Uncle Danny on a bench engulfed by the shade of a large maple tree. They reached into the bag of peanuts, cracked the shells, and fed the small nuts to the pigeons that flocked unafraid around Angelo and Adam while Pompa and Uncle Frank stood a few feet away talking.

Adam giggled wildly. Angelo's mouth was too dry to giggle.

"Uncle Danny...should I tell Uncle Nunzio about, you know, Bookman's?" Angelo whispered.

"Yeah, Champ. But I think Pompa already talked to him about it."

"So, Pompa and Uncle—"

"Know? Yeah. I told them last night."

"Nonna?"

"Yup. And she's probably talking to your mom about it right now."

"Oh, God. I didn't tell Mom yet. I feel like I might throw up."

"Put your head down and take a deep breath." Uncle Danny rubbed Angelo's back.

"Pop, there's Uncle Nunzio," Uncle Frank said.

Pompa smiled and walked toward his friend with his arms slightly away from his sides and palms facing front. The two men embraced, kissed, and then just stood there talking. Uncle Frank walked over and sat down next to Adam.

Pompa looked back toward the boys feeding the pigeons. "Angelo," he called.

"G'head, Champ," Uncle Danny said, ruffling Angelo's hair.

Angelo used his cane to limp to the men. His whole body trembled.

"Happy birthday, *Gattino*." Uncle Nunzio handed a birthday card in an envelope to Angelo. "Let's go sit over there."

Angelo sat between Uncle Nunzio and Pompa on a bench, close enough to watch Adam feeding the pigeons, but far enough away to avoid being heard. He wished he were Adam. He wished this were yesterday and he just stayed in bed. Never set fire to Bookman's.

"Can I open it, Uncle Nunzio?" Angelo squeezed out through sticky, dry lips.

"Sure, kid. It's your birthday."

Angelo removed a card with five new ten-dollar bills in it. "Whoa!"

"Whaddaya gonna do with it?" Uncle Nunzio asked.

"I think I'll save it to buy my mom a TV."

"Yeah?"

"Yeah. Thanks, Uncle Nunzio." Angelo was confused. He thought Uncle Nunzio was mad at him.

"I talked to Pompa and your uncles last night. They said you wanna tell me somethin'."

"Yes, sir." Angelo stood up and faced Uncle Nunzio. When he started to talk, his face and even his words shook. "I was the one who blew up Bookman's." Angelo looked directly at Uncle Nunzio.

"Relax, *Gattino*. We're family. Sit. You did this because of what Bookman said about your mother?"

Angelo sat between Uncle Nunzio and Pompa. "Yes, sir, he said that my mom—"

"*Aspetta*, they told me what he said. And that you didn't know Bookman's and all those stores were my responsibility."

Angelo shook his head and said, "No, sir." *Aspetta* always made Angelo think about the last time he saw his father. *Aspetta, aspetta.*

"What would you have done if you did know?" Uncle Nunzio asked.

"I wouldn't do anything to the store...or where other people could get hurt. That was dumb. But I would do something."

"By yourself?"

"I was the one that did nothin'. So, I had to do somethin', just me...by myself."

"Your uncle told me that you waited four years to figure out what you were gonna do. Never told nobody. Is that right?"

"Yes, sir."

"Not even Bookman. So he don't know you got even?"

Angelo shook his head. "I know."

Uncle Nunzio smiled and nodded. "This kid, thirteen years old, never said a word for four years. Just waitin'. *Perbacco. Gattino*, you ever get mad at me, tell me right away."

Angelo, still frightened, wasn't sure what to say. "I love you, Uncle Nunzio. And I'm sorry I caused you so much trouble."

"I love you, too, kid. Don't worry about nothin'. It's done. Forget about it," Uncle Nunzio said, slapping Angelo on the knee. "Listen to me. You think I'm a tough guy?"

"You're the toughest guy in the whole city...probably in the whole world."

"Although, like you, I ain't so big and yet bigger, stronger men fear me. You know why? Because when they look at me, they see an army. *Capisce?*"

"I think so," Angelo, still nervous, didn't want to get any questions wrong.

"Doin' things all alone, when you don't have to, is stupid, not brave, *Gattino*."

"I was—"

"I know. But if you told me what Bookman said, I would've talked to him. And he would've shit his pants. And from that day forward, he would've treated your mother like a queen. Because whenever he'd see her, or you, he would see me and my army. *Capisce?*"

"Yes, sir." Angelo believed he was beginning to understand something very important.

"*Bene.*" Uncle Nunzio stood up. "Thanks for telling me yourself. Now go disturb those pigeons your brother's feedin' over there."

They got up and began walking toward Uncle Frank, Uncle Danny, and Adam. Angelo hopped ahead a couple of steps, stopped, and turned. "Thanks, Uncle Nunzio."

"Forget about it, kid. It's done. Go enjoy your birthday."

"You sure you can't join us, Boss?" Pompa said to Uncle Nunzio.

"Thanks, Pump, but I'm meetin' Father Joe and the new priest at the Caffè."

The pigeons took flight momentarily as Angelo approached. Pompa and Uncle Nunzio talked softly as they strolled behind him. Angelo felt lighter. Uncle Nunzio didn't kill him. But then he remembered Nonna told his mother. He thought about facing her. And about all the other people who know. Maybe even the police.

* * *

Bra+ Bracciole was Angelo's favorite dinner, especially the way his mother and Nonna fixed it. Pompa worked hard as the senior foreman at the meat market on the West Side so the bosses looked the other way when he brought home a prime cut of beef. Nonna insisted her bracciole be prepared with only the finest bottom round.

She sliced the beef into twelve scaloppini cutlets that she carefully pounded tender and rubbed with olive oil and butter. Upon each of the twelve beef rectangles, Nonna placed a mixture of chopped hardboiled eggs, bread crumbs, grated cheese, minced garlic, pine nuts, fennel seed, basil, parsley, salt, and pepper, all lovingly rolled up like five-inch cigars and tied, seared to lock in the juices, and slow-cooked in Nonna's famous tomato gravy. They simmered for two hours, filling Nonna's apartment and Angelo's head with the aroma of family love. Safety.

When Angelo returned from the park, his mother and Nonna were in the kitchen washing bowls. Angelo's mother looked at him as he limped past the kitchen behind Pompa. Her eyes were rubbed-red and puffy. She looked sad...no, defeated.

All he did—being brave, going it alone, getting even—all of it was to defend his mother, he told himself. He pouted, only briefly, because he knew better. He set fire to Bookman's to redeem his own honor. It was about what he needed. Uncle Johnny was right. Angelo risked his mother's—his whole family's—happiness just to wash away his cowardly moment.

It was twenty past noon, and the men and boys were in the living room watching *Hopalong Cassidy*. Pompa sat in his big chair, stuffing cherry tobacco into his pipe. Angelo and Adam sprawled on the floor, chins on palms, glued to channel four.

Nonna called from the kitchen, "Anna, not now—"

"Ma, please," Angelo's mother said. And then, just as firmly, "Angelo, come with me." His mother, drying her hands with a dish towel, walked past him toward Nonna and Pompa's bedroom.

As Hoppy dismounted Topper, Angelo got up stiffly, grabbed his cane, didn't look at anyone, and followed his mother to the bedroom. Once inside, she closed the door.

* * *

While bracciole simmered at Nonna's on that August afternoon, Father Joe and Father Casimiro met Nunzio Sabino at Caffè Fiora on Grand Street—the heart of New York City's Little Italy.

The Caffè's four sidewalk tables were occupied by neighborhood residents. Inside the Caffè stood an eight-stool chestnut bar to the left and a maître d' pedestal and coat closet to the right. Beyond the bar and pedestal beckoned a sixteen-table, dusk-lit dining room. The décor, understated with ropes, hooks, and paintings, celebrated Genoa's seaport. Two of the front tables had customers, a young couple at one and three men and a woman at the other.

Nunzio Sabino and the priests sat at a round table for six in the back left corner. Nunzio's table. If he was not in the caffè, the table stood empty. It made no difference how many customers waited. The owner, Natale Ventosa, insisted the table remain empty—reserved for Nunzio Sabino. Above the table hung a mesmerizing oil painting of a dark-eyed young woman—Fiora Ventosa, the owner's mother.

Nunzio and the two priests ate scungilli in spicy tomato gravy with hard biscuits. Father Casimiro's taste buds were flying on fire. Such new and wonderful flavors. They drank sparkling water from Italy and talked about the Braves beating the Dodgers yesterday and the sailor who had been shot in the Bronx.

As they sipped anisette-tweaked espresso and ate freshly made biscotti, Nunzio Sabino directed the conversation to a more personal note.

"You wanna talk about the Brooklyn Bridge project?" Nunzio said, nodding toward Father Casimiro.

"He needs to know, too." Father Joe sipped his espresso.

"Well, you were right, Joe," Nunzio said. "They're gonna tear St. Joachim's down. Nothin' can stop it. I'm meetin' with the mayor's guy a week from Wednesday, September fourth. So tell me what's gonna help."

Father Casimiro's eyes went from man to man. He knew that Father Joe was saddened but not surprised. The taste of licorice danced on his tongue and tickled the back of his throat as he sipped his espresso. He spotted the three coffee beans in the bottom of his espresso cup.

"They're for good luck, Robert," Father Joe said as if he read Father Casimiro's mind. "So, we're lookin' at—"

Father Joe watched Mr. Bookman as he tentatively approached their table.

"Wait over there," Nunzio said to Mr. Bookman dismissively. Mr. Bookman walked toward an empty table. "Not there, s*tronzo.* Wait at the bar."

"The bar's closed, Mr. Sabino," Mr. Bookman mumbled, and without waiting for an answer, Mr. Bookman actually bowed, walked to the bar, and slumped on a stool in the dark.

Father Casimiro sipped his espresso to hide his surprise.

"*Pezzo di merda.*" Nunzio nodded toward Mr. Bookman.

"*Ma certamente,*" Father Joe said. "*Che cosa?*"

"*Non ha importanza.*"

"Is he the owner of the store that burned down Friday night?" Father Casimiro said.

"That's right, Robert," said Father Joe. "Do you need to talk to him, Boss?"

"He had no insurance—*stupido*—so now he wants my help to reopen."

"Are you going to help him?" Father Casimiro asked.

"You don't mind askin' questions, huh?" Nunzio smiled.

"He's gaining a reputation for being direct," Father Joe said.

"I'll tell you somethin'. Yesterday, I would've helped him reopen. Today, I'm gonna give him nothin' and tell him to get outta my neighborhood."

"Why? What's new since yesterday?" Father Casimiro asked.

"Nothing's ever new—there's only the history you don't know yet. But, now I know."

"Please excuse me," Father Casimiro said. "I must see to him...comfort him." Father Casimiro walked over to Mr. Bookman and after just a minute or so returned to Father Joe and Nunzio. "He won't talk to me. He just kept apologizing for interrupting us." Father Casimiro found Nunzio both scary and charming. There was an unsettling honesty about him. "Nunzio, what did you learn in less than a day that changed your opinion of Mr. Bookman?"

"He insulted a friend of mine four years ago. Now you know enough," Nunzio said in a cool, unbending voice while he poured another espresso for Father Casimiro. "Where were we?"

"Did you find out anything about the Settlement house?" Father Joe asked.

"No plans to take it down. Whaddaya want from the meeting?"

"The Cherry Street Settlement continues, with me and Father Casimiro running it."

"And ..."

"And I need two months to close St. Joachim's. Right now they're lookin' at the middle of September. It would help if you could stretch that into November," Father Joe said. "I should've talked to you right away."

"You gave it a shot," Nunzio said, waving his hand. "Now we fix what we can fix."

"The demolition of St. Joachim's is one thing," Father Casimiro said, "But surely Father Joe is not at risk of being moved. I mean, if his work in this neighborhood were explained to the bishop, he'd realize it would be a terrible mistake to remove Father Joe."

"Listen, politicians—outside and inside the church—they don't give you what you want because they respect or like you," Nunzio said, leaning toward Father Casimiro. "They give you what you want because they want you to like them. Why? Because you have something they want—money, safety, reputation, and eventually power."

"Not everybody," Father Casimiro protested.

"No, not everybody—not good friends, good family, stand-up guys," Nunzio said. "But most everybody else, kid. Count on it."

Father Casimiro, weighing all he learned, found himself captivated by the portrait of Fiora Ventosa.

"Fiora Ventosa," Nunzio said to Father Casimiro. "She's beautiful, isn't she?"

"Yes, very." Father Casimiro noticed a sad smile on Father Joe's face. "You know her?"

"We both know her," Father Joe whispered.

Without taking his eyes off the portrait, Nunzio said, "She was born in Genoa, Italy, on March 18, 1902. Seventeen years later, she died in this room, right over there. That's it."

CHAPTER FIFTEEN

"This is Merlin."

Angelo and his mother sat campfire-style and shoeless on Nonna's bed. His mother, through tears, recited the story of Angelo burning down Bookman's. Angelo listened, nodded, and cried. An act he thought would symbolize the love for his mother turned out to be an indulgence that hurt the people he loved most. He wished he could go back in time. Maybe this was mostly about him. But he continued to cling to the belief that it was still partly about protecting his mother.

He did what he had to do—Uncle Nunzio understood. He should've been smarter—done something else—he should've made sure no one would ever know. But he hadn't been and his mother knew everything. She even knew that the car accident was a fake. It was painful for Angelo to see his mother so distraught, so disappointed in him. An emotional landslide of inconstant thoughts stampeded from his head to his stomach.

After twenty minutes that seemed like twenty hours, his mother wiped her eyes. "I need you to promise me something right now. I must know that after I put you and Adam to bed, after I lock out the world, you will not, no matter what, leave the apartment."

"I promise."

"No matter what?"

"No matter what."

"Okay, we need to go out there and enjoy your birthday. You're thirteen today. Thirteen."

"No, Mom, not yet. What about that stuff Ernesto said about Dad and—"

"Oh, God, Angelo. Now?"

"Mom, please, I—"

She held his hands. In the past, this always seemed to comfort him, but this time, it was her hands that were trembling.

"On Thanksgiving 1943, I volunteered to help serve dinner for the neighborhood poor at the Cherry Street Settlement. I was there alone, cleaning up..." Anna told Angelo what had happened to her, leaving out details that were too devastating to say out loud to anyone, much less her son. "...No one ever found out who killed the Zara brothers."

Through it all, silent tears coursed down Angelo's face. Anger. Fear. Rage. And through it all, he held onto his mother's damp, quivering hands.

She added, "Your father was haunted by the thought that you might not be his son. Of course you are. A mother knows such things. I know it. And you, my angel, should never doubt it. I'm sorry it's taken me so long to tell you. Do you have questions?"

Unable to speak, Angelo shook his head. He felt weak and profoundly sad.

"You will," she said. "And when you do, whenever it is, please talk to me."

He nodded.

She took him into her arms and held him for a long time.

"You okay, Mom?" Angelo asked.

Anna nodded and said, "Yes. And you?"

"Yeah, thanks for telling me, Mom."

They climbed off the bed. His mother wiped his eyes and hugged him.

"I love you so much, Angelo."

"I love you, too, Mom."

No one seemed to notice as Angelo and his mother walked into the living room. His uncles were sitting on the sofa. Uncle Frank looked through the *New York Times*. Uncle Danny polished his shoes, and Pompa cleaned his pipe in his big, cushy chair. Angelo sprawled on the floor next to Adam in front of the television. His mother walked through the living room and into the kitchen.

Angelo heard his mother and Nonna talking but couldn't make out what they were saying. His emotions ran from sadness to anger to self-pity. He looked around the room. He looked at

Adam. Adam smiled and rested his head on Angelo's back. It was oddly comforting.

"I found it, Pop," Uncle Frank said, looking up from the newspaper. "At one-fifty-five, we got either the Dodgers and Cardinals or the Giants and Redlegs."

"Brooklyn'll be a better game," Pompa said. "Does it say who's on Sullivan tonight?"

"Sal Mineo, Guy Mitchell, Carmen MacRae, and the Milwaukee Braves."

"They gotta hell of a team this year," Pompa said.

"Pompeo, please!" Nonna admonished from the kitchen.

Adam snickered.

Angelo's mother and Nonna prepared a wonderful dinner of bracciole and vermicelli in Nonna's tomato gravy. Scarola. Soffritto—celery, onions, and carrots lightly fried, to which Nonna added garlic, parsley, and sage. And schiacciata, a thin Tuscan bread topped with olive oil and salt. After dinner and Nonna's homemade birthday cheesecake, Angelo opened his birthday presents.

At five o'clock, everyone gathered around the television to watch *Face the Nation*. Pompa returned to his large easy chair and puffed cherry-scented tobacco into the air. Nonna sank into a smaller cushioned chair with a *Life* magazine in her lap. Uncle Frank tipped the straight-backed gooseneck chair precariously against the wall.

"Frankie, that chair's gonna slide and you're gonna crack your head on the wall," Pompa said as dispassionately as he had said it a thousand times before.

"I got it covered, Pop." Uncle Frank didn't move.

Adam was curled up on the couch with his head in his mother's lap as she stroked his hair. Angelo followed Uncle Danny into his room.

"Hey, Champ, come on in," Uncle Danny said. "You okay?"

"Yeah. Are you packin' for the Army?"

"Kinda. I'm goin' through stuff, gettin' rid of some. Come 'ere. Pick anything you want outta my junk drawer." Uncle Danny opened the bottom drawer of his dresser.

Angelo and Uncle Danny sat on the floor staring into the vast riches of baseball cards, T-shirts, balls, a baseball glove, comic books, key chains, and other treasures.

"Really? Anything?"

"Sure. If you could ask for anything, what would it be?"

Angelo thought, looked, and then pointed to a partially visible push-button Italian stiletto with a black pearl handle.

Uncle Danny removed the stiletto from his drawer and looked at Angelo. "Your mother would kill me if—"

"I won't tell." Angelo thought about the discussion he had with his mother. But this was different. "Do you need it for the Army?"

"I got a new one. I forgot this one was still in here. Okay, I said anything, so here ya go." Uncle Danny tossed the closed stiletto to Angelo.

"Thanks! How does it work?"

"Hold it in your right hand. If you're holdin' it right, your thumb should fall on the pea-size silver button."

Angelo positioned the knife in his hand.

"When you push that button, the blade will swing open. But first—"

"I pushed it but nothin' happened."

"Pay attention, Angelo. It's not a toy. As I was sayin', first you check the smaller button below it. See it?"

"Yeah, this one."

"Right. It slides up and down. Up, it's locked; down, it's ready to open. Slide it down."

"Okay, it's down."

"Now push the button."

The blade swung open with a *saalick* sound. "Whoa, how big is it?"

"Closed, it's almost five inches. Open, it's nine."

"How do you close it?"

"See the guard between your hand and the blade?"

"Yeah."

"Right. With your thumb, pull down on the back of the left one."

"It moves. And wow, the blade folds a little."

"Right. Watch your fingers and fold it the rest of the way. It'll click when it's closed."

Click. "Got it."

"Lock it so it doesn't open in your pocket. Good. Now, unlock, open, close, and lock it."

Angelo slid the smaller button down. Pushed the silver button. *Saalick.* He pulled down on the guard and folded the knife closed. *Click.* "I love it."

"Now, this is no ordinary knife, Angelo. This is Merlin."

"Merlin?"

"The wizard, Merlin. It's gotten me outta some tight scrapes. It's magic, like your belt."

"My belt?" Angelo said looking down at the narrow belt he wore to church.

"Not that one, *Patzo.* Your garrison belt. How long did it take you to get that belt just the way you like it?"

"A long time."

"Now when you put it on...how do you feel?"

"Great, I feel like...I don't know...like Mighty Mouse." As soon as the words came out of Angelo's mouth, he regretted saying them.

"Mighty Mouse?" Uncle Danny threw his head back and laughed.

"What?"

Danny's laughter was contagious and Angelo found himself laughing with his uncle. "Mighty Mouse, Angelo?"

"Yeah, you know, he's a little guy, but—"

"Yeah, yeah, I know who Mighty Mouse is. Look, from now on, say Superman, Batman, or something else. No more Mighty Mouse, okay?"

Angelo nodded, giggling.

"Anyway, Mighty Mouse...the point is, it's more than just a belt, right?"

"Yeah, it's a weapon. A belt. Um...it's...you know." Angelo didn't know how to describe how he felt about his belt without sounding silly, especially with this Mighty Mouse thing hanging over him.

"This is Merlin. It's not just a knife," Uncle Danny said.

"Merlin. I get it." Angelo smiled and nodded.

He wasn't sure he understood what his uncle meant, but more importantly, Uncle Danny made him feel like he was his partner in this magic stuff.

"Here's something I made that goes with it. But ya gotta be wearin' a jacket or at least a long-sleeve shirt." Uncle Danny wrapped a leather wristband around Angelo's right wrist. He put Merlin in the three loops on the inside of the wrist. A ribbon attached to the bottom of the wristband ran up under the loops between the knife and the wristband, over the butt of the knife, down the outside of the knife, and under the loops. The ribbon had a loop on the end that hung just below Angelo's wrist.

"If you stick the tip of your finger in the loop and tug, Merlin will fall into your palm."

* * *

The smell of pizza, pasta, and pastry complemented the rumble of chatter and laughter along Grand Street as Father Joe took Father Casimiro on a walking tour of the neighborhood. An open hydrant cooled children as adults swapped greetings and stories on the stoops along the bustling sidewalks.

"How sad, such a beautiful young woman," Father Casimiro said.

"Fiora...heartbreaking."

Father Casimiro wasn't sure if Father Joe wanted to talk about her. The way he said her name was more dreamlike than real. Fiora. "Was it an accident, her dying in that restaurant?"

"Oh, Robert, this is something else you must not repeat. It wasn't a restaurant then."

"When?"

"In 1920...it was the Bailing Hook, a tough bar owned by an ex-longshoreman, Stanley Marco, and his wife Sylvia—who was every bit as tough as Stan. The place was decorated with nets, anchors, and baling hooks hanging all over the walls. It had a long bar and small tables."

"Sounds charming," Father Casimiro said sarcastically.

"In a strange way, it was. The booze was good. The food was tolerable. And the dancers were okay—that is, except for one. Fiora Ventosa was a delicate breeze in a cigar-filled room. And when she danced, the room dropped silent. She was sensational."

"A stripper?"

"Not completely, more burlesque. The dancers would take off this or that but never stripped completely. Each night of the week featured a different dancer. Fiora danced on Tuesday nights. And Nunzio fell in love with her."

"How old was he?"

"Thirteen, like Angelo. We were all kids about the same age. There were five of us—me, Nunzio, Pompeo—Anna's father—George, and Nick. We would sneak in every Tuesday night. Sylvia knew, but let it slide."

"Did Fiora know how Nunzio—"

"Probably. She would sometimes sit with us after her show. Thinking back, she probably thought it was cute, and compared to the rest of the clientele, we were safe, adoring fans. We would sit there and Nunzio would be transfixed. She was seventeen and Nunzio figured a four-year difference wasn't that much. So after watching her dance every Tuesday for seven or eight months, on the third Tuesday in January 1920, Nunzio decided to tell Fiora he wanted to marry her. Seems silly now, but back then...what did we know? Anyway, Nunzio had to work late, so we waited for him and then we beat it over to the Hook."

Father Casimiro loved these stories. They gave him a history, like he belonged to the neighborhood. "Did he tell her?"

"When we got to the Hook, Stan was shoving everyone out of the place, telling them to go home. Somebody, I don't know who, said, 'You kids better not go in there tonight.' We pushed our way in against everybody leaving. There were several overturned tables and a couple of people standing around looking down."

"Looking down?" Father Casimiro dodged several kids running along the sidewalk.

"Sylvia was sitting on the floor crying. Fiora was lying on the floor, covered by a large flannel shirt. Her head in Sylvia's lap. Stan was arguing with a big guy they called the Bear. He was six-foot-six and must have weighed in at over three hundred pounds. He was a foreman on the docks and a neighborhood bully. The Bear stood there in a T-shirt and said to Stan, 'Don't you say nothing, you hear me? Nothing.' Sylvia shouted up at the Bear, 'You sonofabitch, you killed this little girl.'"

"What? She was dead? He killed her? Why?"

"The drunken Bear wanted to see more skin. He yanked her off the dance floor. She fought and he broke her neck." Father Joe lit a cigarette and handed the pack to Father Casimiro.

Father Casimiro lit a cigarette and took a long drag. "Poor girl." Cigarette smoke escaped with the words. He handed the pack back to Father Joe. "Nunzio must have been devastated. You all, just kids, must have been—"

"It was the only time I ever saw Nunzio cry. Ever. It was the most heart-rending, profound sadness I ever witnessed. Nunzio dropped to his knees and touched her face. Meanwhile, the Bear was standing over Sylvia with his two buddies, one on either side of him, and he said to Stan, 'The girl's trash; nobody's gonna miss her. So you and your wife keep your mouths shut.' He reached down and grabbed his shirt off Fiora and started to put it on.

He continued, "That was when I noticed that Nunzio was missing. And then I heard the scream. It didn't sound human. It was pain and fury. It was Nunzio, and he was in midair—he jumped from the top of the bar behind the Bear. In each hand, he gripped a baling hook—he had taken them off the wall. He looked like an eagle screaming in for the kill. The Bear's arms were halfway in his shirt sleeves when the points of the heavy hooks pierced his deltoid muscles from behind. The hooks hit both shoulders and sunk behind his collarbone."

"Dear God." Father Casimiro shivered as he imagined the pain of a thick steel hook sinking into his shoulder muscle.

"The Bear roared and swung from side to side. Nunzio held on tight to the hooks, his legs flying from left to right, back and forth. The Bear's arms were pinned halfway in his shirt. He kept trying to grab Nunzio's legs. But with each movement, the hooks sank deeper."

Father Casimiro was no longer aware of the people pushing past him, some smiling and nodding. The musty beer and sawdust of the Baling Hook filled his senses. He imagined the blood spurting from the hooks, and a thirteen-year-old boy hanging on—fortified by rage. Father Casimiro smoked and listened. "What about the Bear's friends?"

"The two of them grabbed at Nunzio, and that's when we—all four of us—jumped in. I was a pretty good boxer by then, and Pompeo was always a strong kid. Nick pulled a knife, and George grabbed another baling hook off the wall. The Bear's buddies ran out of the place; they weren't up for the fight. After that, the only ones in the Hook were Stan, Sylvia, the Bear, Fiora, and us. The Bear started spinning and coughing up blood. Nunzio just held on. We were trying to get them apart. But the Bear kept spinning, knocking over tables. And Nunzio was like a cape flying from the Bear's shoulders.

"Then, finally, the Bear dropped to his knees, straight down, his arms dead, draped at his sides. As the Bear fell forward, Nunzio pulled on the hooks. The Bear growled and then whimpered as his face cracked the wooden floor. All the time, Nunzio held onto the hooks—pulling. He let go when the Bear rolled over on his back—hooks still buried in his shoulders. He looked straight up at Nunzio."

"He was still alive?" Father Casimiro gasped.

"Only for a moment or two. Nunzio wasn't finished, but Stan grabbed him and said, 'He's gone. You kids get out of here so we can clean up.' Nunzio never fell in love again."

"Did she have any family?" Father Casimiro asked, flicking his cigarette into the gutter. "I mean, Fiora."

"Fiora was fifteen and pregnant with Natale when she arrived in New York from Genoa. The Cherry Street Settlement took her in and after Natale was born, they got her a room with Sylvia and Stan, who hired Fiora to tend bar and dance on Tuesday nights. Fiora Ventosa was born on the third Tuesday in March and seventeen years later died on the third Tuesday in January, and her only family was two-year-old Natale Ventosa. No one ever knew who the father was. Natale was raised by Sylvia and Stan."

"What about the police and the Bear's friends?"

"No police—Stan fixed that. But the Bear's pals came after Nunzio. The five of us were inseparable. Nunzio was, is, a born leader. Battle after battle, victory after victory, we quickly gained a reputation. Eventually other guys wanted to join our gang. By sixteen, Nunzio was the most powerful gang leader in the city. When he was twenty, he bought the Bailing Hook."

"He bought it?"

"Stan had passed away a couple of years earlier, so Nunzio turned it into a pretty good restaurant—no dancing—and re-named it Caffè Fiora. He sent Sylvia money every month to cover Natale's financial needs. He paid Sylvia more than she ever dreamed to run the restaurant. When Sylvia died in '51, Nunzio gave the restaurant to Natale."

"So you became a priest to ..."

"The battles we won were hard fought and people were killed. We all ... I killed," Father Joe confessed. "At nineteen, I decided to become a priest and devote my life to saving as many kids in these neighborhoods as I could in return for God's forgiveness. We have an uneasy relationship—I'm certain God doesn't always agree with my methods, and I have some questions for Him as well. But I'm sticking to the deal."

"What about the other kids? Did they stay in the gang?"

"No. Pompeo is a foreman at the meat market, Spiro became a cop, and George is a foreman on the docks. But on the third Tuesday of each month, the five of us go back there, just like when we were thirteen, but now it's the Caffè Fiora—and we play poker in the back room and talk about how fast time passes."

"Does Natale know?"

"Sylvia told her the whole story. Natale loves Nunzio like a father," Father Joe said as he and Father Casimiro passed Columbus Park and made a left from Mulberry Street onto Worth Street. "This is the end of Little Italy."

As they reached St. Joachim's, Father Casimiro said, "I think I'll walk over to the Settlement. You want to come with?"

"Come with?" Father Joe teased. "Sure, I can use the exercise."

"Does Nunzio ever worry about some ambitious hooligan wanting to take over? Or is that just in the movies?"

"Hooligan?" Father Joe smiled. "Nunzio is the top lion in the pride. He is constantly watched by the ambitious and the aggrieved. He can't show weakness. He can't let a single insult, especially a public one, go unchecked. Continued leadership of the pride requires constant vigilance and no margin of error. None."

"Sounds stressful."

"It is. The only time Nunzio can relax—really be himself, joke around—is with us, the kids who grew up with him, on the third Tuesday of the month."

* * *

The two priests made their way down Catherine Street. A group of people standing in front of St. Joseph's watched a fight involving several Knights within the projects.

"Don't just stand there," Father Joe scolded the spectators, who initially responded by looking around. However, six men reluctantly followed the priests across Catherine.

"Hey, hey, hold up," Father Joe shouted at the scuffle. "Stop it!"

The skirmish was now clearer, but made even less sense to Father Casimiro. Curled in a ball on the ground, a guy in a Knights black T-shirt covered his face and head. The other three Knights in black T-shirts and a teenager wearing a white dress shirt punched, pulled, and shouted at the guy on the ground. The teenager in the white shirt started going through the guy's pockets when he spotted the priests.

"Guys, guys," the white shirt said to the Knights.

"I said knock it off!" Father Joe grabbed the large Knight doing most of the punching. He had Ray on his shirt.

"This big boy is Ray Cotton, Robert." Father Joe shoved him away. "He's one of the Knights' enforcers. A real tough guy."

Ray Cotton was taller than Father Joe and built like an overstuffed laundry bag.

Father Casimiro grabbed a Knight. "Leave him alone. What's wrong with you guys?" He never dreamed he would ever be in a street fight.

The guy on the ground uncovered his face.

"Joe, it's South Street Sammy."

Ray was shouting incoherently and lunged at Father Joe.

Father Casimiro marveled at Father Joe's punch. At least he thought it was a punch. Father Joe's right arm only moved about four inches. The punch seemed to start in Father Joe's right foot and undulated up his leg, rolling through his hip and midsection, which lifted and twisted forward, driving his fist up into Ray's chest. The short punch dropped the Knight flat down into a sitting position. Ray sat slumped on the sidewalk, wheezing.

Then Father Joe reached down and helped Sammy to his feet. Father Casimiro had never seen a priest hit someone before. Never even thought about it. Father Joe didn't seem angry. It was simply a matter-of-fact punch.

"You hurt, Sammy?" Father Joe asked.

"Sammy okay. Thanks."

"He's got one of our shirts," the Knight with Jimmy on his T-shirt said to Father Joe.

"I see that," Father Joe said. "Jimmy Bowman, I believe you've met Father Casimiro."

"Yeah, we met." Jimmy looked at the six men who stood behind the two priests.

"You're a Knight, too," Father Joe said to the kid in the white shirt. "You're—"

"Andy. I met Father Clum—Casimiro, too," Andy said. "Damn right, I'm a Knight."

"Look, Father, he swiped one of our shirts and I bet he gots Ernesto's medallion," Jimmy said. "We was told to find Ernesto's medallion and Marty's shirt."

"How'd you wind up with the shirt, Sammy?" Father Joe asked.

"Them Knights pulled it off the one they beat and threw it away in the bushes. They put my shirt on him and laughed. So Sammy got it outta the bushes and put it on. This one. Then Sammy hide and watch them beat him. Cut him, too."

"Knights don't cut and beat up other Knights. He's nuts. Anyway, it don't matter how he got it," Jimmy said. "It ain't his. He ain't no Knight; he's gotta give it back."

"Sammy, if Andy gives you his white shirt, will you give them the one you're wearing?" Father Casimiro asked.

"Sammy do that."

"Good idea, Robert," Father Joe said.

"I ain't givin' him my shirt," Andy protested.

"Give it up, Andy," Jimmy said.

"No! My mother just bought this; she'd kill me. Forget about it."

"Well, that's up to you," Father Joe said.

"Whaddaya think Ernesto will do to you?" Jimmy said to Andy. "Give up the shirt."

Andy took off his white shirt and handed it to Father Casimiro.

"I don't want no Knight's shirt anyway." Sammy put on the white shirt. "I'm a Popeye."

"What about the medallion?" Jimmy asked.

"Sammy, do you have Ernesto's medallion?" Father Casimiro asked.

"No."

"Search him," Jimmy demanded. Ray, still sitting on the sidewalk, hunched over and puked into his own lap.

"You mean the medallion with the two saints on it? Like the one that Rico wears?" Father Casimiro asked. He recalled Rico showing it to him in front of Bookman's yesterday.

"What do you know about it?" Jimmy said.

"Tell me something, Jimmy. Why would Sammy have Marty's shirt and Ernesto's medallion?" Father Casimiro asked.

"Maybe you're too smart for your own good, priest," Jimmy said.

"Very curious. Don't you think, Joe?" Father Casimiro taunted.

"Very curious, indeed." Father Joe laid a protective hand on Sammy's shoulder. "We'll clean you up and get you something to eat, Sammy. I suggest you boys clean up Ray."

Father Joe thanked the six men behind him. The men nodded and headed back across Catherine Street to the gossip-hungry gathering. Father Joe and Father Casimiro, with Sammy between them, headed toward Cherry Street.

"We ain't finished with you, Sammy," Jimmy shouted.

"No one even called the police," Father Casimiro shook his head.

"Not in this neighborhood," Father Joe said.

* * *

Angelo's mother and Nonna washed the dinner dishes and cleaned the kitchen as *Lassie* ended and it was time to go home. Angelo carried a plate with dinner for Uncle Johnny in one hand and used his cane with the other. Adam carried a piece of birthday cake for Uncle Johnny, and his mother carried Angelo's gifts in a large shopping bag—except for Merlin and the wristband concealed in Angelo's pocket.

"Angelo, what did Father Joe talk to you about after church today?" his mother asked as they entered the elevator in their building.

"He just said he wanted to talk to me, but he didn't want to hold us all up, so he said we could talk at the Settlement some-time." Angelo pushed the button for the fifth floor.

"Did he say what he wants to talk to you about?"

"No, do you know?" Angelo said as his mother unlocked their apartment door.

Uncle Johnny was right there to greet them.

"Oh, you startled me, Johnny," she said. "Is everything okay?"

"Yeah, sorry, but you're not gonna believe this." Uncle Johnny led them into the living room. And there in the corner of the room was a new RCA Victor color television with the channel selector on the upper right-hand side of the mahogany cabinet. It was beautiful.

"Wow!" shouted Angelo and Adam in unison.

"Where did it come from?" Angelo's mother asked.

"Two guys delivered it and set it up about an hour ago. At first, I wasn't gonna let them in, but they said it was from Mr. Sabino."

"Uncle Nunzio?" Angelo's mother said. "But why?"

"The note says, To Mom and Anna, from your son and godfather." Uncle Johnny said.

"Angelo?" she said.

"Uncle Nunzio gave me fifty bucks for my birthday—"

"Fifty dollars?"

"I told him that I was gonna save it to buy you a television. I need to give it back to him now—for my share. Can you give it to him, Mom?" Angelo handed the fifty dollars to his mother. What Angelo wanted most right now was for this day to be over. He wanted to get into bed and lie in the dark. The quiet. He sensed this wasn't the end. Too many people knew.

"I'll give it to Pompa to give to Uncle Nunzio."

"Can we watch our new TV, Mom?" Adam asked.

"First you two boys wash up so you're ready for bed." She walked into the kitchen and put the leftovers and the fifty dollars on the table next to a wrapped birthday present. "Angelo, it looks like your birthday's not over."

"Whoa," Angelo said, seeing the large, rectangular box from Uncle Johnny. "How did—"

"Ben and Henry picked it up for me. But I told them what to get," Uncle Johnny said.

Angelo tore into the paper and unveiled the model kit of a beautiful clipper ship. "Wow. Thanks, Uncle Johnny. This is the *Sea Witch*, the one you said my dad liked."

By ten o'clock, everyone in the apartment was asleep except Angelo. But he was on his way. He thought about the blood-stained kerchief that smelled like lilacs and baby powder, Ernesto's medallion, and the black, push-button stiletto and wristband—all safely tucked into a comic book that he had hidden between his desk and the wall. Angelo smiled as he floated into sleep; a salty night breeze carried the sound of a foghorn and a distant seaport clanging into his room. *Papa...I'll get those Knights back for you, Papa.*

Chapter Sixteen

"How 'bout we try to make it through our first day here without getting killed?"

As overcrowded public schools opened across New York City, the front page of the *New York Times* reported that the Governor of Arkansas, Orval Faubus, sent over one hundred militiamen and state police armed with clubs, rifles, and bayonets to surround Little Rock High School, where racial integration had been scheduled to start that day. The *Times* also reported that the headmasters of Cheam School in England would cane nine-year-old Prince Charles if his youthful exuberance got out of hand.

"Ma, you sure you don't want me to walk Adam to school?" Angelo slipped a new notebook under his arm.

"No, it's his first day." Angelo's mother straightened and tucked Adam's shirt in his pants. "My boss said I could take today off—he's not so bad."

"Angelo. Hey, Angelo!" Tate shouted from the street five floors below.

"I'll be right down," Angelo called back from the kitchen window. "Ma, Mrs. Moran and Barbara are down there, too."

"We're walking over together. Barbara's going into fifth grade."

"Okay, I'm going."

"Not without a hug, you're not. Come here. I hate how fast you're growing up."

Angelo didn't like it right now, either. He was more nervous than he showed.

"Hey, pal, you have a great day." Angelo hugged Adam.

"Angelo, don't forget your cane."

"Ma, please. I'll get killed."

"Okay, but be careful of that ankle. Tell Mrs. Moran I'll be right down.

Angelo walked without the help of a cane and with almost no limp. Although the swelling on his face was down, shades of purplish-blue still splashed about his right eye. He saw Tate and Spiro in front of the building.

"Hi, Mrs. Moran. My mom said she'll be right down. Hi, Barb."

"Hi, Angel-o," Barbara flirted.

Angelo, Tate, and Spiro walked to the Cherry Street Park where Howie, Ren, Sage, Chico, and Ju-Ju were waiting.

"Listen, guys, I've been thinking—life would be better for us, at school, if we were a gang," Ju-Ju said as they walked out of the park. "We need a name and—"

"How about Reapers?" Tate held up his comic book. "Like the Grim Reaper."

"Good name," Angelo said.

"So here's the thing," Ju-Ju said. "Me, Sage, and Chico are going into the eighth grade. Tate, Howie, Ren, Spiro, and Angelo are going into the seventh grade."

"Yeah, so?" Ren said.

"So, I just think I should be the leader," Ju-Ju said. "I mean me, Sage, or Chico, but since I'm the oldest of everybody—"

"I don't want to be the leader," Sage said. "I think Angelo should be the leader."

"Me, too," Tate said.

Angelo's the youngest," Ju-Ju said. "He's not even old enough to be a Knight."

"Yeah, but he's crazy," Howie said. "I'm not sounding on you, Angelo. I mean crazy in a scary, good way. Like running the roofs, talking to the sidewalk, and always jumping in to fight for somebody."

"Like you did for me when we first met, Angelo," Tate said.

"It's okay with me if Ju-Ju's the leader," Angelo said.

"I like Ju-Ju being the leader," Chico said. "But Ju-Ju, if you're the leader, you got to stick up for any us being picked on by anybody or any gang."

I know," Ju-Ju said. "I will. So, am I the leader?"

"All in favor?" Chico said to nods of approval. "It's you, Ju-Ju, you're the leader."

For the last couple of weeks, Sage, Chico, and Ju-Ju told the guys horror stories of anguish and suffering in the seventh grade, and the abundant perils of Junior High School 65. They heard about the various gangs at PS-65 and which teachers were jerks. Where to eat lunch. Where not to hang out. And never, never give up your lunch money—or you would be marked a punk.

The eight friends, walked, talked, and laughed on their way to PS-65. As they approached Doc's Drugstore, Emma Vorgage stepped out in front of them holding a shopping bag. Angelo felt her stare as they parted and walked around her.

"It's you. You're the one." Emma walked behind Angelo, shouting, "Hey, you! I know it was you. The bomb. Hey!"

Angelo felt his face burn as her voice twisted in his stomach. The boys stopped and turned around.

Emma almost bumped into Angelo. "You, am I right?"

Before Angelo could respond, Tate whispered something in Emma's ear. Her mouth dropped open and then closed tight. She stood there, quiet, as the boys continued on their way.

"What was that about, Angelo?" Howie asked. "What bomb?"

"It was about us," Tate lied. "She saw me and Angelo toss some cherry bombs into the back of a newspaper truck."

"What did you tell her?" Angelo asked.

"I told her the Knights made us do it, and they think all the witnesses are dead. So she better shut up." Tate winked at Angelo.

Angelo smiled and the knot in his stomach loosened. He loved walking with his friends. The sound of their shoes hitting the pavement. His own strength and power increased exponentially by the number of friends who walked with him.

The Reapers moved as a singular being and people stepped aside. Angelo heard Sinatra crooning from windows and shops as he walked through the Italian neighborhood. The smell of fresh-baked bread made him hungry again.

"Hey, Ju-Ju, since you're the leader, can you get us some jackets?" Spiro said.

Ju-Ju said, "How am I going—"

"Good idea. Ju-Ju, get us nice ones," Ren said.

Along the edge of Chinatown, as restaurant owners hosed down vegetables on the sidewalks, Angelo smelled ginger and incense and heard the ting-ling-bong music. They walked along East Broadway and passed the library and the Sun Sing Chinese movie theater. Traffic stopped when they crossed the street. Angelo soared on the euphoria of it all—of being, not just with his friends, but part of them, part of the whole of who people thought they were. Angelo spotted PS-65, just beyond the Forsyth Street Diner.

"Good burgers," Chico said pointing to the diner.

"Chico, you gonna join the Knights?" Ju-Ju asked.

"I ain't been asked. Anyway, I'm a Reaper now."

"Yeah, but that's just 'cause it's—"

"Knights." Angelo nodded toward the imposing set of steps at the entrance to the PS-65.

Angelo and his friends watched the group of black T-shirts at the top of the museum-like staircase. Two of the Knights stopped kids going into the school and took their lunch money.

"That's Jimmy Bowman. He's bad news," Sage said as they reached the steps. "The guy with him is Domingo Rio. They're in the ninth grade."

"And that's Liz." Angelo indicated the girl that stopped to talk with Jimmy.

"Liz Brennan, yeah," Chico said. "Also ninth grade. Her and Jimmy are going steady."

The Reapers started up the school steps. Various gang members—Cobras, South Street Boys, Yellow Jackets—peppered the steps. But only Satan's Knights were at the top. Jimmy looked like the king of the mountain.

Jimmy and Liz exchanged words. Angelo couldn't hear what they said but he knew they were arguing. Liz started to walk away.

"She don't like Jimmy robbin' kids." Chico smiled.

Angelo and his friends were almost at the top of the steps.

Jimmy grabbed Liz's arm.

Angelo felt a pull to dash up the few remaining steps to her rescue.

Jimmy looked directly at Angelo as if he could read his mind.

Spiro grabbed Angelo's arm. "How 'bout we try to make it through our first day here without getting killed?" Spiro whispered to Angelo.

Liz pulled free of Jimmy and also noticed Angelo coming up the steps. "Hi, Angelo," she said as she walked away.

Angelo smiled and mumbled, "Hi."

"Whadda you lookin' at?" Jimmy, with Domingo in tow, walked over to Angelo.

"What?" Angelo feigned surprise.

Jimmy continued, "How come my girlfriend knows your name?"

"Sorry, we can't talk right now. We have to get to class," Spiro said to Jimmy while pushing Angelo along.

"Sorry, shit! You go when I tell you to go," Jimmy said. "Let me hold your lunch money. How much you two got?"

Tate stepped between Jimmy and Angelo. Sage, Chico, Ren, Howie, and Ju-Ju quickly surrounded Spiro, Tate, and Angelo. They pretended they didn't know Jimmy was hassling them.

"You guys all in the same homeroom, right?" Sage said to Angelo and the other seventh graders with them.

Jimmy said, "Hey what the fu—"

"Homeroom?" Howie repeated. "Where's that?"

"How ya doin', Jimmy?" Chico said, pushing Angelo, Tate, and Spiro along. "Homeroom time, guys."

"Yeah, it's where you start. You leave your coats, check in, all that," Sage said as he moved the group to the doors and away from the Knights. "You'll figure it out. There's the bell. You guys better get up there."

"Dumb fucks." Jimmy shrugged.

Jimmy and Domingo walked back to the Knights and into PS-65 as a horde.

* * *

Leaving Adam in the kindergarten classroom at PS-1 was more difficult than Anna anticipated.

She leaned against the girls' entrance to PS-1 on Henry Street, waiting for Rosemarie. She longed for a cigarette as she watched Mary open the candy store across the street. Anna wiped her eyes and shook off her sense of clinging to fleeting years. But even her close family—the kids, Johnny, and Rosemarie—didn't eliminate her loneliness. The need to be loved. To be adored. To be held. She thought about Adam starting school and drifted off to when she had first met Mac right here after school one day long ago.

Anna and Mac had fallen in love in the fifth grade. Mac and Johnny had never known their father, and in 1937, their mother had committed suicide. Mac was twelve and Johnny eight. For three months, the boys lived with Father Joe, until Sister Florence, a fifty-year-old nun, diplomatically convinced Father Joe to let her take care of the boys at the Settlement House. Anna, Mac, and Johnny went on to Junior High 65 and then Seward Park High School.

In 1942, Mac joined the Navy. In 1943, a heart attack took Sister Florence, and Nunzio Sabino had gotten Mac a hardship discharge to help care for his brother Johnny. Mac went to work on the South Street piers, married Anna, and fourteen-year-old Johnny moved in with them. In 1948, Johnny joined the Army.

"And now, Mac is gone, Johnny's afraid to leave the apartment, and Adam is in kindergarten," Anna whispered to herself. "My God, who am I?"

"Anna, you okay?" Rosemarie was suddenly next to her.

"Yeah. Just, Adam off to kindergarten and, well—"

"I know."

"Come on, I'll make tea and we'll pretend we're someplace else," Anna said as they walked down Henry Street, passed the boys' entrance, and made a right on Catherine Street.

"There's this new lawyer at the firm. Peter says he's single and thirty-somethin'."

Rosemarie's husband Peter worked as a librarian at a Wall Street law firm. Anna and Rosemarie had grown up together and had been best friends since the second grade.

Anna was quiet as they walked past Bookman's—boarded up and for sale.

"Did you hear what I said?"

"Yeah, new lawyer, single."

"Right. So I was thinking—"

"No, thanks," Anna said.

"No, thanks? Why in the world not?"

"Ro, you're my best friend and you love me. But he's not looking for me."

"Now, how do you know that?"

"A single guy under forty is looking for an eighteen to twenty-nothing-year-old, never been married, no kids, no brains, yes, dear, ask no questions, put up with crap, perky, cutie-doll. Any of that sound like me?"

"This is not just any guy. He's a lawyer."

"So add that the cutie-doll has to be from a well-to-do family. Forget about it."

"So, Anna, not having a good day?"

"Sorry, just...life."

"You still miss him—Mac?"

"You know, Ro, I miss him more now than when he first disappeared. I mean, I missed him then, but I didn't miss the smacks and how he treated Angelo. But now, it's like I only think about the good days, not the rest of it. And, maybe I could've done more to—I don't know."

"You couldn't have done more. But Anna, you can't just keep dating your boss."

"Sure I can, if you don't say it too loud."

"But he's married. It's not going anyplace. You deserve better, Anna. You do."

"Thanks, Ro, but it's what I want right now. I'd rather be the other woman than married to some guy telling me he's working when—" Anna stopped herself. "I didn't mean you, Ro."

"I don't know what's worse...Peter would rather be at work or with another woman. Either way, he doesn't want to be home. Hey, we're supposed to be talking about fixing you up."

"We talked about that already."

"Maybe he's got a good-looking friend and I'll tell Peter I have to work—"

"Ro."

"Talk about a good-looking guy." Rosemarie nodded toward Anna's brother Frank, who was sitting on the front fender of his Bonneville parked in front of Lilly's Spirits.

"You've been saying that since the third grade." Anna chuckled.

"Second."

As they approached Lilly's Spirits, Frank slid off the fender of his car, held out his arms, and said, "Two beautiful women walkin' right to me. Am I a lucky guy or what?"

"I can't believe a girl has not landed him yet," Rosemarie quickly whispered to Anna.

"You got another one of those, Frankie?" Anna pointed to the cigarette in Frank's mouth.

"Sure, but I thought you were down to one a day," he said, putting another Lucky into his mouth right from the pack, lighting it, and handing it to Anna.

"Adam started kindergarten and Angelo PS-65 today."

"Sounds like a two-cigarette day to me. You want one, Ro?"

"No, thanks, Frankie. So, little Danny's in the Army."

"Yeah, can you believe it? Left for basic Friday," Frank said. "I'll miss that kid."

"Me, too," Anna said.

"Anna, I'm meeting with a lead on Thursday," Frank said.

"I told you, as far as I'm concerned, Mac's gone." Anna took a long drag on the Lucky. "I just want to put it behind me." She blew the smoke at the sky.

"I wasn't looking. But if this doesn't pan out, I'm done."

"How are you, Frank?" Rico said as he and another guy walked by.

Frank said, "How's your brother?"

Rico and the other guy stopped. "Improving. No big deal. How you ladies doing?"

"Fine, Rico." Anna looked at the guy with Rico.

"Oh, this here is Jack," Rico said. "Jack, this is Frank. He owns that liquor store, and this is his sister, Anna, and that's... Rosemarie, right?"

Rosemarie nodded.

"Jack," Frank said. "Where you from?"

"I live up in the one-oh—I mean, One-Oh-One West Eighteenth Street. Up on the Westside, you know?" Jack stumbled.

"Yeah, up on the Westside," Frank repeated.

"I've seen you around here before," Rosemarie said. "Do you work around here?"

"No, I'm an accountant. Uptown," Jack said. "Me and Rico are friends from college."

"Yeah, well we have to go," Rico said. "See you around."

"Nice to meet you, Jack," Anna said as Rico and Jack walked away.

"Same here," Jack called back.

"Odd," Frank muttered.

"What's odd?" Anna said.

Frank shook his head. "I don't know. Call it cop instinct, but something ain't right about that Jack guy."

CHAPTER SEVENTEEN
"I always bet on you, Boss."

ngelo and his friends sat at the counter of the Forsyth Street Diner inhaling the smoky smell of burgers on the flat-iron grill. The constant rumble of voices, punctuated by outbursts of laughter, giggles, and shouts, signaled the lunch break for students at PS-65.

The sizzle of burgers screamed and whispered as the cook with a spatula in each hand flipped two burgers at a time. But Angelo was more fascinated by the long ash on the cigarette dangling from the cook's lips, wondering when or, more importantly, where it would fall. Angelo's check, which was nothing more than a slip of paper with the amount due scribbled on it, waited next to his glass. Also waiting were two kids standing in line behind him.

That's how it worked at lunchtime at the crowded, narrow diner. First in got seats at the counter. There were no tables. Next in stood behind a stool. Next stood behind the kid standing behind the stool. Sometimes it was four or five deep. No one dallied. You waited, then ordered even before you sat down.

"Whatcha gonna have, kid?" the counter man shouted over Angelo's head.

"Two burgers, fries, and an egg cream," the kid yelled back.

"Twenty-one," the counter man shouted to the cook. "It'll be right here, kid. I'll fix your egg cream when you sit down." The counter man moved down the counter, taking orders and writing checks.

Angelo had just finished a burger, fries, and a Coke, when an older man in a dirty and tattered army shirt took the stool next to him.

"Here's your toast and coffee, soldier," the counter man said to the old guy. "And your check."

"You got a smoke?" the old guy asked Angelo.

"No, sir. Were you really a soldier?"

"I was, kid, eight years." He turned toward the guy on his right and asked for a smoke.

"Sure," said the other guy.

And as the old soldier was accepting a cigarette and a light from the stranger to his right, Angelo switched checks, spun off his stool, paid for toast and coffee and left. He joined Tate and the guys and they all walked toward the entrance steps of PS-65.

* * *

Nunzio Sabino walked into the Luna Blu in New York's Greenwich Village with all the confidence of a king lion moving among his pride. Guido Pappa, the owner of the restaurant, immediately stopped going through his slips and bills, sprang to his feet, and greeted Nunzio. Ten years ago, Guido was an ambitious waiter with a head for business. He needed Nunzio's help to get his own restaurant. He got it.

"Good to see you, Boss. Are you alone?" Guido asked.

"I'm meetin' some guys from the mayor's office."

"Back there—I'll show you to your table." Guido snapped for a waiter to follow him.

"I see Monsignor Culley is joining us."

"You know him, Boss?"

"Father Joe once threw him outta St. Joachim's."

"Threw him out?"

"Father Joe didn't like how he was treatin' an altar boy, so he grabbed Culley by the ear, pulled him to the open front door, and kicked him in the ass."

"This is bad, I take it."

"I'm here to ask a favor for Father Joe. Whaddaya make the odds?"

"I always bet on you, Boss, but I think you'll need a good glass of wine."

Nunzio Sabino preferred the company of restaurant owners, waiters, and construction workers to politicians, lawyers, and their self-important assistants who pecked around them for crumbs of power.

Plates of baked clams, stuffed mushrooms, eggplant, cheeses, and a large bowl of steamed mussels in a light red sauce were being devoured by the six men at the table as Nunzio arrived.

"You made it." The young man in a white suit and red bowtie looked at his watch and then pointed at the empty chair across the table.

Nunzio looked at Guido. "I think he wants me to sit down."

"*Uno sciocco.*" Guido led Nunzio to the empty chair. He removed Nunzio's paper napkin, gave it to the waiter, and said, "*Lino.*" He then pulled the chair out for Nunzio. "I'll bring you a glass of my wine, Boss?"

"*Grazie.*"

Nunzio's chair remained slightly pulled back from the table. He took out a pack of Camels, removed a cigarette, and tapped it on the table several times. He lit the cigarette with his gold Zippo, crossed his legs, and blew the smoke over his right shoulder. The waiter returned, placed a linen napkin on Nunzio's knee, and handed him a warm, wet towel. Nunzio wiped his hands; the waiter replaced it with a dry towel. When Nunzio finished, the waiter and towels disappeared.

The men around the table sat mesmerized. The bowtie man passed an irritated "What's going on?" to no one in particular. Nunzio waited to see who would talk first.

"Now, then, I'm Andrew Smelt. I'm with the mayor's office," said Bowtie in an affected, Ivy League slur. "He, the mayor, said you were a resident and a representative of the Two Bridges neighborhood and had some questions about the Brooklyn Bridge project."

Nunzio looked around the table at the men slurping mussels and eating eggplant. The sounds of clicking, chewing, and gulping eliminated his appetite. He remained silent.

"The mayor thought it best that the different interests attend so that we could answer whatever questions you might have." Smelt wiped his fingers on a paper napkin.

"*Grazie*, Guido," Nunzio said as the owner handed him a glass of indigo-red wine.

"Ah, as I was saying, the—"

"Who else do we got here?" Nunzio looked at the priest sitting to his left.

"I'm Father Denney. I'm here with Monsignor Culley from the archdiocese—"

Smelt jumped in, "Very well. To my right is Mr. Todd from our budget office, and to my left is Mr. Vernlack from buildings. And, to your right is—"

"I'm Tommy Sullivan, Mr. Sabino. I'm the project manager."

"That's like a general contractor," Smelt added.

"Mr. Sabino knows what a project manager is," Sullivan snapped.

Nunzio enjoyed the tension between Sullivan and Smelt.

"Now, I was saying...oh, let's just get to it." Smelt pouted smugly. "Your concerns?"

"Are you gentlemen ready to continue your order?" the waiter interrupted.

"Fine, yes, indeed," Smelt said. "Well, since our generous taxpayers will be picking up the check, I think I will have—"

"*Aspettare un secondo*," Nunzio said to the waiter.

The waiter bowed and vanished.

"I beg your pardon," Smelt snapped.

"I know it's probably too late to stop the project completely or even move it someplace else," Nunzio began.

"Someplace else?" Smelt said.

"Yeah, someplace where it would not hurt St. Joachim's." Nunzio took a sip of wine.

"It's 1957—you can't stop progress." Smelt shook his head and smirked. "So no, that would be impossible. Is there anything else?"

Nunzio worked hard to conceal his irritation. Few knew him well enough to notice his eyes darkening as anger coiled in his chest. He imagined himself strangling the young man with the red bowtie. "In that case, I ask only that you postpone the project for a coupla months. I would cover the cost of the postponement."

Smelt was incredulous. "Postponement? Demolition is scheduled to begin in—"

"In two weeks—I know." Nunzio put his cigarette out in the small glass ashtray.

"That, too, is impossible," Smelt said. "I'm afraid you're having a bad day, Sport."

Nunzio's eyes seized Smelt and held him as the table became quiet. After a moment or two, Nunzio said, "I also ask that Father Joe Bonifacio stay in the neighborhood and continue his work at the Cherry Street Settlement."

"Enough!" Monsignor Culley said, dismissively waving his right hand. "Mr. Sabatino, I am certain we all appreciate—"

"Sabino," Sullivan corrected.

"Sabino, yes...I'm certain we all appreciate your concern." The monsignor's voice was cartoon shrill and his face flushed. "However, what happens to St. Joachim's, its priests, and its Settlement House is the business of the archdiocese. *When* it happens is between the archdiocese and the city. These matters are not subject to—"

Nunzio Sabino stood up. An uneasy silence gripped the table. He said nothing but simply walked to the men's room. He was alone. He washed his hands and face, giving himself time to calm down. He strolled out of the men's room and walked over to the owner. "Guido, don't give them a check. I will pay for whatever they order."

"*Si, come desideri*, Boss." Guido walked to the front door and opened it for Nunzio.

Nunzio walked out of the restaurant, reached for a cigarette, and realized he had left his pack on the table with his lighter. The smell of car fumes and tar and the sounds of the busy street were a welcome change from the yapping and chomping around the table. He considered going back in—not for the Camels, but the gold Zippo was a gift from Natale.

"Mr. Sabino." Sullivan stepped out of the restaurant. "Your cigarettes and lighter."

"Thanks." Nunzio removed a Camel and offered one to Sullivan, who accepted it. He held the Zippo up to Sullivan first and then lit his own. "Come here."

Sullivan followed Nunzio to the corner.

"Take a look up 11th Street," Nunzio said. "Whaddaya see?"

"Saint Vincent's Hospital."

"Any of your guys remove a nail from St. Joachim's, you gonna find them there."

"Mr. Sabino, none of my guys are gonna do a thing until you say so. Period."

"Yeah?"

"That's right, and it ain't gonna cost you nothin'. I'll absorb the cost."

"Do I know you?"

"No, sir. But I know you. And I want you to think of Tommy Sullivan as a friend."

"Where you from?"

"Hell's Kitchen."

"I'll remember."

CHAPTER EIGHTEEN

"I'm afraid you're having a bad day, Sport."

Deputy Mayor Raymond Clarke tried to wake up as he fumbled to answer the phone.

"Phone, Ray." His wife sighed and rolled over.

"I got it," Raymond rasped. "Hello."

"Mr. Clarke?"

"Yeah. Who's—"

"Gracie Mansion security, Mr. Clarke. The mayor wants you to meet him at City Hall."

"What? What time is—"

"It's 4:00 a.m. Mr. Clarke. The mayor said to bring coffee."

"On my way." Raymond hung up and rolled out of bed. "I have to go—"

"Have fun," his wife groaned.

Raymond Clarke and his wife lived in Peter Cooper Village on Manhattan's East Side. He brushed his teeth, splashed water on his face, threw on a suit, stuffed a random tie in his jacket pocket, and was driving downtown in twenty minutes. He picked up three containers of coffee at an all-night diner and was at the office just minutes behind the mayor.

The mayor and Detective Paul Murphy were sitting at the conference table in the mayor's City Hall office.

"Sit down, Raymond," the mayor said, stroking a black kitten with emerald eyes. "You look awful."

"Here you go." Clarke passed coffee to the mayor and Murphy. "I figured you'd be here, Murphy. What's up?"

"Thanks, Raymond," Murphy said. "Somebody gave the mayor a gift. That kitten."

"It's cute," Clarke said.

"Raymond, my wife's at the shore. I was alone last night," the mayor said.

"His residence was locked and guarded," Murphy added.

"At three-thirty this morning, I woke up to use the john. First, I noticed a chair from across the room was right next to my bed."

"Next to your bed?"

"Yeah, like somebody was sitting there watching me sleep."

"Jeez."

"I go into my bathroom and on the sink is this kitten wearing a white collar and red bow."

"A white collar and red bow?" Clarke asked, not seeing them on the kitten.

"We're checking it out. But, I'm not hopeful," Murphy said. "Everything was still locked up. Secure. Whoever did this was more than just a professional."

"You're telling me someone broke into Gracie Mansion just to leave a kitten in the mayor's bathroom and you have no idea how he...they...did it."

"That's it," Murphy said. "And we don't know the why."

"The why?" Clarke puzzled.

"There are three whys," Murphy said. "The first one is easy—to let us know he can get in anytime he wants. The second why, why does he want us to know that? That's the tough one."

"And third, why a kitten?" Clarke added. "What does the kitten mean?"

"Right," said the mayor. "Free up your morning and figure this out. I'm spooked."

"No problem," Clarke said. "My only meeting is 8:00 a.m. with Andrew Smelt on the Brooklyn Bridge thing."

"Right, right. Smoothing feathers. It'll be fifteen minutes at most...let's keep it."

"No reason for you to be there, Mayor, I can handle it. I'll go through some files with Murphy while we're waiting."

* * *

At 6:00 a.m., Monsignor Culley thought he was in his bed dreaming when his car rolled into a fire hydrant three blocks from his apartment. Although the engine was running, the car was in neutral. Brakes off. The jolt of hitting the fire hydrant caused him to slam against the steering wheel, unintentionally blowing the horn. He slumped back in the driver's seat, still in his pajamas, trying desperately to focus his mind and eyes. He was alone. An empty bottle of Bushmills Irish whiskey was standing up between his legs. His pajamas smelled of whiskey. He smelled of whiskey.

"Hey, pal, you okay?" a man said, opening the monsignor's car door.

"What? How did I get here?" Monsignor Culley asked.

"Here comes a cop," the man said. "I'm afraid you're having a bad day, Sport."

"All right, back away," the police officer said, pushing his way through the onlookers. Leaning through the open door, the cop said, "You tied one on a bit early."

"I'm Monsignor Culley."

"So you are."

Although aware of the situation, Monsignor Culley had no memory of anything between going to bed and hitting the fire hydrant. "I live back there. I don't know how I got here."

"He's a priest," someone in the crowd said. "He said he's Monsignor Culley."

"Enough—now move along, off to work with you," the cop said, breaking up the cluster of pedestrians. "Take your bottle and shove over, Monsignor. I'll drive you home."

* * *

At 7:15 a.m., Andrew Smelt walked along the subway platform. He enjoyed standing out from the crowd. It was one of the reasons he didn't mind taking the subway to and from work. It was also the fastest way to travel from his upper Westside apartment to City Hall. Andrew wore a lightweight beige suit and walked to where the front car would stop. It would be less crowded. Still, a swarm of commuters gathered, lightly bumping and brushing in typical New York fashion.

Smelt leaned over the track to see if the train's front headlight was visible. The train on the other side of the platform thundered and sparked out of the station. It was then, as he was leaning over, that he felt a push—not a New York bump—a good, solid push. As Smelt hit the tracks, liquid splashed on his head—it smelled like whiskey.

"Help me!" Terror gripped Smelt as he scrambled to his feet on the subway tracks. Careful to avoid the third rail, he rushed to the chest-high platform.

"Take it easy, buddy—no train's coming yet." A man reached down, grabbed Smelt's hand, and helped him onto the platform. "I'm afraid you're having a bad day, Sport."

"A little early for the booze," someone else said.

"I wasn't drinking...someone did this to me," Smelt said, his suit stained with black grease and whiskey. "Who pushed me? Somebody pushed me."

* * *

At 8:10 a.m., Clarke left Murphy in the mayor's library looking through meeting minutes, letters, and clippings in an effort to find some connection to a cat or kitten. He headed for his office, where Andrew Smelt, Tommy Sullivan, and Monsignor Culley waited. Clarke allowed fifteen minutes for this meeting and he was already late. But this was an easy one. Smelt should tell him the lunch meeting with Nunzio Sabino went well and everyone left satisfied.

Clarke's secretary looked at him warningly as he walked past her.

"What?"

She responded by rolling her eyes toward his office.

Clarke's head filled with the scent of stale liquor as he entered his office. Smelt, in a soiled suit, perched on the edge of a wooden chair. A seemingly distracted Monsignor Culley slumped at one end of the small couch and Sullivan sat at the other end, looking as perplexed as Clarke felt.

"Andrew, what the hell?" Clarke said.

"Somebody pushed me off the subway platform. On purpose. On the tracks."

"Andrew, you smell like—"

"I know what I smell like. They threw something on me—whiskey, I think."

"Do you know who pushed you? Did you see him?"

"No."

"Are you hurt?"

"No."

"Everybody else okay?"

"Oddly, I, too, had a disturbing morning," Monsignor Culley said and shared the details of waking up behind the wheel of his car to the smell of whiskey. "The bishop suggested I see my doctor immediately. I have an appointment on Monday."

"Mr. Sullivan, your morning?"

"No problem."

"Anything about a cat in any of your experiences?" Clarke asked.

"A cat?" Smelt looked at the monsignor and Sullivan. "No."

"Unless it's black," Sullivan added.

"Black? Why would you say black?" Clarke asked.

"Just joking," Sullivan said. "You know, black cat—bad luck—bad morning. Sorry."

"No, no," Clarke said. "You could be onto something."

"Bad luck had nothing to do with it. I'm telling you, I was pushed," Smelt said again.

"I'm sorry about your morning, Andrew, and yours as well, Monsignor. I don't want to appear insensitive, but I'm sure we are all very busy. So, let's get to the business of this meeting—your lunch with Nunzio Sabino. All went well, I hope."

"Good," Smelt said. "He even picked up the check."

"Mr. Sabino paying that check was not a good thing," Sullivan said.

"Please, Sullivan, you were too busy kissing his ass to notice anything about the meeting."

Sullivan started to get up but Clarke signaled him to remain seated and calm. He did.

"Sullivan would have given that Sabito the keys to the city," Smelt continued. "The monsignor and I were firm. In the end, we steadfastly refused to delay the Brooklyn Bridge project and Sabito left like a petulant child."

"Sabino. His name is Nunzio Sabino." Clarke's head pounded. "What happened?"

"Andrew's correct," Monsignor Culley said. "That man had no business sticking his—"

"Forgive me, Monsignor," Clarke said, holding up his hand. "This was supposed to be an easy schmooze—make him happy, if possible. If not, at least make him feel listened to—respected. Isn't that what I told you, Andrew?"

Smelt cleared his throat, "Well, yes, but he should—"

"Sullivan, what happened?" Clarke walked over to the large window in his office. The tree-lined footpaths meandering through City Hall Park were speckled with people heading to jobs with regular hours and no surprises. He silently chastised himself for trusting Andrew Smelt with this assignment as Sullivan described the lunch meeting at the Luna Blu restaurant.

"Not much else to add," Sullivan finished. "I think Andrew and the monsignor embarrassed Mr. Sabino."

"Embarrassed?" Smelt protested. "Okay, maybe we were a wee bit rude. But he walked away from the table, not us. It was just tough negotiations. He wanted to postpone the project for another month or two. We said no. He walked out. That's it."

"You think that's it?" Clarke said. "Now it's going to cost more than two months—"

"A wee bit rude?" Sullivan said to Smelt. "You said to Nunzio Sabino, 'I'm afraid you're having a bad day, Sport,' as he was—"

"Wait...what? What did I say?" Smelt asked.

"Do you know who Nunzio Sabino is?" Clarke asked.

"Are you sure I said, 'I'm afraid you're having a bad day, Sport,'?" Smelt asked, ignoring Clarke's question.

"Is that exactly what you said?" Monsignor Culley asked.

"Do you know who Nunzio Sabino is?" Clarke repeated.

"A ward captain or something, I would imagine," Smelt said.

"He is a hoodlum friend of Father Joe Bonifacio," Monsignor Culley said dismissively. Then to Smelt, "Were those your exact words?"

"Who cares what his exact words were?" Clarke snapped.

"The man who offered me help this morning," the monsignor said. "When he saw the cop coming, he said to me, 'I'm afraid you're having a bad day, Sport.' Just like that."

"That's what the guy who helped me back onto the subway platform said." Smelt slowly shook his head, as if trying to understand something just beyond his reach. "A hoodlum?"

"How odd," Monsignor Culley said.

"Odd? You think that was odd?" Clarke said, picking up his phone. "Teri, do we have a number for Nunzio Sabino?" Then back to Monsignor Culley, "It's enlightening. Tell me something. Or better yet, let me guess...Sullivan didn't embarrass Nunzio, right?"

Smelt shrugged at Sullivan and the monsignor. "He was kissing his—"

"And you were wearing a red bowtie?" Clarke secured the phone between his shoulder and ear and pressed a growing headache in the outside corners of his eyes with his index fingers. "I should have handled this myself. It would've required less time and less trouble."

"Actually, my bowtie is carnelian...Cornell, you know."

"Of course, and the monsignor would be wearing—" Clarke turned his attention back to the phone. "Yes, that's it...Caffè Fiora...Please see if you can get Mr. Sabino on the line for me. Yes, right now." Then, Clarke muttered, "And neither of you were really hurt."

"Excuse me?" Smelt was clearly taken aback.

"I mean, no train coming, the monsignor's car wasn't doing ninety miles an hour. What was that you said earlier, Sullivan, about the black cat and bad luck?"

"I was just kiddin' around. You know what they say..."

Clarke said, "Yeah, right, black cat, bad luck. But if the bad luck isn't terrible, kind of gentle bad luck, then maybe we're talking—"

"A little...gentle...black cat?" Sullivan squeezed out, shrugging his broad shoulders.

"A kitten," Clarke said and then abruptly turned his attention to the phone. "Mr. Sabino, I'm Deputy Mayor Raymond Clarke. Thank you for taking my call. I just received a briefing of your meeting with three of my staff members along with— Yes, sir, that meeting... No, sir. On behalf of the mayor, please accept my apology for the deplorable way you were— ... I know, Mr. Sabino, I only ask that you make time to meet with me personally. ...No, sir, I will not waste your time. ... No, I don't believe a one-year postponement would be impossible ... if we could just meet wherever and whenever is most convenient for you. ... Yes, on Grand Street. Monday, I will be there. ... Yes, I will bring Tommy Sullivan."

He nodded toward Sullivan, who returned the nod. "No, no one else. In fact, as of this moment, Andrew Smelt no longer works for the mayor."

"I beg your pardon?" Smelt was astounded. "Am I to understand—?"

Clarke frowned at Smelt and gave him a small goodbye wave; into the phone, he said, "That's correct. Thank you, Mr. Sabino."

* * *

At 10:00 a.m., Frank and his ex-partner, Tommy Manuski, were sipping coffee and standing outside the interrogation room at the precinct.

"I hope this guy's got something for you, Frankie."

"So, he thinks I'm a cop working another case." Frank looked through the one-way glass. He missed being a cop. The gathering in the backroom before the shift started, jotting down assignments and "watch fors" in his memo pad. He missed the murmur of cops telling stories and playing cards. The smell of shoe polish, leather, and gun cleaner. He missed the updates before turning out.

Climbing into his seat in their car, he and Tommy took an initial look around their sector before deciding what they were going to eat on that shift. Midnight to eight was his favorite. First couple of hours were filled with disturbances as the bars let out. And then the second-story guys hit the warehouses and lofts. He liked how quiet the city was in the early morning hours. He liked watching it wake up: 5:00 a.m. deliveries, street cleaners, sunrise. Frank Terenzio missed it all—every day.

"That's it, partner. Gary in there's already given me what I need to cut the deal. But he don't know that. He thinks he needs your nod and, believe me, he wants the program. He's been sitting in there for two hours, no coffee or smokes—he's ready."

"So, we go in together and I play him to you," Frank said.

"That's my thinking...hold up," Tommy said. He shouted at a couple of detectives at the end of the hall. "Hartz. Got a minute?"

"Sure." Detective Hartz walked up to Tommy. "What do you need?"

"Frankie, this is Clarence Hartz. We got our gold shields same day. Hartz, this is—"

"Frank Terenzio, your partner," Hartz said, sticking out his hand.

"Former partner," Frank corrected, shaking hands with Hartz.

"Not the way Tommy talks about you," Hartz said. "Frank, all us old guys were around when the crap came down; we have a lot of respect for you. You're an original stand-up guy."

"Thanks, Clar—what do you prefer?"

"My first name's Clarence. Take a guess."

"Thanks, Hartz."

"Frankie, Hartz is working on something in your neighborhood. I told him it'd be okay to drop by and talk to you."

"I've seen you around. No problem. Lilly's on Catherine. Make it a coop," Frank said.

"Thanks, I can use the help. Good luck with this guy. Tommy told me a little about it."

"Ready?" Tommy asked.

"Let's go." The two men walked into the stark interrogation room. Gary was sitting alone at a table for four. Frank was holding two cups of coffee. He sat across from Gary. Tommy sat between them with his own cup of coffee. Frank pushed a cup to Gary, took out a cigarette for himself, and tossed the pack on the table toward Tommy.

"Gary, you're very close to the program." Tommy took out a Lucky, tapped it on the table, put it in his mouth, and lit it. He took a slow, deep drag and blew the smoke out of his nose and mouth as he said, "This is the detective who will make the call. He has a couple of questions and then we're done."

"Whatever you guys want," Gary said. "Thanks for the coffee. Can I bum a smoke?"

Frank nodded. Gary put a cigarette in his mouth and Frank held up his lighter. "I understand you did time with the guy who did a hit on Cherry Street in '51."

Gary took a drag and a gulp of coffee. "That's right. Willie Max. We shared a cell upstate for seven months. He was finishin' an easy deuce for some scam."

"Tell me what he told you." Frank took a sip of coffee and leaned back in his chair.

"Ain't ya gonna write nothin' down?" Gary asked.

"I'll know if you're shitting me."

"Okay, they grab—"

"They?'

"Yeah, there was two of 'em. Anyway, they see this guy, the one they got hired to hit, walkin' along Cherry Street with a kid on Christmas Eve." Gary looked from Frank to Tommy as he repeated the story Willie told him. "The mark was pullin' a shoppin' cart full of Christmas presents. Am I right or what? How am I doin'?"

"Go on," Frank said.

"So Willie and his partner are hidin' behind their parked car. They wait for the kid to pass them, and then they grab the mark and pull him down behind the car. That's when Willie pops him—bang, bang—twice in the head. Blood all over the snow—"

"Okay, I heard enough," Frank said, standing up. "It's crap."

"Wait a minute, guys, I'm tellin' ya what Willie told me."

"There was no blood," Frank said. "If Willie told you that, he was feeding you crap."

"Maybe he was. I don't know. Maybe he wanted to be a big shot inside. You know, make out he was this hit man with a heart. So he says he blows away the father, but lets the kid run away. He said he even picked up the cart that fell over with the Christmas presents in it. Look, guys, maybe he was bullshittin' me, but I ain't—"

"What did you say about the cart?" Frank said, sitting back down.

"Willie said after he hit the mark, the kid tries pullin' the cart. But the cart falls over into the snow and the kid keeps runnin'. So Willie and his partner throw the mark in the trunk."

"What's his partner's name?" Frank asked.

"I don't know. I swear he never said."

"Go on."

"So, Willie's partner, scared shitless, says, 'Let's get outta here.' But Willie walks over to the cart, picks it up, and puts all the Christmas presents back in it. Then he walks back to the car and drives outta there."

"And?" Frank said.

"That's it. That's all of it. I swear to God."

"Tommy, let's talk outside?" Frank stood up.

"Sure."

"So how did I do? Okay, huh?" Gary asked.

"Shhh." Tommy followed Frank out of the room.

"Frankie?"

"The blood is crap. But picking up the cart is one of the holdbacks. No one knew about that," Frank said. "Can you find out where Willie—"

"Where Willie Max lives, works, and plays? Here you go, partner." Tommy handed Frank an envelope. "Gary told me Willie's name and I figured if it was good, you'd want his picture and his address on Baxter Street. Also, he works at the fish market on Fulton, and he spends his leisure time either at the track or at Sonny's Bar and Grill on John Street. No wife. No kids. It's all in there."

* * *

"Any problems, Jokes?" Frank asked as he walked into Lilly's.

"Naw, nothin'. How'd it go?"

"We'll see." Tommy's information was more than he'd hoped for and a surprise. "Right here under my nose the whole time."

"What's that?" Jokes asked.

"Listen, Jokes, I need a couple of hours tomorrow."

"Around noon, okay?"

"Perfect. I'll grab lunch on Fulton Street. Thanks."

"See ya tomorrow, Frankie," Jokes said as he left Lilly's.

* * *

Thursday seemed like the longest day of school all week for Angelo. He was looking forward to heading home and this was his last class.

"Okay, everybody shut up," Mr. Millpod said as he wrote his name on the blackboard. "I will be teaching history and current events. Comparing and contrasting. Therefore, in addition to your history books, I expect each of you to read the newspaper every day. I'll be asking you questions about current events. For example, who is Bobby Fischer?"

"Is he in this class?"

"No, of course not," Mr. Millpod said. "He's fourteen and he was in Tuesday's *New York Times.* Anyone?"

"Where's he from?"

"Brooklyn," Mr. Millpod said.

"Is he in the Scorpions?"

Disgusted, Mr. Millpod said, "Bobby Fischer defeated James Sherwin Monday night to emerge as the winner of the open championship of the New Jersey State Chess Federation."

"So he's not in the Scorpions?"

"Scorpions are from the Bronx," another student said. "Not Brooklyn."

"That's enough," Mr. Millpod fumed. "I might be new here, but I'm from the toughest school in Brooklyn. So I'm not going to be pushed around by any of you punks. Got it?"

"He's the punk," Angelo said to Spiro.

"Yeah. And a jerk," Spiro said.

"What? Did you say something?" Mr. Millpod snarled at Spiro.

"I'm the one who said it, not him," Angelo said.

"Please share what you said?"

"No."

Mr. Millpod grabbed a thick wooden ruler and approached Angelo. "Your hand."

Angelo thought Mr. Millpod smelled like his father. He felt frightened and comforted as he stuck out his left hand, a tight fist, submissively, as he would've for his father.

WHACK! The ruler stung hard across Angelo's knuckles.

"What did you say to your little friend?"

"I said you was the punk," Angelo choked out. He did not say it to be funny or brash; he just said what he had been asked to repeat. He was, at this point, simply the messenger. He continued to hold his fist out.

Classroom giggles.

WHACK!

"Now what do you think?"

Angelo said nothing. He just kept his left arm out straight, fist tight, eyes locked on Mr. Millpod's eyes. Angelo was angry.

"Answer me," Mr. Millpod insisted.

There were no more giggles.

Angelo's dark eyes held Mr. Millpod in a cold hammer-lock. He did not respond.

WHACK!

Angelo stood up, his arm extended, fist tight, red and speckled with blood. Silent.

Mr. Millpod backed up a step. "Now what do you think?"

"Don't hit him again." Tate was standing next to Mr. Millpod.

"What?" a startled Mr. Millpod said. "How dare you? Take your seat?"

"No," Tate said. "And if you hit him again, I'm gonna hurt you."

Spiro stood up. Ren and Howie stood up.

Chapter Nineteen

"Hobos ride trains. Sammy's a bum."

F riday morning, Angelo found himself separated from his friends in the commotion of students hurrying up the front entrance steps to PS-65. The sight of Liz Brennan climbing the steps in front of him slowed Angelo down to a crawl. He watched Liz without really thinking about it. His thoughts were muddled as he assessed the last two weeks. He continued to lag behind as his friends entered the school. He flexed his foot on a step—his ankle felt stronger. He looked up. PS-65 wasn't as bad as Angelo thought it would be.

The sudden shock of a solid shove surprised Angelo and sent his books skidding and tumbling on the steps as he lost his balance and fell.

"What're you lookin' at, asshole?" Jimmy shouted at him.

"What?" Angelo said, getting up and retrieving his books and papers.

"Damn it, Jimmy. What's wrong with you?" Liz helped Angelo pick up his belongings. "Are you okay, Angelo?"

"No problem." Angelo didn't look at her.

"Hey, what's this?" Jimmy held a piece of paper that fell out of Angelo's notebook.

"It's a poem for Miss Coluthia's class." Angelo reached for it. "I need it back."

"Is this a love poem to Anna Coluthia?" Jimmy asked. "It don't even rhyme."

The group of Knights surrounding Angelo laughed. And Liz was witness to his dishonor. He couldn't think. Several Knights pushed him as he tried to retrieve his homework.

"That's it, Jimmy," Liz said. "Give him back his homework right now or we're through. I mean it."

"Break it up," Mr. Gleason, the gym teacher, said coming out of the school. "Angelo, you of all people, what are you doing with Knights? Everybody in the school now."

"Screw you," Jimmy growled, as he crumpled Angelo's homework and threw it at him.

For the first time, at the end of Miss Coluthia's class, Angelo tried to be the first student out. "Angelo, may I see you?" Miss Coluthia said.

"Sure. I'm sorry about my wrinkled home—"

"Your homework is fine. I have it," she said. "I also have a note from the principal, Mr. Holder. He would like to see you in his office."

"When?"

"Right now. Evidently your mother is going to be there as well."

Tate walked Angelo down to the principal's office but Angelo went in alone. He walked directly to the principal's secretary.

"I'm Angelo Pasta—"

Miss Pierce nodded and pointed to the corner behind him, where Angelo's mother sat.

Angelo sat in the chair next to his mother. "Hi, Mom."

"Do you know what this is about?" his mother asked.

"No," Angelo said. "Do you?"

"Ah, Mrs. Pastamadeo, thank you for coming," the principal said as he walked into the reception area from his inner office. "Angelo, please wait out here until I summon you. I want to talk with your mother first. Miss Pierce, you can go to lunch—I'm certain Angelo will be fine out here for a couple of minutes."

Angelo shrugged.

"Excellent," Mr. Holder said. "Now, then, Mrs. Pastamadeo, I'm certain you will agree it is important to deal with this quickly. Please come into my office."

* * *

The smell of the school and the sound of Mr. Holder's voice were unpleasantly familiar to Anna. He was the principal when she attended PS-65, but this was the first time she ever met with him in his office. Anna was suddenly aware of another man in Mr. Holder's office.

"What's this about, Mr. Holder?" Anna asked, still standing. "Miss Pierce assured me that Angelo wasn't hurt or anything like that. What is it?"

"Mrs. Pastamadeo, I would like you to meet our new history teacher, Mr. Millpod." Mr. Holder walked toward a round table. He pulled out one of the three empty chairs. "Please."

"Okay," Anna said as she sat across from Mr. Millpod. "Nice to meet you, Mr. Millpod. You're not from this neighborhood, are you?"

"No, but Principal Holder was kind enough to find an apartment for me in his building."

"Knickerbocker," Anna said.

"Yes, well, I wish we were meeting under better circumstances," Mr. Holder said.

"Circumstances?" Anna looked at Mr. Holder.

"Mrs. Pastamadeo, as you know, the city is in the grip of gang violence. The mayor's office and our police commissioner are very concerned about the problem—"

"What are you talking about, Mr. Holder?" Anna squeezed her handbag in her lap. "What does any of that have to do with my son?"

"Your son and his gang threatened me in my classroom." Mr. Millpod tapped the tip of his finger on the tabletop. "In my own classroom."

"What? Angelo doesn't have a gang."

Mr. Millpod told Anna what had happened in class the day before. How Angelo called him a punk. How he was using a ruler on Angelo's knuckles when Angelo's gang threatened him.

"I feared for my life, so I left my classroom. Just walked right out and went home," Mr. Millpod said. "I came in this morning and told Principal Holder what happened."

Anna stood up, walked to the door, and opened it. Miss Pierce was gone. She saw Angelo slumped in a chair in the large outer office, his fists pushed down in his pants' pockets. He looked so small, so alone—more like six than thirteen. "Angelo."

Mr. Holder said, "Mrs. Pastamadeo, is this wise? I mean we ought to—"

"Mr. Millpod said your gang threatened him," Anna said to Angelo, taking his left hand and examining it. It was yellow and red, and a bit swollen.

"I ain't in no gang." Angelo thought this was not the moment to discuss the Reapers.

"Did you see this?" Anna said, showing Angelo's hand to Mr. Holder, who shook his head. "Go back out there and wait, Angelo, and close the door."

Anna's face was flushed as she returned to her seat at the table. She clenched her jaw. Anger boiled up so quickly it made her mouth dry and bitter. Six years ago, she resolved that no man would ever strike her or her son again. Never. And yet, here he sat. Millpod. She thought about Angelo feeling like he needed to protect her.

"Whether it was a gang or a bunch of friends makes no difference," Mr. Millpod said.

"Mr. Millpod, you told me there was a gang in your class-room," Mr. Holder said with surprise. "In this neighborhood, there is a big difference between gangs and friends."

"When I asked Angelo about his hand, he told me he fell," Anna said to Mr. Holder.

"Well, there you go," Mr. Millpod jumped in. "Obviously, the boy's a liar."

"You piece of shit." Anna stood in front of her chair, palms pressed on the table. She leaned toward Mr. Millpod. "Angelo didn't want me to worry—didn't want me to think he was in danger in his classroom, from his teacher." She imagined delivering a punch to Mr. Millpod's left cheekbone, sending his glasses spinning across the office and dislodging him from his chair. Anna smelled something familiar above the chalk and cleaner as she leaned toward Mr. Millpod. She realized Millpod wore the same aftershave Mac did.

"Mrs. Pastamadeo, Mr. Millpod, please," Mr. Holder said. "For the sake of Angelo's future, we need to discuss this in a calm and rational tone. Mrs. Pasta—Anna, you were a student here. You must understand that sometimes a teacher must discipline a student."

"Fine. Let's talk about discipline and the future." Anna sat back in her seat. She swallowed. "I will talk to Angelo. He should not call a teacher a punk. If he acts up, please call me so that I can properly deal with my son. Angelo should pay attention in class. After all, he's here to learn—"

"That's all we ask," Mr. Holder said.

"I'm not finished. You've been the principal here, what— twenty, twenty-five years?"

"Thirty years this month."

"All that time, you've lived in this neighborhood— Knickerbocker. You know me and my family. My brothers, my father, even my godfather."

"Yes, of course," Mr. Holder said. "Your godfather, um, Mr. Nunzio Sabino, correct?"

"You want to talk about the future? Okay, for the future, disciplining Angelo is my job. My job. Period. If anyone working at this school—teacher, administrator, secretary, janitor, any-one—ever touches my son again, you, Mr. Holder, and that person will have a lot more to worry about than the children attending classes."

Anna stood up and locked a startled Mr. Millpod in her saber-gray eyes, pointed at him, and said, "You. You made a big mistake when you hit my Angelo."

Mr. Millpod's eyes scurried to a dark corner of the room.

After a moment, Anna returned her attention to Mr. Holder. "I'm taking my son to lunch now. Good day, gentlemen."

* * *

Frank walked along South Street and made a right on Fulton. The rush of activity and smell of fish filled the air. Fresh fish were dumped from holds, hosed down, and sold by the piece, pound, basket, and barrel. Frank dodged and bumped his way through the thick crowd. He looked for Willie Max, but instead saw Father Casimiro walking and turning in half-circles, looking up and around.

"Father, you're walking like a tourist."

"Oh, Frank. Good to see you."

"You buying fish?"

"I just checked on Sammy. He's a...a hobo—"

"South Street Sammy?"

"Yes, you know him?"

"Hobos ride trains. Sammy's a bum," Frank said impassively. "He okay?"

"I think so."

"I'm going to grab lunch at Sonny's on John Street."

"Can I come with?"

"No problem. C'mon."

Sonny's Bar and Grill on John Street was a poorly lit, unkempt, and briny establishment that relied on the longshore-man trade, as well as a loyal neighborhood clientele. Mike and his wife Tess owned the place. They had grown up with Frank's parents and had one child. Their son, Michael, Jr., "Sonny," enlisted with Frank. Sonny, a sailor, was killed six months after he shipped out. That's when they changed the name of the bar to Sonny's. The bar was decorated with U.S. Navy memorabilia. Anchors, ropes, model ships, enlistment posters, and the like surrounded the diners and drinkers. The jukebox was filled with songs from the 1940s.

Frank led Father Casimiro to an empty table away from the dark walnut bar.

"What're ya boys wantin'?" the waitress grumbled at their table. "Oh, pardon me, Father. It's hard to see in this place— which ain't always a bad thing."

"That's fine," Father Casimiro reassured her. "I'll have whatever my friend here has."

"A bowl of chowder and a beer—anything but Rheingold, Donna."

"Frankie! I swear I'm goin' blind. You look great."

"You, too, Donna."

"Like I said, the lack of lights in here ain't always a bad thing. Still mad at Rheingold for not crowning Myrna, are ya?"

"She should've won," Frank said.

"Mugs and chowder. Be right back, boys."

"Myrna Rheingold?" Father Casimiro said.

"Myrna Fahey. She was runner up for Miss Rheingold last year."

"Never heard of her."

"She played Margie in *I Died a Thousand Times* in '55. She's in *Jeanne Eagels* and *Loving You* this year," Frank said, looking around the bar for Willie Max. "She's really something. She should've won Miss Rheingold. So, what's wrong with Sammy?"

"A couple of Knights beat him up because he was wearing a Knight's shirt."

"Sammy lifted some Knight's shirt?"

"Didn't make much sense...I don't know. Father Joe and I took Sammy over to the Settlement. Cleaned him up. I'm sure he's fine."

"Here ya go, boys." Donna placed bowls of chowder and beers on the table.

"Willie Max been around?" Frank asked Donna.

"Willie's outta town 'til the end of the month. You want me to say you was askin'?"

"No," Frank said.

"No problem, Frankie. Enjoy the chowder, boys." Donna walked away.

"So, Sammy was wearing a Knight shirt?" Frank said.

"Just didn't feel right."

"I'd trust your gut, Father. You want me to talk to him?"

"Maybe. I have some work to finish at St. Joachim's and then I'm heading to the dance at the Settlement. I'll talk to Sammy in the morning. Stop by the dance tonight if you get a chance."

"No can do, I'm at Lilly's tonight. Enjoy the dance."

CHAPTER TWENTY

"Just say 'yes' if you can hear me."

Angelo and his friends arrived at the Cherry Street Settlement a little early to help set up for the Friday night dance. Angelo knew his mother and Rosemarie, Spiro's mother, would be there, but he was surprised to see his grandfather.

"Mom, what's Pompa—" And then Angelo spotted Uncle Nunzio, George Keller, and Spiro's grandfather—Nick Gostopolas.

"Angelo, you guys push the chairs against those two walls," Angelo's mother said. "A couple of tables will go back there for the food. One up front for the phonograph."

"How come Father Cas ain't here, Mom?"

"He had to finish some work at St. Joachim's; he'll be here later."

As Angelo and his friends moved chairs and tables, several members of the South Street Boys arrived, followed by a couple of Cobras and their dates. Because of Father Joe, the neighborhood gangs, with the exception of the Satan's Knights, considered the Cherry Street Settlement neutral territory. The adults in attendance acted as servers and chaperones.

"Hey, you guys," Nunzio said to the Cobras and South Street Boys. "Give us a hand movin' them tables against the wall and puttin' out the food. And spread the ashtrays around." Nunzio Sabino contributed the food, soda, ice cream, and a phonograph and records to the event.

"No problem, Mr. Sabino," one of the Cobras said.

And they all went to work. Angelo knew that they looked up to Nunzio Sabino. He would make a point during the evening to be seen talking to Uncle Nunzio.

* * *

Father Casimiro loved being alone in the church. But he was also anxious to get to his first social at the Cherry Street Settlement. As he prepared to leave, he kneeled in the center aisle facing the large crucifix in the front of the church. He crossed himself, brought his hands together, dropped his head, and closed his eyes. Suddenly, he sensed he wasn't alone. He opened his eyes, but by then a heavy sack was over his head and being pulled down his torso. He heard restrained giggles. The smell of damp canvas abruptly replaced incense.

"Hey!" He stood up but was immediately hit across the shins by a broomstick. The pain was so intense that for a moment, the interior of the oversized Army duffle bag lit up bright white. A second blow hit him behind his knees, dropping him to the floor. He heard cheers—children cheering. The end of a stick jabbed him hard in the stomach. For a moment, he thought he was going to pass out. He was completely inside the large duffle bag now and was being turned upside down, as the open end was tied shut.

Father Casimiro was shivering with fear. He couldn't get enough air. "Oh, God, please help me. Be here with me." He tried to collect his reason. His courage. His breathing became easier. He focused on listening to their voices. He could tell that there were at least four of them.

Father Casimiro brought his arms up, covering his face and head. He was hit again. He heard the cheers. They were just boys—kids. His pain mercifully surrendered to numbness. The hitting stopped. "Who are you? What do you want?"

"Shut up. I ask the questions, Priest," a boy's—maybe a man's—voice said. "Just say 'yes' if you can hear me."

"Yes." Father Casimiro tensed his body, expecting more blows. They didn't come.

"Just two questions. If you get them right, we're gone. Who has Ernesto's medallion?"

"I don't know. All Sammy said was that he found a gold coin and sold it for a dollar. He didn't say to who and he didn't say anything about a medallion."

"I believe him," the voice said. "Question two, where's Sammy?"

"I don't know." Father Casimiro wasn't prepared for the blow to his chest. He stiffened, covered his face, tried to anticipate the next blow.

"That, I don't believe," the voice said.

Father Casimiro took the second and third blows on his shoulder. Cheers and giggles.

Another voice, a younger boy, said, "Cut him, Raz."

"Shut the fuck up. You, pull your car up to the front of the church and open the trunk. The rest of you guys grab the bag. Priest, you make one sound and we're gonna start stickin' blades through this bag. Let's go."

"Our Father..." Father Casimiro began to pray in a whisper as he felt the duffle bag being lifted, carried, and then tossed into the trunk of a car. He heard the trunk lid close above him.

As the car drove off, Father Casimiro tugged at the mouth of the duffle bag. It was securely tied from the outside. At least they weren't hitting him. The car stopped. He stayed very still. He felt the bag again being lifted and then dropped on the ground. He groaned.

"Grab them bricks. The big rocks over there, too," a voice said. "C'mon, c'mon."

Father Casimiro heard shuffling and sensed movement all around him. "God loves all of you and He forgives you, as I do. Please stop now!"

"Come 'ere, open the top. The rest of you guys throw all that shit in when Ray opens it."

Father Casimiro was bounced onto his shoulder with his legs twisted above him. He saw the top of the duffle bag open, and quickly covered his face as an avalanche of bricks and rocks came in on top of him.

"Tie it and throw it in the river. C'mon, before some Popeyes spot us."

"The river?" Father Casimiro said.

The bag was quickly tied shut. He felt it being dragged. Bricks and rocks were tumbling over him. He was going to drown inside this duffle bag.

"No, wait! Please!" Father Casimiro shouted. Expecting to be hit for speaking, he covered himself. There were no strikes, just continued dragging. Tumbling. Giggling. Then it stopped.

"Last chance—where is Sammy?"

"I just don't know. Please, God is here, don't do this."

"Throw him in the river."

He sagged in the middle of the duffle bag as they lifted the two ends and swung it.

"One, two," the kids said.

"Wait, please," Father Casimiro said. "My God!"

Father Casimiro heard the kids shout, '...three,' and felt the release of the duffle bag. A moment of flight was followed by the terrifying sensation of falling.

"No!" Father Casimiro shouted. He heard fading giggles. And then splash and thud. He hit water—it was seeping into the duffle bag. But he just as quickly hit ground, punishing his shoulder and back again. At first, hitting ground so quickly didn't register.

Shallow water.

He scurried around the bricks and rocks in the darkness of the bag. He had to get out before they realized he hadn't sunk. He was oblivious to his pain and injuries as he crawled in the two feet of chilling water that soaked into the bag.

He found the neck opening and began to tug and pull at it, but it was tied shut. He used the edge of a brick to scrape the side of the canvas bag over and over until he made a small hole. He stuck a finger through it and pulled. Nothing. He went back to the brick and scraped and cut at the hole. It grew. It was working.

Finally, Father Casimiro was able to tear a large enough hole to squeeze through. He was out of the bag and crawling in a shallow inlet of the East River. He saw the black shape of a pier above him against the night sky. He stood up and sloshed toward the pier. A ladder was attached to a stanchion. He gripped it and began to climb. His pain resurfaced and shot around his knees and straight up his back and into his ears.

"My God, please." Father Casimiro moaned.

"Hey," a young man's voice came from above. "Harry, get a couple of the guys."

"Please, no more." Father Casimiro's pain broke his hold on the ladder and he splashed backward into the river and darkness.

* * *

Rock and roll music, laughter, and chatter filled the Settlement's gym. Angelo and his friends stood on what became primarily the boys' side of the room, talking above the clamor as others danced. Various perfumes carried by cigarette smoke swirled around Angelo's head. He spotted a couple of girls from his class on the other side of the room as he told his friends about his trip to the principal's office.

"Mr. Millpod told the principal that we were a gang," Angelo said.

"How does he know about the Reapers?" Tate asked.

"He don't know," Angelo said. "He was just guessing."

Tate said, "This Knight, you remember the one that was with Liz Brennan—"

"Jimmy," Ju-Ju said.

"Jimmy, right. He asked me if I wanted to join the Knights. So I said, 'I already got a gang, the Reapers. He asked who the leader was and I said it was you, Ju-Ju."

"You said no to joining the Knights?" Ju-Ju said. "What did Jimmy say?"

"He said, 'Fuck Ju-Ju.' So I said, 'Say that to his face.'" Tate looked at the other guys. They all nodded, except for Ju-Ju. "Just kidding, Ju-Ju, I didn't tell him to say it to your face."

"Don't fool around, Tate. Did he say anything else about me?" Ju-Ju asked.

"No, why?"

"Because Jimmy asked me to join the Knights today, and I said maybe. That's what I wanted to tell you guys. I think we can all join."

"What about the Reapers?" Tate said.

"But these are the Knights," Ju-Ju said.

"I'll never be a Knight...not ever," Angelo said. "I hate those guys."

"What about you, Chico?" Ju-Ju said.

"I was the one who said you should be our leader," Chico said. "What kind of leader leaves his gang for another one?"

"But we can all be Knights together," Ju-Ju said.

"I ain't going," Chico said. "Angelo should be our leader, not you."

"Guys, let's just think about this," Ju-Ju said. "Angelo, you understand—"

"No," Angelo said. The only thing I'm thinkin' about is asking Audrey to dance." Angelo looked across the dance floor at Audrey Vadunka.

"Take a shot. G'head, ask her," Tate said.

"Okay, I'm going to do it." Angelo crossed the dance floor toward Audrey. She was talking to several girls on the other side of the room. He stopped in front of her. The girls stopped talking and looked at him.

"You wouldn't want to dance with me, would you?" Angelo's lips kept sticking to his teeth as he pressed out the words.

"Hi, sure," Audrey said as the needle dropped on *Earth Angel*.

"I'm Angelo. We were in the same class at P.S. 1 and now I'm in your class at PS-65." Angelo rubbed his hands on his pants as he followed her onto the dance floor.

"I know who you are, Angelo. I'm Audrey."

"Audrey Vadunka," Angelo said, holding her as they moved in small, lingering circles."

"That's right." She rested her head on Angelo's shoulder.

She smelled like lilacs and baby powder. *The angel*, Angelo thought.

"Did you say something?" Audrey asked.

"You smell like an angel," Angelo said without thinking.

Audrey pulled back a bit and looked at him. "You're sweet." She returned her head to his shoulder and moved closer.

Angelo could feel every part of her touching every part of him. They moved together. His hand on her back. Her leg moving against his. He wanted the song to go on forever. He wanted to die for her.

"Where do you live?" Angelo asked.

"Fifty-four Catherine. First floor, front."

"First floor, front?"

"I saw you the other night, Angelo," Audrey said into his neck, sending a tender electric charge along his spine.

"Yeah?"

"When you fell into the bushes, I climbed out of my window and put Band-Aids above your eye, and my kerchief on—"

"You are the angel," Angelo said as the music stopped. "I hate that the song's over."

"You're so funny—you just say stuff."

"So why'd you help me?" *A Sunday Kind of Love* filled the room and they continued to move in small circles.

"I like you. Listen, Angelo, I wish I could stay longer, but I told my father I'd be home early. He's not—anyway, my friends are waiting. Gina lives in my building."

Angelo looked at the two girls, Gina Rizzo and Sass Monahan, looking at him and Audrey. "Okay. Hey, thanks for dancing with me and for saving my life."

"I don't think I saved your life, Angelo." Audrey smiled.

"Are you going to come next Friday?" Angelo asked as she walked away. She stopped and walked back to him.

Audrey took his hands in hers just for a moment. "Yes." And then she walked away.

"Me, too," Angelo muttered. As he walked toward his friends, someone grabbed his arm.

"Angelo, come dance with me," Liz Brennan said.

Angelo looked toward the door, surprised that his first thought was that he didn't want Audrey to see them. She was gone. He couldn't believe that he was now dancing with Liz. He looked over at his friends, who were gawking, mouth-opened, stunned.

"Hi, Liz," Angelo said.

"Angelo. I didn't want to bother you when you were dancing with your friend. She's really cute. I just wanted to apologize for Jimmy messing up your homework," she said as they danced. "He's such a jerk sometimes."

"No problem. Thanks for helping me." Angelo saw two South Street Boys bolt into the dance. They didn't look happy. They stopped, looked around. Everyone stopped dancing. Angelo was sure there was going to be a fight. He held Liz's hand and walked her toward his friends. "Popeyes. They're looking for somebody."

"Who?" Liz looked around the room.

"Hey, Angelo, you're the new leader of the Reapers," Howie said.

"I am?"

"Yeah, we all voted, even Ju-Ju—he wants to be a Knight," Tate said.

The two Popeyes walked directly to Father Joe, who was standing with Pompa and Uncle Nunzio. They talked, nodded, and then Father Joe quickly followed the South Street Boys out of the Settlement.

* * *

A sedan, motor running with three South Street Boys in the front seat, waited on Cherry Street. Father Joe sat in the back between the boys, who had escorted him out of the Settlement.

"Tell me what you know," Father Joe said as the car took off.

"We're playin' cards in the shack on mud pier," the boy on his left said. "You know it?"

"Yeah, shallow water, mud, trash, rats," Father Joe said.

"That's it. Anyway, I went out to take a leak off the pier, and there's this guy comin' up the ladder. It's dark. So I called for a flashlight and a couple of Popeyes. Then he yelled, 'No more, please,' and fell off the ladder—landed flat on his back in the water. We go down and that's when we saw who it was. We found a duffle bag, blood inside, rocks, you know. It's in the trunk. Knights...they like baggin'. Five Popeyes took Father Cas to Beekman, then we came for you."

"How's he doin'?" Father Joe asked.

"He's pretty shook up. I don't know. I think they just wanted to scare him. But we're gonna stay with him for a while just in case. It ain't right what they did."

* * *

Frank finished with a customer, walked outside Lilly's, leaned against his car, and lit a cigarette. The street was quiet with a lovers' summer-night breeze. Frank felt less lonely outside in the night than inside Lilly's. People thought he was one of those guys who liked being alone. He liked that and wished it were true. Frank saw a familiar face coming up Catherine toward him.

"The boss fire you, Frankie?" Hartz walked up to Frank. "Nice ride. Yours?"

"Good to see you, Hartz. Yeah, she's my Bonnie. I got a backroom with a television, best coop in the neighborhood."

"Sounds good, but right now I'm looking for some help."

"On the Bookman fire?"

"Frankie, cop to cop, I don't give a shit about the fire. The only witness talking skipped."

"Skipped?"

"Apartment's empty except for the keys left on the sink. A neighbor said Harold and Emma packed their '52 Olds with everything it could carry at 5:00 a.m. and drove away."

"That's it?"

"Bookman's cold." Hartz nodded. "How's your nephew doin'?"

"He's okay." Frank smiled. Hartz was letting him know that he knew Angelo set fire to Bookman's, and it wasn't going any further. "Thanks. So what do you need?"

"I'm using the fire to stick around the neighborhood. But I'm coming up empty. The night of Bookman's fire, a cop was supposed to touch base. He never showed."

"Undercover?"

"With Satan's Knights. Just a kid, fresh out of the Academy."

"Maybe he has to lay low."

"Maybe. I like the kid...he's a good cop."

Frank dropped his cigarette and stepped on it. "Got a picture of the cop?"

"I was hoping you'd ask." Hartz handed a picture to Frank. "Here, keep it. Like I said, I can use the help, just keep it close."

"I need to show it to somebody."

"What are you thinking?"

"Well, there were two possibilities. But looking at the picture, I can nix the first one."

"What's the second?"

"A local, South Street Sammy, saw a dispute between some Knights. Probably nothing, but anyone sees you talking to Sammy, they'll know it's not about the fire. Plus, Sammy gets spooked easy. I'll show him the picture without saying it's a cop."

"What was the first possibility?"

"Yeah, I need to tell you about that, anyway. It just came to me when we were talking. The other day, I was talking to my sister and her friend right here and Rico Cruz comes by, one of the leaders of the Knights."

"I know who he is."

"He stops to say hello with this guy. Clean cut, said they graduated from college together. Said his name was Jack. I knew he wasn't from the neighborhood, so I asked him where he lived. He said, 'I live up in the One-Oh,' then he quickly said, 'I mean One-Oh-One West Eighteenth Street.' He said he was an accountant."

"And you don't buy it?"

"I couldn't put my finger on it. But this talk of undercover business triggered something." Frank lit another cigarette and gave one to Hartz. "Who would say he lived in the One-Oh?"

"I don't getcha," Hartz said. "Anyone living in the Tenth Precinct would—"

"Most people would say, 'I live on the Westside.' Or, 'I live at One-Oh-One West Eighteenth Street' right off the bat. A few might say, 'I live in the Tenth Precinct.'" Frank took a long drag on his cigarette. "But who would say, 'I live in the One-Oh'? Not Tenth, One-Oh."

"A cop. They own a cop."

"Bingo! And he ain't the guy in this picture. Get pictures of cops in their twenties living in the One-Oh. Maybe Jack? Maybe college? And I'll pick out Rico's buddy."

"Will do. How'd the snitch turn out?"

"A solid maybe," Frank said.

"Tommy said it had something to do with your brother-in-law."

"He disappeared back in '51, on Christmas Eve."

"My undercover said something about a Christmas hit involving someone named Willie. I looked at the last couple of Christmas killings, but I didn't go back to '51."

"Willie's the right name."

"I'll go through my notes again."

CHAPTER TWENTY-ONE

*"When I hear the beast, I'm always frightened,
but I run toward his growl."*

Jimmy and several other Knights were standing at the top of the steps to PS-65 as another school day was about to begin.

"Ju-Ju, whaddaya doin' with Reapers? You belong to us now," Jimmy said.

Angelo looked over at Ju-Ju, who shrugged an awkward smile at his friends. "G'head, it's okay," Angelo said.

Ju-Ju nodded toward Angelo and headed up toward the Knights.

"What the fuck's the matter with you? You don't need the Poet's permission to hang with us. You ain't no Reaper no more; you're a fuckin' Knight," Jimmy shouted at Ju-Ju and gave him a shove. "Go make me some money."

"I'm glad I didn't join them," Tate said as they continued up the steps.

"I'm glad you didn't, too," Angelo said. "Father Cas got out of the hospital yesterday."

"I hope he's okay," Tate said.

"Tate, I like us being the Reapers. Maybe we should write it on our jackets."

"Write it on our jackets? What about your mom?"

"I told her we made it up to stay out of the Knights. She was okay with that. She hates the Knights as much as I do."

Inside the school, Tate elbowed Angelo and pointed at Ju-Ju talking to another kid. The kid shook his head and started to walk away but Ju-Ju grabbed his shirt. Thinking that Ju-Ju might need help, Angelo and Tate walked over.

"Hey, Ju-Ju, what's going on?" Angelo said. And then to the other kid, he said, "I know you—you're in my class. Gerard, right?"

"Yeah, right," Gerard said. "I like how you stood up to Mr. Millpod, but I ain't giving up my lunch money."

"Damn right you're not," Angelo said.

"They're watchin' me," Ju-Ju said. "It's part of being a Knight."

"Forget about it. He's in my class. G'head, Gerard, I'll see you later."

"Angelo, I have to come up with two dollars a week for Jimmy," Ju-Ju said as Gerard walked away. "I keep anything over that. I got to pay for my jacket, shirts, all that stuff."

Suddenly Jimmy was there, shoving Ju-Ju away from Angelo and Tate. "Get goin'."

"Audrey's going to be at the dance on Friday," Angelo said to Tate, while watching Ju-Ju disappear with Jimmy and several other Knights. He felt like he should stick up for Ju-Ju. But Ju-Ju picked the Knights.

"Maybe Audrey can fix me up with Gina, and we can all go out sometime," Tate said.

"Good idea. I'll ask her."

* * *

At 10:30 in the morning, Father Casimiro walked along Catherine Street with Father Joe. He felt as though his chest and back were being squeezed.

"How are you doing, Robert?" Father Joe said. "You still up for this?"

"It's good to be outside in the air. But I feel like a ninety-year-old man. So first we talk to Frank and then lunch with Mr. Sabino, right?"

"Nunzio, right. If you're up to it."

"They said I should get some exercise. Walking will help."

Father Joe opened the door to Lilly's.

"Good morning," Frank said. "I've got some fresh coffee and crullers."

"Sounds great." Father Joe plopped into a chair.

"What's the damage?" Frank said to Father Casimiro as he brought over a pot of coffee and three cups.

"Pretty lucky. No broken bones," Father Casimiro said.

"Were you able to identify—"

"Nothing." Father Casimiro saw Frank and Father Joe exchange glances. He knew they could tell he was scared. All he wanted now was to be home—back in Milwaukee.

"Do you remember voices? What they said? Names? Sounds?" Frank casually asked as he brought the crullers over and sat with them.

"Just something about Sammy and the medallion. Looking for him."

"Did you talk to the cops?" Frank asked.

"No. I was planning on going home to Milwaukee for my father's birthday." Father Casimiro stared at his coffee. "So I can't spend time with the police right now."

Father Joe said, "Maybe we should talk about this another time, Frankie."

"Sure, no problem." Frank took out a pack of Lucky Strikes, pulled one out, tapped it on the table, and put it between his lips. He tossed the pack on the table. "Did you bump into any Knights while you were in the hospital?"

"I didn't tell him about that yet," Father Joe said.

"About what?" Father Casimiro asked.

"Friday night, after you were admitted to the hospital, about two dozen of Nunzio's guys walked through the projects with iron pipes and baseball bats, cracking knees and elbows of anyone wearing a Knights shirt. Eleven Knights wound up with broken bones that night. On Saturday, they went through again and clipped another seven Knights. On Sunday, you couldn't find a Knight with a search party. Then, somebody from the Knights must have talked to Nunzio, because he let up on them. That's it," Frank said.

"He hurt those boys because of me?"

"Absolutely not. Long ago, Nunzio told the Knights not to harm St. Joachim or the Cherry Street Settlement. They violated that when they grabbed you inside St. Joachim," Father Joe said.

"I don't want to hurt your feelings, but what Nunzio did had nothing to do with you."

"That's a true fact," Frank said. "If they grabbed you after you left St. Joachim's—no problem. Like Father Joe said, it wasn't about you."

Father Casimiro was still trying to process all of this when Father Joe asked, "So, Frankie, what did you need?"

"I'd like to talk to Sammy, but I haven't seen him around lately. Then I remembered Father Casimiro told me he was checking on him when we met on Fulton Street."

"He's in a loft over on Front Street. Robert checked on him Friday. Popeyes have been keeping an eye on him," Father Joe said. "We'll take you to him. Would tomorrow be okay?"

"Whenever you can do it. Just let me know and I'll get Jokes to watch the place."

"Will do, Frankie. We better get going."

Frank gave an understanding nod.

"You're going back to Milwaukee?" Father Joe said as they walked away from Lilly's. "Do you need any money?"

"No. I'll get a bus ticket. I will still get there in time for my father's birthday." A hint of autumn carried on a September breeze ruffled Father Casimiro's hair. The air smelled crisp and tasted like apples. He missed Wisconsin.

"I'll say—your father's birthday is September 20, right? You have nine days to get there."

Father Casimiro's stomach dropped. "Look, Joe, I'm sorry. I'm still a little...I just need a little time to think things through. Put it all in perspective." Father Casimiro knew Father Joe could tell he was rattled. Scared. His desire to work in this neighborhood and learn from Father Joe had dissolved in a duffle bag.

"Perspective?" Father Joe smiled and shook his head. "We have a little time before we meet Nunzio. Can you climb a couple of flights?"

"Sure."

Father Joe led Father Casimiro inside a tenement next to St. Joseph's church and up the stairway. Halfway up the four flights, Father Casimiro stopped and put his hand on his side. He took a deep breath. He was still in pain and the effort of the climb was taking a toll.

"Let's rest a moment, Robert."

"No, no. Just a little slower."

Finally, they were alone on the roof.

"Over there," Father Joe said.

Father Casimiro stopped as Father Joe walked right to the rim of the roof's airshaft and sat down with his legs dangling off the edge. Father Casimiro wasn't a fan of heights. They gave him a weird, sick feeling. He eased up closer and sat cross-legged behind Father Joe.

"Sit right here next to me." Father Joe patted the roof to his right.

"I'm a bit uneasy."

"I know. Me, too. I hate heights." Father Joe patted the roof again. "Right here. Let your feet drop into the airshaft."

Father Casimiro inched his way to the lip of the roof without standing. He swallowed hard and dangled his legs over the edge. He looked down. A disharmony of muffled voices and clatter rose from the clothesline-crossed shadows. Father Casimiro pressed his palms down against the warm tar and leaned back. This helped his lightheadedness a little. "Airshaft?"

"Yeah, we have to talk softly. Our voices carry down there."

"Please understand, Joe. About my putting it in perspective—I just have to get over what happened. Put it behind me."

"Of course, I understand. A terrible thing, both painful and frightening, happened to you—you saw the face of the beast."

"What?" The last thing Father Casimiro wanted was a lecture.

"I know, I know, you were bagged in your own church, beaten, and thrown in the river's muddy water. Terrible thing. That's what they did to you, but that's not what happened to you."

"I just need—"

"Two and a half weeks ago, your first day here, we had pizza at Mo-Mo's, and you thanked me for giving you this opportunity to work with me. You remember?"

"Of course."

"Do you remember what I said to you, Robert?"

"Um...sorry, no, I don't." Father Casimiro blushed even more deeply.

"Listen to me. You took this opportunity and you did good. And now it is time for you to leave and discover new opportunities."

"You're that certain I won't come back." Father Casimiro was both relieved to end this experience and annoyed that Father Joe knew he was running away.

"How do you feel sitting here on the edge?"

"Terrible. Woozy. Frankly, I'd be very happy to sit anywhere else."

"This is the neighborhood, sitting here on the edge with that woozy feeling in your stomach. You don't get used to it. You don't get over it. And you don't put it behind you. What you need to do is understand yourself in it." Father Joe stood up. "And that, my dear friend, you have not been able to do. Come, let's get off this roof."

Father Casimiro just sat there. Five minutes ago, he would have given almost anything to get off this roof. But now something held him there. "What did you say?"

"Let's get off the roof."

"No. At Mo-Mo's, when I thanked you for the opportunity to work with you?"

"I said, 'I need you here. We are needed here.' And I believe I said, 'There's much to do.' That's what I said. Come on, Robert, there's nothing to prove by sitting there."

"Joe, I'm trying to understand, but I fear I keep missing the point. All I need is—"

"This is not a classroom. I don't have time to give you what you need." Father Joe sat back down and dangled his legs over the edge again. "I brought you up here because you said you needed a little time to think things through, and to put it all in perspective. This edge is the perspective. You said you need to put this behind you. You thanked me for your opportunity. Now you tell me you keep missing my point and what you need is...What? What do you need, Robert?" Father Joe lit a cigarette.

Father Casimiro was overwhelmed by the scolding barrage. "I don't want to pick sides. I want to help and comfort everyone. I want to save the Knights, not fear or despise them...and that's what's happening to me."

"What happened to you on Friday was terrible on many levels. But children in this neighborhood have been bagged, beaten, raped, and murdered. Children. Satan is here, in this neighborhood, in those projects, and he is scaring, hurting, and recruiting our children. They need me to stand between them and the beast. When I hear the beast, I'm always frightened, but I run toward his growl. Because that's where I'm needed."

Father Casimiro nodded. "That's what you meant by the difference between what they did to me and what happened to me. I became a coward because of what they did."

"A coward? Ha! I meant no such thing. I told you what happened to you. You saw the face of the beast, and it scared you. As it would anyone. You think Satan will appear the way you imagine him—all horns and on fire? Forget about it. He will plunge you into darkness and drag you out of your church. His fingernails will crack against your bones like sticks swung by kids. His growl will sound like children giggling. And he will be merciless. That, Robert, is what happened to you. You stepped between the beast and Sammy. You're in his way as he tries to recruit our children. It should scare you. But a coward? Did you tell them where Sammy was?"

"No."

"Then you're one of the bravest guys I know. Everybody's scared, but a coward would have given Sammy up. You faced the beast...you don't have to face him again. He won't follow you to Milwaukee. He likes this neighborhood." Father Joe stood up. "Let's get off this roof."

Father Joe led Father Casimiro out of the tenement and toward a black Cadillac Brougham parked near the corner. Nunzio and another man stood next to the car talking.

Father Casimiro said, "Isn't that—"

"Nunzio and his driver. We're going to the Drake for lunch. Nunzio lives there."

The driver held the back suicide door open for Father Casimiro. Father Joe walked around the car and let himself in the back. Nunzio sat in the front.

"Hey, how ya doin' there, Father? You got bopped a little, huh?" Nunzio lit a cigarette as the car headed uptown along the Bowery.

Father Casimiro looked out of the window at the small hills of trash pushed along the curb. Flophouses. Bums everywhere.

"Could've been worse." Father Casimiro was surprised by his own answer. An hour ago, he thought it was the worst thing that could ever happen to him. But although Nunzio sounded sympathetic, he also made it seem like no big deal. Father Casimiro had never been beaten up before. No fights. Not even in school. Earlier, it seemed an outrage.

Now, it was a thing, like Angelo getting hit by that car. Just a thing. He was still wrestling with what Father Joe said to him. All along, he thought about being here as something that was happening to him, something he dreamed of getting. He never understood, until this moment, that he was something that was happening to the people in this neighborhood.

"It's been a bad week for priests," Nunzio said. "The paper here says an archbishop somebody was arrested in Hungary."

"Groesz," Father Joe said. "Archbishop Jozsel Groesz...I heard."

"Okay, here's somethin' else," Nunzio said. "You ever hear of havin' ten votes to one and the one wins?"

"What?" Father Joe said.

"Here, in the *New York Times*, page 32. Listen to this crap: The chairman of the United Nations Security Council announced a count of votes Tuesday afternoon. Ten of the council's members had been in favor of admitting South Vietnam to the United Nations. One member was in opposition. Now I have no idea what or where South Vietnam is...but one outta eleven guys said no, and it's no? Here, take a look." Nunzio passed the newspaper to the back seat.

"Joe told me you live in a hotel." Father Casimiro said, staring out of the car window. After Cooper Square, the Bowery was behind them and they were heading up Fourth Avenue. Tenements and some trash still lined the streets, but most of the bums and flophouses were gone.

"I have a suite at the Drake. It suits me. So why'd they do it?"

"They were tryin' to find out where South Street Sammy was," Father Joe said to Nunzio. "He knew but never told them."

"Yeah? You took a beatin' for a bum?" Nunzio nodded. "You ever give up the collar, you can come work for me."

"The collar suits me." Father Casimiro felt stronger around these men. After 14th Street, Fourth Avenue became Park Avenue South. And less trash lined the gutters.

"Kid, my friend Joe back there taught me a long time ago—it ain't about what happens to you—it's how you handle what happens to you that counts. Looks like he got the right partner."

Father Casimiro liked the sound of that...even beyond his fear. "Thanks."

"Let's get business outta the way," Nunzio said. "First, you should know that your buddy Monsignor Culley had somethin' to do with closing your church."

"Culley." Father Joe nodded.

"You got a rabbi in the church, Joe?" Nunzio asked.

"In Rome. I've been meaning to write to him."

"A rabbi?" Father Casimiro shook his head.

"An influential friend." Father Joe smiled. "Must've been a tough meeting."

"Not after Culley was cut from the herd," Nunzio said. "I met with the deputy mayor on Monday—Raymond Clarke—he needed help with the bridge and tunnel union. I fixed it and told him to have the mayor meet with them. This way, the mayor gets credit for stoppin' the strike."

"It was in the news," Father Casimiro said. "The mayor met with a delegation yesterday and averted a strike. It was right there in today's *Times*."

"Yeah, I know. Anyway, the best I could do was buy a year for St. Joachim, and you both keep the Cherry Street Settlement." Nunzio turned in his seat and smiled at Father Joe.

"We got a year? I never—that's terrific. *Grazie, mio grande amico.*"

"I got a bottle waitin' for us at the Drake. We'll drink to one more year," Nunzio said, and then looking at Father Casimiro, "How 'bout you, tough guy? Or would you rather drink to your Braves beatin' the Pirates last night in Milwaukee? What a game...Aaron and Mathews, consecutive homers in the fourth."

"Are you afraid of anything?" Father Casimiro asked Nunzio as the car crossed 50th Street. Trees, bushes, and planters filled with flowers separated the northbound traffic from the southbound along Park Avenue. Well-dressed women walked small dogs down pristine sidewalks. Men in suits. Smiles. Awnings and doormen.

"Me? No."

"Nothing scares you?"

"You didn't ask me that. You asked if I was afraid ... what I fear day to day. But, have I ever been scared? Yeah, I've been scared. But it never stopped me from doin' what I gotta do."

"Not even afraid of dying?"

"No. We're all gonna die, pal. Some men hide in the corner tryin' to avoid it as long as possible. Joke's on them 'cause they never lived in the first place. Me, I'll go out swingin' with one hand and throwing a kiss with the other. They'll know I was here." Nunzio took a long drag on his cigarette and looked directly at Father Casimiro. "Friday got you thinkin' about fear and dyin'? Whaddaya worried about? The devil ain't got a shot. You got the light on your side."

"The light." Father Casimiro leaned his head back on the seat as the car made a U-turn on 57th Street—the Drake was on the southbound side of Park Avenue at 56th Street. "I'm staying."

As the car pulled up in front of the Drake, Father Joe placed a hand on Father Casimiro's shoulder. "Give this more thought."

"No. I understand now. I want to face him again."

* * *

At 2:00 p.m., Rico was finally alone with his two brothers. The three of them sat at one end of the conference table in the Knights' apartment.

Rico said. "I just learned that Marty was a cop."

"What?" Ernesto stood up.

"Ernesto, sit down," Hector said. "You sure about this?"

"Positive. My friend Jack the Cop just told me. He'll let us know what's happening."

"What should I do?" Ernesto asked.

"Nothin'. We wait for more information," Hector said. "Meantime, do nothin'."

"Good advice," Rico said. "So please tell me why our guys bagged a priest and threw him in the river." Rico pressed his palms against his eyes as he sat back. "What's going on?"

"First off, we didn't know about Marty being a cop," Hector said. "Second, there are times when you make nice and times when you show muscle. This was a time for muscle."

"Yeah, well, I was the one that had to go make nice and apologize to Nunzio."

"Who told you to apologize?" Hector asked.

"If I didn't, half our guys would now be in the hospital and the other half would be hiding under their beds. Anyway, who said this was a time for muscle?"

"Me. That's who. And just in case you forgot, I'm in charge of this gang."

"Fine, Hector. You're right—you're in charge. Fine." Rico stood up and walked toward the door. "I should've checked with you before I talked to Nunzio. Lesson learned." Rico's plan now was simple. Let the plates fall and move to Brewster with his girlfriend—she'd be thrilled.

"Where you goin'?" Hector asked Rico.

"I wanted to meet with you and Ernesto to find out why— why we bagged a priest, why we don't care about pissing Nunzio off, why we're doing what we're doing. But you don't owe me an explanation. You're the leader and whatever you do, you do."

"C'mon back, sit down," Hector said. "I just got a lot of shit right now."

"Hector, do whatever you want—I don't need to know." Rico remained at the door.

"Sammy knows what Ernesto did to Marty. He's a witness. And that new priest is protecting him. He knows somethin'. We just scared him—he's gonna run home. You'll see."

"Maybe, but what Casimiro knows, Father Joe knows, and Father Joe's not a runner," Rico said. "And then there's Nunzio Sabino."

"I've been workin' on somethin' that'll make Nunzio Sabino go away."

"Go away?" Rico stopped himself. "What am I doing? Hector, whatever you say goes."

"I hate when you pout."

"Pout?"

"Come on, sit down," Hector said. "We got a lot to talk about."

CHAPTER TWENTY-TWO
"Beware the kitten in the shadows, for a lion follows."

"**W**ait, before you leave...," Mr. Millpod pleaded in a failed effort to halt the stampede of students responding to the final bell of the school day.

On their way home, Angelo, Tate, and Spiro walked along East Broadway toward Catherine Street. Under the Manhattan Bridge, Spiro said, "Hey, there's Ju-Ju up ahead."

Angelo looked through the crowd walking in front of them. "Looks like he's with—"

"Ju-Ju!" Spiro called before Angelo could say "Knights."

Jimmy turned and started walking toward Angelo, Tate, and Spiro. He was pulling Ju-Ju by his arm. Eight other Knights followed them. A circle of kids immediately formed around the three Reapers and ten Knights.

"Hey, Poet, you owe Ju-Ju here an apology," Jimmy said. "For interrupting him when he was just tellin' me what an asshole you were."

"What?" Angelo was confused.

"Ju-Ju thinks you're an asshole, and so do—"

"No, I don't," Ju-Ju protested and was shoved out of the way by another Knight.

"Then apologize to me. Say, 'I'm sorry, Mr. Bowman.'" Jimmy shoved Angelo.

Nervous laughter sprinkled through the crowd.

"Jimmy, can you never just relax?" Liz Brennan said.

Angelo looked at Liz for a split second. Jimmy slammed the spine of a textbook into Angelo's face. Blood rolled from Angelo's nose and tears trickled from his eyes. Angelo threw himself at Jimmy, but was grabbed by one of three cops who pushed their way through the crowd.

"All right, show's over," a cop said as he moved the crowd along.

"Hey, the Poet's crying," Jimmy said. "They ain't Reapers—they're Weepers."

"Weepers," another Knight said, laughing.

"Who hit you, kid?" a cop asked, handing Angelo a handkerchief to hold on his nose.

Everyone became quiet.

Angelo avoided everyone's eyes—especially Liz's—and said, "I fell."

"Look, kid, we're here to help you," another cop said. And then, grabbing Jimmy by the shirt, he said, "This the punk that hit you?"

"I fell."

"Fine," the cop said. "Get out of here, all of you."

"Weepers. Weepers," was repeated as the Knights walked away.

* * *

Angelo, Tate, and Spiro stopped in Mo-Mo's on the way home. Morgan immediately brought the boys into the kitchen, where he cleaned Angelo's face.

"It ain't broken," Morgan said. "Sit here with this ice on your nose for twenty minutes."

"Okay if we split?" Tate asked. "I gotta shape up at the *Journal*...try to make a buck."

"No problem," Angelo said. "Uncle Nunzio's dropping off Yankee tickets at Lilly's about five, I'll grab a few. See you later." He watched Tate and Spiro leave.

Morgan went about making pizza and Angelo slumped in a chair with his head back.

"You can take it off now," Morgan said. "Sit in a booth. I'll bring ya a slice and a Coke."

Angelo sat in a booth facing the door.

The bell on the door tinkled as Ju-Ju walked in and sat across from Angelo.

"Hey, Angelo, I'm really sorry about—"

"It wasn't your fault. Jimmy's got it in for me. What did I ever do to him?"

Ju-Ju shrugged. "I'm quitting the Knights. It ain't like I thought. Not like us."

"Good."

"I got an idea. We need Reaper jackets, right?" There's some motorcycle jackets, like in *The Wild One*, with nothin' on them in the Knights' apartment. And, they don't know I have a key. I stole it from one of the older guys sleeping a bad night off."

"What if somebody's there?" Angelo's "edge" adrenaline kicked in.

"When somebody's there, they leave the door unlocked for the younger Knights. So, if it's unlocked, I go in and leave right away. You hide in the stairwell. But if it's locked, then nobody's there. We go in, grab a dozen jackets and anything else we want, and beat it. So?"

"What about Knights hanging around outside?"

"If they're in the front, we go out the back. If they're all over, we'll stash them in my apartment upstairs until it's safe."

Angelo liked the idea of ripping off the Knights. In some sense, at least in his own eyes, it would redeem him...just like keeping Ernesto's medallion. "Let's do it."

* * *

The back entrance to 10 Catherine Slip was free of Knights as Angelo and Ju-Ju strolled into the building. Ju-Ju checked the apartment door while Angelo hid in the stairwell.

"C'mon, it's locked and the hall is clear. Ready?"

"Ready."

Ju-Ju unlocked the apartment door and closed it behind him and Angelo. Ju-Ju walked around a small bend in the wall.

"The shit is in the bedroom closet," Ju-Ju whispered as Ernesto was returning to the living room with a bottle of whiskey.

"Who the fuck are you?" Ernesto grabbed Ju-Ju.

Angelo wasn't past the bend. He was going to try to run out of the apartment, but heard Ernesto approaching rapidly. The door to a small coat closet adjacent to the front door was slightly ajar. Angelo slipped into the closet, just as Ernesto seized Ju-Ju. Angelo did not try to close the closet door for fear that it would be seen. He just stood very still.

"I'm Ju-Ju, a new Knight. Jimmy asked me to join. I'm new."

"I know you. You live in the building, right?" Ernesto said.

"Right. I thought we could come in. I mean us new guys could use the apartment."

"Right now, it's just for me and my brothers. So get the fuck out."

Angelo heard the door open and close. Just him and his brothers. He listened as Ernesto walked into the other room.

"How'd he get in?" someone asked.

"Jimmy probably forgot to lock it." Ernesto said. "It's locked now."

Angelo heard someone say, "Rico, stick around 'til Christmas. Three months. Then if you still want to leave the Knights, no problem. Okay? Meanwhile, tell me what you think."

"You want to know what I think? Okay. Ernesto, pour me a drink while you're there."

Angelo heard the sound of liquid being poured into glasses.

"Okay, Hector, we need to stop thinking of the Knights as a gang and more of an organization that Nunzio Sabino could depend on."

"I already told you, we ain't gonna have to worry about Sabino anymore."

"Hector, this is a mistake and I—"

"Rico, we're gonna have our friends running Sabino's organization. How is that—"

"Too many things could go wrong. Call it off before it's too late and let me get us back on track with Nunzio Sabino."

Angelo moved his ear closer to the opening in the closet door, causing it to squeak at the same time there was a thud on the front door.

"Now who the fuck is in here? Didn't you lock the door?"

"Yeah, I locked it. I'll take a look around."

Angelo saw Ernesto open the closet door.

Angelo backed up inside the closet as Ernesto started to lean in. Another thud on the front door drew Ernesto's attention away.

From the dark of the closet, Angelo saw Ernesto open the front door. "Hey, take your ball and get the fuck out of this hallway."

"Ernesto, what's going on?" Rico said.

"Just some kids playing ball in the hall. They're gone."

"Good. Lock up and come back here."

"And put the chain on."

Angelo saw Ernesto examine and lock the apartment door. He closed the door and fastened the chain. And then he closed the closet door.

Angelo pressed his ear against the now-closed door to listen better.

"As I was saying ... it off ... now," Rico said.

"It's already...late for that. I mean, after Nunzio is outta the way...workin' with new...and there will be a lot more for us."

"What do you mean, too late?" Rico said.

"Tunnel brothers gonna kill him...Biff told me no more contact 'til...under the bridge...Ray and some of our...rid of the body," Hector said.

Body? Nunzio is stopping by Lilly's with Yankee tickets...he's probably there right now. Angelo scrambled out of the closet, unhooked the chain, swung the front door open, and ran out of the apartment. He could hear Hector saying, "What the fuck?... the door..."

Angelo thundered from the building and ran alongside the little park toward Uncle Frank's store.

"Hey, Angelo!" It sounded like Ju-Ju, but he wasn't going to stop now. He spotted Uncle Nunzio's black Cadillac in front of Lilly's. Nunzio got into the front passenger seat and closed the door. The car started to pull away.

"Hey!" Angelo yelled. The car kept moving. He angled his run to cut the Cadillac off. But the Cadillac was now picking up speed on the other side of the street. *Shit. I gotta get hit by a car again. I'll hit the front passenger door and bounce off.*

In the past, Angelo had been careful to play this game with slow-moving cars, cars slowing down near a corner. The Cadillac wasn't slowing down. Angelo took a deep breath and shot across Catherine into the path of the Cadillac.

Angelo was almost at the Cadillac's front passenger door when the driver hit the brakes, throwing off Angelo's timing. Angelo was now headed for an encounter with the front of the Caddy. He tried to slow down and twist to the side. *This is gonna hurt. I can do this.*

Angelo managed to barely avoid a head-on collision. He put his hand on the right front fender just behind the headlight as the Cadillac skidded sideways toward him. The momentum of the car propelled Angelo up and along the hood.

Angelo was surprised by how easily he ascended the windshield and slid across the roof of the black Cadillac Brougham. He tasted blood and burning rubber as the tires screeched to a stop. He tumbled off the driver's side of the Cadillac onto the hood of a parked car several shops past Uncle Frank's store. He rolled off the hood, onto the sidewalk. *My nose is bleeding again.*

People were rushing toward him.

"Tell Frankie his nephew got hit by a car again." Angelo heard someone say.

"Angelo," Uncle Nunzio's driver, Mike, was bending over him. "Kid, I'm sorry. I didn't see ya 'til the last second. You're all bloody. Jeez, maybe you shouldn't try to get up."

"Get my Uncle Nunzio here, please," Angelo whispered to Mike.

"Angelo, how bad you hurt?" Uncle Frank said.

"Please, get Uncle Nunzio. Please," Angelo said.

"Right here. I didn't know it was you," Uncle Nunzio said. "You flew right over my car."

"Uncle Nunzio, I have to tell you something," Angelo whispered.

"Angelo, I have you covered," Uncle Frank said.

"If it's all the same, *Gattino*, I gotta go do somethin'," Uncle Nunzio said. "I'll be back."

"No. Please, Uncle Nunzio, please just listen to me. Please."

"Angelo, what's wrong?" Uncle Frank asked.

"Okay, *Gattino*," Uncle Nunzio said. "Mike, I'll be a minute. Keep the motor runnin'."

Uncle Nunzio followed Uncle Frank as he carried Angelo into the store. Uncle Frank stretched Angelo out on the couch in the back room.

"How bad?" a man's voice came from behind Uncle Nunzio.

"I don't think too bad, Hartz," Uncle Frank said. "This is my Uncle Nunzio."

"I'm fine, I'm fine, really nothing bad," Angelo said.

"Okay, good, like I said, I gotta be someplace," Uncle Nunzio said.

"No. Uncle Nunzio, I got hit by your car on purpose, to tell you something."

"Yeah. What's so important?" Uncle Nunzio said as the three men looked at each other.

"The Tunnels are going to kill you," Angelo whispered while sitting up.

"*Gattino*, you hit your head a little too hard." Uncle Nunzio laughed as he walked away. "But just in case, I promise to stay outta the tunnels."

"One of them's named Biff," Angelo shouted.

Uncle Nunzio stopped. "Biff?" He walked back to Angelo.

"Yeah, Biff is one of the Tunnel brothers...I think."

"Biff is one of the Tonello brothers. They're in my car right now."

"Don't go, Uncle Nunzio. They're gonna take you under a bridge and kill you."

"Biff set up a meeting at 6:00 p.m. with some big politician... at their cousin's bar...under the Brooklyn Bridge. I figured I'd drop off the Yankee tickets and get there a little early." Uncle Nunzio looked at the other two men. Then back to Angelo. "Tell me what you know, *Gattino*."

Angelo told the three men what he heard from the closet in the Knights' apartment.

"I gotta get Mike outta the car—the Tonello brothers are in the backseat."

"I'll get him," Uncle Frank said. "You can't go out there. If Angelo's right, it's you they want. They might take their shot."

"I'll go," Hartz said. "I'm a cop, and I—"

"You're a cop?" Uncle Nunzio said.

"Relax, Mr. Sabino. Yeah, I know who you are. Frank's a friend of mine. And anyway, time's taught me to take the long view."

"The long view?" Uncle Nunzio said.

"Later," Hartz said. "Right now, I'm a cop who witnessed the accident. I go over to the driver, flip my tin, tell him to turn off the car, and step out. I tell the Tonello brothers to stay where they are. I bring Mike in the store to sign a statement. Stuff like that. Cop stuff."

"They got guns back there, Cop," Uncle Nunzio said.

"The name's Hartz, and I got one, too."

"Be careful, Hartz," Uncle Nunzio said. "Frankie, I need to make a call."

"Phone's there in the corner." Uncle Frank sat next to Angelo and patted his face clean with a warm wet towel. He handed Angelo a bag of ice, and said, "Lie back and put this on your nose. I'm going to the front to keep an eye on things."

"Thanks, Uncle Frank."

"I won't call your mother. I don't want her running down here 'til we figure out what's going to happen," Uncle Frank said. "You really okay? That ankle?"

"I'm fine. Really, I'm surprised, too." Angelo heard Hartz and Mike come into the store.

Uncle Nunzio finished his call and rubbed Angelo's hair as he walked by to greet Mike.

Mike said, "Nunzio, this cop, I don't know what—"

"Mike, his name is Hartz, and he just did you a big favor." Nunzio filled Mike in, told him he just made a call and three cars were on the way. "It's like an angel intervened...an angel named Angelo. He's runnin' to Lilly's to warn me and we're right there just when Angelo's crossing Catherine. What are the odds? Mike, me and you were dead tonight. Un-fuckin'-believable."

"Nunzio, you better stay in the back. They might get wise and bust in here," Mike said.

"Frankie," Hartz said as the men walked into the back of the store. "You got a gun?"

"Shotgun and a thirty-eight, right next to me," Frank said.

"I got a forty-five," Mike said.

"Mine's a thirty-eight," Uncle Nunzio said.

"Thirty-eight," Hartz said.

"I got a belt," Angelo said getting up. "I'm good with it."

The men smiled, but didn't laugh. Uncle Nunzio walked over to Angelo, laid him back down, kneeled in front of him, and whispered, "Rest, *Gattino*. But get that belt ready."

"*Gattino*?" Hartz repeated to Frank.

"It means a young cat or kitten, but not literally...it's more complicated," Frank said. "In Naples, they say, 'Beware the kitten in the shadows, for a lion follows.' The kitten in the shadows is *Gattino*. It's a term of endearment that Uncle Nunzio gave Angelo. I'm thinking it fits."

The men returned to the front of the store. In less than ten minutes, Angelo's nose stopped bleeding and he heard Uncle Frank say, "We got some traffic out here."

Angelo walked into the front of the store and through the window saw three Cadillacs next to Uncle Nunzio's car. Frank was outside in front of the store with Hartz. Angelo walked outside and stood next to Uncle Frank. Uncle Nunzio was talking to Mike and two other guys.

Angelo heard Mike say, "They got Biff in the back of one car and his brother in the other car. Four of our guys are in each car to keep them company. They'll find everybody that was involved in this."

"Good," Uncle Nunzio said. "Nicely done."

"We got two more guys for our car and another car with four guys. We're stayin' at the Drake with you 'til we know every-thing," Mike said to Uncle Nunzio as the two cars with the Tonello brothers took off. "You ready to go, Boss?"

"Just a minute." Uncle Nunzio walked back to Angelo. "You know what time it is, Angelo? It's ten after six. Right now, this very minute, I would be dead. You saved my life, *Gattino*. You risked your life to save me." Uncle Nunzio kissed the palms of Angelo's hands. Then he got in the back of his car and the two Cadillacs took off for the Drake.

Angelo was filled with pride. The only thing that could have made this better was if he had actually died saving Uncle Nunzio. He knew Uncle Nunzio liked him. But now he felt special. And he was soaking in the moment.

"I'll call your mother," Uncle Frank said. "Can you walk okay?"

"Angelo, I'm going to walk you home," Hartz said. "Here are the pictures you wanted to look at, Frankie. Be right back."

"Uncle Frank, I need a couple of those Yankee tickets...I promised Tate."

"Here're your tickets, and try not to get hit by a car crossing the street. Keep an eye on him, Hartz—he seems to have a problem with that lately."

* * *

Jimmy held Ju-Ju's arm as they stood facing Hector, Rico, and Ernesto in front of 10 Catherine Slip.

"What's goin' on?" Ray Cotton said, walking up with several other Knights.

"The plan's dead," Hector said. "We watched it die from here...four Caddys. They split up the Tonello brothers. Okay, Rico, you were right. There, I said it. So whadda we do now?"

"The Tonello brothers will tell Nunzio's guys everything." Rico sat on the chain surrounding the grass and lit a cigarette. "And then we're going to die."

"You still wanna talk to him?" Jimmy pushed Ju-Ju toward Rico.

"You're friends with that kid, Angelo, right?" Rico said.

"So what? I didn't do nothin'," Ju-Ju said.

"When you came into the apartment today, were you alone?" Rico asked.

"Yeah, Ernesto saw me. I was alone," Ju-Ju said. "Right, Ernesto?"

"I didn't see nobody else," Ernesto said. "You should've locked the door, Jimmy."

"I did. Jimmy said."

"Bullshit, then how—"

"Please," Rico said. "Ju-Ju, did you see anybody else in the apartment, besides Ernesto?"

"No, just Ernesto and the guy on the bed." Ju-Ju took a risk—lied—to confuse things. He was hoping they weren't sure if anyone else was in the apartment. He was able to see one of the bedrooms from where he was standing in the apartment when Ernesto saw him. The door to the bedroom was ajar—no one was on the bed. But he took a shot.

"In the bed?" Rico said, looking around. "Who was in the bed?"

"Not in the bed, on the bed, lying across it," Ju-Ju lied. "He had one of our black T-shirts on so I figured it was okay. But I don't know who he was; I'm new."

"Rico, we saw Angelo runnin' past the little park just before he got hit by Nunzio's car," a Knight said. "Ju-Ju called him, but he didn't stop."

"What was he running from?" Rico asked. "Ray, go in the apartment and see if the bed looks like somebody was on it."

"We didn't see where he came from, don't even know why he was runnin'," the Knight said. "But that Caddy knocked him in the air. Looked like he got killed."

"I hate coincidences," Rico said. "Search the kid."

Ju-Ju stood silent, scared, as Jimmy reached into his pockets and came out with the key.

"See, I told you I locked it. This kid's got a key," Jimmy said.

* * *

Hartz walked back into Lilly's after taking Angelo home. "Did you get a chance to look at the snapshots?"

"This is the guy who was with Rico." Frank tapped his finger on a picture of a young cop.

Hartz picked up the photo and read the information on the back. "Jack Herbert Stipple, Assignment: Headquarters. And he lives in the One-Oh—on West 20th Street, not 18th. Very good work." Hartz gathered up the other pictures spread out on the counter. "The Knights own this guy and at HQ, he would've known about Marty. Son of a bitch."

"South Street Sammy walked away from his loft," Frank said. "But he'll show up. We'll get to the bottom of this."

* * *

After dinner, Angelo, his mother, his brother, and his Uncle Johnny sat around the table and talked about their day.

Angelo's mother said, "You must've been frightened, Angelo, but that didn't stop you. You saved Uncle Nunzio's life."

"Thanks, Mom."

Uncle Johnny smiled. "I'm really proud of you, Angelo."

Angelo wanted to tell them that mostly he was scared. From his encounter with Jimmy to taking off his belt in Uncle Frank's back room, waiting for the Tonello brothers to shoot their way in. But he just smiled and said, "Thanks."

"Can I watch TV now?" Adam said.

"Yes, come, I'll turn it on for you," Angelo's mother said.

Angelo left and headed up the hall to his room. He retrieved Ernesto's medallion and went to Uncle Johnny's room and knocked.

"Come in," Uncle Johnny said. "You okay?"

"You knew about what happened to my mom?"

"Terrible. Awful thing."

"Yeah, that's why my dad never liked me, huh?"

"No. Your dad loved you. He started drinking too much. That's what made him nuts. Your face looks a little beat up. The car clip you on the nose?"

"Jimmy Bowman clipped me on the nose. Liz was there. I got distracted. And he whacked me with a book." Angelo shook his head. "Right on the nose. Dumb."

"What'd you do?"

"Nothing. All the stuff you taught me. I went blank. And then the cops—well, first I kind of cried, you know tears came out, and then the cops showed up." Angelo showed Uncle Johnny the medallion. "Will you hold this for me?"

"Where'd you get it?"

"South Street Sammy gave it to me the night I did Bookman's. He said he found it. I don't think he knew what it was...it was all dirty."

"Just give it back to Ernesto," Uncle Johnny said. "Why keep it?"

"At first, I liked having it because of how Ernesto embarrassed Mom that night. Remember, he asked Adam if he wanted to hold it, and—"

"Yeah, I remember."

"I want him to be sad that he lost it...and for me to know I'm the one making him sad. I'll give it back sometime, but if he finds out I have it—"

"Who knows you have it?"

"Just Tate...he won't tell anybody...and, maybe Sammy, if he knows what it is. Anyway, if he finds out, I don't want to punk out and give it to him. So if I have to ask you for it..."

"Angelo, you're not going to punk out. Why would you even think that? What happened between you and Jimmy today? From the beginning."

Angelo told him what happened. "...then Jimmy told me to say, 'I'm sorry, Mr. Bowman,' and shoved me."

"He shoved you? Why didn't you do something when he asked for the apology before he shoved you or after he shoved you? A kick, something?"

"That's when I got distracted by Liz. She said—"

"Angelo, why?"

"I can't kick," Angelo said. "That's how a girl would fight."

"The person who taught me how to end fights—how to win, to stay alive—was a woman name Mary. We met in Korea and she could kick my ass and all them Knights at the same time."

"A girl taught you to fight?"

"Mary." Uncle Johnny waved his hand and walked over to the window. "Pay attention to what's happening around you. They were going to kill Nunzio, and you're worried some asshole might laugh at how you look when you fight? Let me make it clear for you. You don't want to be dead when the fight's over. Period. You still think there are rules? You think they're playing?" Uncle Johnny shook his head and added, "Look, if you're not going to use what I teach you, don't waste your time learning it. Study hard and get out of this neighborhood as fast as you can. But whatever you do, start thinking smart."

But Angelo wasn't thinking about what almost happened to Uncle Nunzio. He was thinking about what two Knights did to his mother. To his family. "You're right. I'll use it, Uncle Johnny. Teach me to end fights like Mary." Angelo paused for a moment, then added, "I still can't believe I cried, though."

"I was in the Army with a guy who cried all the time. It didn't stop him from fighting. He just cried a lot."

"Yeah, but I got to see these kids every day. You know how I told you we named ourselves the Reapers? Well, they started callin' us the Weepers instead. Because of me crying."

"Keep it."

"Keep what?"

"The Weepers, I like it. In fact, I like it better than the Reapers. Use a teardrop as your symbol. Write Weepers on the back of your jacket. Take it away from them. Take pride in it. Make it yours. They'll be confused and you win. And when people ask you why, say we weep for the families of our enemies. Give me your arm—I'll tattoo you."

Angelo rolled up his sleeve. Uncle Johnny took a pen off his desk and wrote Weepers on Angelo's shoulder and drew a small teardrop falling from the "s."

Angelo looked in the mirror. "Weepers. I really like it. I like it better than the Reapers, too. Something about it. What?"

"I'll tell you what," Uncle Johnny said. "It says, *Fuck you*, that's what."

"Weepers."

CHAPTER TWENTY-THREE
"He knows, but for some reason, we're still alive."

Father Casimiro didn't look in the duffle bag dribbling crimson in the rain. Father Joe did that and nodded. "Sammy."

"I got a positive at 7:46 a.m. by Father Joseph Bonifacio," a police officer said, scribbling in his memo pad while another cop held Father Joe's umbrella over them.

Father Joe poured holy water from a small bottle into the bag as he pleaded in Latin for the salvation of South Street Sammy's soul on this dreary, misty-rain morning.

Father Joe, Father Casimiro, and a small gathering stood over the duffle bag, heads bowed in prayer. Father Casimiro felt a shiver as he watched Angelo, Adam, and several of Angelo's friends walk by on their way to school. They stopped for a moment and watched as two men in yellow raincoats carried a stretcher into the park, lifted the duffle bag onto the stretcher, and carried it back to the morgue wagon waiting near the park entrance.

When they were finished, Angelo and his brother and friends continued on their way. Father Joe thanked the cop, took the umbrella, and led Father Casimiro out of the circle and across the street to Frank's liquor store. Seeing the blood seeping through the duffle bag was a grim reminder for Father Casimiro. He knew the terror, if not the pain, Sammy must have experienced. He wondered if the killers giggled as they beat Sammy, like they did when they beat him. He was glad he hadn't left. And he better understood Father Joe's uneasy relationship with God. Father Casimiro was now more angry than frightened.

Frank handed the two priests coffee. They sat at the small table.

Frank said, "Was it...?"

"Sammy." Father Joe nodded.

"Must be bad," Frank said. "First cop there looked in the bag and lost his breakfast."

"It's awful." Father Joe shook his head. "Let's change the subject before I change my career? I saw the FOR SALE sign on the shoemaker's shop next door."

"He wants to retire to Florida." Frank shrugged. "Now he just needs to find a buyer."

"After they bagged me," Father Casimiro said, "you asked me if I remembered anything. Voices, anything. And I acted like a jerk."

"You weren't a jerk." Frank said. "You were just rattled."

"Just now, standing there looking at the bag, I remembered one of the kids sounded like that Jimmy, the one who stopped me the first day I—"

"Jimmy Bowman," Father Joe said.

"Right. And I remember two names, one kid was called Ray and another was called Raz," Father Casimiro said.

"Ray Cotton was that big guy I hit the day we stopped them from beating up Sammy," Father Joe said. "And Raz would be Ronnie the Razor. Ray and Raz are both a couple of nut cases close to Ernesto. Jimmy Bowman is their apprentice. Makes sense they'd be together."

The phone rang; Frank walked over to the counter and picked it up. "Lilly's."

"Frankie, this is Donna from Sonny's."

"What can I do for you, Darlin'?" Frank smiled and winked at the two priests.

"One of the girls here, Janet, just called and asked me if I could cover her shift tonight 'cause Willie Max gets home this evening and wants to take her out on the town. I remembered that you were lookin' for him, so I thought I'd give ya a ring."

"You Sweetheart, I owe you."

"He's pickin' her up at eight. That's all I know. Frankie, ya gotta promise me you won't tell anyone I told you."

"I promise, Sweetheart. Not a word." Frank tapped the phone cradle a couple of times and then dialed.

"Jokes, it's me. Can you cover Lilly's tonight...about 5:30?"

* * *

Rico squinted through the streaks left by the tick-smear-tick of his windshield wipers as his car slapped through puddles along First Avenue. Hector was in the front passenger seat and Ernesto was in the back. "It's almost 10:00 a.m.—let's get breakfast at the Lipstick Diner up on 61st Street," Rico said.

"Jimmy told me Sammy said he gave a gold coin to another bum for a buck," Ernesto said. "You believe that?"

"Maybe, if he didn't know what it was," Hector said. "But I still think that kid Angelo might know something. Ernesto, didn't you say you saw him that night?"

"Yeah, and he saw us with Marty."

Rico shook his head. "Why'd they have to kill Sammy?"

"Who the fuck cares? He was a bum," Hector said. "What about Nunzio?"

"We have to get Nunzio's trust back so we can stay alive and start making some money again," Rico said. "And, if the coin is Ernesto's medallion, the good news is, it ain't with Marty. It's either with another bum or...I don't know. Maybe Angelo does know something about it. That kid Ju-Ju could just ask Angelo."

"We beat him up and threw him outta the Knights, remember?" Ernesto said.

"Yeah, but maybe he wants back in," Rico said. "Start looking for a parking place."

"What's the harm in just asking Angelo?" Hector said. "A spot on the right."

"I see it," Rico said. He backed into the parking spot just a few feet down from the Lipstick Diner. "Ask Angelo? It could be that easy."

"If Nunzio knows about us and the Tonello boys, how come we ain't dead?" Hector said.

"During the three days Nunzio was off the street, every one of Nunzio's guys you talked to disappeared, including the Tonello brothers. He knows," Rico said. "But for some reason, we're still alive. My cop is trying to set up a meeting for me with Nunzio— we'll see."

• * *

By the time lunch rolled around, everyone in the school knew that South Street Sammy was dead. Angelo, Tate, Spiro, and Ju-Ju walked down the steps of PS-65 toward Audrey, Gina, and Sass.

"Audrey," Angelo called as he walked in front of his friends.

"Hi, Angelo, I hope you're going to the dance tonight."

"Sure. Maybe we can all hang out there together. I mean, if you want to."

"That would be nice, Angelo. That was terrible about Sammy, wasn't it?"

"Yeah, I liked Sammy." Angelo stared at the sidewalk.

"Look's like Ju-Ju's hangin' with the Reapers." Jimmy with four Knights walked up.

"We're the Weepers now, remember?" Angelo said.

"You gonna cry again? This time for a bum?" Jimmy said.

"Screw you, Punk." Even Angelo was surprised that he said that to Jimmy. But he was angry. It was a different kind of anger. It felt deeper, more permanent. It was about what happened to his mother. And what happened to Sammy. And he was tired of being afraid of Satan's Knights. Still, it surprised him to call Jimmy a punk. He felt a little out of control.

"What did you say?" Jimmy reached for Angelo.

"He said 'Screw you, Punk,'" a man said before Angelo could respond. The man was one of nine Popeyes walking toward Jimmy and the four Knights with him.

"We're Knights," Jimmy said as he and the other Knights backed up the stairway.

"Where you goin'?" a Popeye said to Jimmy. "Kid's right, you are punks."

"Poet," Jimmy yelled at Angelo. "I'm comin' for you."

* * *

Jokes made it to Lilly's by five. Frank thanked him and drove over to Baxter Street, where Willie Max had an apartment. He parked a block away—a little too close, but since it was raining, Frank was willing to risk it. While Willie was out of town, Frank secured a key from an old contact and looked around Willie's fourth-floor apartment. Willie had locks on his windows and a bolt lock and chain on the apartment door. This would make it tough to get in if Willie were home and unwilling to open the door.

Frank hoped to get into Willie's apartment before him and wait inside. He also hoped that Willie would come home before going over to Sonny's Bar to pick up his date. Otherwise Frank had a long night ahead of him, and maybe the complicating factor of Willie bringing the woman back to his apartment. But this was no different than police work—planning, patience, and luck.

Frank took off his shoes on the second floor and put them in a shopping bag he brought with him. Also in the bag were two sets of handcuffs and six feet of clothesline. He walked up to the fourth floor in his socks—not wanting to leave a trail of wet footprints, Frank knocked at the door. No answer. He tried the key. The door opened—no deadbolt or chain.

Closing the door, Frank looked around the apartment. The door to the bedroom was ajar. He pushed it open. A partially unpacked suitcase was on one of two chairs in the bedroom behind the door. He found a loaded forty-five automatic and stuck it in his waistband. After checking out the rest of the apartment, he returned to the bedroom. He made certain that the door was in its former position and sat in the empty chair. From his vantage point, he could see the apartment door between the hinges on the spine of the bedroom door. He put his shoes back on, placed the forty-five in his lap, and waited.

It was almost seven o'clock when Frank heard a key in the front door lock. He watched. Willie Max came in, closed the front door, and engaged the bolt and chain. He was alone.

Willie used the bathroom and then came into the bedroom. Frank stood up and cracked Willie on the left ear with the butt of the forty-five. Willie wobbled and twisted toward Frank as he fell sideways. Frank took the opportunity to kick him in the groin. Probably unnecessary, but this was the guy who had killed his sister's husband and scared the hell out of Angelo six years ago.

Willie was down, gasping, and curled into a fetal position. He was dazed. Frank grabbed Willie by his hair and dragged him into the kitchen area. "You took a father away from Angelo and Adam."

"What...wait." Willie passed out.

Frank rolled Willie onto his stomach and handcuffed his wrists behind his back with the cuffs running under Willie's belt. Frank also cuffed Willie's ankles together. He made certain the cuffs on Willie's wrists and ankles were overly tight. Frank also cinched Willie's belt excessively tight. He wanted him disoriented and uncomfortable. He lifted Willie into a wooden chair. Frank tied the clothesline around Willie's neck, ran it down the back of the chair, under the chair, and tied it to the ankle cuffs, pulling his feet back.

Frank put a pot of coffee on the stove and lit a cigarette while he waited for Willie to regain some sense of awareness.

"What—oh, man, oh, that hurts. Hey, look, pal, take whatever you want. Oh, man, wait—I know you...you're...you're from the neighborhood. The liquor store. You're—"

"Good, you're coming around." Frank sat in a wooden chair in front of Willie. He sipped his coffee. He liked it black, without sugar, and very hot. He took a final drag on his cigarette, dropped it on the floor, and stepped on it. "Willie, tell me all the people who helped you kill Mac Pastamadeo and why. The why isn't all that important. It's just a thing with me. Even when I was a cop, I always wanted to know why. The other guys would—"

"Get the fuck outta here. I never killed nobody. Do you know who I am?"

"Close your eyes." Without waiting, Frank tossed the hot black coffee in Willie's face. It sizzled a sunburn red. "You should've closed your eyes, like I said."

Willie started to scream, but Frank reached out with his powerful right hand, gripped Willie's larynx, just behind his Adam's apple, and choked the scream silent.

"I'm blind," Willie coughed and hacked out. "My face...oh, hurts, oh. God." Black-cherry blood oozed from his left ear— where Frank had struck him with the gun earlier.

Frank walked over to the stove and poured himself another cup of coffee. He looked around the kitchen and found an ice pick. Frank returned to his chair. Willie squeezed his eyes closed and opened them. "Screaming won't help," Frank said. "First, no one in this building or neighborhood gives a shit, and second, I'll choke it out of you. Understand?"

"I can't see too good." Blood and spittle came out of Willie's mouth when he spoke. "Don't. I mean, please don't do that again. I think you got the wrong guy here."

"Willie Max, right?"

"Yeah, right, but—"

"Christmas Eve 1951, Cherry Street. You were the shooter." Frank stuck the ice pick between Willie's legs into the wooden chair. It made a *boink* sound and the handle swung back and forth for a moment. Willie stared at it while Frank lit another cigarette and then sipped the coffee. "You're going to die tonight, Willie," Frank said matter-of-factly. "But first we're going to talk. Do you remember what I want to know?"

"Okay, wait. I was there, but I wasn't the shooter. I swear to God I never killed nobody."

"That's not what your friends in the joint said."

"I bullshitted them so they'd think I was a torpedo—tough, you know?"

"Willie, if you can convince me of that, you just might live through this night. But I will know if you lie to me. And then you will experience pain and death."

"Got it, no lies. But first, will ya please loosen the cuffs? They hurt like hell."

Frank put the cup of coffee on the floor and secured the cigarette between his lips. He pulled the ice pick out of the chair, put the point on top of Willie's right knee, and with his full weight, pushed down. The ice pick punctured the top of Willie's right knee, and sank in up to the wooden handle. Willie screeched in pain as the sharp point penetrated flesh, muscle, and cartilage and pierced the skin on the back of his leg. Willie screamed. Frank choked the scream silent and Willie shuddered, dropped his face, and cried.

"Willie, you think I want to be your buddy? Maybe make chit-chat?" Frank grabbed a handful of hair and lifted Willie's chin off his chest. "You killed my sister's husband. My nephews don't have a father. Now, do you remember what I want to know?"

Willie nodded. Eyes tearing, nose running, he rasped, "Yes."

Frank pulled the ice pick out of Willie's knee and stuck it back in the chair between Willie's legs. Blood began to drip from the right cuff of Willie's pants. "So, tell me the story," Frank said pleasantly, picking up his coffee.

"Please don't hurt me no more," Willie said. "Please, I'm gonna tell you everything I know, I swear. Just, please don't hurt me no more."

"The story, Willie."

"Back in December of '51, Stan said to—"

"Stan?"

"Stan Primo. Me and him go way back to our days in the Knights. So we're havin' a couple at Sonny's and Stan asked me if I wanted to make a quick five hundred. I said, jokin' around, 'Who do I gotta kill?' He said, 'A guy you work the ships with.' I'm acting like a tough guy, so I said, 'No problem.' That's when he tells me it's Mac Pastamadeo. He wants me to keep an eye on him. Watch where he goes, shit like that. He said some Knights will be lookouts for us, he'd do the hit, I just gotta be there in case he needs backup. I asked, 'When do I get the five hundred bucks?' He said, 'When it's done.'"

"Who's payin' for this?"

"Gene Viola, he's the—"

"I know who Gene is. You sure it was him?"

"Positive. I didn't know right then. Stan told me on Christmas Eve."

"Which Knights were involved?"

"No idea. Stan handled that."

"Why'd Gene want Mac dead?"

"Gene was the middleman. I'm pretty sure it was Bennie Bets who paid for the hit. You know the fat guy who owned the newsstand on Catherine and Cherry?"

"Yeah, the bookie. He died the next day, on Christmas."

"Mac owed him big time, almost ten grand. From what I heard, he wasn't even payin' off the nut, just floatin'. Mac hits a number for four grand, he gives Bennie three, and Bennie's pissed. Go figure." Willie shook his head. "Anyway, like you said, a day after the hit, Bennie dies of a heart attack. No surprise, big as Bennie was, but if we would've waited another couple of days, I don't know, maybe the contract—"

"So that's the why," Frank said. "Mac owed Bennie money and pissed him off?"

"That's what Stan thought. I don't know if that's all there was to it."

"What happened that Christmas Eve?"

"Me and Stan were drinkin' at the South Street bar, you know, at the Journal?"

"G'head."

"Stan gets a call from a Knight who said Mac is on Cherry Street and they're watching from the projects. So we leave the bar. Very quiet night, snow all over. We walked to Stan's car parked on Cherry Street alongside Knickerbocker Village. It's covered with snow. We're about to clean it off when we hear voices. I look up Cherry Street and see Mac and a kid walkin' down the street.

"I say to Stan, 'That's our mark, but he's with a kid.' Stan patted his coat pocket and said, 'I got heat.' We duck down on the driver's side of Stan's car, you know, in the street. Stan takes his gun and a silencer out of his coat pocket. Who walks around with a silencer in his pocket? I said, 'We gotta wait for him to be alone.' But Stan said, 'Maybe Viola will give us a bonus for two.' That's when I knew it was Gene Viola. So, we wait for the kid to skip by and then we grab the mark—"

"Mac."

"Right. Sorry, we grabbed Mac and pulled him down behind Stan's car."

"Not a chance you two could have grabbed Mac without his..."

"No. That's right, I forgot. We went around to the back of the car after the kid passed, and Stan pointed the gun at Mac and whispered, 'Come here.' Mac looked around and Stan pointed the gun at the kid."

"You piece of shit."

"I'm just tellin' ya what happened. Don't get pissed. Please."

"G'head."

"Mac leaves his shopping cart, full of presents, and walks over to us. That's when we pull him down. Then the kid screamed, lookin' for his father. Stan starts to point his gun at the kid again. And Mac whispers to Stan, 'You want this to be easy, leave the kid alone and you get no problem from me. You take a shot at the kid and I'll rip your heart out right here.'"

"That sounds like Mac."

"This guy, Mac, had balls. So the three of us crawl back alongside Stan's car, in the street, while the kid is cryin' for his father. Stan's getting impatient, afraid a car's gonna come by or somethin', and started to get up. Mac grabbed his arm and said, 'Wait.' Well, the kid must've heard something because he jumped up and—"

"Mac said 'Wait' to Stan. You sure that's what he said?"

"Yeah, he said, 'Wait, wait,' twice like—no, he said it in Italian. Um, *aspetta*, that's it, Mac said, '*Aspetta, aspetta.*' Anyway, the kid took off. He must've knocked the cart over 'cause the presents were all over the snow. Stan opened the trunk and told Mac to get in."

"And Mac just climbed in?" Frank said.

"Stan said to Mac, 'We let the kid go, but you fuck with us now, and I'll find that kid and your wife and kill them both.' So Mac said, 'I told you, I ain't gonna give ya problems.' But he walked over to the shopping cart instead of getting in the trunk. Stan said, 'Hey, what the fuck?' And Mac just held up his hand. What balls. Mac picked up the cart, put the presents back in, dusted them off, took some cookies out of his pocket and put them on top of the presents, and then he climbed in the trunk.

"Mac looked at Stan and then me; he just lay there on his side. Like he was tryin' to memorize our faces. It was creepy. He didn't even look scared. Then, *thub, thub*—two shots—and Stan slammed the trunk closed. Scared the shit outta me. I didn't know Stan was gonna shoot him right there. I threw up all over myself.

"Go on." Frank remembered the cookies and the vomit.

"I was gonna get in the car, but Stan said, 'Get outta here, you're a mess. I'll pick up the money and dump the body myself. I'll meet ya at Sonny's in a couple of hours.' So I cleaned myself off with snow and went to Sonny's, you know, on John Street, and waited 'til they closed. Never saw Stan again. The fuck kept my cut and split. No surprise, huh?"

"Actually, I am surprised. Stan leaves town for five hundred bucks. It doesn't sound like he was afraid of you. You ever try to find him?"

"I went to see Gene Viola the next day. Christmas. He's having a party and is pissed that I knocked on his door. He takes me outside, like I'm some piece of shit, and asked how I knew he was involved. I said, 'Stan told me.' Anyway, Gene said, 'Stan stopped by last night and showed me Mac—dead in his trunk. I gave him the fifteen hundred and he left.' Fifteen hundred. The fuck even lied to me about how much we were gettin' paid."

"Where'd he dump Mac?"

"No idea. Really, not a clue. Gene'd probably know. I told you everything I know. I swear, that's the whole thing. Never saw Stan again and never saw my five hundred."

"You never tried to get your money from Gene?"

"Are you kiddin' me, or what? We're talkin' about Eugene Viola; he works for Nunzio Sabino. Just like Stan. I don't need that kind of trouble. Forget about it."

"Willie, I'm not going to kill you, but if you're lying to me, I'll find—"

"Why would I lie about Nunzio Sabino? I'm dead. Dead. I'm just more afraid of you than him right now. But I'm dead. Fuckin' easy five hundred."

Frank had always believed that Nunzio's connection to Pompa, Anna...his whole family, was stronger than anything else. Frank picked up Willie's phone and dialed his father's number.

"Hey, Pop, meet me at Lilly's in ten minutes. It's important." Frank hung up. He uncuffed Willie and said, "Get some sleep. You look terrible."

Frank left with his cuffs, rope, and Willie's gun and ice pick in the paper shopping bag.

* * *

Anna talked with Rosemarie, Father Joe, Father Casimiro, and Nunzio at the Settlement as neighborhood teens danced to *Sincerely* by the Moonglows. She watched Angelo dance with Audrey and smiled. "They look so sweet," Anna said.

"My Spiro said she's a really nice girl," Rosemarie said.

"Uncle Nunzio, is my Angelo in any danger since the Tonello brothers thing?"

"I don't think so, Anna. Rico wants to be my friend. But just in case, I got a couple of guys keepin' an eye on Angelo...from a distance, so he don't know."

"Thank you," Anna said. "Ro, let's walk over and say hi to our boys."

"You mean talk to the girls dancing with them."

"Yep, come on. Do you know their names?"

"Audrey is with your Angelo and Sass is with my Spiro. Be nice, Anna."

"Of course. Let's invite them up for tea sometime."

As Anna and Rosemarie walked over to their sons, the three men smoked and talked about the Asian flu, which was an epidemic in New York, and the World Series between the Braves and the Yankees starting October 2nd.

Father Casimiro liked being accepted by these men. The kids now called him Father Cas. It made him feel like a fixture around the Cherry Street Settlement and in the neighborhood. He walked the streets and through the projects, no longer wide-eyed, but with a stolen sense of history from Father Joe's life. He also had a sense of mission—to stare down the devil.

CHAPTER TWENTY-FOUR

"I like takin' the long view."

Angelo, Adam, and Tate walked along Catherine Street toward their schools. As they passed the little park, Angelo looked at the ground in the far corner of the park where South Street Sammy had died just one week ago. Angelo felt an emptiness he never knew Sammy filled. "Sammy was okay."

"Sammy was okay." Tate patted Angelo's shoulder. "Angelo, Gina told me that Audrey really likes you. She said not to tell you."

"Yeah? What else did she say?"

"What else did she say? She's worried about you standing up to Jimmy. Gina's brother Bobby said Jimmy was one of the guys who killed Sammy."

"What? Who killed Sammy?" Adam asked while picking up an orange and red maple leaf that scooted in front of him. "Angelo, isn't this pretty? I'm going to give it to my teacher."

"It's real pretty." Angelo shook his head at Tate. He hoped Adam wouldn't ask again.

Tate nodded. "Do you like school, Adam?"

"It's okay. Yesterday we had to hide under our desks for the air drill."

"An air raid drill," Tate said. "Angelo, did Audrey say anything about me and Gina?

"No, but if Gina's telling you secrets about her best friend, she must like you. You want me to ask Audrey?"

"No. If it ain't good, it's done," Tate said. "At least I got the dream right now."

Autumn was early but in full radiance. Its breeze felt clean on Angelo's face. He tasted the crisp morning. The air smelled innocent and the sun sprinkled through red, rustling trees.

"Audrey said they'd meet us in front of P.S. 1 and walk to school with us," Angelo said.

"Why did somebody kill Sammy?" Adam asked.

"Sammy just died, Adam, that's all," Angelo lied.

"I found gum stuck under my desk yesterday when we did the air drill," Adam said. "It was good...but kinda hard."

"Yuck, Adam," Angelo admonished. "Don't eat stuff you find. Oh, man."

* * *

Later that morning, Frank's father dropped into Lilly's Liquor Store with a box of pastries and two containers of black coffee. "Frankie, I'm guessing you need a cup of coffee?" Pompa put down the coffee and picked up the newspaper. "Look at this—the feds said Chesterfield's went too far when they said their cigarettes weren't bad for you. Speaking of cigarettes..."

Frank walked around the counter and sat with his father at the round table he kept in the front of the store for drop-in friends. He tossed his Lucky Strikes on the table toward his father. "All I got are Luckys, none of them safe Chesterfields. Listen, Pop, I know it's only been a week since Willie Max told me about Nunzio, but—"

"Be patient, Frankie. You'll know when you know."

"Ain't he concerned that Willie'll call Gene Viola?"

"Viola's still in California. After we talked last Friday night, I called Nunzio, told him about Willie, and that we needed to have breakfast the next morning. Anyway, Nunzio's guys picked up Willie right after I talked to Nunzio...he's on top of this, Frankie."

"Pop, do you think maybe Nunzio—"

"Impossible. Could not happen. Nunzio is my friend. Hey, it looks like we're about to have a religious experience."

"I'll put up a pot of coffee," Frank said as Father Joe and Father Casimiro walked into Lilly's. Frank wasn't sure what to think. He did all he could for six years. Now, reluctantly, he had to leave it in his father's hands.

"There's a sold sign on the shoemaker's next door," Father Joe said. "Who bought it?"

"I didn't even see the sign," Frank said. "Sold already? Good for him."

"Frankie, you got a payin' customer," Pompa said as Hartz walked into Lilly's with two containers of black coffee.

"Hey, everybody," Frank said. "This is my friend Detective Hartz. Hartz, this is my father—Pompa, this is Father Joe and Father Casimiro. Pass the coffee around, Hartz; I'm makin' more. I'll grab another chair from the back."

"I'll get it," said Father Casimiro.

"I heard about South Street Sammy buying it last Friday," Hartz said. "I'm guessing he was the contact?"

"Bingo. But no prize," Frank said. "You can talk freely in front of this group, Hartz."

"You wanted to show Sammy a picture?" Father Joe said. "Let's take a look."

Frank looked at Hartz and Hartz nodded and shrugged.

Frank tossed the picture on the table. It went from hand to hand. No one remembered seeing him.

"Don't give up, pal," Pompa said. "You never know when somethin'll turn up."

"Look at this crowd—you're gonna have to start charging admission, Frankie," Nunzio said, walking into Lilly's. Then Nunzio looked at Father Joe, winked, and said, "It's all set."

"Terrific, Boss," Father Joe said. And then to Father Casimiro, he said, "We're all glad you didn't go back to Milwaukee. And, to formally welcome you to the neighborhood, we will hold tonight's dance in the Cherry Street Park."

"That's a wonderful idea," Father Casimiro said. "But how does holding—"

Nunzio said, "A friend in Milwaukee sent me a thousand brats and a couple of barrels of Schlitz beer. The sodas and other stuff are from right here in New York. I also got several guys who cook the Italian sausage at the San Gennaro Feast to set up their grills in the Cherry Street Park starting at five o'clock tonight. How's that for a Milwaukee-style welcome?"

"It's...perfect," Father Casimiro said. "I don't know what to say. You guys—"

"Here." Father Joe smiled and handed his handkerchief to Father Casimiro. "Don't embarrass me."

* * *

At 5:30 p.m., Angelo and his friends followed the sweet, smoky smell of sizzling brats into the Cherry Street Park. Angelo spotted several guys from the neighborhood, including Morgan, cooking up brats on open grills. The smell wafted through the neighborhood, luring the curious, as well as those in the know, to the park.

"Hey, Angelo, Tate, Sage, guys," Father Casimiro called, wearing a Milwaukee Braves baseball cap. "Welcome. Grab a brat and a soda. All compliments of Mr. Sabino."

"You have guts wearing that hat, Father Cas," Angelo laughed.

"I didn't put it on until I was in the park."

Angelo noticed that the park shed was open for electrical power. Music and chatter floated on a brisk evening breeze as Angelo and his friends joined Audrey and her friends.

Angelo watched Father Casimiro walk over and sit at a table with Uncle Nunzio, Pompa, Uncle Frank, Father Joe, and Spiro's grandfather.

"This is fun," Audrey said to Angelo. "Your Uncle Nunzio is very generous."

"Yeah, he is."

In the Still of the Night started couples dancing. Angelo looked at Audrey, she took his hand, and they danced.

After several dances, Angelo saw Hartz walk into the park. Hartz walked over to Uncle Nunzio's table. Angelo remembered how Hartz helped Uncle Nunzio. But he also knew Hartz investigated the Bookman fire. *Please, God.* His stomach tightened. As much as he wanted to hide, he also wanted to know what it was about.

"I'll be right back," Angelo said to Audrey and walked to Uncle Nunzio's table. Tate automatically followed Angelo. By the time they got there, Hartz was sitting and smoking.

"I'll see what I can find out for you, Hartz. I owe ya," Uncle Nunzio said, apparently unaware of Angelo and Tate. "But if what you want is a collar—"

Hartz leaned in and said, "No, no collar. What I want is a reckoning."

"You got anything?" Uncle Nunzio asked. "A day? A place? Anybody see anybody?"

"Nothin'." Hartz shook his head. "My gut says Knights, but I got zip."

"Who saw him last?" Uncle Frank passed the picture of Marty to Uncle Nunzio.

"Probably your friend Sammy," Hartz said. "Poor guy."

"Saw who?" Angelo asked, leaning over Uncle Nunzio's shoulder to see the picture. The man in the picture looked familiar.

"Oh, jeez, Angelo," Uncle Frank said. "I didn't see you guys there."

"Um, Detective Hartz," Angelo said, "this is my friend, Tate."

"Good to meet ya, Tate." Hartz shook Tate's hand. "Just call me Hartz, boys."

"Who's that?" Angelo said nodding toward the picture.

"A friend of mine," Hartz said. "He was just found...dead."

"I'm sorry," Angelo said. "He looks familiar."

Hartz looked at Angelo. "If you can think of...anything, I'd appreciate it."

"Oh, yeah. I know where I saw him."

"Where?" Hartz said. Everyone at the table stopped talking.

"Okay, I'm probably going to get in trouble, but since he was your friend," Angelo said. "Remember the night that Bookman's burned down?"

"Yeah, I was supposed to meet him that night," Hartz said. "He never showed up."

"I saw him that night."

"Sit down, boys," Hartz said as everyone shifted over to make room. "Angelo, I promise you will not get in trouble. Am I right, gentlemen?"

Everyone nodded.

"That don't matter. He was your friend, like Tate—"

"What did you see that night, Angelo?" Uncle Frank said.

"That night, I went for a walk through the projects at about two in the morning."

"At two in the morning? Alone?" Father Casimiro looked around. "Alone?"

"Yeah. Anyway, as I'm walking past the little park, the light from the lamppost was right on that guy in the picture. He was wearing a checkered shirt."

"They found him wearing a blue and yellow checkered shirt—wrong size," Hartz said. "G'head, Angelo."

"There were these two guys, I couldn't see their faces too good, but they were wearing Knight T-shirts and were standing in front of him. One of the Knights was Ernesto; he was talkin' and slappin' the guy, your friend, on the head. The other Knight I figure was Ronnie the Razor, 'cause I could see he was holding a straight razor, you know, like the barber uses."

"You couldn't see his face too good, but you know it was Ernesto?" Uncle Frank asked.

"He wore a medallion around his neck and it was shining in the light."

"So do Hector and Rico," Father Casimiro said. "Rico showed me his medallion. I think it was the morning after the fire at Bookman's. So how'd you know it was Ernesto?"

Angelo loved this attention. "I knew it was Ernesto because on my way back from my walk, the three guys were gone. But I would've walked right into some other Knights if South Street Sammy hadn't pulled me into the shadows. The weird thing was, Sammy was wearing a Knights' T-shirt with the name *Marty* on it."

"Marty is my friend's name."

"Joe, remember my first night here? We were walking down Catherine and we saw Sammy?" Father Casimiro said. "Wasn't he wearing a blue and yellow checkered shirt?"

"You could be right," Father Joe said.

Father Casimiro looked around at the other men and said, "Well, he was talking to us and urinating in the street. I had never seen anything like that before. Anyway, I think it was his shirt, because he told us some Knights had taken his."

"That's right. Sammy was wearing a Knights' T-shirt with *Marty* on it when we pulled the Knights off him," Father Joe said. "But, Angelo, I still don't know how you knew it was Ernesto—oh, I'm afraid I might know."

"So I thanked Sammy and gave him a dollar I just happened to have in my pocket. And he gave me a dirty gold coin. It turned out to be—"

"Ernesto's medallion," Father Casimiro said.

"Right."

"And odds are, Sammy told Satan's Knights that you have it," Father Joe said.

"Well, now we got somethin'," Uncle Nunzio said. "Angelo, when you saw the three of them in the park, did they see you?"

"Oh, yeah."

"So it's not just the medallion they're interested in. They know Angelo is a witness to somethin'," Uncle Nunzio said. "He could put them together."

"True," Hartz said. "Did Sammy see them that night?"

"Yeah, Sammy told me they were asking this guy, Marty, if he told the cops about Hector and Willie."

"So Hector was the Knight contact," Uncle Frank said.

"If Sammy told them I have the medallion, how come they haven't come after me yet?" Angelo asked. "It's been over a week since they killed him."

"Good question," Hartz said.

"Because they want my friendship." Uncle Nunzio stood up and started to leave. "That piece of shit Viola told me no Knights were involved. He made a jerk—"

"Easy, Nunzio," Hartz said. "If you jump-crazy, your enemies will scatter and make plans."

"Hartz is right, Boss," Pompa said. "Viola crossed you, but—"

"No fucking buts. I want to—"

"Nunzio," Father Joe said. "This is what you and I talk about...this is what can kill you...stop. Swallow it. Did you hear what Hartz said?"

"I did. That's smart, Hartz." Nunzio sat back down.

"Nunzio, you said the Knights want your friendship," Hartz said.

"That's right. So maybe we got an opportunity here," a cooler Nunzio said.

"What are you thinking?" Pompa asked.

"Okay, this is just for the guys around this table," Uncle Nunzio said, and everyone looked at each other and nodded. Even Angelo and Tate. "There's this crooked cop, hangs out with Rico, tryin' to set up a meeting with me and Rico."

"Officer Jack Stipple," Hartz said.

"Very good, Hartz—you should be a detective." Uncle Nunzio smiled. "I've been blowin' him off. Rico wants me to believe that he and his brothers had nothin' to do with tryin' to ice me, and they wanna be friends. This is what the cop said. So I figure they don't know Angelo was in the closet when they were talkin' about hittin' me."

"So?" Pompa said.

"So, I'll meet with Rico. I make Rico think all is okay and that I can make this Marty thing go away. He ain't gonna see an arrest and Hartz will convince Officer Stipple that the case is closed so he'll believe me. He don't know the only reason his brothers are still alive is 'cause I owe you, Hartz. And now they got no reason to worry about Angelo. Meanwhile, I get Rico to give me the names of the guys who killed Marty. He ain't gonna give me his brother, but we already know that. After that, if it's all the same with you, Hartz, I'll take care of my business."

"I like getting Angelo off the hook," Uncle Frank said. "Maybe you should remind Rico about the Knights keepin' their hands off Anna and her kids."

"Oh, I'll remind him," Uncle Nunzio said.

"I'll pass some bullshit to Officer Jack Stipple, about the Marty case being closed," Hartz said. "And Nunzio, Stipple is mine, so let's talk before you take care of your business."

"No problem. I like takin' the long view." Uncle Nunzio took a drag on his cigarette. "And Frankie, about that other thing...I'll let you know when I know."

"Thanks," Uncle Frank said. "Oh, Angelo, tell your mom I got tickets to that new play. I'll take you and her when it opens next week. I have two extra tickets if she wants to invite anybody else."

"What play?" Hartz asked.

"*West Side Story.*"

"Yeah, at the Winter Garden," Uncle Nunzio said. "It should be terrific."

"Thanks, Uncle Frank. I'll tell her."

As the talk drifted to the Yankees and Braves, Angelo and Tate stood up and Angelo said, "We're going back now, okay?"

"Who's that cute girl you're dancin' with?" Uncle Frank teased.

"Forget about it." Angelo laughed and walked away with Tate.

"Hey, Angelo," Hartz called after him. "I owe you."

"No problem." Angelo waved.

Tate patted Angelo's back as they walked toward Audrey and Gina.

"Angelo, look around," Tate whispered. "The other gangs are checkin' you out."

Angelo saw Popeyes, Cobras, and other gang members watching him walk away from a meeting with Uncle Nunzio. He felt like a star, but acted nonchalant. He just talked to Tate— about going to Coney Island tomorrow and stuff like that—as they returned to their friends.

CHAPTER TWENTY-FIVE

"I better start carrying Merlin."

A fter church on Sunday, Angelo's mother and Adam went to Nonna's apartment. Angelo went home, changed clothes, checked on Uncle Johnny, and left to hang out with his friends. Tate met Angelo in front of their building and they headed over to Cherry Street together.

"Hey, Angelo, here comes Ju-Ju. Should we wait for him?"

"Naw, he's back in the Knights and Jimmy's with him."

"I don't know why after that beatin' they gave him."

Angelo and Tate swaggered into the Cherry Street Park and into the welcoming ritual of hits and bumps from their friends.

"Look at this, Angelo." Sage nodded toward the park entrance.

Jimmy and Ju-Ju walked up to the entrance of the park and stopped. Jimmy stood outside the chain link fence as Ju-Ju approached.

"Hey, guys." Ju-Ju's greeting received shrugs. "Angelo, Jimmy wants to talk to you."

"What's he want?" Tate asked.

"Just wants to talk. No big deal."

"Okay, tell him to come in." Then, without waiting, Angelo waved Jimmy over.

Jimmy looked around, as if uncertain the wave was meant for him. He shoved his hands into his pants pockets and walked over to Angelo.

"Look, I know we've had problems in the past, Poet, but I'd like to forget about it," Jimmy mumbled. "No reason why we can't get along."

"Okay." Angelo was relieved.

"I wanna ask you for a favor," Jimmy said.

"What?"

"We think you might know where Ernesto's medallion is. He wants it back. Can you get it back for him?" Jimmy said. "Me and Ju-Ju will go with you to get it...right now."

"No."

"No?" Jimmy leaned toward Angelo as if he didn't hear him correctly. "No, what? No, you don't know where it is? Or no, you don't wanna go get it right now?"

"Just no to you right now." Angelo was sorry he added the "right now"—it sounded weak. He needed to reassert himself as a leader. "Tell Ernesto I'll think about it."

"Are you fuckin' nuts or what? Ernesto will come down here and rip your head off," Jimmy said. "Smarten up, Poet—if you know where the medallion is, tell me and I'll go get it."

If Angelo was to be the leader of the Weepers, he needed to flex some muscle right now. Angelo maintained eye contact with Jimmy. "You heard what I said."

Jimmy blinked. "How 'bout a trade or I buy it? Whaddaya want for it?"

Angelo looked around at the Weepers. "I'll think about it."

"Good. Let's go get the medallion now, then later, you tell me what you want for it."

Angelo knew Jimmy didn't want to leave without the medallion. He swallowed hard.

"He said he'll think about it," Tate interrupted. "So that's it."

"Is that it, Poet?" Jimmy said.

"I have to think about it," Angelo said, still maintaining eye contact.

Jimmy's face was blood-boiling red. He looked around at the other Weepers as they stood up and slid off wooden picnic tables.

Angelo was impressed with Jimmy's self-control. He could tell how angry he was and yet, like a stage performer, Jimmy took a bow, walked backwards a few steps, turned, and walked out of the Cherry Street Park with Ju-Ju in tow.

"Something's up," Angelo said to Tate.

"Maybe."

The cheetah moved brazenly into lion country. Intoxicated by his own boldness, he drank from their river. He sniffed their air—dread. His yellow eyes cut a path through the thick jungle—something was coming through the darkness. His instincts kicked in...be alert.

I better start carrying Merlin.

* * *

Rico was looking forward to telling his brothers about his meeting with Nunzio. He wanted them to appreciate his relationship with Nunzio and his special ability to negotiate. They would be grateful to him for smoothing things out.

Rico and Jack the Cop met Hector and Ernesto at the zoo in Central Park. They meandered along the serpentine footpaths as Rico talked about his meeting with Nunzio.

"Nunzio said Jack the Cop could be there. Anyway, it went great," Rico said.

"Yeah?" Hector said. "How great?"

"The Tonello brothers told Nunzio's people who Hector was one of the guys behind the attempt on his life. But I convinced him that they were full of shit. Right, Jack?"

"Rico's right," Jack said. "You know—why would Hector want to change your organization? He's got his own. And he likes doing business with you—that kind of stuff."

"So then I asked Nunzio, what would it take to put this behind us and go back to making money? Nunzio said he's expanding his operation and could use us beyond just the projects."

"But then we're under his thumb," Ernesto said.

"Ernesto's got a point," Hector said. "Then this is like Nunzio's gang instead of mine."

"What?" Rico expected applause. He took a deep breath and said, "Look, you asked me to stick around 'til the end of the year. I agreed. You needed my help when your hit on Nunzio fell through. I'm the one getting us out of that shit. Now you're telling me what?"

"We're not tellin' you anything," Hector said. "We're walking and talking. What else?"

"He said if we're going to work for him, we must stop hammering people whenever we want. It draws too much attention. I played dumb and said, 'What are you talking about?' He said, 'Sammy the bum, that cop Marty, and beating up Father Casimiro.'"

"How'd he know Marty was a cop?" Ernesto asked. "And anyway, it ain't none of his business what we do to who. See, that's what I mean."

"Nunzio knows about everything. Period." Rico rubbed his eyes. "But he agrees that it's none of his business. Right, Jack?"

"That's right," Jack said. "Nunzio said it was none of his business who you killed or beat up or why if you don't want to work for him."

"But if we do work for him, we must stop drawing heat," Rico said. "Then he said, 'I can make the Marty and Sammy problems go away. But I ain't going to keep doing that; it uses up favors. So go talk to your brothers and let me know.' That's it. That's what he said."

"Getting rid of the Marty problem would be a big deal," Jack the Cop said. "I can tell you there's a lot of heat coming down at headquarters over Marty."

"I like makin' the Marty problem go away," Ernesto said. "But we can just knock off Angelo and the two priests and then there ain't no witnesses and the Marty problem goes away."

"You kidding me or what?" Jack the Cop said. "You knock off Angelo and a couple of priests and you'll have every cop in the city looking to nail you. Witnesses will be crawling out of the woodwork—and what the cops don't have, they'll make up. You would be done. Forget it."

"Hey, who asked you?" Ernesto said.

"We would also have a Nunzio problem," Rico said. "Are we still on the same planet?"

"Fine," Hector said, staring into the eyes of a caged lion. "Okay, we'll play nice. But I ain't gonna be this lion. I'd rather go down on fire than to be caged."

"I ain't scared and caged," Rico shot back. "Being smart ain't being afraid."

"We'll try it your way for now," Hector said. "C'mon, Ernesto—I hate the zoo."

Rico watched his brothers walk away and sighed.

"You didn't tell them that Nunzio asked you about Marty," Jack the Cop said.

"I don't know if Nunzio wanted to see if I trusted him or if I'd rat out my brother. Anyway, if I told them he asked about Marty, what do you think Hector would've done?"

"But you didn't tell Nunzio anything," Jack said.

"I know that. But, what would Hector do?"

"I don't know."

"Me, neither...that's why I didn't tell him."

* * *

Frank, Pompa, and Father Joe walked to the Caffè Fiora on Grand Street. Nunzio had asked them to meet him there. When they arrived, instead of being seated at Nunzio's table, they were shown to the back room, where Nunzio and his friends played cards. Frank assumed—hoped—this was about Mac.

The room lacked the charm of the restaurant. However, in addition to two card tables, several overstuffed chairs, and two couches, it had coffee, a bar, and a buffet. Most importantly, it was private. Natale Ventosa assured them that no one would even check on them.

"So if you need something, buzz." Natale pointed to the phone on the bar.

"Thanks, Sweetheart." Nunzio kissed her cheek and she left. "Help yourself, gentlemen. You know your way around this room as well as I do."

Even though Frank wasn't an official member of the third-Tuesday poker club, he had spent enough time here to feel comfortable.

"What's up, Boss?" Pompa asked.

"Pomp, we're here to talk about Mac," Nunzio said. "I thought about who should be here. Right or wrong, this is what I came up with. So sit, eat, drink, and we'll talk."

After a moment, Nunzio said, "Frankie, everything Willie told you, he believed to be true, and some of it was...and some of it wasn't. For example, Bennie Bets had nothin' to do with it."

Father Joe said, "So what happened, Boss?"

Frank continued to be intrigued by the fact that these men still called Nunzio "Boss." When they had been all kids, his father explained to him that Nunzio had been the boss of their gang.

"I wouldn't admit this to anyone else, but I don't know everything goin' on in my organization—I should, but I don't. Here's what I do know: Gene Viola, Stan Primo, and Bennie Bets all worked for me. So let's first clear up Bennie. Mac owed Bennie three grand. But because Mac was married to Anna, I would not allow Bennie to muscle Mac. And sometimes that pissed Bennie off.

"Now, one day—early December '51—Mac hit the number, got four grand, like Willie said. But Bennie only got three hundred, not three thousand, from Mac. Bennie came to me angry as shit, and I gave him twenty-seven hundred. So, Bennie got three grand but—"

"That's why he was still pissed at Mac," Frank said. "But he told people Mac gave him the three thousand."

"Right. Bennie was a good soldier. He did what I told him." Nunzio lit a cigarette. "Bennie died of a heart attack on Christmas...simple as that."

"Now let's talk about the people who were involved with Mac's disappearance," Nunzio said. "As we all know, following the death of Camillo Zara, his widow, Fabia Zara, and her twelve-year-old daughter, Angie, moved to Naples, Italy. In 1950, Fabia Zara married off Angie to Aldo Emetico, a sixty-year-old international banker and businessman in Naples, for the promise of revenge for the killing of her sons, Iggy and Remo."

"Shit—I never considered Fabia," Frank said. "She was gone."

"I simply felt sad for her," Father Joe added.

"And I believed Viola when he told me the Knights had no role in Mac's disappearance," Nunzio said. "But they did, as

Frankie found out, and Hector was the contact in the Knights, as Angelo learned from Sammy."

"So this banker, Aldo, knew Gene Viola?" Pompa asked.

"Aldo is a close business associate of Timothy Jewels. Jewels handles overseas investments for me and my organization through Gene Viola. Viola vouched for and brought several former Knights into my organization, like Stan Primo and the Tonello brothers."

"So Aldo approached Jewels to help fulfill his promise to Zara?" Frank said.

"Exactly. Aldo put up the money—five thousand dollars—and Jewels brought the deal to Viola, who hired Stan Primo to do the hit. And Stan got Willie Max and Hector to help," Nunzio said. "And, I'm guessing they were all in agreement about the hit on me, although the Tonello brothers never gave Viola up."

"Willie thinks Stan ran out on him," Frank said.

"Christmas Eve 1951, Stan stopped at Gene Viola's, just like Willie told you, Frank. Stan opened the trunk and Viola saw Mac dead. So he gave Stan fifteen hundred."

The three men nodded.

"My guys ain't allowed to freelance. Willie knew that—that's why he figured I okayed it. The truth is, I didn't know any of this until last week. So in January of '52, my guys find Stan's car parked at one of our construction sites on Long Island. At first, they think nothing of it. But the car just sits there, so they get curious and pop the trunk. And there he is—Stan Primo, naked with four bullet holes in his face. The car was like an icebox, so he was pretty well preserved. I figured somebody was tryin' to send me a message. Maybe another family. Who knows?"

"I remember you talking about that back then," Pompa said.

"Me, too," Father Joe said. "You were waiting for something else to happen."

"Yeah, and nothin' ever did. Viola didn't step up and tell me anything 'cause he knew he broke the rules. He just let me worry about it. We weren't gonna call the cops and nobody knew how long the car had been there. So we buried the car with Stan in the trunk, right there, under what is now the Island Bank in Little Neck. Meanwhile, Pete took over for Bennie Bets."

"Wait a minute," Father Joe said. "So where's Mac?"

"I do not know...yet. But I'm bettin' he walked away from there, with Stan's gun, wallet, shirt, pants, and coat."

"Holy shit, you're saying Mac's alive?" Frank said.

"Could be," Nunzio said.

Father Joe asked, "Did any of your guys tell Mac about Fabia—"

"No. Stan didn't know and Gene Viola never saw him again out of the trunk. But I don't know what Mac thinks—if he's alive."

"So, in addition to Mac and us, there are six people who know the hit failed," Frank said.

"Five guys," Nunzio said. "Viola and the guys in this room."

"I was talking about Jewels, Willie, Gene, Aldo, Fabia, Angie...who else?" Frank said. "I'm assuming Viola told—"

"I don't think Viola told anyone. Even Willie didn't know," Nunzio said. "I think he just kept the money and said nothing. So, since Willie's gone, it's just us, Viola, and—if he's alive, Mac—who know the hit failed."

"Gone," Frank repeated.

"Gone."

"If Mac's alive, we need to find out where he is and what he's thinking," Pompa said.

"I talked to Anna back in August," Father Joe said. "I felt like there was something she wouldn't tell me. I asked her, 'Anna, what am I missing?' She said, 'You don't want to know.' A few days later, she told me that she was relieved that Mac was gone. 'No more beatings,' she said. I'm not so sure she wants us to find him, Pomp."

"How many times I wanted to do something...but no, I told myself don't interfere between a husband and wife," Frank said.

"Not just you, Frankie," Nunzio said. "All us tough guys were lookin' the other way."

Everyone nodded.

* * *

Johnny, wearing only pajama pants, stood on his hands, his feet barely touching the wall, as he pushed himself up and down. The moonlight cutting through his window chiseled his rope-like muscles and cast a shadow of a huge scorpion moving in for the kill again and again. Angelo, mesmerized by the image, stood in the doorway of his uncle's room.

Johnny sensed his presence and, without stopping, said, "Come in, Angelo."

"Uncle Johnny, will you teach me to knife fight?" Angelo sat on Uncle Johnny's bed.

Uncle Johnny flipped into a standing position and sat in his chair. "What happened?"

Angelo told him about Jimmy asking for the medallion.

"Why don't you just give him the medallion?"

"I need to think of a way that doesn't make me look like a punk. Will you teach me to—?"

"Go get your toy knives."

Angelo returned with three different rubber knives. "These okay?"

"Perfect. There's two rules about knife fighting. Of course, you should try to avoid a knife fight. But if you can't, then rule one is, you're gonna get cut, so you decide where."

"What?" Angelo said. "But if I win...?"

"You're gonna get cut, even if you win. Second rule has three Ds: distract the dragon, defang the dragon, destroy the dragon. I'll teach you one method of knife fighting. Unless you're plannin' on goin' pro, you don't need more. Okay, take one of the knives and get into a fighting stance."

Angelo picked up a rubber knife and held it loosely in his right hand between his thumb and three fingers with his pinky sticking up. He tossed it from hand to hand.

Uncle Johnny laughed.

"That's how they fight," Angelo said. "Even in the movies about gangs."

"I'm your opponent. What's your target?" Uncle Johnny picked up a rubber knife.

Angelo playfully poked at Uncle Johnny and said, "Your chest, stomach, neck." Angelo tossed his knife to his left hand and before he could catch it, Uncle Johnny caught it and stuck it down the front of Angelo's pants. It was the fastest thing Angelo had ever seen.

"And that's how quickly you could die in a knife fight," Uncle Johnny said.

"Show me what to do."

"Okay. First hold the knife like a spear or an ice pick, not like a sword. Pretend you're gonna stick it in the floor. So, make a fist, like you're boxin'. Good. Hold the knife in your right hand so that the tip is pointin' at the floor, not your face. The sharp edge of the blade is pointed toward your opponent. Open your left hand. Good. Turn your body slightly so that your left shoulder is a little closer to your opponent than your right shoulder. Excellent. Notice you can still punch with both hands. Knife fighting isn't just using knives. It's fighting plus a knife. Punch, kick, elbow, grab, everything...plus a knife."

"What were the three Ds?"

"First is distraction. You saw Liz and Jimmy bopped your nose. He knew you were distracted. Watch his eyes, but don't look at his eyes. He'll trick you. Focus on where his tie knot would be if he was wearin' a tie. But pay attention to everything around you, especially his eyes. The instant he is distracted, you must spring."

"Distracted by what?"

"Anything. A woman shouts from a window. A cat meows. Liz walks by. You'll see it in his eyes. I knew a street fighter who had the words *YOUR MOTHER* tattooed on his stomach. If he was in a tough fight, he'd pick up his shirt and sure as shit, the other guy would read the message and before he could figure out what it meant, he was clocked. Any distraction. But remember—a good fighter is watching you."

"Distraction—distract the dragon. What's the next D?"

"Defang the dragon—disarm him. Your first target is his knife hand. Not his heart, stomach, whatever else you said. Don't go for the kill until he's disarmed. Cut his knife hand," Uncle Johnny said. Turning Angelo's palm up, he added, "On the inside of your forearm here, from your elbow to your pinky, are lots of nerves." Uncle Johnny released Angelo's hand and said, "Hold your knife like your friends on the street."

Angelo went back to his old street stance. And quicker than he could blink, Uncle Johnny grabbed the back of his right hand, rolled it over, and passed his rubber knife over Angelo's right forearm.

"Jeez!" Angelo exclaimed.

"Now you're disarmed," Uncle Johnny said. "The third D is dead or destroy."

Angelo felt Uncle Johnny's rubber knife tip strike the right side of his neck. "I'm dead."

"Practice—you'll get better and faster instead of dead."

CHAPTER TWENTY-SIX

"You can tell a lot about a guy on a roof."

A ngelo couldn't put his finger on it, but the atmosphere felt ominous. He wasn't being pushed or even taunted by Jimmy or the other Knights. But he could feel it just the same. Ju-Ju repeatedly begged him to give up the medallion. He told Angelo he feared something bad would happen. Nothing had—but that was all about to change.

Friday morning, Angelo was with his friends halfway up the steps in front of PS-65 waiting for the bell to announce the start of the school day. At the top of the steps, Jimmy was standing with a group of Knights. And, as usual, Jimmy and Liz were arguing.

"Why does she like him?" Angelo said to no one in particular.

"Girls like bad boys," Howie said.

"Not all girls—" Audrey said, but was silenced by the sound of a slap.

Angelo saw Liz's bloody lip as she fell on the cement steps toward the Weepers. Jimmy shouted incoherently at her, fists tight, as he walked toward Liz. Audrey, followed by Angelo and others, ran toward Liz.

One of the Knights grabbed Jimmy's arm, but he shoved the other guy aside. Audrey reached Liz first and put her arm around her. Angelo, Gina, Tate, Sage, and others followed close behind. Before they could get to Audrey and Liz, Angelo saw Jimmy grab Audrey by the arm and jerk her away from Liz.

Jimmy held Audrey for what seemed to be an eternity as Angelo struggled to get to her. He felt like he did in dreams, when the steps he tried to climb became soft tar sticking and holding him back. Jimmy slapped Audrey on the left side of her face. Audrey fell against Tate and Gina, and the three tumbled into a heap.

Tate scurried to his feet.

Angelo landed a hammer fist to the tip of Jimmy's nose that knocked Jimmy backwards off his feet. Before Angelo could land another punch, several Knights grabbed him. Weepers pushed through to help Angelo. A pulsating commotion crowded the steps of PS-65.

"Let me go," Angelo barked. "You're a punk-ass coward, Jimmy. You're real tough with girls and bums. Let go."

"Hey, Jimmy, the kid sounded on you bad, man." One of the Knights reached down to help Jimmy up. "He sounded on you. Your nose is bleedin', man."

"Hold it! Hold up!" Jimmy screamed, his voice cracked. He rubbed his face and stared for a moment at the blood on his hands. "You little fuck. You're dead. I don't give a shit what Rico or nobody says. Me and you, right now...but not here. I don't want nobody stoppin' it. No bell, no teacher, nothin'."

Angelo could see Audrey through the crowd holding the side of her face and crying. He looked back at Jimmy. Pure rage focused Angelo. He looked across the street, pointed to the roof of the red brick tenement directly across from PS-65, and said, "That roof, now."

Angelo pushed through the crowd and toward the tenement. Tate, three other Weepers, and Jimmy with a dozen Knights followed.

Angelo heard Jimmy say, "I'm gonna kill this little shit—I mean it. Four of you guys stay down here on the stoop. Don't let nobody up 'til I come down."

Weepers and Knights stepped out onto the roof with some caution, except for Angelo. He was first to hit the roof and he felt like he had just come up from underwater. He was home. He quickly looked around. There were no guardrails. The roof sloped up slightly toward the edge, but nothing to hold you back. The borders of this roof were defined by the edge facing PS-65, the other roofs of varying heights, and alleys of different widths. This was Angelo's kind of roof. He could tell Jimmy was uncomfortable.

"Okay, here's what we're gonna do," Jimmy said. "Weepers and Knights will make a circle in the middle of the roof, like a boxing ring."

Angelo walked away from Jimmy and right to the edge facing PS-65. He saw Audrey and all the other kids looking up. Someone pointed at him and a loud cheer rose from the street.

Angelo turned his back to the street, still standing on the edge, and reached out to Jimmy. "Come take your bow, Jimmy."

"After I kick your ass." Jimmy motioned for Angelo to join him in the center of the roof.

"Come kick my ass. I'll even close my eyes." Angelo spread his arms apart.

"You're crazy. You're gonna fall." Jimmy looked at the Knights. "He's gonna fall."

"You afraid of the edge?" Angelo said. "You can tell a lot about a guy on a roof."

"Jimmy, he sounded on you again, man," a Knight said.

Jimmy walked toward Angelo, fast at first, but slower as he got near the edge. He inched up to the rim of the roof a few feet to Angelo's right. Jimmy looked down. Cheers came up. He backed away from the edge and moved sideways toward Angelo.

This was not what Angelo envisioned. He wanted Jimmy next to him—facing each other—both on the edge. He took a deep breath and squeezed his eyes shut. He let his breath out slowly and opened his eyes halfway.

They could reach out and touch each other's fingertips. Angelo's back was to the street. *Look at his neck but pay attention to his eyes. Breathe.*

Jimmy pulled a gravity knife out of his pocket and flicked it open.

Angelo turned slightly sideways with his left side closer to Jimmy. He searched for his knife with sweaty fingertips. He couldn't find the pull ribbon. *It must have twisted when the Knights grabbed me.*

Jimmy smiled.

Angelo put most of his weight on his right foot, which was closest to the edge. So close that the back of his right heel was dead even with the brim of the roof. He drew his left foot closer to his right. His knees were bent in what Uncle Johnny called a cat stance.

Angelo's left hand was open. His right hand was wet with sweat and twisting as his fingers struggled to find the ribbon under the sleeve of his jacket. He needed to release Merlin.

Jimmy poked the knife at Angelo.

Angelo almost instinctively backed up. *Don't forget the edge of the roof.* He slapped Jimmy's right hand away with his left hand.

Jimmy was becoming bolder. Getting closer. He poked at Angelo's stomach, trying to make him back up and off the roof. Angelo took a cut on his chest. Jimmy smiled.

Jimmy inched closer to Angelo with the point of his knife leading the way.

Angelo heard the roof door bang open and without taking his eyes off Jimmy's neck, he saw a Knight charge onto the roof, look around, and then run over and stop right behind Jimmy.

"Jimmy, you better finish this quick," the Knight said. "Two of Nunzio Sabino's guys pushed their way through downstairs and are on their way up."

Angelo kept his focus on Jimmy's neck but watched for the slightest distraction.

Jimmy pressed the knifepoint against Angelo's chest, as if to hold Angelo right there. And then Jimmy's eyes went to his left to see the messenger and the door to the roof. His head moved just a fraction.

The first D—distraction.

Angelo fired his right arm under Jimmy's right arm and raised it in a clockwise circle with such force that Jimmy's knife hand crossed over his left arm. And in that moment, Angelo crouched low and stepped past Jimmy's right side with his left foot.

Jimmy started his swing back to his right as Angelo stomped on the outside of Jimmy's right ankle with the side of his right foot, causing Jimmy to screech in pain and wobble to his right. At the same time, Angelo drove his right elbow into Jimmy's lower back.

Jimmy lurched forward and right. He stumbled. Jimmy twisted, trying to stop. His knife dropped and stuck in the tar at the lip of the roof. Angelo saw panic and embarrassment in his eyes. It was the look of someone who just slipped on ice in front of a crowd. Jimmy's mouth opened wide as momentum caused him to step off the roof.

"Bye, bye, Jimmy." Angelo smirked and rushed to the edge in time to see Jimmy falling face to the sky. Jimmy's eyes were wide and straining to the side, as if he wanted to see where he was going. His arms seemed to reach for the roof edge and his fingers were spread apart. His mouth contorted into a silent scream.

A fire escape waited below him. The outside iron railing of the fourth-floor fire escape caught Jimmy across the lower back. He made a strange explosive sound, like air rushing from a balloon. He flipped forward, his knees cracked on the iron floor, and he tumbled head first through the stairwell opening. Jimmy's face bounced on the iron steps, his neck jerking back again and again, as his limp body raced down the punishing steps. His arms twisted absurdly as he smashed into the third-floor fire escape landing. He stopped there. Impossibly distorted.

Angelo was mesmerized. In all the times he imagined himself falling, he never thought it would be so horrific...so real. Still, all he felt was relief. "Come kick my ass, Jimmy."

"You okay, Angelo?" Tate asked as he pulled Jimmy's knife out of the tar, closed it, and offered it to Angelo.

"Keep it," Angelo said, still standing there. Through the corner of his eye, he could see two men standing near the door.

A scream came from the third floor apartment.

"Angelo, we better get outta here," Tate said. "You okay?"

The Knights ran down the stairway of the tenement. The Weepers waited for Angelo.

"Yeah, I'm good," Angelo said.

"Okay, let's get off this roof before the cops get here." Tate started toward the door the Knights had used, where the Weepers were waiting.

"Not that way," Angelo said. "There's going to be tenants, police, and teachers all hangin' around that stoop to grab anybody comin' out. Follow me. We'll come out of a different tenement, one that's down the street and around the corner. Then we'll walk back over to school like we don't know nothing'."

"Kid's smart—follow him," one of Uncle Nunzio's guys said. "We'll go down the building next door, that roof over there, and make sure nobody says nothin' about you guys."

"C'mon." Angelo ran across the roofs and the Weepers followed him.

* * *

Timothy Jewels always treasured his visits to the ancient seaside city of Pozzuoli, Italy. Because of its beauty, and because it was a time to relax and enjoy the company of Aldo Emetico, his old friend and business associate. But this time was different. Gene Viola was concerned about the sudden disappearance of Willie Max, who could connect him to the hit on Mac. Then there was the botched attempt by the Tonello brothers to kill Nunzio Sabino. This wasn't a time to panic, it was simply a time to make plans and get everyone's story aligned. While Jewels was in Italy, Viola would fly back to New York from California and smooth any ruffled feathers Nunzio might have. Viola was always good at that.

After arriving at Aldo's home, dropping his bag in the guest room, and freshening up, Jewels joined Aldo, Fabia, and Adele, a young woman from Aldo's bank, in the large front room. Aldo and Jewels sat in leather chairs facing the two women on the sofa. Two dozen candles provided the only light in the room. The dark walls were filled with original oils of the Bay of Naples.

"Aldo, your precautions are premature," Jewels said.

"Maybe. For now, I got my wife a new name, and I'm moving her to London. She has a job waiting for her in the branch of my bank there, plus an apartment and a bank account all in her new name. No one at the London bank knows who she really is."

"What is that heavenly aroma?" Jewels asked.

"Angie's favorite antipasto is in the oven," Fabia said. "Two minutes, they'll be done."

"Where is Angie?" Jewels asked.

"She is upstairs packing a bag. Adele here will accompany Angie—I mean, Heather Potter"—Fabia smirked—"to London to help get her settled. And I will join her when my new papers are ready...one or two days."

"Fabia, you must stop telling people Angie's new name," Aldo said.

"Please, this is Timothy," Fabia said. "She should be down any minute. Wait 'til you see her red hair...she is beautiful."

"This is all so unnecessary," Jewels said. "Viola will handle this."

"Good," Aldo said. "Then everyone will come home. Let's drink to unnecessary caution. Roberto!"

"Yes, sir. *Cosa posso fare per te?*" Roberto said.

Jewels recognized Roberto as Aldo's driver and servant of many years. "It is good to see you, Roberto."

"*Grazie*, Mr. Jewels. *E anche voi.*"

"Roberto, *portare una bottiglia del mio miglior grappa*," Aldo said, and then to Jewels he said, "I asked him to bring us my best bottle—"

"Of grappa." Jewels smiled. "I got the grappa."

"You look tired, Timothy," Fabia said. "Was travel difficult?"

"It was long, but comfortable."

"I better check on my antipasto—we can't have them burn—"

"*Mi scusi, chi vuole che la grappa?*" The man walking into the room with the bottle of grappa and a gun was not Roberto.

Adele yelped.

"Shhh, *silenzio*," the man said.

Aldo stood up. "*Chi sei?*"

Jewels stood up. "What's going on? Where's Roberto?"

"Are you American?" the man asked.

"Yes. Who are you?" Jewels asked.

"I am Lanzo Basso, and I will try to speak English for you."

"I'm Aldo Emetico, the banker, and this is my home."

"I know who you are," Basso said.

"Do I know you?" Aldo asked.

"I am Gomorrah."

"My God...where's Roberto?"

"Dead...like you."

The *thub-thub* from the silenced gun knocked Aldo back into his large chair. Blood splashed on the front of his white shirt and trickled down his face from the hole in his forehead. With one loud and final exhale, Aldo's chin hit his chest.

"No, please, spare my daughter, Angie." Fabia threw her arms around Adele.

"No, no, I'm...my na—" Adele's words were cut short by two more thubs, one for Fabia's forehead and one for Adele's left eye.

Jewels watched the two women fall into a tangled, bloody bundle and wondered if Adele's unwitting sacrifice would save Angie's life. "Hold it! Stop! I'm Timothy Jewels, and I work for a very powerful man in America, so you bet—"

"Signor Nunzio Sabino said to say hello," Basso said. "And goodbye. *Ciao e ciao.*"

Jewels smelled burning antipasto but did not hear the next thub.

* * *

Nunzio's car pulled up behind Viola's car at the arrival exits at Idlewild Airport.

"Mike, you stay with the car." Nunzio turned to the two men in the back seat. "You guys wait over there by the doors."

"You want an umbrella, Boss?" Mike asked.

"Nah, it's only a drizzle."

Viola's driver, Victor, was holding an open umbrella and leaning against the front fender facing the airport doors as Nunzio pushed through a crowd of travelers and walked up to him.

"Victor, let's sit in your car a minute," Nunzio said.

"Holy Jesus, Boss, you surprised me," Victor said. "Sure, Mr. Sabino, whatever you say."

After the two men climbed into Viola's car, Nunzio said, "How long have you been Viola's driver?"

"Twenty-six years."

"Where are your loyalties?"

"To you, Mr. Sabino."

"Who do you work for?"

"You."

"You okay with a new position in my organization, maybe with more money?"

"More money, less money, I do what you say."

"*Benissimo*," Nunzio said. "You bring Viola out and put him in the backseat. I'll be back there. You see those two big guys near the airport doors?"

"Yes."

"That's Anthony and Donato. They will be riding with us. You will just follow Mike. Don't say nothing to Viola about me being out here. It's a surprise, okay?"

"Okay, Mr. Sabino. He's coming, so I go get him now."

"Good."

After a few minutes, Victor and Viola walked out of the airport. Victor put Viola's suitcase in the trunk and then opened the back door for Viola, who started to get in but then stopped when he saw Nunzio. Anthony was now behind Viola and gave him a small push. Viola sat between Nunzio and Anthony. Donato sat up front with Victor.

"Victor, let Mike pull around in front of you and then just follow him."

"Yes, sir, Boss."

"Welcome home, Gene," Nunzio said.

"Nunzio, I came back early to fix everything. It's all a big misunderstanding. First, I—"

"Shut up, Gene. I want to enjoy the ride."

The five men traveled in silence. Nunzio looked out the window—all the traffic, flashing lights, the sounds of horns and sirens all covered with rain. This mess meant nothing if you could see through it. This was his life and he loved it.

After twenty minutes, Viola said, "Nunzio, please, let me talk to you."

"What about?"

"I know a couple of my guys messed up," Viola said. "But I'm on top of it. Where are we going?"

"We're almost there."

"Where?"

"Are you a child? Shhh."

After a couple of minutes, Viola said, "Look, I know I need to cut Jewels. He's the—"

"Did you enjoy California, Gene?" Nunzio said. "I bet it beats this chilly rain."

"What? Yes...Nunzio, we've been friends...together, for thirty years."

"I know. Remember when you first came to work for me, you said, 'Nunzio, you can have any car you want—why do you drive a DeSoto?' You remember?"

"Yeah, you said you trusted the DeSoto."

"No. I said, I don't do the driving. Mike does, and I trust Mike."

"I don't get the difference."

"I know," Nunzio said. "We're here."

"Bruno's Salvage Yard?"

"Yeah, now you get to pick your favorite car. Look around, any car you want. Chevy, Ford, I don't see a DeSoto, but there's a Cadillac over there. You want the Cadillac, Gene?"

The rain was now less than a drizzle and the air smelled like wet tar and diesel fuel.

Anthony and Donato wrestled Viola to the ground and wrapped and rolled him in a large tarp. "Where do you want him, Boss?"

"Since he ain't picking, put him in the Chevy—it's closest." Nunzio had a salty, bitter taste in his mouth.

"Nunzio, please, at least talk to—"

"Lay him on the backseat and throw his suitcase in there with him," Nunzio said.

"Jesus, there's a shitload of roaches in this car," Anthony said.

"No, not with the roaches!" Viola shouted.

"Are you shittin' me?" Nunzio said. "Because of you, they're gonna lose their home and maybe die. They should be yelling to keep you out, you piece of shit. Put him in there."

"Nunzio, I can help you. I know some stuff," Viola said.

"Gene, I'm gonna shoot you in the eyes so these roaches can hide in your head when we crush your corpse in this car. *È fottuto traditore*. Give me that towel for splatter."

Nunzio put the towel over Viola's face and pressed the barrel of the gun hard against his right eye. "This one first."

"Nunzio! Please! Nun—"

Nunzio didn't use a silencer. He wanted all the noise the gun could make.

* * *

Frank opened the door of Lilly's just as his father walked up. Nunzio and Father Joe got out of Nunzio's Cadillac carrying a box of pastries and walked toward Frank.

"Got some hot coffee in there, Frankie?" Nunzio asked.

"Just made a pot." Frank locked the front door after the men were in, put the Closed—be back in an hour sign on it, and pulled the shade. "Is this about Mac?"

"He's alive. He's in Italy," Nunzio said.

Pompa said, "All this time. Alive."

"Coffee. I'll get the coffee." Frank poured four cups of coffee and put a bottle of brandy on the round table in the front of the store.

Father Joe opened the box of pastries and took out a piece of rum cake. "It would appear that he has been in hiding for fear that his family would be in danger if Bennie Bets knew he was alive. I guess the news of Bennie's death hadn't reached him."

"How do we know this?" Frank asked.

"I know it." Nunzio took a cannoli out of the box. "Pomp, I got an idea. Before we say anything to Anna about Mac bein' alive, we need to know what Mac has become. Which is hard to do from here. So one of us must go to Italy and talk to Mac. Face to face, and that person is Father Joe."

"Why me?"

"First, it can't be me. Mac might think I'm the guy who wants him dead. If either Frankie or Pomp go, everybody—including Anna—is gonna wanna know why. But Father Joe goin' to Rome, everybody's gonna say, 'How nice.'"

"Why not tell Anna?" Frank asked.

Nunzio said, "Once we tell her, she's gonna start askin' questions. 'What's he doin'?' 'What's he like?' 'Whaddaya think he wants to do?' 'Maybe I should go see him.' Stuff like that, and right now, we got no answers for her. So I give Father Joe two round-trip tickets. One ticket for New York to Rome and back, and the other ticket for Rome to New York and back."

He continued. "Father Joe talks to Mac. If he thinks it would be best for Anna if Mac came back, and if that's what Mac wants to do, he gives him the ticket. Mac's flight from Rome is the same as Father Joe's return. That way, we know if he's coming. If, after he gets here, Anna says no, then he can stay in this country or use the ticket to fly back. But Anna don't have to say nothin' until Joe checks out Mac, and Mac decides he wants back. Whatever happens, one of us will tell Anna about Mac as soon as Father Joe gets back."

"Where is Mac?"

"He's in Costafabbri."

"I know the town—it's just outside Siena," Father Joe said.

"There's an *osteria* on the main road," Nunzio said. "A friend of a friend, Luca Cipriano, owns it. Mac has breakfast there every Thursday and Friday morning at eight."

"When do I go?"

"If we are in agreement, you'll be in Rome on Monday. I figured Rome, in case you wanted to visit your rabbi at the Vatican."

"Okay with me."

"Good. A car, driver, and bodyguard will meet you at the airport. They'll take you anyplace you wanna go. They'll arrange for hotels, restaurants, anything you need. Wherever you are, they will be sure to get you to Costafabbri on Thursday for breakfast. The driver and bodyguard both know Luca. You will leave for New York from Rome on Friday."

"I still have family in Pienza. It's a beautiful city in the sky." Father Joe lit a cigarette. "It's not far from Costafabbri. Maybe I'll go there on Wednesday."

"That's the town with the church that's gonna fall off the mountain?" Nunzio said.

"That's the one. But only half the church."

"Listen," Frank said, "I have to tell you—I'm willing to say the past is the past. But if he touches her again, I'll kill him. He needs to know that before he comes back."

"I'm her father; I'm the one who'll—"

"I owe Angelo my life. So, no offense, but I'm better at this kinda thing than any you guys," Nunzio said. "The past is the past, but he lays a hand on Anna or her boys, he will disappear forever. Period. So, whaddaya say?"

Everyone nodded.

"I'll pass along the warmth expressed here when I see Mac." Father Joe laughed with the other men. "You guys keep an eye on Casimiro while I'm gone. Don't let him hurt anybody."

Frank smiled and nodded. And then to Nunzio he said, "I heard you bought the shoemaker's shop next door. The windows and door are all covered and it sounds like—"

"I'm building a liquor store. I heard they need a good one on the block." Nunzio winked.

* * *

At 5:30 p.m., Rico walked into the Knights' apartment, grabbed a beer, and slumped in a chair in the living room. Hector, Ernesto, Ronnie, and several other Knights were sitting around drinking and smoking.

"What am I missing?" Rico said. "I just finished telling Nunzio we would follow the rules. Now I find out Jimmy had a knife fight with Angelo. What the hell's going on?"

"Jimmy just went nuts," Ernesto said. "He's dead."

"Dead?"

"Yeah, Jimmy's the one that's dead, not Angelo."

"Thank God," Rico said.

Hector shook his head. "Your cop friend have any news about the Marty thing?"

"Shit, I forgot all about Jack." Rico stood up. "I saw him on my way in. He said he has something. I told him to wait and I'd see if you and Ernesto were around. Come on."

Rico and his brothers joined Jack in his car, which was parked along the projects on South Street.

"What's the news, Jack?" Hector asked once the car was moving.

"I'll just drive around the block so nobody interrupts us. It's not much, but it's good. I know Nunzio said he could make the Marty thing go away, but I was doubtful. I didn't figure even Nunzio had the power to make a cop killing disappear. But yesterday, I see this detective, his name is Hartz—he's been looking into the Bookman fire and Marty—anyway, he's pissed. Turns out, the brass just told him to drop the Marty investigation. They told him it was closed."

"Yeah?" Hector said.

"Yeah. I guess he needed somebody to talk to. Anyway, he tells me they reassigned him to look into Nunzio Sabino. Evidently, Sabino is expanding his operation. I didn't push him. I just said, 'If there's anything I can do to help, just give me a call.' He thanked me. That's it."

"So not only is the Marty thing cold," Rico said, "but we might get inside information to pass along to Nunzio."

"Exactly." Jack pulled up to where he had picked up the Cruz brothers. "Guys, this is good."

"Yeah, great, but I still want my medallion back," Ernesto grumbled. "Maybe that Ju-Ju kid will get it without breaking your freakin' rules, Rico—I told him to ask Angelo."

* * *

Angelo walked into the dance with his friends. He was aware of eyes following him and hushed conversation. The story going around was that Jimmy was showing off on the roof this morning before school and just fell—a sad, but not uncommon, accident. He wondered how many knew about the fight. His emotions bounced from fear to excitement and back to fear. He thought about Jimmy and wondered what would happen next.

"Ju-Ju wants to talk to you about trading the medallion for something," Spiro said.

"Ernesto has this great baseball card collection goin' back to '51," Howie said. "Or trade it for a couple of their jackets—we need Weeper jackets."

"You don't want their jackets," Father Casimiro said, walking up to them. "You guys should get your own. I heard about Jimmy falling off the roof this morning—how awful."

"Is Uncle Nunzio here tonight?" Angelo said.

"Maybe later. So have you decided on your club's colors?"

Angelo said, "Maybe purple with gray letters—you know, outlined in black so they stand out—and a golden teardrop."

The Weepers nodded.

"Nice. I'll tell you something, if I were a kid in this neighborhood, I'd want to hang out with you guys. I'd want to be a Weeper," Father Casimiro said.

"Really, how come?" Angelo exchanged smiles with his friends.

"Look at you guys. You have Negroes, Spanish, Italian, Irish...everything in just twelve kids. And you really care about each other. The world could learn something from you guys," Father Casimiro said as he walked away to rejoin Father Joe.

The music was playing and soon Audrey showed up with her friends. They didn't hesitate; they joined Angelo and the guys. They were a group.

As Angelo listened to Tate telling the girls what Father Casimiro said, he felt he was heading toward something important, something that would change him forever. He noticed Audrey looking at him. He returned her smile. They danced.

"I think Liz really likes you," Audrey said.

"Nah, she's older than me," Angelo said.

"That doesn't matter. Don't you think she's pretty?"

"She's okay. She's always wearing those neckerchiefs like Dale Evans."

"Dale Evans? Those are hickey scarves...forget it, let's just dance."

Angelo considered asking Audrey to go steady. He feared it would scare her away. Ruin everything. Like Tate said—at least now, there's the dream.

* * *

As he rejoined Father Joe, Father Casimiro thought about the line between good and bad that once seemed so clear. Not here, not anymore. Nunzio Sabino helped St. Joachim, and his presence at the Friday-night social attracted lots of gang members, and those were good things. Father Casimiro felt himself changing, growing. For the first time in his life, he believed he was living on purpose.

Father Casimiro thought about the first time he had seen Angelo standing on the edge of that roof. So alone. "Why does Angelo stand on the edge, Joe?"

"As I promised his mother, I talked to Angelo about that and other stuff. My guess is that his entire relationship with his father was on the edge."

"But how can that be comforting?"

"Because it's familiar. I think the edge reminds him of how he felt around his father. It feels like his father."

CHAPTER TWENTY-SEVEN

*"If you drop a rock into the East River,
the ripples will go all the way to Italy."*

Before Father Joe left for Italy, he told Father Casimiro about meeting Mac there. It was agreed that information would go no further.

Father Joe spent his first night in Italy at the Vatican. He dined and talked with old friends. He spent Tuesday evening and Wednesday morning in Pienza. He loved Pienza's piazza, with its town hall. He embraced family still living in this breathtaking small city in the sky. It was 53 degrees and a light rain had just ended. Father Joe looked over the wall and was awestruck by a rainbow between him and the valley. "I am actually somewhere over the rainbow," he said to himself and smiled. It was as beautiful as he remembered.

Father Joe spent Wednesday night in Siena. He walked the red-brick Campo to Siena's black-and-white-marble duomo, the magnificent cathedral. He prayed there and then dined with his bodyguard, Giordano, and driver, Naldo, in a converted Carthusian monastery, now a restaurant on Via Certosa in Siena. The meal of ribollita—a thick, rich soup of cabbage, beans, herbs, and vegetables—and arosto misto—mixed meats and spicy sausage—was unhurried and delicious.

The next morning, they drove along a dusty, winding road. They stopped briefly to avoid several wild boars in their path. Father Joe took in the Tuscan countryside rolling past him—the tall, black-jade cypress trees standing guard over fields promising red poppies in the spring. This charming painting was simply the road to Costafabbri.

At 8:20 a.m., Father Joe's car reached the osteria owned by Luca Cipriano in Costafabbri. Naldo pulled off the road and down the driveway to the left of the osteria.

"I will wait here with the car, Father," Naldo said. "Giordano will go in with you."

Giordano led Father Joe back up the pebble and dirt incline to the front door of the *osteria*. It was a misty morning and although cool, it wasn't as chilly as his beautiful Pienza. Father Joe heard the car turning around so that they would be facing the road when he was ready to leave. He wondered if all this precaution was necessary. After all, he was just a priest. They walked past the open window to the kitchen and Father Joe was pleasantly surprised by the tranquil aroma of tomato sauce at this hour. But this was Italy and the smell of basil, olives, and leisure perfumed the air.

Giordano pulled open the door and entered in front of Father Joe. The *osteria* was dimly lit with a long, olivewood bar to the left and a couple of tables along the right wall. Beyond the tables to the right was a doorway, behind the bar on the left was another doorway, and straight ahead was the bathroom. The tables were empty. Two men sat at the bar talking to the bartender. They stopped and looked at Giordano and Father Joe.

"Luca, *vieni*," the bartender called over his shoulder.

A pleasant, slim man in his thirties entered from the room behind the bar. He looked at the priest and Giordano for a moment and then said, "*Prete*, ah, Sir Nunzio Sabino?"

Sir, Father Joe thought. That's reserved for royalty. Not bad, old friend.

"*Si, signore*," said Giordano. "Luca Cipriano?"

"*Si*." Luca walked over, bowed to Father Joe, and pointed to the door beyond the tables.

"The man you are looking for, Father, is in the dining room through that door," Giordano said. "I will sit at a table near the door away from you. But close enough to watch. Okay?"

Luca walked into the dining room first and pulled a small table and one chair near the door for Giordano.

"I bring caffé," Luca said to Giordano.

"*Mille grazie*."

The dining room was stark. No pictures. No decorations. Just a large, square room with a dozen tables. In addition to

Giordano, only two tables were occupied. Five men played cards at a table near the back of the room. A man sat alone at a table in the front corner near a window.

Luca nodded toward the man sitting alone.

"*Grazie.*" Father Joe smiled and walked toward Mac.

Mac gave no indication that he was aware of Father Joe approaching. He remained hunched over a flat dish of tomato gravy, tearing bread with his hands. A chunk of cheese and a cup of coffee rested to the right of his plate. A cigarette burned in an ashtray to his left. He read a narrowly folded English-language newspaper.

"Mac," Father Joe said. There were three empty chairs at the square table; Father Joe selected the one across from Mac. He wanted to look directly into his eyes as they talked. Father Joe was aware that Luca had followed him. "Luca, please get me whatever he's having."

Mac stared at Father Joe as Luca bowed and left.

"Father Joe?" Mac's eyes slid to the bodyguard, then back to Father Joe.

"Mac, I came here to talk with you."

"I know you're not here to kill me." Mac put down the newspaper and took the cigarette out of the ashtray. He tapped off the long ash and took a deep drag.

"All the people involved in the attempt to kill you are dead." Father Joe lit a cigarette.

"Bennie?"

"Dead, but he had nothing to do with it."

"Nunzio?"

"Nunzio had nothing to do with it, either. But a couple of his guys and the Zara family did, and when Nunzio found out, he cleared the deck." Father Joe blew smoke in the air. He stared for a moment at the scar running from above Mac's left eye, splitting his eyebrow, continuing down to his cheek, and turning toward his left ear. "That's a hell of a scar."

"You should see the other guy."

"I heard."

"I can't believe you're here. You wouldn't be shitting me about Nunzio?"

"If Nunzio wanted you dead, the gentleman sitting alone near the door would have danced with you a long time ago. I didn't come all this way to bullshit you."

Luca delivered food and coffee to Father Joe and disappeared again.

"Tell me about Anna and the boys."

"Not *the* boys, *your* boys. Your sons. Angelo and Adam." Father Joe stared into Mac's eyes. "They're great kids, and you don't deserve them or Anna, for that matter." Father Joe looked toward heaven and shook his head. "The boys?"

"Please tell me about Anna, Angelo, Adam, my brother, everybody. Everything."

For almost an hour, Father Joe filled in the history of time lost.

"I suppose Anna's remarried by now."

"She should be. But she's not."

"How's my brother doin'?"

"Okay...he has some problems, but Anna is taking care of him."

"Anna is?"

"She promised you she would, so she's doing it. When Johnny came home, we all told her she had enough to do raising two kids all alone, she didn't need the extra...well, you know Anna—she promised you she would take care of your brother and that was that."

"Does she know you're here talking to me?"

"No. Anna doesn't know if you're dead or living with your mistress. And Angelo, your son, blames himself for your disappearance—he thinks he should have taken better care of you when he was seven. He still walks over to that spot on Cherry Street trying to find you." Tears welled up in Father Joe's eyes. He took a long drag on his cigarette, then sighed the smoke out in a stream. "How have you been these years, Mac?"

"I always thought I'd live forever. That there would be time to make amends for what I've done. That Anna would understand, forgive me, and love me like when we first got married. And then one day I looked in the mirror and saw me. What the hell happened to my life?"

"You. The guy you saw in the mirror—you—happened to your life. Mac, you and Anna were friends since you were kids. I was there, I remember. Best friends madly in love. After what happened to Anna, you could have been a standup guy and helped her through the tough times, the nightmares. But instead, you decided to add to her nightmares. You could have embraced your son, been a real man, a father. You could have helped him grow up in the projects that he feared. But instead, you decided to add to his fears. For some reason, that truly surprised me—you decided to wallow in self-pity and take your anger out on Anna and Angelo. You had a choice, Mac. And you picked asshole. That's who you saw in the mirror."

"I forgot what it's like talking to you. You never pulled your punches, not in the ring and—"

"And not with the people I love. And no one's ever tested my love the way you did. So, are you still an asshole or what?"

"Funny thing, that night six years ago when me and Angelo were walking with the cart full of presents, it was like I saw him for the first time. This sweet kid trying so hard to get close to me. Happy. Catching snowflakes on his tongue. I decided enough's enough, I have to change."

Father Joe recalled Anna telling him that Mac never said a kind word to Angelo, except the night he disappeared, when Mac told Angelo he was a good kid. "Then why did you leave?"

"The guy who shot me missed twice—well, he really didn't miss, as you can see—but neither bullet was fatal. This one was a ricochet." Mac ran his thumb along the scar on his face. "The one in my chest, he fired down into the trunk. In and out, it left two holes in me. Blood but not much damage—I wiped the blood all over my face. He drove me to some guy who looked in the trunk. I played dead—nobody checked my pulse...nothin'. *Stupido.*

He went on. "Then he drove me to a construction site. Opened the trunk and this idiot grabs me with both hands to pull me out. I open my eyes and I'm lookin' at his heat right there, stuck in his pants in front of me. I grab it, make him undress 'cause my clothes are bloody. I put him in the trunk. He told me he worked for Nunzio, and that if I killed him, my whole family would die. Then he told me he could get me a deal. I told him goodbye and shot him, I don't know how many times."

"Four times in the face," Father Joe said.

"Right. I closed the trunk and changed clothes. I took his wallet; this guy had over fifteen hundred bucks on him. I threw the gun and my clothes down the construction pit and covered them with snow, dirt, and rocks. I washed off my face, chest, and hands in the snow."

"Okay, but why leave the country?"

"'I figured if I disappeared, they'd think I was dead and they'd leave Anna and Angelo alone. So I bought my way into Italy. Worked the docks up in Genova for a couple of years. Made friends with a guy who's converting estates into tourist housing down here. He gave me a construction job." Mac lit a cigarette. "I wish I knew nine, ten years ago how good I had it. How good my life was. When I get blue, I just remind myself that once upon a time, Anna loved me. That's more than most guys ever get."

"That's true."

"You think she ever thinks about me?"

"What are you asking me? If she misses the guy she married? Yes, I think she does. But not the guy who beat her and her little boy," Father Joe said. "Have you remarried?"

"Me, no. I keep looking for Anna in every—well, you know."

"But when you were with Anna, you had a couple of girl-friends."

"Not at first. After the thing, everything changed."

"The thing? The rape and beating happened to Anna, not you, Mac. And then you happened to Anna and that was 'the thing' that caused everything to change. You. Am I getting through to you? I'm only going to say this one more time—Anna was in love and married to her best friend. When she needed him most, he crawled into a bottle and a mistress. You stopped being her best friend. It was you, Mac, not the Zara brothers, who changed everything." Father Joe signaled for Luca and ordered some brandy.

"You're right," Mac said. "She needed me and I acted like an asshole. I wish you would've kicked me in the ass back then."

"Me, too. In fact, Nunzio, Pompa, Frankie, and I all accept some responsibility for not breaking your arms and legs years ago. And we have vowed never to let any man, and I mean any man, strike Anna or her boys again."

Father Joe nodded to Luca as he delivered a bottle of brandy and two glasses. Luca cleared the table and left. Father Joe poured brandy in both glasses. He handed one to Mac, they raised their glasses, and then swallowed the warm, soothing liquid. "Frankly, I don't think Anna would put up with it again."

"So who else knows I'm alive and in Italy?"

"Nunzio, Pompa, Frankie, and me. I'll tell Anna when I get back."

"What will you tell her?"

"I don't know, Mac. I really don't know."

"Will you tell her how sorry I am? And that I will die loving her the way she loved me before—before I picked asshole?"

"I'll tell her you said that, Mac." Father Joe pulled an envelope out of his jacket pocket and placed it on the table. "I'm leaving for New York tomorrow. I'll have coffee here at seven in the morning and then my car will take me to Rome."

"Father Joe, there's no way I can go back. Too much time. Too much of an—"

"Let me finish." Father Joe put two cigarettes in his mouth as Mac nodded and poured more brandy in both glasses.

Father Joe lit both cigarettes and handed one Mac, who sat back to listen.

"In this envelope is a round-trip ticket to New York and all the necessary papers you'll need, compliments of Nunzio. If you want to come back, I want to know why. Meet me here at seven tomorrow morning and you can tell me. If you come to New York, you will stay with me. I will talk to Anna. If she wants to see you, fine. If she doesn't, that's that. You can return to Italy or do whatever you want."

"Father Joe—"

"Shhh, I don't want to know now. Because it's not just up to you, it's up to me. So take the night to think about it." Father Joe pushed the envelope to Mac. "Take this—if you don't come, cash in the ticket and keep the money."

Father Joe stood up and so did Mac.

"Thanks for comin', Father Joe. I miss you."

"It's good to see you, Mac. I miss you, too." Father Joe embraced and kissed Mac on both cheeks.

Giordano stood as Father Joe walked toward him.

* * *

Rico heard the 7:00 a.m. foghorn and inhaled a salty sea breeze as he and Jack Stipple walked along the projects side of South Street. They talked about the need to control Hector and Ernesto if they hoped to get a bigger piece of Nunzio's pie.

Rico was startled by a black Cadillac Brougham that came to a sudden stop alongside them. "Nunzio's car," he said unnecessarily.

The front passenger window lowered and Nunzio's driver, Mike, leaned across the front seat and said, "You, get in."

Rico and Jack moved toward the car. Rico squinted, trying to see through the dark, tinted window as he reached for the back door.

"Just Rico, and in the front. You're ridin' shotgun, pal," Mike said. And then to Jack, he said, "You, cop, stand over there so I can see you. Make sure nobody bothers us."

The window went up and Rico climbed into the front passenger seat. As he did, he saw Nunzio sitting behind the driver and noticed a guy hidden in the shadows behind the passenger seat—his seat. He figured the guy behind him was probably one of Nunzio's captains. Rico knew this was not good. The driver, with a newspaper on his lap, twisted in his seat to face him. Rico was certain there was a gun under the newspaper and one in his back. He checked the car doors. He could jump out if he needed to, he thought. If he had enough time.

The doors locked. The car didn't move.

"Where you two guys goin'?" Nunzio asked.

"Me and Jack always have breakfast at the South Street Diner on Thursdays."

"Breakfast...Thursday," Nunzio mumbled. "Mike, what time is it in Italy right now?"

"Um, around 1:00 p.m., Boss. I think it's about six hours later there. You thinkin' about the breakfast meeting? It's done by now."

"*Bene*," Nunzio said, and then to Rico, "The kid who fell off the roof...he was a Knight?"

Rico started to turn as he said, "Jimmy Bowman, yeah, he's dead—"

"Don't turn around. Talk to the windshield," Nunzio said.

"I understand he fell tryin' to cut Angelo Pastamadeo. Angelo is like a grandson to me. Do you understand that?"

"Yes, I know. The official report said that Jimmy—"

"Knock it off. Are you in control of your guys or what?"

"Yes, sir." Rico's mouth was bone dry and tasted like stale beer. "Look, I will make—"

"Do you know who is in charge of you?" Without waiting for an answer, Nunzio said, "I am. I am in charge of everybody who works for me. And, I wanna know everything that's goin' on. Some bosses don't wanna know. Not me. I wanna know everything. It ain't rattin' when one of my soldiers tells me about another soldier breakin' the rules or planning to kill me. I wanna know everything. Good news and bad news. Do you understand me?"

"Yes, sir, you can trust me."

"Trust you? Before I trust somebody, that person has to prove he is worthy of my trust. You remember I asked you who killed Marty the cop?"

"Ronnie Mendez—we call him Ronnie the Razor—Ray Cotton, and Jimmy Bowman. They killed the cop. Marty the cop, the one you asked me about."

"Just those three guys...not your brother?"

"Look, Mr. Sabino—"

"Forget about it, get out."

"Wait, I have something else for you, Mr. Sabino."

"Oh, yeah? What?"

"There's a cop, a detective looking into your organization."

"You sure?"

"My friend, over there—you remember him, Mr. Sabino— Jack Stipple, he's a cop at police headquarters. He's the one who put us wise to Marty being a cop."

"I remember," Nunzio said. "He was with you when we talked. He turns on his own."

"But he wouldn't turn on me...or you. I trust him and he's in the know."

"And your friend Jack told you a detective is stickin' his nose into my organization?"

"That's right." Rico was excited. He was now scoring points with Nunzio. He had contacts inside the police department and that was something even Nunzio respected.

"Did Jack tell you the name of the guy lookin' inside my organization?"

"Hartz, Mr. Sabino. Detective Clarence Hartz."

"You did good tellin' me, Rico. Now tell your brother Hector and your cop friend Jack over there to meet me at the Caffè Fiora tomorrow at 11:00 a.m."

"Me, too, right?" Rico was taken aback by this. He was always the contact, the middleman. He didn't like Hector having a direct line to Nunzio.

"No, just the two of them. Tell 'em not to be late. Now get out."

* * *

Detective Hartz remained silent in the back seat of Nunzio's car as Rico exited. It was hard for Hartz, sitting right behind Rico, to hold his anger. One of his own—a fellow cop—had given him up.

He waited until the black Cadillac was moving once again and said, "You'd think I was too old to be disappointed."

Nunzio said, "Anytime somebody turns on us—people like you and me that think we're so smart about other people—we are surprised and disappointed. Forget about it."

"But a cop turning on another cop." Hartz shook his head.

"Hey, pal—it ain't what you wear, it's what you are. You put a uniform on a monkey, it's still a fuckin' monkey. Keep your long view, Hartz." Nunzio lit a cigarette and handed the pack to Hartz. "Relax, pal, have a smoke. Now we know."

"Let's talk." Hartz lowered his window an inch and blew smoke into the morning.

* * *

Angelo, Tate, and several other Weepers were climbing the steps of PS-65. They still had ten minutes before school started on this cool Thursday morning.

"Hey, Angelo, wait up." Ju-Ju came running over to Angelo and the Weepers. "Ernesto is still really pissed about his medallion...Angelo, there's a train coming."

"So what's new?"

"He said to tell you he ain't gonna ask you about his medallion again. Why won't you tell him where it is? I'm scared for you."

"Let's challenge the Knights to a punchball game for the medallion," Tate suggested.

"Punchball...why not?" Ju-Ju said.

"I was just kidding," Tate said.

"Yeah, but maybe it's not a bad idea," Angelo said. "And if we beat them, Ernesto gives us his baseball card collection, or money, or something. You think they'd go for it, Ju-Ju?"

Ju-Ju said, "The Knights have never lost a punchball game against anybody. When?"

"Tomorrow after school, five o'clock, in the Cherry Street Park," Angelo said. "Weepers against Knights...punchball."

Weepers were nodding. This is what Angelo wanted—it was no longer between him and Ernesto. If the Weepers lost the punchball game, he would not be a punk returning the medallion.

"I gotta go check," Ju-Ju said. "But I think it's a good idea."

Angelo said to Tate, "You think the cops know I was fighting Jimmy on the roof?"

"No way. That was smart how you led us across the roofs to a different tenement."

"Yeah, the cops stopped everybody coming out of the building Jimmy fell from," Spiro said. "Nunzio's guys got there right away...nobody's gonna rat on nobody—not in this neighborhood. The only people who know for sure are the Knights and us."

"What do you mean?" Angelo asked.

"I just meant you have a rep now as the kid who beat Jimmy—that's a good thing, Angelo," Spiro said. "But nobody really knows except the guys who were on the roof."

"Right, and in this neighborhood, no one cares enough to dig...you know that," Sage said. "You got nothin' to worry about, Angelo. Forget about it."

But Angelo was worried. The reputation wasn't as fortifying as he thought it would be. If he just stayed in bed that morning instead of blowing up Bookman's, he never would've seen Ernesto, the Razor, and Marty. Sammy never would've given him the stupid medallion. He did that one dumb thing—Bookman's— and other stuff kept happening...Like his father once told him, "If you drop a rock into the East River, the ripples will go all the way to Italy." He wasn't kidding. Everything's connected to everything. Papa.

CHAPTER TWENTY-EIGHT

"No collar...just a death sentence."

I t wasn't the Caffè Fiora that made Jack Stipple uneasy. It was walking in with Hector that troubled him. Up to this point, he was dealing through Rico, who was a bright, likable guy, so making side money off the Knights seemed not so...dirty. However, working directly with Hector made him feel low and sinking deeper. His cop instincts told him this was a mistake.

"Listen, maybe we shouldn't go in," Jack said.

"You kiddin' me or what?" Hector opened the door to the Caffè Fiora.

As they entered, six large men frisked them and took away Jack's gun and badge. "You'll get these back when you leave," one of them said. "Follow me."

Nunzio was seated and having coffee; a man stood at his table. "Sit," Nunzio said to Jack and Hector, pointing to the chairs.

"Should I come back later, Boss?" the man standing next to Nunzio asked.

"No, finish, Ralph." And then, pointing at Jack and Hector, Nunzio said, "These guys work for me now."

Jack and Hector looked at each other.

Ralph said, "So this guy up in Hell's Kitchen ain't cooperating—he's sayin' his guys work just for him. We got teamsters about to move on him but he mentioned your name, Boss. So that was the call just now. They don't believe him but—"

"But they wanna be sure," Nunzio finished for Ralph. "What did this guy say about me?"

"He said he hoped you thought of him as a friend."

"Oh, yeah? What's his name?"

"Tommy Sullivan," Ralph said.

"Tommy Sullivan." Nunzio nodded. "You tell them he's a good friend of mine. Leave him alone and fix anything they broke. G'head, I gotta talk to these guys."

Ralph disappeared and the six large men divided and retreated to two nearby tables.

"You guys want some coffee?" Nunzio asked Jack and Hector.

"No," Hector said. Then pointing to the picture of Fiora, he asked, "Who's the broad?"

Nunzio shook his head. "Hector, I thought it was time we talked. Rico said you're ambitious. That's good. There's a lot of money to be made outside the projects."

"What's a lot of money?" Jack asked.

Nunzio looked over at one of the large men at the neighboring table and said, "Pepe, who we got in the second car for this afternoon?"

"Nobody yet, Boss. Who do you want?"

"I think I got 'em."

Jack said, "This afternoon?"

"Yeah. If you're not too busy, you can be my number two," Nunzio said. "I'm gonna pick up some cash. I like havin' a backup car with four or five guys just in case somethin' goes wrong. For which the usual pay is ten percent of the cash."

"How much are we—"

"Ten percent comes to a little over fifty thousand."

"Fifty?" Hector actually licked his lips.

"You're not getting the usual ten percent," Nunzio said. "This is a test run. You do good, you'll get five thousand. Next time, we'll talk about more."

Jack nodded. "What do we have to do?"

"Good," Nunzio said. "Jack, you remember where my car met you and Rico on South Street? Be there at four o'clock. There will be two cars; I will be in the first one with a couple of my guys. The second one is yours. I want you drivin' just in case some traffic cop pulls us over or whatever else happens where we might need a cop to flash his tin. Hector, I want you plus three of your tough guys, no kids. Who you got?"

"Rico would be good," Hector said.

"You kiddin' me? Rico's a talker. C'mon, you got the muscle for this or what?"

"Yeah, you noticed that about Rico," Hector said. "Okay, I'll get good guys."

"Who?" Nunzio said. "I wanna know everything. That's how I got here."

"Ernesto's good," Jack said.

"How 'bout the Razor and the big guy who pushed Father Joe around?" Nunzio said.

"Ray Cotton," Hector said. "Yeah, he's good."

"Four o'clock. You two, Ernesto, Ray Cotton, and the razor guy. Don't be late."

* * *

Rico was hurt and angry. The first big job with Nunzio and he wasn't included. He paced around the living room of the Knights' apartment. Hector, Ernesto, Ray, and the Razor lounged on the sofa and in overstuffed chairs. "What did Nunzio say exactly?"

"I told you what Nunzio said three times. He wants me, Ernesto, Ray, and Razor. Oh, and Jack the Cop. And that's it. Anyway, you gotta get Ernesto's medallion at five o'clock. Am I right? What time you got now?"

"Two o'clock." Rico could tell that his brothers were enjoying his exclusion. "Fine."

"Why you poutin'? The medallion's important, you said so yourself. Am I right?"

"I ain't pouting. Ju-Ju told Angelo the punchball game is on. He also told him that he must have the medallion with him and we will bring Ernesto's baseball cards."

"You don't need the cards. You get there with twenty of our guys, surround the Weepers. And while they're shakin' and shittin', you take the medallion. That's it. That's all."

"That's it, that's all?" Rico mocked. "We promised Nunzio—hands off Angelo."

"Not a problem," Hector said. "The kid's gonna be so scared, he'll beg you to take the medallion. We'll meet you there right after the job. Nunzio said it'll take forty minutes, tops—start to finish. If we get to the park before you, I'll take the medallion from the kid."

"No," Ernesto said. "If we're back in time, I'll take my own fuckin' medallion back."

"If we're not back until after you get the medallion, Rico, you wait there for me and we'll walk back here together with the medallion and five G's," Hector said. "How much do we give your friend Jack the Cop for drivin'?"

"Two hundred should make him happy." Rico would have said a thousand, but Jack was going with them, and that also angered Rico. "Why don't we offer Angelo a few bucks, it might make things go easier?"

"Nunzio is right. You're a talker," Hector said.

"Hector, maybe the Razor should stick with Rico in case, you know," Ernesto said.

"Not a bad idea. We got four guys without him and no way Angelo is gonna say no to the Razor," Hector said. "Okay, Razor, you're goin' to the Cherry Street Park with Rico. Oh, and take Big Mark and Andy—nobody's gonna say no to them, either."

"I don't need nobody watching over me." Rico was flabbergasted. He was just being smart. He could be tough when it mattered—when he wanted—but smart was better.

"I'm gonna go for a walk," the Razor said. "Rico, I'll meetcha in the small park with some of our guys at four-thirty so we can all walk over to Cherry Street together."

"Sure. Fine." Everything Rico dreamed the Knights could become was coming true without him. He had been banished to the corner where, if he was a good little boy, he might be permitted to watch it all unfold. This had all been his idea. His plan. "Fine."

* * *

It was the end of the school day and kids poured out of PS-65. Angelo looked over to where the Knights hung out and saw Domingo, Andy, and other Knights looking at him. They'd given him more room since the fight on the roof. It was cool and he turned his jacket collar up.

"Hi," Angelo said to Liz as he took another look at the Knights.

"Hi. Jeez, it's cold for October," Liz said. "Don't worry about them. They don't know what to make of you. And neither do I."

Angelo asked, "You okay?"

"Jimmy's mother is always crying," Liz said. "I just can't go see her anymore. Would it be okay if I hung out with you guys?"

"Sure, that would be great," Angelo said.

"Hi, guys." Audrey walked up to Angelo and Liz. "What's great?"

"Hanging out with you guys," Liz said. "I have to get going. See you later."

"See, she likes you, Angelo," Audrey teased as Gina and Tate joined them and the four walked along East Broadway.

"Me and Tate are going to Mo-Mo's for a slice. We got the punchball game at five," Angelo said. "You want to come?"

"No, we're meeting Sass here," Audrey said, stopping in front of the public library.

"What for?" Tate said.

"Tate, the assignment for history class," Gina said. "And you promised you were going to get a library card. Come on up with us; it'll take just a second."

"Oh, yeah, I guess I should do that. You got a library card, Angelo?"

"Yeah, it's a good idea, Tate. G'head, I'll wait here for you."

"We'll see you at the dance after the punchball game, right?" Audrey said.

"Yeah, we'll be there." Angelo watched the library door close behind them.

"Angelo. Hey, Angelo, gimme a hand here, will ya?" someone called from the alley next to the library. Angelo walked over to the mouth of the alley and strained to see without going in.

Two guys grabbed him from either side as a third grabbed him from behind; they carried him into the alley and released him in a small clearing near the far end.

"Right here, shit for brains," said Ronnie the Razor, waiting in the alley.

Angelo faced four Knights and one of them was the Razor. Before he could react, a punch to his lower back buckled his knees. Another Knight swept his feet and Angelo hit the ground flat on his back.

"Search him for Ernesto's medallion," the Razor ordered.

"Nothin'," one of the Knights said after they went through Angelo's pockets.

"Screw Rico's promise," the Razor said. "Let's bucket him."

Angelo was lifted off the ground by the Knights, turned upside-down, and pushed head first into a partially filled garbage can. His chin slammed into his chest as decaying trash spilled over his face. The smell of rotting fish and fear brought vomit into his mouth. He choked it back down. He was scared and for a moment, thought he might be dreaming. A second garbage can was brought down over his legs. He was squeezed into a tight ball with his knees touching his face. He was having trouble breathing. His heart was beating in his eyes. The trash cans overlapped each other and they were being compressed further.

"Hey, Angelo, can you hear me in there?" the Razor said. "This is your coffin. We're gonna bury you alive in this bucket of trash."

Angelo tried to respond. "Wait, no, I'll give you the medallion." But it came out muffled into his chest. He was scared. He tried to kick free but the garbage cans held together.

"Bang them together with them boards and bricks over there. We'll bury this in the Jersey dump. My car's at the end of the alley," the Razor said. "Nobody will ever find him."

Angelo's head was filled with pounding and banging as the trash cans compressed further. He could taste blood and more vomit in his mouth. He smelled urine. The pounding continued. He was coughing and gasping. The banging on the garbage cans continued.

Angelo's entire body was trembling. He released a muffled scream.

The banging stopped. Angelo heard shouts—a scuffle? The garbage cans were being rocked and pulled apart. He saw Tate looking down at him, and two big guys.

"They were going to bury me alive," Angelo said. He was covered in vomit and garbage. Blood dotted his face. And he was shivering.

Tate and the two big guys lifted Angelo out of the garbage can and onto his feet. Tate wiped Angelo off with some newspapers, old towels, and a sheet he found in a box of trash.

"Where'd the Razor and the other Knights go?" Angelo said.

"Two are down for the count over there," one of Uncle Nunzio's guys said. "The guy they call the Razor and another guy beat it outta here like rabbits. You okay, kid?"

"They were really going to kill me," Angelo said, still shaking. "How come you guys are always around when I'm in trouble?"

"Your uncle asked us to keep an eye on you...but from a distance, so you don't know," one of Uncle Nunzio's guys said. "I gotta tell you, kid, that ain't easy with you. I think we need to be a little closer. But I'd appreciate it if you don't let on to your uncle that you know. Okay?"

"No problem," Angelo said. "Thanks."

"Can you walk?" Tate asked.

"Yeah. Can we go to Mo-Mo's so I can clean up a little?"

Tate and Angelo, with Uncle Nunzio's guys behind them, walked into Mo-Mo's.

"Bring him around here," Morgan said. "I'll clean him up."

"I'll be okay now," Angelo said to Uncle Nunzio's guys.

"Okay, kid, we'll be around."

"Tate, can you wait for me?" Angelo said heading to the back bathroom.

"I ain't goin' no place."

In the bathroom, Angelo held his breath the way Uncle Johnny showed him. He still trembled, but not as bad.

"Who did this to you?" Morgan asked as he finished examining Angelo's face and head.

"Ronnie the Razor and some other Knights."

"Ronnie the Razor," Morgan said. "Let's see, he's about nineteen or twenty now. When he was ten, they called him Porky Ron. He was a pudgy little guy."

"Maybe," Angelo said. "But he ain't little now."

"You gonna have a couple of bruises, but you'll live," Morgan said.

"Thanks to Tate and Uncle Nunzio."

"Tate, take this pizza to a table for you boys. And grab yourself a couple of Cokes."

* * *

At 4:00 p.m., Jack Stipple walked toward Hector, Ernesto, and Ray, waiting at the appointed spot on South Street. Jack still had that nagging feeling that trouble was coming. He told himself to shake it off. This was the start of real money.

As he got to Hector, a black Cadillac pulled up, followed by a black Ford. The driver of the Ford got out and walked over to Jack and handed him the keys.

"How yous doin'? I'm Pepe, remember? You got your badge, Cop?"

"Yeah, I got it."

"Good, you're drivin'. All you gotta do is follow us. The Ford is for the four of you. Was there supposed to be five?"

"No, four's right," Hector said.

"Besides the cop, who's got heat?" Pepe asked.

"Me," Hector said.

Ernesto and Ray shook their heads.

"No problem," Pepe said. "We got extra in the Caddy. When we get there, I'll run a couple of guns back for you two guys. Hopefully nobody will need 'em."

"Where we goin'?" Jack asked. "In case I lose you."

"You lose us and you lose your money and your future. We'll drive slow for you, cop."

"I'll keep up."

"Okay, I'll be in the front car with the boss. Don't none of you do nothin' dumb. No matter what, be cool and let the cop here handle any problems that come up. Got it?" Pepe didn't wait for an answer—he walked away and got in the shotgun seat of the Caddy.

Jack got behind the wheel of the Ford and Hector sat in the front next to him. The Caddy pulled out and headed south, staying under the speed limit. Jack followed.

"Hey, Hector, how do we know Nunzio is in the Caddy?" Ernesto asked. "That don't even look like Nunzio's Caddy. I think he's got a Brougham. That's a '56 sedan."

Good question, Jack thought.

"What difference does it make what kind of car? Anyway, I can see somebody in the back seat," Hector responded.

"Yeah, but how do ya know it's Nunzio?" Ernesto said.

"You think with us pickin' up this much money he wouldn't come?" Hector said.

Jack stayed close behind the front car as they continued down South Street. Just past Fulton, the lead car turned left onto one of the East River piers containing a warehouse the size of a three-story apartment building. The lead car stopped and a uniformed man approached them. After a moment, the uniform nodded and walked back toward Jack.

"Who do we have here?" the uniform said, looking in Jack's window.

"I'm on the job," Jack said.

"Oh, yeah? Let's see your tin."

Jack showed him his badge.

"Okay, officer." The uniformed man walked toward the warehouse and waved to two other uniforms, who pulled open the large doors.

"This place is huge," Jack said.

"They used to run trains in there," Hector said. "Now just those big trucks."

The Caddy drove slowly into the warehouse. Jack followed, and the large doors closed behind them. They continued to the far end of the warehouse and stopped. Large wooden crates were stacked on both sides of the four-car-wide center aisle.

In his rearview mirror, Jack saw the three uniformed guys walking toward the cars. It made him feel safer—cops watch out for cops. He thought about Marty and was sorry, but he had done what he had to do. Besides, he hadn't known they would kill him.

Pepe, carrying two guns, walked back to Jack just as the three uniforms reached him.

"I think these guns are for you guys," Jack said to Ernesto and Ray.

"Stay in your car," Pepe said. "The Caddy's gonna turn around and pull up here. You drive down to the end almost touchin' the wall. But try to stop before you go into the river."

"Are those for us?" Jack said, nodding at the guns.

"Yeah. I'll give 'em to your guys when they're outta the car. G'head, pull on down. We'll walk behind you," Pepe said.

Jack pulled ahead. Now in his rearview mirror he saw the four men following him on foot. "They got this all figured out. I wonder how many times they picked up cash here. It's got to be millions of dollars."

As Jack passed the Cadillac, now pointing in the opposite direction, he noticed a driver and someone in the back seat. Nunzio?

"Okay, turn off the car," Pepe said to Jack. "Good, give me the keys and everybody out."

A uniform was at each of the car's doors except for Jack's door—Pepe stood there. He opened Jack's door and the other three doors opened simultaneously. Jack handed the keys to Pepe and stepped out of the car.

"Whadda we do now?" Hector asked.

"Let me see your gun," the uniform said to Hector.

As Hector reached for it, the uniform pressed his gun against Hector's ear.

Jack Stipple's mind was racing. He needed to understand what was going on. He told himself he was a cop. He could work this through. He needed to take control of the situation. He wasn't really part of this, and anyway, they wouldn't kill a cop.

Pepe and the three uniforms pointed guns at Jack Stipple and his crew. A uniform removed Hector's gun. Pepe removed Jack's off-duty .38.

"Let's check the trunk, cop," Pepe said. "C'mon."

Jack followed him to the trunk, as did the others. In the trunk was a small canvas bag. "What's in the bag?" Hector said.

"Take a look," Pepe said.

Hector removed one of the small packages from the bag. "Heroin? We're selling—"

Pepe raised Jack's gun and fired one shot into Hector's forehead. Hector went down.

Big Ray Cotton started to cry.

Ernesto looked at his brother, dead before he even hit the ground, still holding the heroin. He turned toward Pepe, whose next shot shattered Ernesto's chin. Ernesto looked like a grotesque cartoon character without a lower jaw. The next bullet split Ernesto's right eyebrow. He fell straight backwards like a slapstick comic.

Ray dropped to his knees and begged to be spared.

"Fuck," Jack said.

"Whaddaya complainin' about, cop? You're the hero. You pretended to wanna buy heroin. These guys showed up in a stolen car with the stuff. You tried to arrest them but they opened fire on you. See, that's why I'm usin' your gun. The uniforms here were witnesses."

Ray was praying between sobs until Pepe shot him in his left ear. Ray fell dead sideways, his hands still clasped together.

The uniforms checked each body to make certain the Knights were dead.

"I don't suppose I get to attend the medal ceremony for my heroism," Jack said.

Pepe fired Jack's gun two more times into a crate. "You gotta miss sometimes, cop."

"You just screwed up your whole plan," Jack said. "Everybody knows I never miss."

Pepe thought for a moment and then laughed. "I like you, cop; you're funny. Your car, by the way, is parked outside. Very good police work, cop. You might even make detective." Pepe turned to the uniform holding Hector's gun. "Gimme that gun." And then to the other two uniforms, "You two fire those guns a couple of times and give 'em to those two dead guys. Hector will be holdin' this one."

"Look, Pepe," Jack said in a calm voice. "We can make a deal here. You don't want to do this. They always conduct an extensive investigation when a cop is killed."

"I think we got that covered." Pepe held Hector's gun out butt-first toward the Cadillac. To Jack's surprise, when the back door opened, out stepped Detective Hartz.

"Thank God." But then it all made sense to Jack. "Hartz, you told me that stuff to see if I would pass it along—if I would rat you out. You didn't drop the Marty case—this is the Marty case. No collar...just a death sentence. Am I right?"

Hartz took the gun from Pepe, and with ghostly vacant eyes, he looked at Jack.

Jack nodded and murmured, "Fuck me."

CHAPTER TWENTY-NINE

"It's what you do when you're afraid that counts."

After pizza, Angelo's fear turned into anger. "I have to check on my uncle."

"I'll walk you home," Tate said. "You okay, Angelo?"

Angelo nodded and stood up, without shaking. "Thanks, Morgan."

"No problem," Morgan said. "You boys take care out there."

Angelo and Tate walked home in silence. As they walked into their building, Tate said, "I'll wait down here for you."

"Thanks, Tate."

When Angelo walked into his apartment, Uncle Johnny was sitting at the kitchen table with a cup of coffee.

"Are Mom and Adam still at Nonna's?" Angelo asked.

"Yeah, they should be there for a couple of hours. What's up?"

Angelo told his uncle about the Razor and garbage can. "You think the Razor's going to come at me again?"

"Maybe not if you give him the medallion."

"Yeah, but the punchball game today is for the medallion."

"Angelo, the Knights are going to show up but not to play punchball or any other game."

"I know."

"I can end this right now and chase those fucking Knights away."

"I know. And it sounds good, but I have to face this. I need to do it for me."

"I am so impressed with you, Angelo, and I understand. Just please be smart—no games."

"Thanks, Uncle Johnny, I will."

* * *

Angelo and Tate walked out of their building and to the Cherry Street Park.

"My uncle doesn't think the Knights are going to play punchball. Do you think they're gonna?"

"No, but I'm hoping I'm wrong. I'm glad I gave Uncle Johnny the medallion to hold. Those Knights searched me. Here, hang on to it until I ask, okay?"

"Sure, no problem," Tate said. "What's Nunzio gonna do with that store?"

"I don't know. He keeps telling Uncle Frank it's a liquor store just to break his shoes."

"Hey, it looks like all our guys are here," Tate said as they walked into the park.

Angelo was obsessed with his anger at both himself and the Razor. He recalled Uncle Johnny's telling him that "every soldier is afraid, but it's what you do when you're afraid that counts—that separates the hero from the coward." He realized that the Razor had not made him a coward; the Razor just made him afraid.

"What I do when I'm afraid is up to me," Angelo said to himself.

"What happened to you?" Spiro said, looking at Angelo.

"We got jumped by some Knights over on East Broadway," Tate said.

"You don't look too beat up," Howie said to Tate.

"Angelo did most of the fightin'."

Angelo smiled.

"Why'd they do it?" Sage asked. "We're gonna play punchball."

"My Uncle Johnny don't think they're gonna really play."

"Ju-Ju said they would." Howie bounced a pink Spalding ball. "I got a new Spaldeen."

"My uncle don't trust Ju-Ju," Angelo said.

"Me, either." Tate was writing his name on the wooden bench with his pen.

"I think Uncle Johnny was right. Take a look."

Angelo and the rest of the Weepers were struck by the sheer number of Knights in black jackets walking into the Cherry Street

Park. He quickly looked around for Uncle Nunzio's two guys, but all he saw was a sea of Knights.

"Shit," Spiro said. "I bet there're twenty or thirty guys."

The Knights made a circle around the Weepers. Rico, Big Mark, Andy, and the Razor stood together with their backs to the Cherry Street Park entrance.

The Razor took the ball away from Howie and threw it over the fence.

Angelo had never hated anyone more than the Razor at that moment. He turned his back to the Razor and whispered, "Tate, take your pen and write RAZOR on the back of my hand." Angelo stuck out his right fist.

"What?"

"Tate. C'mon."

"Somebody better give me that medallion," the Razor said. "Or Angelo's dead."

Tate made the vertical line for the R. "Wait," Angelo said. "Write PORKY RON'S and under it write MAMA."

"Are you crazy? He'll—"

"Just do it."

Tate finished. "If he kills you, or hurts you real bad, I'm gonna kill him. I swear it."

"Angelo, you can't hide, I can smell you." The Razor got big laughs from the Knights.

"Thanks, Tate." Angelo showed the Razor his palms as a sign that he was unarmed. He didn't want to show the Razor the back of his hand just yet. Angelo walked up to Rico and said, "I thought we were playing punchball for the medallion."

"We ain't playin' shit," the Razor said. "Just give me the medallion."

"I'm talking to your boss," Angelo said. And then to Rico, "Ain't I?"

"Yeah, kid, but the Razor's right. There will be no game. Be smart. Give me my brother's medallion and nobody will get hurt. It'll be over."

Angelo looked at Ju-Ju standing with the Knights. "You're with them?"

"Please just give him the medallion," Ju-Ju said.

Angelo was afraid. But his anger helped him take charge of his fear. He swallowed hard and said, "No. No game, no medallion."

The Razor shoved Angelo with such force that Angelo's feet left the ground. The cold cement was unforgiving as Angelo fell feet-in-the-air-flat-on-his-back. Snickers quickly spread among Knights.

Angelo was embarrassed but then caught himself. No one else is here. *Focus on the enemy.* He'd been afraid too long. Bookman, his father, Knights...what they did to his mother, Sammy, the garbage can—an ecstasy of wrath washed over Angelo. He stood up.

The circle widened.

Angelo saw Uncle Nunzio's two guys standing behind Rico and felt their strength.

The Razor opened his silver straight razor with the care of a surgeon. "I ain't Jimmy."

Tate quickly jumped between Angelo and the Razor. "You gonna fight me, not Angelo."

"Hell, I'll fight both of yous," the Razor said to applause.

"I have to do this, Tate." Angelo patted Tate on the shoulder and in a whisper said, "Like with Bookman. I have to."

Tate nodded and reluctantly moved into the circle of Weepers and Knights.

"Fuck." Rico put his hands on his head and looked to the sky.

Angelo started to shake. He held up his index finger to the Razor.

"You need a minute? G'head, take your minute," the Razor said.

Angelo stood very still. He dropped his chin to his chest and put the audience out of his mind. He took a deep breath and let it out slowly. His shaking stopped. He felt for the ribbon. It was there. He lifted his head, opened his eyes, and focused on the Razor's neck.

The Razor didn't look as fearsome as he did a moment ago. Angelo flicked the ribbon with his finger. Merlin magically appeared in his hand. He unlocked it, pushing the button the way he had practiced in his room. *Saalick.* Merlin sprung to ready.

The Razor seemed surprised as he got into a typical street-fighting stance—bent at the waist, blade loosely held out in front of him. He tossed his silver razor from hand to hand, to the cheers of his fellow Knights. "I'm gonna slice you up for what you did to Jimmy."

Angelo focused on the Razor's neck, but watched his eyes. He held the knife in his right fist the way Uncle Johnny taught him—point toward the ground, sharp edge toward his opponent. He drew his right foot back into a cat stance.

"The kid don't even know how to hold a knife," the Razor said to giggles and applause.

Angelo watched for the first D—distraction.

The Razor made a couple of menacing gestures that took Angelo by surprise. But each time, Angelo learned something about the Razor and returned to his cat stance.

The Razor moved toward Angelo.

With his weight on his right leg, Angelo snapped his left foot forward, bulleting his toe into the Razor's shin.

"Ow, you little fuck! You fight like a girl." The Razor moved back and bent more at the waist to reach Angelo.

Like Mary, Angelo thought.

The Razor was getting cockier as he moved around Angelo like a performer.

Angelo waited, focused.

The Razor made a breathtakingly quick pass, cutting a slit in the front of Angelo's jacket.

"Whoa," Angelo said instinctively.

"You like that?" The Razor smiled and made another pass but missed.

Now, Angelo thought. Now. He rolled his right fist down and to his right, exposing the three words—PORKY RON'S MAMA—for the Razor to read.

The Razor's eyes went to Angelo's hand and back quickly.

Not yet.

Then the Razor frowned, as though he just realized what it said. His eyes locked onto Angelo's right hand.

This was the moment. Now.

In one smooth move, Angelo grabbed the back of the Razor's right hand with his left hand, rolled it palm up, and quickly brought the sharp edge of Merlin across the Razor's exposed wrist. Angelo sliced a deep red crevice into the Razor's flesh.

The Razor squealed as his hand involuntarily contorted and his fingers splayed open. The silver razor slipped between his twitching fingers and fell to the ground.

It worked. I did the second D—defang the dragon—disarmed. Angelo began his swing back. "Think Elvis," Uncle Johnny had said. "It's all in the hips. Swing left, then swing right, and the point and edge will be ready to smite."

As Angelo swung back, the point of Merlin headed toward the right side of the Razor's neck. With the speed of a frog's tongue capturing an insect, Angelo poked Merlin into the side of the Razor's neck and pulled it back. It sank in just shy of an inch, causing a thin line of blood to snake down the Razor's neck.

Angelo could have buried Merlin deep into the Razor's throat. He could have killed him...he wanted to. *Third D— destroy.* But at the last second, something stopped him.

Angelo took two steps back but remained in his cat stance holding Merlin. His heart was pounding against his chest. His mouth tasted like beach sand. Breathe. He took a deep breath but stayed focused on the Razor.

A chilly silence filled the park.

The Razor appeared more incredulous than in pain. He stood for a moment, holding his right arm, which hung slack in front of him, bleeding. He stared at Angelo and then looked at his silver razor on the ground. He dropped to his knees and, trembling, made a feeble attempt to reach for the razor.

Angelo quickly moved forward and kicked him in the face. The Razor fell backwards, his legs bent under him.

Angelo kicked the silver razor to Spiro, who picked it up.

The Razor rolled onto his side, sat up, bent over, and coughed blood into his lap.

Angelo's heart was still racing. He took a deep breath and walked over to Rico. "If you ain't gonna play punchball, get out of my park."

The Weepers quickly flanked Angelo on both sides, but faced the Knights. Tate stood next to Angelo facing Rico, Andy, and Big Mark.

"How old are you, thirteen? Nobody ever beat the Razor. Nobody. Andy, go help the Razor," Rico said. "But look around you, kid. My Knights would love nothin' better than to crush you and your friends right now."

Ju-Ju took off his black jacket and stood with the Weepers next to Gerard.

"You're a Weeper now?" Ju-Ju said to Gerard.

"Yeah."

"Rico, we gotta get Razor's arm stitched up—it's bleedin' bad," Andy shouted.

"Wrap it with a piece of shirt," Rico said. "This is real life, Angelo." A current of agitation ran under Rico's calm tone. "We're not playing a game. You didn't kill the Razor and that's good. But it makes me think that you don't really get what's going on here. You don't get this whole thing. Us...the Knights."

"You little punk, we're not gonna take your fuckin' milk money." Big Mark grabbed Angelo's hair with his left hand and reached inside his jacket with his right hand. "I'm gonna blow your fuckin' head—"

Uncle Nunzio's guys moved forward.

A gunshot shattered the moment. It was the loudest anyone in that park had ever heard. The right side of Big Mark's head burst like a water balloon as his body—right hand still on the gun under his jacket—crumpled into a bloody ball where he was standing. Weepers and Knights alike let out cries and twisted in circles. Rico dropped to his knees and looked around.

"Holy shit."

"Oh, my God."

"What the fuck? Rico, whadda we do?"

Most of the Knights ran out of the park; the rest were flat on the ground with the Weepers in a helter-skelter jumble.

Nunzio's guys, with their guns drawn, were on either side of Angelo, who was still standing. "Don't worry, kid."

"Where did that come from?" Rico's voice cracked as he stood up.

And that's when Angelo saw them. Uncle Johnny's war buddies, Ben and Henry, were standing behind all the Knights and Weepers on the ground. They were facing Angelo with their arms folded. Without turning his head, Angelo's eyes moved to his building across Catherine Street. His eyes went to his floor and then to Uncle Johnny's room. The window was open and the room was dark. He looked back at Ben and Henry. Ben gave one slight nod.

"It's cool," Angelo said to Uncle Nunzio's guys. "The shooter is—"

"We know."

"The guy who grabbed me was going for a gun." Angelo stood up. "Tate, Weepers, get up. It's okay."

Andy, who was helping the Razor, reached inside his jacket.

Rico overheard Angelo and shouted, "Andy, no weapons. Nobody pull a weapon."

Andy put his empty hands up in front of him.

Angelo looked into Rico's eyes. "Don't fuck with the Weepers."

Rico looked back at him. Angelo's eyes weren't wide, or angry, or sick with triumph. They reminded Rico of the eyes of the dead fish at Vernon's market.

Uncle Nunzio suddenly appeared behind Rico. "*Gattino*, give Rico the medallion."

Rico, obviously startled, spun around. "Nunzio."

"What did you call me?" Uncle Nunzio leaned an ear toward Rico.

"I mean, Mr. Sabino."

Angelo was surprised and comforted to see Uncle Nunzio. Without hesitation, Tate handed the medallion to Angelo. Angelo handed Ernesto's medallion to Rico. "Uncle Nunzio, the cops might be coming 'cause of the gunshot. Shouldn't you—?"

"No cops for at least another hour, *Gattino*."

"I have to meet Hector here," Rico said. "I thought he—"

"Listen to me very carefully and then do what I tell you," Uncle Nunzio said. "The only reason you're not dead right now is that one of my guys was in your apartment when you told your brothers that they should cancel the hit on me."

"The Knight that Ju-Ju saw on the bed," Rico said. "A Knight was really on the bed?"

Angelo knew there had been no Knight on the bed. He told Uncle Nunzio the story Ju-Ju made up to cover for Angelo. He was impressed with how Uncle Nunzio used that information to make Rico insecure about trusting his own Knights.

"Hector, Ernesto, Ray, and your cop friend are dead. You'll read about it in tomorrow's paper," Uncle Nunzio said. "So you're the leader of these Knights."

Rico looked like he was going to be sick. He counted only seven Knights, including the Razor, who were still in the park. All of the Weepers were still there. "I can get more Knights down here just waiting to—"

"Shut up." Uncle Nunzio lit a cigarette. "What do you wanna do, Angelo?"

"I want to settle this tonight."

"Good idea, *Gattino.*"

Angelo looked at Rico. "Is this thing between your guys and mine settled now?"

Rico looked at his Knights and then back to Angelo.

Uncle Nunzio said, "All of it's gonna be settled, one way or another, right here, right now, Rico. So, you gonna be smart or join your brothers? Do what you gotta do. But do it now."

Rico looked at his brother's medallion. "Were they be-headed?"

"What?" Uncle Nunzio looked irritated. "What's the matter with you?"

"Like Saint Justus and...forget it," Rico said. "You know, Angelo, when Ernesto was six, seven, he was a frightened little boy. I could've saved him back then...could've run away. Then one day, I couldn't save him anymore...but he was still scared... always scared."

"Is it settled?" Angelo said.

Rico turned and shouted, "Knights, I got Ernesto's—" he swallowed hard. "—medallion. We're finished here. You two guys help Andy with the Razor—"

"Tell them to put the dead guy and the Razor in the trunk of the blue Chevy behind my car," Uncle Nunzio said.

"But the Razor's fine. He'll be okay," Rico said.

"You just do what I tell you."

"You guys put Big Mark...and the Razor in the trunk of the Chevy over there." Rico looked at Angelo, took a deep breath, and nodded. "It's settled...you're thirteen. You have any idea where you're heading?"

Angelo shrugged. "To the dance."

Rico shook his head and joined the other Knights flowing out of the Cherry Street Park and into the projects. Muffled pleas and sobs came from the trunk of the Chevy as it drove away.

"He didn't mean tonight." Uncle Nunzio took Angelo aside. "*Gattino*, listen to me. When you fail to kill your enemy in battle, you do not turn an enemy into a friend; you create a more determined enemy and some doubt in your friends. Tonight, the Weepers defeated the Knights. People will talk about this. Other gangs will want to take your reputation. After tonight, if you're gonna be the leader of the Weepers, you gotta be able to do what you gotta do. *Capisce?*"

"I know...I will," Angelo said.

"Okay, *Gattino*. Let's go back. You know what happened here tonight?" Uncle Nunzio asked as he and Angelo rejoined the other Weepers.

Angelo thought about Uncle Nunzio's question. *I defeated the scariest Knight ever—the Razor. The Weepers faced down the Knights. I know I can do what I gotta do, even if I'm scared. I'm not a coward.* He knew that the Razor would not be back. The Knights and Weepers were forever changed. Angelo thought of all this and then said, "Nothing. Nothing happened here."

"*Bene.* You okay, *Gattino?*"

Angelo nodded. He needed time to think about all of it. He needed to talk to his friends about nothing. He needed to slow dance with Audrey and get lost in her gentle scent.

Uncle Johnny lowered his M1C sniper rifle in his dark bedroom and gazed out at the night. He nodded toward Ben and Henry as they drove off in a dark sedan.

CHAPTER THIRTY

"It depends on what the Weepers become."

"ANGELO, ANGELO," Tate called from the street at five after eight Saturday morning.

Angelo left his Cheerios and went to the window. "Hey, Tate, what's going on?"

"C'mon down—you gotta see this."

"What?"

"No. You gotta come down now."

Angelo looked at his mother, who shrugged and nodded, so Angelo bolted out of his apartment and down the five flights to Tate. "What?"

"What? The new store next to your uncle's—oh, just c'mon." Tate ran up Catherine Street with Angelo following.

Uncle Frank was standing outside when Angelo and Tate got there. It was beautiful. The letters painted on the glass window spelled W-E-E-P-E-R-S in gray letters outlined in purple. Since gangs were against the law, under the WEEPERS at the bottom of the window, in the same color, it said S-A-C, for Social and Athletic Club.

"Here you go, Angelo." Uncle Frank handed Angelo a ring with twelve keys on it. "Uncle Nunzio also gave me a key, just in case of—I don't know what."

"Whoa," Angelo said. "Uncle Frank, did you know?"

"Nope, not until this morning when Uncle Nunzio dropped off the keys. He said to tell you it's rent-free for three years, then you gotta negotiate a rent with him. He also said it's a down payment on saving his life."

"Let's go inside." Angelo unlocked the door.

Inside were sidewalk tables and chairs, a couple of sofas, indoor tables and chairs, and a television set. It was beautiful.

"Oh, Uncle Nunzio said for you to look in the closet," Uncle Frank said.

Angelo opened the closet. There on hangers were twelve purple jackets with WEEPERS on the back in gray letters outlined in black, and a gold teardrop falling from the S. Below WEEPERS, in the same colors, were the letters SAC. On the front of each jacket was a name in gray outlined in black with a gold teardrop falling from the last letter in the name. Angelo pulled the one that said Tate off the hanger and tossed it to his friend. Then he took his off the hanger and slowly put it on. He put his hands in the jacket pockets. He felt better than when he first put his garrison belt on. The jacket represented the collective courage of all the Weepers. It was his flag...his honor.

"How's that jacket feel?" Uncle Frank asked.

"Like Superman's cape," Angelo said.

"Uncle Nunzio said in addition to those heavy jackets, you have a dozen lightweight jackets and two dozen T-shirts in the boxes over there." Uncle Frank pointed to the closet. "Future members have to buy their own. Same with the keys—there're twelve on that ring."

"Tate, we have to get the guys," Angelo said. "And wait 'til Audrey and Gina—oh, man, is this great or what?"

"Is it great or what? Hey, there's Father Joe," Tate said. "Father Joe, look at this."

"I love it," Father Joe said, carrying a box of pastries. "Nunzio told me about it last night at the airport. But you're still going to attend the Settlement house...right?"

"We promise. Did you have fun in Italy?"

"It was wonderful, boys. I'll come by your club and tell you all about it later. But now I must talk to your mom. Is she upstairs?"

"Yeah."

Uncle Frank walked out with Father Joe. "You got a visitor out here, Angelo."

"A visitor?" Angelo walked to the door. In front of the club sat the white dog.

"Tate, it's that dog. Let's let him sleep in the club at night, especially when it's cold out."

"Yeah, our club dog," Tate said. "We'll feed him, walk him. You know, everybody will take care of him. What's his name?"

"How 'bout Sammy?"

"Sammy's good."

* * *

Father Joe handed Anna the box of pastries, which she opened and placed on the table along with two cups of coffee. Johnny was in his room reading to Adam so that Father Joe and Anna could talk privately.

"Anna, I don't know the best way to tell you what I must, so I am just going to blurt it out and try to fix it later." Father Joe placed a pack of cigarettes and a lighter on the table.

"What is it?" Anna said, sliding an ashtray over to Father Joe and sipping her coffee.

"I want to say three things before you interrupt me. Okay?"

"Okay."

"First, Mac is alive."

Anna looked at him in stricken silence.

"Second, all of the people involved in the attempt on his life are dead."

With trembling hands, Anna took a cigarette out of Father Joe's pack on the table. Father Joe lit Anna's and one for himself.

"And third, he stayed away for six years thinking he was protecting you and the boys from harm. And now that the threat is gone, he would very much like to talk with you. To tell you how sorry he is for the way he treated you, and I suspect how much he loves you."

Anna was silent for a long time. "Where was he?"

"Italy. He returned to New York with me."

"Did you know that before you left?"

"Anna, whatever you say will be the way it will be. If you never want to see him again, you never will. If you want to talk with him, you can."

"Tell me about him. What you said. What he said."

Father Joe spent an hour talking to Anna about his conversations with Mac at the *osteria*, the drive to Rome, and the flight home. Finally, he told her that Mac was staying with him and would not bother her or even attempt to talk with her unless it was what she wanted.

"Do you believe him?"

"Yes, I do. If I didn't, I would not have brought him back with me, and you and I would be having a very different discussion."

"You need to let me think about this. All of it."

* * *

Father Casimiro was having coffee with Frank in Lilly's, waiting for Father Joe to stop by after he talked with Anna.

He looked up from the newspaper. "The paper says that Hector, Ernesto, and Ray Cotton were heroin dealers."

"I saw that," Frank said.

"A cop tried to stop them. There was a shootout—a shootout. And the cop, Hector, Ernesto, and Ray are all dead. It says your friend, Detective Hartz, is in charge of the investigation. A shootout?"

"It's too bad about the cop, but the Knights can use some thinning out," Frank said.

Father Casimiro closed and folded the newspaper. "Is it true about the fight last night? I mean about Angelo and the Razor?"

"They fought and Angelo won, if that's what you mean."

Father Casimiro hesitated for a moment but then asked, "Is the Razor dead?"

"The Razor was alive when he left the park."

"How's Angelo handling it?"

"Angelo seems fine."

"And Anna?"

"Anna and Adam were at my parents' last night for dinner. She thought Angelo was going to play punchball and then go to the dance. Me, too. That's also what Angelo thought."

"So Anna doesn't know about the fight?"

"She knows there was a fight instead of a punchball game and that Angelo won. She doesn't know it was with knives."

"Weren't you worried? I mean, what if the Razor—"

"Like I said, I didn't know about it ahead of time or I think I would've stopped it. I say 'I think,' because sooner or later, something had to happen. The Knights were getting bolder. And, anyway, a couple of Nunzio's guys had Angelo covered."

The bell on the door announced Father Joe.

"How'd it go?" Father Casimiro asked.

"Better than it might have."

"Will she see him?"

"She wants to think about it."

"Understandable," Frank said.

Once they left the liquor store, Father Casimiro said, "Joe, we saved Angelo from the Knights and the other gangs. But we both heard about what happened last night in the Cherry Street Park. So do we count this as a success? Did we save him?"

"Good question, Robert. I guess it depends on what the Weepers become."

Father Casimiro and Father Joe walked past the Weepers' storefront and waved to the boys inside.

* * *

Tate waved to Father Joe and Father Casimiro as they walked past the club. "Angelo, everybody at the dance last night was talking about you. I mean, you beating Jimmy was cool, but nobody ever beat the Razor."

Angelo felt an electric charge go through him. "We beat the Knights. We have to wear our jackets to school on Monday."

"Monday? I'm wearing mine now." Tate put his Weepers jacket on.

"Tate, look at this, we got a bathroom with a shower."

"These sofas are great. And the kitchen has a stove, a new icebox—"

"Look at this, a meeting room with a long table and twelve chairs around it. Tate, please tell me I ain't dreaming."

"You ain't dreaming. Let's go get the girls."

"Yeah, here's your key." Angelo locked the club behind them.

"Angelo, 'cause of what you did last night, the Weepers are the coolest gang—"

"Club."

"Yeah, club, in the whole neighborhood," Tate said as the two friends walked up Catherine. "You okay?"

"I'm good. But, we need to think about getting some guns."

"I guess after last night, we know a couple of Knights have guns. But that will change us."

"We've already changed, Tate."

"Could your Uncle Nunzio help us get some guns?"

"Maybe."

"There they are." Tate pointed to Audrey, Gina, Liz, and Sass standing in front of 54 Catherine Street. "Gina!"

"Audrey!" Angelo waved, eager to show off his new jacket... and status.

Chapter Thirty-One

"Milwaukee explodes with joy."

On Sunday, Anna sat with her family where they always sat in church, in the third pew from the front on the right. She watched but didn't really listen to Father Joe go through the 9:00 a.m. Mass. Nonna sat at the end of the pew, Anna sat next to her, then Adam, Angelo, Frank, and Pompa.

Anna closed her eyes and inhaled the scent of incense. She was exhausted. Staying awake all night had not yielded an answer to what she ought to do about Mac. Certainly her sons needed a father—but not one who hit them. And no one would ever hit them—or her—again. She thought about how nice it was in the beginning. She prayed for God to tell her what to do.

"You should talk to him, dear," a voice startled her from behind.

She whirled around, "What?"

"Your boy," the woman behind her whispered. "He's licking that woman's fur collar in front of him. He'll surely pick up germs. You should talk to him."

Anna looked at her boys. Adam had his face buried in the woman's fur collar. Angelo appeared to be on the verge of laughter. "Adam, stop that—sit back. Angelo, shhhh."

"I should talk to him," she whispered to herself. Anna waited for Father Joe to look at her and then she nodded. Anna intended her nod to simply signal her desire to catch Father Joe alone after Mass—to discuss a place where she could meet with Mac— Perhaps Father Joe's office.

To Anna's surprise, Father Joe smiled and, with his chin, indicated the back of the church.

Anna's eyes led her head in a slow turn. A man was in the last row with his jacket collar turned up and his head down. He sat alone in the middle of the pew.

Mac? Anna thought and then looked back at Father Joe, who simply nodded once. She whispered to her mother, "I'll meet you outside."

Anna walked to the back of the church. Her boys were too captivated by the woman's damp fur collar to care about where she was going. She stopped behind the last pew and walked toward the solitary man. As she got closer, she knew it was Mac. He looked like the little boy she had grown up with. He had hurt her. But they had once been best friends and he now looked lost.

She took a deep breath and whispered, "Mac."

He turned to look at her. His dark eyes glistened in pools of pending tears. In all the years she had known him, she had never seen him cry. The terrible scar on his face was highlighted and colored by the stained-glass windows.

"Outside," Anna whispered.

The air was chilly for October and they shuffled back and forth in small steps as vapor punctuated their words. They sometimes looked at each other but mostly avoided eye contact as they talked across the street from the entrance to St. Joachim's church.

"There's so much I want to say to you, Anna. I'm so sorry."

"Mac, not once in six years did you contact me. What is it you want now?"

"You want a smoke?" Mac held his Lucky Strikes toward her.

Anna shook her head.

Mac lit his Lucky and repeated the events of that Christmas Eve in 1951 to Anna.

Anna had heard all of it from Father Joe, but she wanted to hear it from Mac. She watched him—watched his eyes—looking for clues to his soul. She wondered who he was—the man she trusted or feared. Or had he changed completely? She watched him as he talked and smoked.

"...I thought the only way to keep you safe was for everyone to think I was dead. But now I know you are no longer in danger."

"So you came back because the danger was gone?"

"I stayed away because of the danger. I came back because of...you and me."

"You and me?"

"The thing is, I know this might sound strange, but the you part of you and me was easy. I mean, you're terrific, Anna, and I never, ever for a second stopped loving you. And as terrific as you were, I used to feel that I deserved you. That we were right for each other, you know?"

Anna nodded slowly, more in thought than agreement.

"Anyway, at some point, after I became—as Father Joe put it—an asshole, I knew I no longer deserved you or your love."

"But now you're back."

"Now I think I deserve you again."

"Oh, do you?" Anna surprised herself with the sarcasm in her tone. But then, he wasn't picking up where he left off six years ago. He was courting her. She controlled the moment.

The clamor from across the street signaled that church was over. Anna saw her family coming down the church steps and looking around. She knew they were looking for her. Angelo suddenly stood very still halfway down the steps. He walked toward Anna as if in a trance. Without thinking, Anna took hold of Mac's arm; he stopped talking and followed Anna's eyes to Angelo. Mac flicked his cigarette into the street.

Anna could tell people were talking to Angelo but he just continued to move through the crowd toward her. He crossed the street and stopped directly in front of them. His eyes were now clearly fixed on Mac.

Angelo mumbled something.

Anna looked at Mac. And then, bending toward Angelo, she said, "What, Sweetheart? What did you say?"

Without taking his eyes off Mac, Angelo said, "I knew it. I just knew you would come back. I knew it." And then, more like a seven-year-old than the thirteen-year-old leader of the Weepers, Angelo added, "I'm sorry, Papa."

Dams of steel would have been incapable of holding back Mac's tears any longer. His throat released a chirp of air as tears burst free, escaping down his cheeks. He folded Angelo into his arms. Angelo buried his face in the shoulder of Mac's jacket.

For the first time, Anna saw Mac embrace their son. She pressed her lips tightly together.

* * *

During the following week, Mac spent his nights with Father Joe. But his days were spent with Anna, Angelo, Adam, and Johnny.

Anna and Mac talked about the last six years. And as Anna's comfort grew, they talked about the beatings, drinking, and gambling. Mac told Anna that he would rather die than ever raise a hand to her or Angelo again. Anna simply nodded.

They walked through the neighborhood, they laughed, and, more importantly, they argued. They had argued when they were kids. They had argued all through their relationship. And the arguments always underscored their mutual respect and love. It was only during Mac's "asshole days" that arguments would end in violence.

"What's SAC mean?" Mac asked Anna.

"Gangs are against the law now, so they call themselves social and athletic clubs."

"Lots of gangs?"

"More than ever. The mayor calls it an epidemic. Movies are about gangs—*Blackboard Jungle*, *Rebel Without a Cause*, *The Wild One*. Even a new Broadway play opened at the end of September about gangs, *West Side Story*. I took Angelo. It was great, but gangs are everywhere, Mac. Everywhere."

"So what're they doin' about it?"

Anna shrugged. "The Times said there's a proposal to put cops in every school."

"Cops in schools. Christ."

"That and banning certain comic books, button knives, gravity knives, stuff like that. No really good ideas."

Anna and Mac talked about when they were kids and how much they loved each other. How important they always thought it was to laugh at themselves. They reminded each other of their special relationship.

* * *

Angelo had a turbulent week. At first, he was simply ecstatic to see his father again. But day by day, his fantasies about his father were overwhelmed by his memories. It seemed as if his father had changed, but unlike his mother, who knew and remembered the old Mac, Angelo lacked that point of reference. Instead, he relied on his mother and Uncle Johnny to tell him about his father before Angelo was born. Still, he was on guard for his father's temper eruptions, just like before.

Each night, his father, mother, brother, and Uncle Johnny would have dinner together before his father left to spend the night with Father Joe. Angelo studied his father, trying to reconcile his memories, fantasies, and this new reality. And his father reduced Angelo's newly acquired self-image. He felt more like a kid except when he was at the Weepers' club.

Angelo's week at PS-65 was his best ever. On Monday, Angelo and his friends wore their Weepers jackets to school. When they arrived at the steps to PS-65, several Knights moved out of sight. Kids pointed at Angelo and whispers filled the air. Angelo loved it. As the Weepers climbed the steps, other gang members exchanged nods with them. At the top of the steps, Angelo stopped and looked across the street at the tenements.

"That's the roof Jimmy fell off of," Angelo said. "Don't it seem like a long time ago?"

"It kinda was," Tate said.

"Hi, Angelo." Audrey and her friends walked up to the Weepers at the top of the steps. "Hey, Angelo. Hi, Spiro." Liz joined them. "Everybody's talking about you guys."

"Yeah?" Howie said.

Gina said, "Even more than the shootout with the Knights and that cop."

"You coming over to our club after school, Audrey?" Angelo asked. He saw Liz over Audrey's shoulder. She was talking to two girls, but she was looking at Angelo.

"Sure, we'll all come by," Audrey said. "I hear you guys have a dog. What's his name?"

"Sammy—he likes hanging out with us."

"Ah, great name," Liz said.

* * *

On Friday, all of Father Joe's poker buddies, including Nunzio, were in attendance at the Settlement dance and social. Rosemarie, Anna, and Mac were also there.

Father Casimiro said, "So, Mac, are you staying? Did you find a job?"

Father Joe shook his head. "You'll forgive my partner, Mac. He has a reputation for being a little direct."

"No problem," Mac said. "Nunzio got me a construction job. It's steady work and pays better than the ships. I got an appointment with a guy on Monday—Tommy Sullivan."

Father Casimiro said, "So you and Anna are—"

"C'mon, dance with me," Anna said and led Mac to the dance floor.

"Robert," Father Joe smiled and said. "You ever hear a little voice telling you maybe you shouldn't say this or that?"

"Are you kidding me?" Pompa said. "You should've seen him at the game yesterday, Joe. It was good you couldn't make it— what a shame. Anyway, Me, Nunzio, and Father Cas are sitting there in Yankee Stadium with sixty thousand other fans and the Yanks go down five zip to the Braves. Last out in the ninth, dead silence all around us, except for your partner, who's jumping up and down cheering. I swear, I thought we were gonna get killed. Am I right, Boss?"

"That crazy priest." Nunzio shook his head. "I'll never go to another game with him."

"I heard about that." Father Joe laughed.

"Well, they're happy in Milwaukee," Pompa said. "Milwaukee explodes with joy, right there on the front page."

"Give me that paper," Father Joe said. "I'd rather talk about Hoffa being elected to head the teamsters."

* * *

Anna talked to Rosemarie about her mixed feelings toward Mac and trying again with him.

"Ro, in August, when I talked with Father Joe, he told me about how he learned to play pool."

"Pool?"

"How it was all about controlling two inches," Anna said. "He told me I can't fix everything at once."

"It's true, Anna," Rosemarie said. "Mac moving home would affect Angelo, Adam, everyone. Even Johnny. Have you said anything to Mac about you—"

"Don't go there, Ro."

"I think you need to take some time with this. Talk to Mac about how you feel and about taking it slow. See what he says."

"Good advice, Ro."

* * *

On Sunday, after church, Anna and Mac walked along Roosevelt Street.

"Does Angelo know what happened that night?" Mac said. "Why I left?"

"Yes, and so does Adam. Look, Mac, I know you want to come home. And there's a part of me that would like to just say yes, but this affects more than just us. Do you understand?"

"You mean the boys?"

"Yes, our boys, my family, me...I want us to keep seeing each other, talking..." Anna took a deep breath. "I need time. We all need time. Understand?"

"I got time. And no other plans."

Chapter Thirty-Two

"It was too soon and too late."

In the early evening on Monday, after purchasing groceries at the A&P on Market Street, Mac, Angelo, and Adam headed home. Even without snow and lights, walking along Cherry Street, with his father pulling a shopping cart—this time filled with groceries—reminded Angelo of that Christmas Eve six years ago.

As they walked along Cherry Street, Angelo stayed close to his father's side while Adam skipped ahead. Angelo wasn't going to risk losing his father again. The smell of baked pies swirled in Angelo's head. The tang of peppermint teased his tongue as he crunched on candy and walked toward Catherine Street and the projects.

There was a chill in the air so Adam wore Angelo's old dark-blue winter jacket with the two embroidered white reindeer facing one another across the jacket's zippered front. Angelo wore his Weepers jacket. As he watched Adam, he saw himself in 1951. But the cars weren't snow-covered mounds and the projects ahead didn't look so menacing.

From a window in Knickerbocker, the Rays sang *Silhouettes.*

"That A&P we were just in opened in '51," Angelo's father said. "Nice it's still there."

"That was before I was born," Adam said and then quickly added, "Look over there...they're scary bogeymen, huh?"

Angelo spotted several Knights in black jackets across Catherine hanging out in the little park. "They're just punks, Adam."

His father nodded as he pulled the cart filled with groceries.

As they got closer, the Knights backed away.

The large male lion led the two young males of his pride through the savanna. Hyenas watched from a safe distance as the three lions strutted toward them. The hyenas continued to back away into the shadows of the jungle. The young males looked at the king of the pride for approval. He gave it. It was good to be a lion.

"Angelo, do you think it'll snow for Christmas this year?" Adam said, running in circles in front of Angelo and his father.

"If it does, I'll teach you to catch a snowflake on your tongue."

Angelo's father stopped walking.

Angelo spun around and looked at him. "Papa?"

"Nothing's wrong. What you just said reminded me of another time—"

"Are you going away again?" Angelo asked.

"No. Never."

"Even if I screwed up? Do you know about Bookman's?"

"I know all about it," Angelo's father said. "I was the one that screwed up, not you, son. If I was here, you wouldn't have felt like you had to take care of your mother. I let you down."

"You couldn't help it. Those men—"Angelo's heart suddenly raced into his throat, he swallowed, took a deep breath, and then said, "You called me son."

"You're my son. And no father has ever been prouder of his son." Adam walked back to them. "Angelo, Adam, I was wrong for a long time. No excuse, just wrong. I have it in me to be a pretty good father. Not perfect but...pretty good."

"Does that mean you're moving back home?" Angelo asked.

"I did wrong. Bad wrong. So your mom needs to take her time. You, too—give it a lot of thought. Meanwhile, I'll be coming over and hanging around. Okay?"

"Okay." Angelo was still having trouble reconciling his memories with his desires.

"So do I call you Daddy?" Adam asked.

"You can call me Dad, Father, Pop, Papa, Daddy, whatever you guys want."

"Can we call you Daddy-O?" Adam asked, covering his mouth to prevent giggling.

"Daddy-O?"

"It was in a movie called *Blackboard Jungle*," Angelo explained. "Adam's just bein' silly." Angelo knew that meant Adam was becoming more comfortable with his father.

"Well, I said anything, so I guess if you want to call me Daddy-O, you can."

"Can we call you Hoppy?" Adam laughed.

Angelo shook his head but had to laugh, too.

"Hoppy? Why Hoppy?" his father asked.

"You said anything," Adam said. "Can we call you Lulu?"

"Oh, I get it—you're a wise guy." Angelo's father got down on one knee, grabbed Adam, rolled him on the sidewalk, and tickled him into irrepressible laughter.

"Angelo," Adam called between chuckles.

Angelo wanted to jump on his father, bring him down to both knees, and get in on the tickling. But he didn't. It was too soon and too late. Adam, plagued by contagious and abandoned laughter, twisted toward Angelo. Angelo couldn't help chuckling a little with his brother. But he just stood close and watched.

THE END

ACKNOWLEDGMENTS

Much appreciation to my family: Thank you to my wife, Judy Olingy (my initial reader) and our son, Josh, for their encouragement and for reading and commenting on too many drafts of chapter one to the end. Thank you to Erica Chiarkas, my daughter and line editor, who patiently tried to teach me the difference between a comma and a semicolon, a dot, and a dash. And thanks to my son, Nick Chiarkas, who also read and edited the final draft. Thanks also to my son, Christopher Chiarkas, for his encouragement and for creating my website, and to my daughter, Adrienne Marchioni, for all her encouragement. Thanks also to my brother, Mario, my brother John, and Carol Hill for their advice, encouragement and support.

Thank you to Christine DeSmet, who stayed with me from page one to "THE END," offering valuable criticism and encouragement. In addition to being an author herself, she is the director of the writer's program at the University of Wisconsin Extension. Her curriculum for writers includes the extraordinary "Write by the Lake" program each spring in Madison. Thanks also to Laurel Yourke of the University of Wisconsin's writing program.

For reading early drafts of the opening chapters, thank you to Marilyn Kliman, Bob Moris, Jane Olingy, Randy Kraft, Krista Ginger, Gina Pruski, Barbara Gorman, Kellie Krake, Kelli Thompson, and Joni Varese. Thank you to Dr. Heather Potter and Attorney Liz Brennan for allowing me to use their names. Thank you to Dan and Julie Berkos, and Tommy Thompson, for their kind words and encouragement.

Thank you to my publisher, Kira Henschel of HenschelHAUS Publishing, without whose guidance, knowledge, and wisdom, you would not now be reading *Weepers*.

I am also grateful for the support and encouragement of my brothers (Ralph BD, Bill, Doug, James, Jeff, John, Mark, Mitch, Pat, Steve, Tom, and William) in the JDS Society of Madison, Wisconsin.

Thank you to Mary Elizabeth Brown and the Center for Migration Studies in New York City; to Mariam Touba and the Archdiocese of New York; to Syndia Cruz and the New York City Housing Authority.

Thank you to Master Mary Murphy of Villari's Shaolin Kempo Karate on State Street in Madison.

Thanks to Tom Kenney, my NYPD partner, for teaching me more about the law in action, good judgment, and common sense than all my formal education.

Thank you to Penny C. Sansevieri and her brilliant team at Author Marketing Experts (AME) for helping *Weepers* reach to more places than I every could have imagined.

And I thank God for granting me more second chances than I deserve.

ABOUT THE AUTHOR

Nick Chiarkas grew up in the Al Smith housing projects in the Two Bridges neighborhood on Manhattan's Lower East Side, where *Weepers* takes place. When he was in fourth grade, his mother was told by the principal of PS-1 that, "Nick was unlikely to ever complete high school, so you must steer him toward a simple and secure vocation." Instead, Nick became a writer, with a few stops along the way.

How many mothers are told their child is hopeless? How many kids with potential simply surrender to desperation? Nick wrote *Weepers* for them.

Today, Nick Chiarkas, Wisconsin State Public Defender Emeritus, is an acknowledged expert in the areas of leadership and management of governmental entities, specifically in the criminal justice field.

For twenty-two years, Dr. Chiarkas was the Director of Wisconsin's State Public Defender Agency. Under his leadership, the agency received three consecutive awards for excellence. In addition, he was the founder of *Justice Without Borders*, was an adjunct professor of law at the University of Wisconsin Law School, and was a visiting lecturer in law at Justus-Liebig-Universität, Gießen, Germany.

Previously Dr. Chiarkas served as the Chief Counsel to the United States Architectural and Transportation Barriers Compliance Board; Deputy Chief Counsel and Research Director to the

President's Commission on Organized Crime; Deputy Chief Counsel to the United States Senate Permanent Subcommittee on Investigations; Professor of Law; Professor of Criminology; a New York City police officer; and a U.S. Army paratrooper, 101st Airborne Division, .

Dr. Chiarkas has a doctorate and master's degrees from Columbia University; a law degree from Temple University; a master's and bachelor's degree in Criminal Justice from the John Jay College of Criminal Justice; a post-graduate certificate in Computer Systems Analysis from New York University, and was a Pickett Fellow at the John F. Kennedy School of Government at Harvard University.

Dr. Chiarkas worked with Israel in establishing and enriching Israel's first National Public Defender Agency; with Japan as it introduced a public defender system; with the U.S. Department of Justice in examining indigent defense in the United States, including New Orleans following Hurricane Katrina; and with the National Legal Aid and Defender Association in assessing defense services in Michigan and Ohio.

He was also part of the planning team for the U.S. Department of Justice's 2010 Symposium on Indigent Defense in the United States. In 2012, Dr. Chiarkas developed the public defenders protocols for Afghanistan, and in 2013, he examined Delaware's justice system for the Sixth Amendment Center.

In 1996, Dr. Chiarkas became the nation's first public defender to receive the "Law Enforcement Commendation Medal" awarded by the Sons of the American Revolution. In 1999 and 2000, Wisconsin Governor Tommy Thompson recommended to the National Governor's Association that Dr. Chiarkas be named the National Public Executive of the Year.

In 2001, the author was elected to the Alumni Executive Council of the Kennedy School of Government at Harvard University, and to the Board of Directors for the Wisconsin Forward Award, Inc. In 2002, Dr. Chiarkas received the Outstanding Professional Award by the Wisconsin Law Foundation, and in 2006, he was elected to the Board of Directors of the

National Legal Aide and Defender Association. Three years later, Dr. Chiarkas was the Dorsey Award winner for outstanding public defender by the Government Lawyer Division of the American Bar Association. In 2010, he received the Eisenberg Award, the Governor's Commendation Award, and the State Public Defender Board named the Innovative Leadership Award after Dr. Chiarkas to be awarded annually to an outstanding leader within the State Public Defender agency. Emeritus status was awarded to Dr. Chiarkas by the Wisconsin State Public Defender Board in January 2012.

Among Dr. Chiarkas' publications are five law books, three books dealing with criminal organizations and enterprises, two articles, translated into Japanese, published in Japan by the Japan Federation of Bar Associations on "Public Defenders" and "Legal Ethics."

Weepers is his first novel. Forthcoming fiction includes: *Nunzio's Way*, *Black Tiger Tea*, and *Blue Bounty*.

The author would be delighted to hear from you. Please visit his website: www.nickchiarkas.com.

CPSIA information can be obtained
at www.ICGtesting.com
Printed in the USA
FFHW01n1614211018
48827666-53013FF